Working Girls

Maureen Carter

First published in Great Britain in 2001 by Flambard Press
www.flambardpress.co.uk

This edition published by Crème de la Crime Books in 2004
Crème de la Crime Ltd, PO Box 445, Abingdon,
Oxon OX13 6YQ

Typesetting by Yvette Warren
Cover design by Yvette Warren
Front cover photography by A. Inden. Zefa Visual Media,
www.zefa.co.uk
Printed and bound in England by Biddles Ltd,
www.biddles.co.uk

ISBN 0-9547634-0-8

A CIP catalogue reference for this book is available from the British Library

www.cremedelacrime.com

About the Author

Maureen Carter has worked extensively in both print and broadcast journalism. She worked on newspapers and commercial radio before joining BBC TV News and Current Affairs.

As well as being a reporter, Maureen co-presented BBC's flagship *Newsnight* programme and went on to become one of the first women news producers outside London when she edited *Midlands Today*.

She is now a freelance writer and narrator. Her work has been short-listed in the Crime Writers' Association's New Writing Competition. She is currently working on further DS Bev Morriss novels.

Maureen lives in Birmingham and is married with one daughter, Sophie, who could be a useful contact in future – she's going to university to read criminology!

Author's note

My thanks go to members of Wolverhampton's Vice Squad who helped with much of the research. Since then, part of the squad has been renamed and is now known as Child Protection.

For friendship and faith, I thank: Edwina van Boolen, Christine Green, Frances Lally, Suzanne Lee, Corby Young and Peter Shannon.

For his unfailing encouragement and expertise, I thank my editor, Iain Pattison. And for that wonderful phone call, my thanks to Lynne Patrick.

To Sophie

PROLOGUE

The one streetlight that had been working had just gone out.

"You and me both," Shell muttered, words lost in a wide-mouthed yawn. She hadn't had a punter for two hours and it was so cold she couldn't feel her toes. Four creased and grimy tenners were lining the soles of her shoes. It was all she had to hide for opening her legs to two blokes she didn't want to see again, let alone screw. She couldn't go back with a puny £40. Her feet wouldn't touch. Charlie had told her he wanted a monkey by Sunday, and he wasn't someone you dared cross.

A flash motor turned the corner, cruised towards her. She was no good with car names but even Shell knew a BMW when she saw one. For a second she panicked, then told herself not to be stupid. They weren't all pimpmobiles; loads of normal blokes drove Beemers. The car was almost at the kerb now. She took a calming breath, then another. She'd have this last john, then knock it on the head for the night. She licked her lips, hoped they weren't blue.

Her white ankle-length coat was unbuttoned, her fists thrust deep in the pockets. She pulled it open even further as she approached the car. Long, blonde hair fell across her face as she leaned forward to look inside. The practised smile froze on her face. It couldn't be? Why hadn't she listened to Vicki?

"Get in." It wasn't a request.

Shell put a hand to her heart, scared its pounding would crack a rib. Her glance was everywhere but on the driver. She was looking for an exit; knowing there was no way out. Flight or fight?

Either way she was fucked.

She sighed, opened the door, sliding across the seat. It was warm inside and apart from her body's odour, she smelt rich leather and classy aftershave. They drove in a silence she didn't dare break. They moved away from the back streets now, heading for the ring road, joining other traffic. There was a tall tower – all steel and glass – to Shell's left. On top was a read-out in neon red. It flickered every few seconds, flashing through time, temperature, date. Shell followed it with her eyes: 20.19; 4°C. She had to crane her neck: 13.

"It's Friday, innit?"

He responded without looking. "So?"

"Unlucky for some, innit?" she whispered.

1

"Michelle Lucas. Fifteen. Throat wounds. Dead nine hours. Approx."

Detective Sergeant Beverley Morriss couldn't keep the anger out of her voice so she was saying as little as possible. She watched her boss, Bill Byford, check his watch, aware that her body language more than compensated for the verbal shortcomings. Her arms were clamped round her body, a Doc Martened foot tapping the rock-hard earth, her normally fluent features fixed in a stony stare.

It was a little after 8.30am. She'd arrived twenty minutes earlier, alerted by the school caretaker who'd found the body. He was now under sedation. Michelle Lucas had been left to bleed to death, on the edge of a scummy pool, on one of the coldest nights of the year. It was yet another image that Bev would have to learn to live with.

"You all right, Bev?"

"What do you think?" She turned her face to Byford. In itself, the question wasn't insolent. Its delivery was definitely borderline, and judging by the look the Detective Superintendent was returning, she might have just overstepped the mark. It wouldn't do to get on the man's wrong side. Supportive senior officers were like snowmen in the desert. She gave a half-smile to break the ice, and cracked it further with a full apology. "That was out of order. Sorry, guv."

She was relieved to see a softening of his features but it didn't alter the harsh reality of the violence before them.

"Fifteen, you say?"

Bev heard the doubt in Byford's voice. She wasn't surprised.

The victim appeared older. The long blonde hair, the on-the-pull clothes barely concealing the womanly curves. Bev's initial estimate had been late teens, early twenties, even.

"Some kids grow up fast, sir."

She watched as he edged closer. They were in a dip and the body, screened by shrubs, wouldn't have been visible from the footpath. She flinched as she saw Byford recoil. She didn't blame him. Any decent man would. The girl's long legs were splayed and stained. The tacky, crotchless knickers, more shocking than her near-nakedness. There was dried blood and excrement on the inside of her thighs: the stink of human waste, in every sense. Bev averted her eyes, not out of embarrassment or disgust but in respect for the girl's shattered dignity.

"Animals," she hissed.

"What did you say?"

"Nothing."

Aware he was still watching, she tried focusing on routine procedure rather than what appeared to be random savagery. She turned the pages of her notebook, but the tremor in her hands did little to calm her thoughts.

"Come on, Bev, what is it?"

She glanced at this big man who always had an eye for the small detail. But how could she tell Byford what was wrong when she could hardly explain it to herself? All she knew was that in eight years on the force, nothing had hit her so hard as the senseless obscenity of this young girl's death. And she'd seen worse, far worse. She'd cracked sick gags at murder scenes along with the rest of them. It was a defence mechanism, essential for survival, but it was more than that. It was part of the culture: fit in or fuck off.

Bev had no intention of looking weak. "No prob, guv," she answered softly.

She knew his nod of acknowledgement was as convincing as her words of assurance but they were all she had at the moment. She broke eye contact, glanced down at the notes of her brief interview with the caretaker. Byford resumed his scrutiny of the scene.

She waited in silence, knowing he wouldn't want to talk until he'd absorbed the details, the camera in his brain snapping a series of pin-sharp stills. She'd worked with him for nearly three years, was familiar with his ways, followed most of them. He was fifty-two, but she reckoned he'd only started to look it in the last eighteen months or so. The black hair was greying but there was still plenty of it. Bit more of him too, she realised. She hadn't noticed the slight paunch before. Mind, at six feet two he was hardly Michelin man. Even if she could see his face, it wouldn't tell her what he was thinking. She wondered anyway. His kids were grown up, but he was still a father.

"Parents?" he asked.

Her eyes widened. If he was into clairvoyancy, she'd soon be out of a job. As to Michelle's lineage, the words Bev had in mind were four-lettered and not the kind you'd use in front of granny. She gave a snort instead: a Morriss special.

He lifted an eyebrow. "Do go on."

She noted the sarcasm. Not like Byford, that; he must be picking up bad habits.

"Mother and Father of the Year award?" she asked. "Missed it by a whisker."

She consulted her notes again. "According to the caretaker – a bloke called Jack Goddard – Michelle was in care. She was taken in when she was about twelve." She paused, recalling the tears on Goddard's leathery cheeks. "He didn't recognise her at first."

"Hardly surprising," said Byford.

She glanced round at the sound of a car door being slammed. She hoped it was the scene-of-crime boys, or they'd be getting it in the neck from Byford. Even more than that, she hoped it wasn't Mike Powell.

"Anyway," she continued, "Michelle was in Year Ten. Goddard

says she was a nice kid. Had a heart of gold. Do anything for anyone."

She was pretty good at interpreting Byford's eyebrows; at the moment they were in his hair-line.

"There must be hundreds of kids at the school. How come he knows so much about Michelle Lucas?"

"Everyone knows Michelle," said Bev. "She was the original *Home Alone* kid. Only her ma didn't just take off on holiday, she took off, period. The story goes that Mrs Lucas's boyfriend was playing mummies and daddies with Michelle. The mother blamed the girl and buggered off with the bloke. Michelle's been in children's homes ever since. Goddard says it was all anyone round here talked about for ages. He reckons – considering everything – she was doing okay. He couldn't believe it when he found her lying here."

There was no doubt. Bev looked at the body again. The girl's flesh was as unnaturally white as the fake-leather coat. The red slash across her neck was a grotesque parody of her scarlet-painted lips. The only other colour was in the eyes. They were the deepest blue Bev had ever seen. She so wanted to close them for her. Like she wished she could slip the kid's shoe back on. It was lying to the left of the body; presumably, it had fallen off in a struggle. It looked cheap and shiny, the badly scuffed heel ridiculously high.

"And I bet she loved them," whispered Bev.

"Say something?" Byford asked.

"Not really."

"Okay, let's get back to Goddard. What was he doing over here?"

"This bit of the park belongs to the school." Bev nodded over Byford's shoulder. "You can just make out the building through the trees." She paused, though there wasn't a lot to see from this distance. "Anyway, some old boy left this area round the pool to Thread Street in his will. The school uses it as a nature centre.

Teachers bring the younger kids over to look at the wild flowers, the pond life. Goddard comes here regularly. Safety checks mostly. You know the kind of thing: broken glass, used condoms, rusty syringes."

"Very rustic."

She gave a token smile. "Anyway, it's private land. You're supposed to be a key holder. Doesn't stop people getting in though. The railings aren't that high. Youths mostly. The odd wino. Whatever. They slip in, down a few beers, shoot up, sleep it off."

"How many legitimate key holders?"

"I'll get a list off the trustees. But as long as you live in the area and can afford £120 a year…"

She waited while he looked round. The park wasn't large and in the middle of February it certainly wasn't lush, but it didn't take much imagination to realise that in a few months it would be stunning.

"I had no idea the place existed," Byford said.

It was well concealed, lying between Thread Street comprehensive at one end, and a row of high street shops at the other. Its sides were bordered by private properties, neither as imposing nor as expensive as they had been twenty years back. The park was all that remained of a once vast estate, owned by the once mighty Bogart family. It was a rural throwback, a stone's throw from the inner city.

"No reason you should," said Bev. "I only know 'cause my dad used to come here for the fishing. I got dragged along to bait the hooks. All those tins of maggots, I can see them now."

She grinned at his obvious unease until she realised it probably had nothing to with the dubious delights of her childhood pursuits.

"It begs a question though, Bev. Just how many people do know about it?"

The query went unanswered.

"Wotcha. Sorry. Couldn't find the bloody place," an approaching voice boomed.

"Shit," Bev muttered. It was supposed to be sotto voce but it wasn't sotto enough. She smiled a 'sorry' at Byford. Not that the expletive was directed at him. It was aimed at the tall, well-dressed blond currently inching his way gingerly down the slope to join them. Bev hid a smirk as DI Powell checked the heels of his expensive Italian shoes.

She *knew* it was a cliché: young female cop on shite terms with sexist, senior male officer. She knew it. Only trouble was, Mike Powell lived and breathed it.

"Morning, Mike," Byford greeted him. "Trouble with the motor?"

Bev wondered if he was taking the piss. Powell's time-keeping was as dodgy as a sundial's in the dark but it could have been a dig at the DI's elderly Alfa Romeo.

"No way!" Powell said. "She goes like a dream."

"Wet, no doubt," murmured Bev.

He ignored her; nothing new there. "No. I got held up by the SOCO boys. They'll be here any time. They're just unloading. They weren't sure how to get here, till I put them right."

"That was good of you," Bev smiled, "seeing how you couldn't find it yourself." She knew it was childish, but he was a self-serving prat. The whole station was aware of their loathe-bait relationship. It had intensified after last year's board when he'd been made up to inspector. Even a few of the blokes reckoned Bev had been robbed.

"I used my initiative. You should try it some time, Morriss."

"Surprised you know where it is." The words were lost as she turned her head, making a mental note to get more nicotine patches. In Bev's book, the man should carry a health warning.

"There they are, guv." Three white-suited figures emerged from a clump of winter-spindly trees. What with the suits, the protective masks and the steel cases, it was like an X-files shoot.

"It'll be worth checking taxi firms, Bev."

Byford was at it again: mind-reading. Not really. She knew it was a pretty obvious route. They'd have to question anyone who was out and about at the relevant times. Mind, they had to narrow those down. That's where Harry Gough would come in: another player who was making a late entrance.

Byford's mobile rang and she wandered over to have a few words with the crime scene lads. It was small talk mostly, while they prepared police tape, loaded cameras, lined up the gear. Gathering forensics was a painfully slow business, and Bev's sense of urgency was in overdrive. She made her way back as soon as she spotted Byford tightening the belt on his trench coat. It was a sure sign of his imminent departure.

"I'm going up to the school to have a shufti, Bev."

"Okay, guv." She didn't blame him. It was freezing out here.

"Obviously, the priority now is to find out what Michelle was doing in the park, and who she was with. We need to know who saw what; when; where. You both know what's needed."

Bev wasn't so sure; Powell was concentrating on his shoes, probably wondering if he'd ever get the stains out.

"You hang on here, Mike. Anything they turn up," Byford nodded at the SOCOs, "I want to know about it. And make sure Goughie gets a move on with this one. Bev..." He paused, as if considering, "You can use your initiative."

She sneaked a glance at Powell's face which appeared to consist mostly of mouth.

"That's after you've filled in the inspector."

"Any time, guv." She knew Byford had a soft spot for her, but he rarely made it so obvious. She shouted a somewhat belated "Catch you later" at his retreating back.

"Talking of catching things," Powell baited. "Where are the worms, Morriss?"

"You what?"

"Early birds and all that..?"

"Yeah. Right." She wasn't rising this time; getting to the scene first had nothing to do with brownie points. She lived closer; simple as that. She turned away, concentrated on the activity around the body. Michelle Lucas's brutal death was attracting a lot more interest than her short life. A photographer was taking shots from every angle; then there'd be the movie version; then there'd be the close ups: samples and swabs extracted from every orifice. As for what would happen on the slab – Bev didn't even want to think about that.

"Where the hell's Goughie?" Powell demanded. "There'll be a few worms on her, if he doesn't hurry up."

"Watch what you're saying." The man was an arsehole.

"No point getting all sensitive, Morriss. Look at her."

"I've seen her. I was here before you. Remember?"

"You'll have clocked it already then, won't you?"

She narrowed her eyes. "Clocked what?"

"Come on, Morriss. Where's your inititative? You don't need me to tell you. It's staring you in the face."

She knew what he was getting at, just couldn't believe he was going there. "Enlighten me."

"Look at her, Morriss. She was a tom."

Bev hated the expression. It was police-speak – police like Powell, anyway. "If you mean she was a prostitute, why don't you say so?"

"What? 'A rose by any name..?' Call her what you like, Morriss, she was a whore."

He was probably right. Bev had recognised the possibility the minute she'd laid eyes on the body. But right now, that's all it was. And even if it was confirmed – so what?

"That makes all this okay, then, does it?"

"I didn't say that."

"Didn't you?" She wanted to knock the smirk off his face.

"It goes with the territory, Morriss. It's a meat market out there."

Even without last year's secondment to vice, Bev knew she had a sensitivity that Powell – and most of the blokes, come to that – would never achieve.

"Listen, Cliché Man, you're talking bollocks."

"Oh! Pardon me! I didn't realise I'd been granted an audience with Mother Superior."

He bowed his head in mock supplication. Bev turned on her heel before she said something she wouldn't regret, but he grabbed her arm.

"A few weeks on tom-watch doesn't give you divine insight, Morriss."

She shook him off before making eye contact. "Vice squad. Six months. Acting Inspector."

"Have it cracked by breakfast then, won't you?" Powell countered.

"Breakfast? I should be so bloody lucky." The voice was unmistakeable. Bev greeted Harry Gough with a warm smile. She'd never quite got used to a Del-boy soundalike who was the spit of Richard Burton.

"The sodding alarm didn't go off. There I am having a bit of how's-your-father with the luscious Sarah Montague. Next thing I know, one of your geezers is on the blower telling me to come as fast as I can. I ask you. What's a bloke to do?"

Bev laughed. Goughie was so old school, he was classic. He'd be hanging up his scalpel in eighteen months and nothing was going to change the old boy now. As far as Harry was concerned, PC was either a young bobby or a saucy postcard. Bev didn't have a problem with that; at least it was in-your-face, not between-your-shoulder-blades.

"So what did you do, Mr Gough?"

"Shot out of the sheets and prayed to God I'd have the same nocturnal visitation tonight."

She smiled. Despite his advancing years and regressive attitudes, Goughie was as good as pathologists get. One of his juniors had once told Bev that his nickname at the morgue was Psycho. It was payback for all the times he called them 'a bloody shower.'

"What've we got then?" he asked, peeling on surgical gloves.

She ran through what little they knew, watched as Gough's expression changed half a dozen times. Eventually, he knelt by the girl's body, not caring whether the slowly thawing earth soiled his dark suit. The initial examination was by sight, seemingly long moments spent in visual study and assessment. It was Gough's way – like the guv, she realised. She watched the man's ice-blue eyes linger over every contour and crevice. They widened and narrowed, registering and recording.

Powell's tuneless whistling was beginning to bug her. *Like a Virgin* was either a deliberate wind-up or incredibly crass. She glared furiously but he was studying his watch.

"In a hurry, lad?" Gough asked. Bev hid a smile; Goughie never missed a trick. "More haste, less speed, young man. You know what they say?" The pathologist met Powell's eyes. "Softly, softly, catchy monkey."

"Start at the zoo then, shall I?" It was an attempt at humour. Powell was the only one laughing.

"Not funny, sonny." Gough said. "Why don't you cut the comedy and get on with the job?"

It was unfair but Powell had asked for it. Bev did her UN peacekeeping bit.

"What can you tell us, Mr Gough?"

"The body's a punch bag. Poor kid. None of the marks are that recent: three days, maybe four. She could have fallen. More likely to have been a fist, or a boot. I'll know more when I get her on the slab."

Bev had already noted the bruising on the shin and inner thigh, filed it under *pimp*?

"Cause of death's pretty obvious," Powell proffered.

Bev glanced at the pathologist. Even tiptoeing on Goughie's

territory was not to be advised. Words like *fool* and *angel* rushed to mind.

"Really, Inspector?" said Gough. "Do share."

Bev's eyes widened as Powell mimed a throat being cut.

"How terribly illuminating." Gough turned his back on the DI. "As Doctor Powell has kindly pointed out, Bev, a slashed throat is not conducive to good health. Especially in this case. The blade's gone through the jugular and the carotid. She was killed here. You can see how much blood she's lost, how it's spurted, the spray it's left. I'd say she didn't have a clue. There's little sign of a struggle, no defensive wounds. She was attacked from behind, taken by surprise and dead by the time he lowered her down."

"He?" Bev asked.

Gough paused, considering. "Could have been a woman, I suppose. No great strength needed. Especially, as I say, with the element of surprise."

She nodded. "Any thoughts on the weapon?"

"Sharp, that's for sure. Look at that wound."

Bev had seen enough. "Doc Jordan reckoned about nine hours?"

"Gone already, has he?" Gough asked.

Paul Jordan was on the GP call-out list. A new boy, or he wouldn't have left the scene without having a word with Goughie.

"Yeah. Emergency call," Bev white-lied.

"I'll not argue with him. Not yet anyway." Gough rose, removing the gloves. "I'll do the biz this afternoon."

She watched Gough climb the slope; she'd miss the old boy when he retired.

"I'm going up to the school, Morriss. Have a word with the guv."

Powell was easier to read than a primer. "Okay," she said. "'I'll hang round a while. See what they turn up."

As well as the SOCOs, a team of officers and dog handlers was scouring the park for any trace of Michelle Lucas's last movements. They'd be bagging butt ends and bus tickets, spent matches and crumpled packets; every scrap of humanity and sign of life, to try to unearth a pointer to the girl's death.

Bev walked away from the body, noticed again the scuffed shoe. She thought of glass slippers and fairy stories and sighed. Michelle was no Cinderella and any prospect of living happily ever after had been written off in the first chapter.

She frowned, went down on one knee, something had caught her eye. She glanced round for a twig, used it to prop up the shoe then peered closer. Lining the sole was a stash of cash. Ten-pound notes. Dirty money. Bev shook her head. Finding this particular piece of evidence gave her no pleasure. Out with the vice, kerb trawling, it was the first place they looked. It was the oldest trick in the book of the oldest profession. And it cleared up any remaining doubt that young Michelle Lucas was a fully paid-up member.

2

"Any of you lot seen Shell?"

Five pairs of young eyes reluctantly left their appreciation of Orlando Bloom's glistening pectorals and glanced towards the door.

"'ere, Vicki. Come and get a load of this." The invitation was issued by a skinny girl with bright red hair and a nose stud. But Vicki Flinn had laid eyes – and other body parts – on more naked flesh than Stud and the other kids had wolfed down TV dinners. She was unmoved by *heat's* latest centrefold, spread as he was across a corner table at the Copper Kettle caff.

"I'm in a rush, Rose. Any idea where she is?" Vicki asked.

Maybe the nasal attachment gave the girl an authority denied the others, but Rose was clearly their mouthpiece. "We ain't seen her for ages. She ain't been in school all week. You 'ang round with 'er more than us, anyroad."

Vicki frowned. It was true. She was a couple of years older than Shell. Been on the game that much longer. Shell was the only one who'd shown any interest. Rose and her cronies got what they wanted from shoplifting, not dropping their knickers. Kids who lived at home and had family – such as it was – didn't want to know. Shell was different. She and Vicki had big plans. They were going to work the streets together, get some readies, then leg it. They'd get out of Birmingham, start a business some place: hairdressing maybe, or a sandwich bar. First she'd got to get Shell away from Mad Charlie.

"You sure she ain't been in?" It was nearly 10am. They were supposed to have met outside the Odeon at nine, go to Mac's for a bite to eat, then pick up a few bits and pieces in town. Rose's attention was elsewhere; one of her badly-bitten nails was tracing a line round Orlando's navel. "Rose! Are you listenin'?"

"I've told you once," she glared. "You wannit in writin' or sumfink?"

Given the girl's patchy school attendance, Vicki reckoned that was well optimistic. She stood in the middle of the floor, chewing her bottom lip, working out the next move. Her red leather skirt was only slightly longer than the leopard print blouson she'd nicked off the market. There was a ladder running up the inside of one black stocking.

"You want somethin'?"

Vicki turned. The question came from a huge woman with a washed-out face behind a none-too-clean counter. Her hair looked like a mauve meringue. A nylon cap was perched on top, but it was only a gesture towards public health regulations. Any beneficial effect was largely negated by the smouldering cigarette dangling from the side of her mouth. Vicki curled her lip.

"You're jokin', ain't you?"

The woman plonked sausage-shaped fingers on the mounds of fat floundering around the vague location of her hips. "I ain't Benny 'ill." Vicki watched the cigarette keep time with the woman's mouth, apart from odd flecks of ash that were floating towards the Eccles cakes. "And if you ain't buyin' you can bugger off. I don't want your sort in 'ere." She extracted the dog-end and ground it underfoot. "And get a move on or I'll call the Old Bill."

Vicki knew that after a quick once-over, the woman had jumped to several fast conclusions. She dragged a hand through her Gothic crop and tugged the hem of her skirt. Her stick-thin legs were none too steady atop pink plastic wedgies. The place wasn't crowded and it wasn't the Ritz but she felt a blush creeping up her neck and over her face. The miserable cow. There was no need to talk to her like that. She felt like giving her a mouthful and throwing a cup of cold tea in her ugly mush.

Still, the old bag had given her an idea. In the girls' line of business, cops were an occupational hazard: she reckoned her mate had been nicked. It'd be a first for young Shell. She smiled picturing the girl cooling her heels in a police cell down at Highgate nick. She'd better get herself down there, find out when they were letting Shell out. The overnight accommodation might well have been at Her Majesty's pleasure, but it sure as hell wouldn't have done a lot for Ms Lucas's.

3

Thread Street Comprehensive had seen better days. Then again, mused Byford, hadn't we all?

The Superintendent was on an impromptu walkabout. He was searching for signs to the head's study and at the same time, taking in pointers to the state of the school. Five out of ten, could do better, was his initial verdict. Its paintwork was having a mid-life crisis; ubiquitous, grey vinyl flooring was stained and skid-marked; discarded sweet wrappers lurking in corners, keeping the dustballs company. Byford was taking mental notes and trying not to make assumptions. He still hadn't tracked down the study. He was beginning to think it was a deliberate ploy to keep the little dears at bay; either that or the little dears had been playing silly beggars with the signposts.

There was no point in following his nose; everywhere he went was the same strange smell. It was difficult to pin down but encompassed cheesy socks and stale curry.

"Can I help you?" A cut-glass voice that evoked Home Counties' home comforts had no difficulty carrying the length of the corridor.

Byford turned. A tall woman, late thirties, not unattractive, was standing in a doorway. She was wearing a well-cut, dark blue trouser suit but there was nothing masculine about her. He wondered how long she'd been watching him.

He retraced his steps. "Detective Superintendent William Byford. I'm…"

She glanced at her watch. The movement was meant to be noticed. "Yes. I've been expecting you. I'm Elizabeth Sharpe. Headteacher. Will this take long?"

He bit back his first response. He might regret it later. "Hope not. Let's make a start, shall we?"

"Follow me." She spoke without smiling. He trailed behind, feeling like a recalcitrant schoolboy. Again, he noticed her height. He was six-two and she wasn't much shorter. She was big-boned but not fat: not yet. There was a faintly regal air about her. She was walking at a sedate pace with her head held high and her shoulders back. He could imagine her waving from the back of a Bentley. Perhaps it came in handy when dealing with hundreds of truculent kids.

She reached her study, held the door open to let him pass. No sweaty footwear or bearded vindaloo here. It was more furniture polish and air freshener.

She gestured him to a chair and talked as she walked across her own spotless floor. "It's quite beyond me. Absolutely unbelievable. Michelle Lucas. Dead." She didn't actually utter, "And on school grounds," but the words hung in the air. "You're sure there's no mistake?"

How many times had he heard that? "Quite."

Her eyes were a pale-blue and her gaze hadn't left his since he'd sat down. Byford wasn't a fan of unremitting eye contact. He put it in the same league as an overfirm handshake.

"Thank God it's Saturday," she said.

His face must have betrayed his reaction and she lifted a hand to quell a protest he hadn't voiced. "I didn't mean it like that. It's just… well, at least the children are at home. By Monday perhaps…"

He watched as she returned an errant strand of chestnut-coloured hair to an otherwise obedient bun. His first impression was wrong, he realised now. She was older.

"We'll need a room," he said.

"A room?"

He might just as well have been asking for a handbag. Byford nodded. "Just for a few days. The main incident unit will be at headquarters but we're going to need something nearer the scene."

"But surely..." She put a hand over her mouth. He noticed that the red nail polish was chipped and make-up was caught in the creases around her eyes. At this distance, it was highlighting the defects she hoped to hide.

He tried an encouraging smile. "We may get an early break. But it's not something we can bank on. We have procedures and we have to implement them as soon as we can."

"Yes." She didn't sound convinced.

"A girl's been murdered, Mrs Sharpe. We have to find out who did it."

"Of course. It's just that the whole thing is so distressing. We have exams coming up. An OFSTED next term. The children will be..."

Byford was picturing Michelle's body. "One of those children has been murdered."

Her mouth tightened slightly. He thought she was about to argue but she said nothing.

"What can you tell me about Michelle Lucas?"

She walked to the sash window behind her desk, stood with her back to it and casually ran a finger along its dust-free ledge.

"What have you learned already?"

He shook his head. "That's not important. I'm interested in what you can tell me. I need to know everything about her. Who her friends are. Where she went. What she did."

"Surely you don't think someone here..?"

"I don't think anything at the moment, Mrs Sharpe. All I know is that a girl is dead and whoever killed her is still out there."

Her eyes widened. "My God."

He looked at his watch. The gesture wasn't lost. She returned to the chair, sat back with legs crossed, hands in lap. "Michelle was a lovely girl. Especially when you consider... Well, her life's not been easy."

He bit back a remark about her death.

"Are you aware she was in care, Superintendent? She'd been at Fair Oaks Children's Home for about two years. Michelle was abandoned by her mother. There were rumours of abuse. Violence."

"Rumours?"

"Nothing ever got to court." She looked at her nails. "And… Michelle…"

"Michelle?"

She forced a smile. "Let's just say there were times when she had a vivid imagination."

Byford scratched his left eyebrow. It was a warning – to anyone who could read the sign.

Elizabeth Sharpe leaned foward, rested her elbows on the desk. "Michelle liked to be the centre of attention, Superintendent. It happens a lot with children from broken homes. They need to be noticed. They want everyone to like them. Sometimes they make things up… I suppose it's compensation for what they've lost."

Spare me psycho-crap, thought Byford. "And Michelle…"

The silence was uneasy. He had no intention of breaking it.

"Michelle could be very caring. Very helpful."

"But?"

She shrugged. "Mostly when there was something in it for her."

Sounded like every teenager Byford knew. "For instance?"

"Oh, little things. Offering to tidy up after class to get out of a detention. Carrying a teacher's bag to her car – so as to get a lift into town. That sort of thing."

His withering expression suggested it was hardly major league.

She pursed her lips and upped the ante. "She smoked in school. And several times, my staff suspected she'd been drinking."

"What about drugs?'"

"Not in school. But… she took rather a lot of unauthorised

absences."

Byford nodded. Bunking off they called it in his day. It was time to get on. "I'd like a list of her teachers and how they can be contacted. If you can think of any pupils she was particularly close to – put their names on it as well."

"I've already made a start." She handed over a file. He wondered why he wasn't impressed with her efficiency. "You'll need to speak to her Head of Year, Henry Brand. He works very closely with the children in his care and he's been on the staff here for many years."

"Right. Thanks. I'll keep you informed."

She smiled for the first time. "Actually if you don't think you'll need me…"

He waited. Was the woman incapable of finishing a sentence? "It's just that when your man called at my home this morning, I was actually on my way out…"

He nodded but said nothing.

"It was no problem, of course. I don't live far. I have to pass school to get to the course anyway."

"Course?" He had visions of lecture halls and seminars.

"Golf. Woodley Manor. There's a tournament on today."

He was shocked, wondered if he had the right, had to stop himself bridling. "Don't let me keep you, Mrs Sharpe. If we need you, we can always catch up with you on the green."

She narrowed her eyes. "I don't think that will be necessary, Inspector."

He ignored the deliberate demotion. "In a murder inquiry, anything might be necessary, Mrs Sharpe."

He remained silent, again wanting her to break it, wondering how she would. She sighed. "Michelle will be missed. She was very popular here. A lovely girl…"

Not for the first time, Byford thought that what Elizabeth Sharpe didn't say was more interesting.

"But?"

She stood, held out a hand. "Nothing. I don't believe in gossip and tittle-tattle."

Byford shook her hand, trying not to feel that he was being dismissed; trying not to feel the antipathy and hostility she had, perhaps unwittingly, aroused. He couldn't work her out; couldn't get a handle, to borrow one of Bev's favourite sayings. He made a mental note to point Bev in the woman's direction. His sergeant had a knack for cutting to the chase by cutting out the crap (her words again). Byford reckoned she could sniff out bullshit in a rose garden. "Before I go… we haven't sorted a room."

"Use the one next to mine. It's yours as long as you need it. If I'm not on school premises…" She paused, wanting to make a point but unwilling to spell it out. "I'll be at home."

He nodded: point taken. She walked him to the door, halted before opening it and placed a hand on his arm. He hoped the shock hadn't reached his face.

"My staff and I will do everything we can to help. No one deserves to die in this terrible way. Whoever killed Michelle needs to be caught. And the sooner the better."

The man tightened his grip on the girl, pulled her in close.

"I am not happy, Cassandra."

There was a wide smile on his face but it didn't get anywhere near his narrowed eyes. To a casual observer, they were love's young dream, snatching a Valentine's Day kiss in a shop doorway. No one was near enough to hear; he'd made sure of that. "If you're lying to me, I'll kill you. You do understand?"

He licked his lips, brushed them gently against her cheek then released her.

"Honest to God, Charlie. It's the truth. Straight up."

He laughed, sending out waves of garlic and tobacco fumes. He wasn't much taller than her own five-six, but workouts and weight training made every inch count. Cassie had fallen for his dark good looks. She'd always fancied blokes with long hair, especially pony tails. She couldn't stand the sight of them now. He put his finger to her mouth. "You'd better hope so, Cassandra, baby."

Cassie Swain wished she was a baby: a babe-in-arms. None of this would be happening if her stupid, crazy mother hadn't swallowed a load of paracetamol then thrown herself in the river. Cassie wouldn't be living in some poxy kids' home. She'd never have heard of Charlie Hawes, let alone whored for him. And she wouldn't be standing here now, scared shitless with wet knickers.

She took a step back. Why had she ever let him anywhere near Michelle Lucas? The sledge-hammer had added weight to his argument; he'd been swinging it at her knee caps. She tried to smile but her mouth hurt.

Cassie had long realised that Hawes had only wormed his way into her affections as a way of getting to Shell. Shell Lucas was a real looker: a nice little earner. Charlie had a string of girls but Shell was the youngest. And Cassie had led him right to her.

A year ago now it was. They'd started sharing a room at Fair Oaks and Shell wanted to know where Cassie was getting her swank clothes and posh jewellery. Charlie was dead generous in those days. Groomed his girls well. Till he got them where he wanted them: up against fat beer guts and inside thick wallets. Shell was his richest picking.

Cass'd had a load of grief from Shell's mate, Vicki Flinn. Vick had gone apeshit. She was on the streets herself but she couldn't be doing with pimps, especially Mad Charlie. Vick had been doing her best to protect the girl. At this moment, protection was the last thing on what passed for Charlie Hawes's mind.

"Soon's I see her, I'll get her over to you, Charlie."

"Yes," he drawled. "You do that."

It was easier said than done. Cassie hadn't a clue where the silly little cow was. One thing was certain: she hadn't slept in her own bed last night. Cassie had covered for her at breakfast: lying to the staff, coming up with some old tosh about a migraine. They looked out for each other at Fair Oaks. But getting on the wrong side of Charlie Hawes was something else.

She watched as he pulled up the collar of his brown leather trench coat then tightened the belt. Word was that he'd used it to top some crackhead. Probably just big talk but right now – Cassie really didn't want to know.

4

"We need the pimp, guv."

Byford nodded, sat up straight and put his hands behind his head. Bev reckoned it must be the school environment; he normally had his feet on a desk and the chair tilted. She noticed they'd made themselves at home; there was a great smell of coffee in the room and DI Powell had what looked like biscuit crumbs round his mouth. She'd mention it later, wind him up. Maybe.

She'd just brought them up to speed on finding the stash of cash in Michelle Lucas's shoe, and, right now, the priority was finding out what sort of a scumbag had put a fifteen-year-old girl on the game.

"Any bright ideas?" Byford asked.

Bev sighed; plenty of dark thoughts. All the way from the park, she'd been thinking about her time on vice, and the difficulties in getting to the average pimp.

Locating the coffee maker was a cinch by comparison. She made her way over and poured, still lost in thought. Every day she'd go in and see the fixed smiles of a bunch of slimeballs who made life hell for girls like Michelle. Grainy photographs of six suspected pimps had been pinned to a wall of the squad's cramped quarters. It was the closest they'd come to nailing the bastards.

In every case, the pimp had been fingered by one of his women, and in all but one instance, those same women had subsequently withdrawn their statements and refused to give evidence. Bev could hardly blame them. The initial desire to turn a man in quickly turned into terror of the consequences. It was one thing for a woman to be beaten, burned and buggered; it was something else when her family, even her kids, were threatened. And prison didn't stop the bastards. They had lackeys on the outside more than willing to lend a hand, or a boot, or a baseball bat.

It was no wonder they were all smiling in the snatch-shots, Bev thought. They believed – unlike their girls – that they were untouchable.

She took a sip of coffee, aware that Byford was waiting for input. She sipped again; it was good. Two shots of caffeine and she could still only come up with one thought. "If it's okay with you, guv, I'd like to talk to the girls. I'll probably get the bum's rush but it's got to be our best chance." It was a weak link but it was the only one they had.

"Go on," Byford prompted.

"There's a group of them. They work a patch near the park. It's causing a lot of grief cause it's so close to the school. The people who live round there are well narked. They've been trying to get the girls moved on for ages."

"Moved one on, haven't they?" Powell held out his empty mug to Bev. "Two sugars, love."

"Pot's there, sweetie," she said automatically. "I don't know if it was Michelle's beat. I've never seen her there, but it's got to be the first place we try."

Byford nodded. "Sounds good, Bev. Get out there, soon as you like."

She'd have to chase a few addresses first. It was a bit early for the girls to show their faces. They'd be sleeping it off. She stifled a yawn; must be thought association.

"Late night, Morriss?"

"Early shout, Inspector."

"Come on you pair," Byford said. "Save the energy. You'll need it. There's going to be plenty of late nights for everyone until we get this cleared up."

Bev swigged the last of her coffee and looked round for her

shoulder-bag. It was a vast depository of junk with the odd essential item thrown in, and she was always promising herself she'd sort it. "I'm off then. I'll catch you later."

"I'll walk out with you." Byford got to his feet. "See what else you can get here then get back for the briefing," he told Powell. "I want everyone back at Highgate by say, 10.45."

"What about the press?" the DI asked. "The *Star's* been sniffing round and I've had the radio people on the phone."

"Best place for them," Byford said. "I'll have to talk them eventually. But not now. The priority's getting the team up to speed. And finding everything we can on Michelle. The mother and that boyfriend of hers will have to be tracked down. And one of us is going to have to go over to Fair Oaks. Michelle was there longer than any of the other places. Even so, they'll all have to be checked. We'll get to as many of the teachers as we can before Monday. They'll be able to tell us who her friends are. Strikes me, it's the kids who'll be able to tell us more than anyone."

"Do you want me back at Highgate as well?" Bev hoped he'd say no. She was keen to get to the girls.

The phone rang. He lifted a finger. "Byford." The conversation lasted less than a minute.

"That was Vince. He's got a young woman called Victoria Flinn at the front desk. She wants to know if we've got a friend of hers locked up. A friend called Michelle Lucas."

Bev slung her bag over her shoulder. "On my way."

Vince Hanlon's avuncular appearance was deceptive. In reality the desk sergeant was like a drill at the dentist's: indispensable and just as sharp. There were only three stripes on his arm but, as Bev was well aware, a wealth of experience nestled in the rolls of flab under his belt.

So said, the sight that greeted her when she emerged from the revolving doors at Highgate nick was as arresting as catching Hannibal Lecter in a vegan restaurant. Big Vince had deserted his customary lair of the front desk for less familiar territory. He had his arm round a skinny girl, young enough to be his great-niece, who looked as streetwise as an A–Z.

He waved a hand at the floor. "The lass slipped. It shook her up a bit."

Bev glanced at the lass's footwear. Lucky: she could have broken her neck. The girl hadn't looked round, hadn't moved away; if anything she'd snuggled even closer to Vince. Her proximity to his paunch was having visible effects. Bev's lips twitched as he pulled a huge white handkerchief from a trouser pocket, mopping sweat from his corrugated brow. His eyes darted round like a drowning man's in search of a life jacket. "Thank God you're here."

At last, the girl glanced round, curious to see what Vince's saviour looked like. Saint Bev was in her late twenties, five foot six, nine stone, with chin-length hair the colour of Guinness and a face that her mother called beautiful. She bestowed what she hoped was a suitably beatific smile, but the girl pulled a face and a few seconds later was floundering again in a mound of flesh that could have been Vince's chest or abdomen; there was no perceptible demarcation. It was a wind-up. The girl was enjoying this.

Vince wasn't. He tried to put a little distance between them but she was clinging like cotton-wool to Velcro. Bev was in no hurry to tear her away: break the news and break her heart.

The game soon lost its appeal. The girl looked up and smiled. "Feel a bit better now." She moved away and ran a hand over her rear. "Mind, me bum hurts."

"Bev here'll look after you," he said.

"Rather talk to you, Vince."

Vince? Bev shot him a look. He was having a hot flush. Another time, it would have been funny. She sighed. The girl was still studiously ignoring her, so Bev moved nearer the desk and skimmed through the notes Vince had made before his temporary foray into community relations. She found what she was looking for and turned to face the girl. "Victoria?" She waited for an acknowledgment. It didn't arrive. "I'm DS Morriss. Bev Morriss. Come on, love. Let's get a cup of tea."

Bev took a step back as the girl swirled round, eyes flashing. "I'm not your love. And I don't want a soddin' cup of tea."

Good start, thought Bev.

The girl pointed a finger with a badly-bitten nail. "I'm not talking to no one in this place. I've come to pick up Shell." She looked at Vince. "When can I see her?"

Vince shrugged, nodded towards Bev. She jerked her head, signalling the girl to follow her. "We need to talk."

Something in Bev's voice pre-empted another verbal attack. Vicki stared, nodded, said: "Okay."

"We'll be in number three, Vince."

"Hey! I ain't done nuffin'."

Bev smiled reassurance, at the same time registering the fact that Miss Flinn clearly knew her way around Highgate nick. "I know that, Victoria. But we need somewhere private."

The girl nodded again, gave what Bev suspected was a smile. Bev had to stifle a grin as the girl reached up to plant a kiss on Vince's cheek. "Ta, Vinnie. And I will have that cup of char. Four sugars. And a couple of Hob Nobs."

Bev noted the relief on Vince's face. He was back on an even keel. Tea was no problem. Sympathy for a sexy slip of a girl floundering in his arms and playing havoc with his equilibrium was something else.

Bev had reckoned on a bit of ranting and raving, a few screams maybe. But not this. Vicki was silent, still, as motionless as her best mate in the morgue. Perched on the edge of the desk, Bev watched a solitary tear slide past the girl's nose and drop from the bottom of her chin. It was the only discernible movement. She was seventeen, going on seven. A kid who wanted to go home to mum. That's if she had a mum – or a home. Bev would give her right arm to know what was going on behind those huge blue eyes.

"When did you last see Michelle, love?"

Vicki was staring into space. Had she heard? Was she in shock?

"D'you want a doctor, Vicki?" Bev stroked the bony shoulder. "Is there anyone I can call?"

Another tear. Another damp trail.

Bev knelt in front of Vicki, took her hands. They were cold and could be cleaner. She cupped them in the warmth of her own. No reaction. Bev might have been invisible. She rose, gently helped the girl to her feet. They were much the same height. It was probably the only thing they had in common. Bev searched her face, looking for answers to a million questions. It was blank. A plain cover for the hurt and pain Bev knew were there. She drew her close and stroked her hair, spoke the only words she could think of. "I'm so sorry, Vicki. So very sorry."

It was like the snap of a hypnotist's fingers. The girl circled her arms round Bev's waist and cried like a baby. "Why Shell? Why little Shell? She was only a kid."

The words came between shuddering breaths and pitiful sobs. Bev held her tightly, waiting until she was calmer.

"That's what we have to find out, Vicki. Then we can nick the bastard who did it. Get him behind bars where he belongs. But we're going to need your help."

Bev held her breath. It could go either way. Asking a girl to grass on a pimp was tantamount to putting her neck on the block. Bev counted silently to ten, then twenty. She hit twenty-nine before Vicki pulled away. Bev saw the fear in the girl's eyes, and she saw the grief, and she saw something else: fury.

"You've got it." Vicki brushed away a tear with the heel of her hand. "And then you can throw away the fucking key."

"Call for you, guv. Some git with a shoulder on his chip."

DC Darren Newman? Sounding tetchy? Rare as a clockwork CD was that. Byford snatched up his extension, wondering who'd managed to wind up the famously phlegmatic Dazza. "Superintendent Byford."

"Listen up. And listen good. You've had enough warnings."

Byford ran a finger along his eyebrow. He didn't know the voice but the drift was all too familiar. "Who is this?"

"It doesn't matter who I am. Just hear this." That wouldn't be difficult. A megaphone was quieter, even without the loud Birmingham accent. "The tarts. In Thread Street. They've got to go. We've had enough. And if you lot don't do something, we will."

"I don't think that would be advisable, Mr..?"

"We don't want advice. We want action. We've been asking long enough. You'd soon do something if you lived round here. Cars crawling, engines revving, doors slamming; all hours of the day and night. You wouldn't like it if your wife was insulted every time she went to the shops. Decent women can't step outside their own door. Kids are coming home from school with used condoms. Slags are wrapped round every lamp-post. I'm telling you, copper. It's got to stop."

Byford glanced at a note Dazza had just put in front of him; the caller must have given young Newman an ear-bashing as well. He mouthed an 'okay' and continued, "Tell me, Mr… are you speaking on behalf of some sort of organization?"

Dazza had simply written the word: CUTS? It rang an immediate bell with Byford. It was the group Bev had mentioned. Now he came to think of it, there'd been a few stories in the local rag. According to the *Star*, Clean Up The Streets was cutting-edge community action. Forget Neighbourhood Watch – this was full-scale surveillance.

The group had first hit the front page just before Christmas. It was mainly composed of dissenters from the residents' association, plus a few die-hard rent-a-gobs and a handful of bored youths with nothing better to do. The *Star* had carried an interview with the campaign co-ordinator and, later, covered a protest rally in the park. The uniforms had been keeping tabs. The verdict, after a couple of months, ran along the lines of mouth and trousers, bark and bite. Perhaps, Byford thought, it had cut teeth.

"We want our streets back, Mr Superintendent. And we'll be out in force every night until we get them."

"That sounds like a threat."

"It's a promise." He paused. "They're vermin, spreading filth and disease. They need putting down. The sooner the better."

Byford relaxed his fist before he damaged his circulation. Every time he closed his eyes he saw Michelle's bruised and bloody body. It was fortunate that Big Mouth was on the end of a phone. Fortuitous or foresighted? Bad timing or excellent?

Byford wished he could see the creep's face. Could the man already know what he was about to tell him?

"You'll be seeing a good deal of police activity over the next few days."

"Oh yeah?" The voice was giving nothing away.

"There was an incident in the park this morning."

Byford listened for a pause; tried not to read too much into it.

"Good. Best news I've had all week. Told you didn't I? Get rid of all the little scrubbers. One down – one less to go."

Byford was alert to every nuance in the man's voice. Was it too casual? Too forced? It was certainly too quiet; the Superintendent was listening to the pips. Byford put the phone down deep in thought. Mouthie had a lot to answer for. First: how did he know there'd been a murder? And second: how did he know the victim was a prostitute?

"Chance of an early collar, Mr B?"

The throwaway line was a Matt Snow special: heavily baited.

Byford raised his eyes to the ceiling and held out an imaginary piece of string. The gesture was wilfully misinterpreted as Snow played to the press gallery. "Obviously not, lads. Must be the one that got away."

A few reporters sniggered. The quip wasn't one of Snow's best but as the Crime Correspondent of the *Evening Star*, he was the biggest fish in this particular pool.

Byford looked round the room, acutely aware of the poor turnout. None of the nationals had shown and network TV hadn't sent. He hoped they'd take pictures from regional crews and that stringers would file to the Sundays. It was five hours since Michelle's body had been found and none of his officers had come up with a lead.

He'd called the news conference reluctantly – for once courting the media exposure that he more often shunned. He was struck by the irony. Any other time and they'd be over him like a rash, but now? It was Saturday, early afternoon and he was up against weekend cover, reduced output, shorter bulletins. The *Star* had the biggest circulation here; he'd have to try to keep his cool with Mr Snow.

"Can't see anything remotely amusing in the death of a young girl, Matt."

The reporter shrugged as though the point was debatable.

Byford conferred with a stern-faced press officer seated to his right, then turned back to the half dozen hacks who had made the effort.

"Bernie Flowers here has a photo of the girl. He's got copies for all of you. Grab one on your way out and go as big as you can. It's a couple of years old but it's the best we can do."

Not true, of course, but he baulked at releasing pictures taken after death. He hoped it wouldn't come to that. The photo he was looking at now had been supplied by Elizabeth Sharpe. Michelle was in school uniform: well scrubbed face, cheeky grin and bright eyes. Words like promise, and waste, innocence and evil came to Byford's mind. Those he spoke were more mundane.

"It's vital we trace anyone who saw Michelle after six on Friday evening."

Bev had established the cut-off point. She was still interviewing Vicki Flinn but had already passed on the information that the two girls had spent most of Friday together. They'd parted just after six with Michelle saying she was off to put in a few hours. It was the last known sighting.

"What was she doing in the park?"

Byford had a feeling that Matt Snow already had an idea. "That's one thing we've yet to establish."

"With anyone, was she?"

No one was fooled by Matt's indifferent delivery. The reporter was well aware of the anti-vice campaign: he'd devoted more than enough column inches to CUTS.

Byford adopted a similar tone. "Don't know yet."

Snow brushed the fringe out of his eyes. He was small and wiry, had a wardrobe full of cheap brown suits. He put Byford in mind of a hyperactive shih tzu.

"Assaulted, was she?"

"We're waiting on the post mortem."

"Got a motive?"

"Not yet."

"Found the knife?"

"Nice one, Matt." The cause of death hadn't been revealed.

Snow winked. "Worth a try."

Byford's studied silence indicated the attempt's failure. The reporter held out his hands, body language which Byford read as, "Give us a break, man, I'm only doing my job." He didn't much care for Snow's verbal version, conveyed with an affected matiness neither man had ever felt.

"Aw, come on, Mr B. We ain't gonna win any awards with this little lot: girl dead; witnesses sought. Not much to go on, is it?"

Byford shook his head. "I'm staggered that even you, Mr Snow, regard a brutal murder as a mere career move."

"Brutal?" The animation was unmistakable. "Can I quote you on that?"

Byford pursed his lips. "Quote me on that, and I'll bloody kill you."

The hacks laughed. Bernie cracked his face. Even Byford had to stifle the ghost of a smile, despite the fact that, just for a second or two, he'd meant every word.

5

SCHOOLGIRL HOOKER SLAIN IN PARK

"Slain?" Cassie Swain's vocabulary was as slender as her grasp of car maintenance. She pointed at the headline, repeating the mystery word. Her aggrieved tone implied suspicion of a universal conspiracy aimed at highlighting her academic shortcomings. "What the frig's that?"

"It's old fashioned for dead, innit."

The not entirely accurate enlightenment was handed down by Cyanide Lil who flogged fags and papers from a grimy kiosk on a corner of the High Street. Cassie stopped by most days for ten Embassy and a packet of Polos. Still fully to master any of the three Rs, Cassie rarely bothered with the newspapers. But this evening's late edition of the *Star* had attracted a second glance and was about to receive her undivided attention.

Lil had a School Certificate mouldering away somewhere at home and was well-equipped to help Cassie with the finer points in smaller print. The intellectual high ground was not a position she often occupied. Lil was making the most of it. She lit an untipped Players, screwed up her eyes against the smoke and cleared her throat.

Cassie was staring at the old woman's greasy grey hair and the long deep lines on her nicotine-coloured face. Rumour had it, she'd seen off three husbands and not one through natural causes.

"You lissnin' or what?" Lil snapped.

"Sorry. I was miles away."

"You'll wish you were in a minnit."

Cassie concentrated as Lil read Matt Snow's deep-purple prose. Her face paled as her kohl-rimmed eyes widened. She seemed to Lil like a panda having a panic attack.

Shell Lucas done in, in the park. Cassie couldn't believe it. Christ, she wished she'd never come back now. She'd been earning a few bob in Wolverhampton. An Away-Day the girls called it. Have-It-Away-Day, Cass reckoned. She'd done a punter on the way there, three pulls on the patch and a blowie on the train back. Ninety quid, easy. More to the point, it had kept her away from Charlie Hawes. Unlike Shell. Poor cow.

"Bloody hell, Lil." Cassie was recalling Charlie's fingers round his belt that morning. She lifted a trembling hand to her mouth.

Lil's eyes narrowed as she took another drag. A column of ash fell across Michelle's smiling face; she'd made the front page but only a single column, head and shoulders.

"If you know anything, girl – get yourself down the cop shop."

Bile was burning the back of Cassie's throat; she feared she might faint or throw up. "Me? Why the fuck should I know anythin'?"

"You and her were at Fair Oaks. I've seen the pair of you together often enough."

Shit. Cassie hadn't thought of that. She wasn't going back tonight. The Bill'd be all over the place.

"I know nothin', right?"

"It ain't me you have to worry about, kid."

"You what?"

"It's the bobbies you're going to have on your back."

Cassie was wrestling with a couple of scenarios: answering questions from the police, then answering to Mad Charlie Hawes.

The call wasn't even close.

"Straight up. I'd tell you if I knew, Bevvie."

Bev weighed the fragile rapport she'd gradually been

forging with Vicki Flinn over the day, against the heavy-duty panic whenever their conversation touched on Michelle's pimp. On balance, Bev believed the girl: she'd said she hadn't a clue where the man lived. It was a pisser but at least they had a name now; however unlikely. It had taken ages and there'd been the inevitable crossed-lines and incredulity over the whole whores/Hawes biz, but Vicki was adamant it was for real. Bev gave her the benefit of the doubt on the basis that only a dummy would make up the dubious moniker 'Hawes' for a pimp. And whatever else Vicki Flinn might be, Bev was pretty sure the girl was no air-head.

The name had been run through the usual checks and come out clean. Still, it was a start, and more than Bev had ever managed when she was with the vice squad. The two most crucial lessons she'd learned then were: 99.9 per cent of women on the game are run by pimps and, all 100 per cent are more afraid of a pimp than the police and punters put together.

Vicki was that rare commodity: a solo player. She was still shit-scared.

"I've never known where Mad Charlie's house is, see. No one does. Except the girls he's groomin'."

Grooming. Bev shook her head. An improved appearance was the last thing a girl with a pimp was likely to get. "How many's he got?"

Vicki shrugged. "Dunno. He ain't exactly in Yellow Pages."

Bev speared a puny grey prawn covered in pink gunge. They were in the canteen again. They'd spent the last six hours either talking in interview three or sampling the carbohydrate kicks on the sixth floor. Bev had hidden a smile as Vicki licked her lips and headed for the toad in the hole. A few square meals was a small price to pay for the wealth of information the girl was coming out with.

Bev had passed on everything relevant as soon as it emerged: confirmation of Michelle's background and information on her recent history. Byford was well-pleased but Bev was still working on the big one: the whereabouts of Charlie Hawes. "So you've no idea where this bloke's place is?"

Vicki shook her head.

Bev watched as she dunked a sausage in a lake of brown sauce.

"Where you staying tonight, Vick?"

The fork stilled for just a second. "Dunno. Don't fancy the squat somehow. Not yet anyway."

Neither would Bev. "Friend with a floor?"

She screwed her nose. "Nah. Might see if me ma'll let me kip down for a bit."

"Your ma?" Bev's jaw hit the lino. "You told me your ma was dead."

"Yeah. Well." At least she had the grace to look sheepish. "I didn't know you then, Bevvie."

"With you," Bev feigned enlightenment. "You only tell porkies to pigs you don't know."

Vicki laughed. "Porkies. Pigs. Good, that."

Bev made a face. Vicki got the drift. "Yeah, yeah. Okay. Anyway the old lady's gaff's a no-no if her toy boy's around."

"Toy boy?"

"Steve."

Bev waited for more but Vicki was chasing the last piece of batter round her plate. "It's still your home, Vick."

"Yeah. Let's just say two's company where that pair's concerned. Except for the baby, of course."

"Baby?"

"Lucie. She's a right little doll. Come as a right shock, though. I thought the old lady was past all that nappy changing lark."

"How old's your ma, Vick?"

The girl turned her mouth down. "Thirty-two, three? Something like that."

"Well ancient." Bev sniffed.

"You got kids, Bevvie?"

She shook her head. She had the maternal instincts of a Sumo wrestler. "I still can't see why you can't go round, Vick."

"Got chucked out on my arse, didn't I? She caught him givin' me the eye. Next thing – I'm out on my elbow."

Bev kept up with the anatomical references but they still didn't make sense. "I don't get it. You get slung out. And he's still there?" Shit. Didn't anyone have a proper home these days? A mum and dad; meat and two veg? Bev's parents hadn't been perfect but they had been there. Okay, so the old man had been down at the pub as well, but he didn't come back all rat-arsed and flying fists. Her mum was still cut up and he'd been dead five years. The chances of them showing her the door were bigger than winning the Lottery – twice. Bev had left home years ago, and Emmy Morriss was still peeved.

"What happens if this bloke's there, then?"

Vicki was removing all traces of sauce with the last of her bread and butter. "Somethin'll turn up."

Bev was toying with the idea of the spare room at her place. She knew all about keeping a professional distance but maybe that was the problem. Everyone Vicki had ever known kept a distance. Maybe she should mention it to Mave? Mave'd had the odd PG in the past. Very odd, come to think of it. Anyway, crossing bridges and all that. She'd wait and see. "Want a lift?"

Vicki grinned. "Gonna put the flashers on and do the old naa-naas?"

"You've been watching too much telly." She scraped the chair back. "You comin', or what."

Vicki looked up and slowly crossed her legs. "Nah. It's just the way I'm sitting."

Bev shook her head, gave a wry smile. The kid had lost her home but was clinging to a sort of sense of humour; there was a grin from ear to multiple-pierced ear. The girl's beam gave way to a sudden frown.

"What is it, Vick?"

"I don't know where Charlie hangs out." She tapped the side of her nose. "But I know a girl who does." Vicki rose, tugged at the skirt clinging to her thighs. "First we have to find her. Then we get her to talk."

Vicki's eyes shone; her excitement was catching. A girl groomed by Mad Charlie would have a sack load of goodies. Bev was hoping that Charlie's Girl was one of life's sharers.

"In a word, guv: diddlysquat." Bev puffed out her cheeks. It was late. She was knackered. Her high hopes of tracking down Vicki's mate had been dashed. Not even a companiable nightcap – half a finger of Famous Grouse – in the boss's office was compensation. She'd hit every dive in town and drawn blank after blank. "As Vicki put it, guv: the bird has flown." 'Fucked off,' was what Vicki had actually said. Bev was giving edited highlights; Byford could be iffy about bad language.

"Done a runner more like," he said.

She took a sip of scotch, not sure she liked where he was going "How do you mean?"

"You know as well as me, Bev, these girls don't want to talk to cops at the best of times." She waited as he reached down to retrieve a copy of the local rag from an overflowing bin. "This is hardly that."

It was the *Star*'s final edition. Michelle Lucas's image was splashed across five columns, complete with coffee stains and tea leaves. Bev shook her head: the girl's murder was already yesterday's news. She took it from him, skimmed through Matt Snow's so-called exclusive. She shook her head again and gave a suitable snort. The only thing he hadn't made up was the girl's name, and even that was misspelt. "My God," she said. "What happened to all that stuff about not speaking ill of the dead?"

Byford wasn't speaking at all. She glanced up: he was leaning back, eyes closed. She yawned, laid the paper to one side. It had been a long day. And night. And the prospect was more of the same. There was already a mountain range of paper work: statements from the dead girl's teachers, friends, staff at the home. Then there were the door-to-doors, the crank calls and the usual string of confessions from the local nutters. Two Jack the Rippers had left blood-stained letters at the front desk.

She looked at Byford again; had he dropped off? She cleared her throat, stage whisper style.

"I'm resting my eyes," he murmured.

She smiled; he was as knackered as her. He'd been leaving the building as she arrived but had seemed keen to turn round and hear how the evening had panned out. Perhaps, like her, he didn't always fancy going back to an empty house.

She downed the scotch and was debating whether to slip out when he got to his feet.

"Come on, Bev. You look shattered. Go home. Get some sleep. I'll walk you to that arrangement of corroded metal you call your car."

She held the door, waiting while he logged off and extinguished lights. "Dunno about shut-eye," she said. "I certainly had my eyes opened tonight."

"I'm intrigued. Go on."

The walk to the car park was accompanied by a lively account of Bev's venture into the city's low-life night life. Vicki had been an invaluable, not to say voluble guide. Despite the disappointment, they'd had a few laughs; more than that, Bev reckoned they'd got on really well. The girl had a wicked sense of humour and a tongue like a needle; it was sharp and had Bev in stitches. She was talking Byford through the best bits but he wasn't exactly rolling in the aisle. "What's up, guv?"

"Nothing. Carry on."

"Anyway, Vick says…"

"Vick seems to have had a lot to say tonight."

There was a hint of something in his voice; the emphasis he

put on the girl's name. Bev couldn't pin it down and the glance at his face didn't help. "Problem with that?"

"You make it sound like a girls' night out, Bev." There was no mistaking the disapproval this time.

She took a deep breath, told herself to chill. "That's not fair and it isn't true." She added a reluctant "Sir."

"She's an informant and a potential witness, not a mate. There's a professional distance to keep."

She was furious. He had no right. She wasn't some bloody rookie. Then thoughts of futons and spare rooms flashed in her head. Okay, maybe he had a point. It didn't lessen her anger; made it worse. Now she was cross with herself as well as him.

His face softened. "It's a gentle reminder, Bev, that's all."

They were almost at her MG. An inept spray job with insufficient black paint had added a certain *je ne sais quoi* to the original shade of chicken-crap sallow. The Midget looked like a malformed hornet, but she'd christened it Trigger in an optimistic attempt to inject horsepower. She unlocked the door, aware Byford was still by her side. Maybe he regretted the earlier stuff.

"I'd like to meet the girl, Bev. You've given her quite a build-up." He smiled.

Bev nodded. It was an apology of sorts but she was still smarting. He was still hovering. "Come on, Bev. I have faith in you. You know that."

She relented. He was a good bloke and he had her interests at heart. She smiled. "Ta, guv. I reckon I know how to handle her. Trust me on this."

"Sure. I think she could be crucial to the inquiry, as well, Bev. She was very close to young Michelle. When are you interviewing her again?"

"Tomorrow, hopefully."

"Hopefully?"

She heard what he was not saying: that 'hope' wasn't enough. But a definite meet had been difficult to set up. She'd dropped

Vicki round the corner from her ma's but it was no guarantee she'd spend the night there. "She's almost NFA, guv. She said she'd get to Highgate as soon as she could. If there's a problem, she'll give me a bell."

"You gave her your number? Your home number?" He was more surprised by that than by Vicki's no fixed abode status.

Bev crossed her fingers; hated porkies. "Nah. Here. Front desk'll get a message to me." She watched him open his mouth to remonstrate, then presumably changed his mind. In Bev's mind was an image of Vicki, tottering on her wedgies down an unlit street to a house she could no longer call her home. Bev felt she'd let the girl down, should have stuck up for her in the face of Byford's criticism. She knew it was irrational but tried to redress the balance anyway.

"She's a nice girl, boss. She's had a rough time. Been through a lot of shit."

"Think of Michelle. Another nice girl. Dead. Covered in it. Be careful, Bev. That's all I'm saying."

The words rang in her head all the way home.

6

"The bells…the bells."

Bev staggered out of bed, completing her impromptu Quasimodo with a bleary-eyed lurch towards the alarm. The clock, a fraternal Christmas present, was blaring from behind rainbow curtains on the far side of the room. She hid it in a different place every night. The daily enforced fumble in the dark meant less chance of a return to the duvet.

She yawned, headed for the bathroom. It might be Sunday, but Bev's gut told her it was not going to be a day of rest. She studied her face in the mirror over the basin.

"Now look, punk. Are you gonna have a good day?" She paused, did a passable Clint Eastwood: "Or are you gonna have a good day?"

The morning mantra was more Felix Barry than Dirty Harry. Felix tried hard to teach her Tai Chi. Not hard enough. The job kept getting in the way. Still, Felix was a fervent proponent of positive thought and verbal reinforcement. Bev reckoned anything was worth a try.

A pee and a shower, and it was back to the boudoir to grab a suit. Days of dithering in front of the mirror were long gone. She now wore blue. Blue. Or occasionally: blue. Picasso could have painted her wardrobe. She still hadn't sewn the button on her skirt's waistband and was scrabbling round for a safety pin when there was a hammering on the door.

"Hold on. I'm coming."

It had to be Mave. Who else was going to come calling before seven on a Sunday? It was. She breezed in bearing a plate of bacon sandwiches and trailing a blend of Persil and Players.

"Get these down your neck. You can't operate on an empty stomach."

Bev grinned. There was enough to keep the BMA going for a fortnight. "You're a star, Mave. Know that?"

"Milky Way, me, mate."

Some people have neighbours; Bev had Mavis Holdsworth. Think Joan Collins on income support, out of Oxfam. Mave looked on Bev as the daughter she'd never had.

"What's up?" Bev asked.

"Me." Mave said as if a single syllable was sufficient.

"And?" Bev grabbed the kettle.

"I'm up when I should be in bed. It's supposed to be my day off." Mave was the manageress and queen of the Washwell Deluxe Laundrette and Dry Cleaners.

"And?" Bev waved Mave's resident mug in the air – interpreted the shrug of narrow shoulders and chucked in a tea bag.

"Rita's called in sick again, hasn't she?" Mave worked with a woman who had more time off than a stopped watch.

"Never mind. Least it's not far to go."

A flight of stairs to be precise. Their maisonettes were above a row of shops that included the launderette, a dodgy vid store and a deli to die for.

Mave pointed at Bev, pointed at the bacon butties and took over the teamaking. "I wouldn't care, but it's not the first time." She did care. Mavis chewed gum incessantly; her mouth was going like a piston.

Bev was munching smoked back and Sunblest. She could only nod. Besides, she didn't want to get involved. Not that Mave seemed to notice.

"Twenty hours a week she's s'posed to do. By arrangement with me."

The woman was positively bristling. Nose out of joint? Or something more? It wasn't like Mave to take a downer on anyone. Looking on the bright side and seeing the best was

Mave's style. It was the unswerving cheerfulness that had endeared her to Bev in the first place. That, plus her propensity to pick up the odd bit of gossip with the ease of an industrial hoover.

"A sickie's a sickie. Not much you can do." Bev said.

Mave stuck her gum on the side of her mug and took a gulp of steaming tea. "It's one thing after another, Bev. Bruised ribs. Sprained wrist. Detached retsina."

"Retina."

"Same diff."

A Greek Adonis, bearing crystal glasses on a silver tray across a golden beach, flashed before Bev's eyes. "Not quite."

"I mean, Bev, how many doors can one woman walk into?"

"What you saying, Mave?"

"She's either swinging the lead," Mave finished the tea and retrieved her Wrigley's, "or some bastard's swinging it at her."

"Shit!" Bev had caught sight of the clock on the cooker. "I've got seven and a half minutes to get to Highgate."

The woman's face fell. "Sorry, Mave. Do you want me to have a word with her? Rita, isn't it?"

Mavis sniffed. "She won't talk. I've tried to get her to open up. She won't say a word."

"I can have a go." Bev smiled as she shrugged into her jacket. "They don't call me silver-tongued Morriss for nothing, y'know."

"Pay them, do you?"

That was more like it. Bev winked. "Cheeky tart."

"Cassie Swain's our best bet." Bev looked round, encouraged by a few nodding heads.

The whole team was now up to speed – a meagre two miles a fortnight, she reckoned – and a subdued Byford sat back, having just thrown the briefing open. Bev was on her feet at the front, chucking in her two penn'orth. "The girls were the same age.

Went to the same school. Shared a room at Fair Oaks."

"Not all they shared, is it?" Bev recognised the voice, forced herself not to show a reaction. Twenty bodies were crowded into the incident room and, without looking up from her notes, she'd bet eighteen pairs of eyes were now focused on Mike Powell. She'd spotted him earlier, leaning against a side wall, examining his nails.

"Not sure what you're saying." She tried to match his casual delivery, but her heart sank. She wasn't in the mood. She was tempted to sit, decided to stand her ground. Everyone knew the girls were on the game but what was Powell playing?

"Both in the same line of business, weren't they?"

Eyes were back on her now. It felt like the centre court at Wimbledon. She tried to ignore the crowd; kept her voice level. "And that makes them what? Stupid? Unreliable? Liars?"

"It makes them tarts. Lie as soon as look at you. False names. Fake addresses. That's when they're talking at all. When it comes to pimps – they've all taken a vow of silence."

She was aware of bums shifting; of her own foot tap-tap-tapping and a trickle of sweat, cold down her back. She'd met a handful of cops who openly admitted hating whores; bragged about it; wouldn't touch vice with a sterile barge pole. But Powell? She had zilch time for the man, but she wouldn't have put him in that underclass. He was probably just on the bait.

"And we all know why," she said. "They're shit scared. If a girl opens her mouth she gets a size ten in it. That's if she's lucky and doesn't wake up in Casualty."

"Yeah, yeah." She waited, there was clearly more to come.

"Blame it on the blokes. The toms are all little pussy-cats, aren't they, Morriss?"

There were a few sniggers but the man was so dense, the double entendre was probably unwitting. Bev shook her head, aware they were waiting for a one-liner; a Morriss special, but instead of Wimbledon, this was beginning to resemble something out of *Gladiators* – and guess who was the Christian?

Byford was getting to his feet; thank God.

"That's it," he snapped. "A young girl's been murdered. For whatever reason, she was on the game. If anyone has a problem with that, they'd better say so. Now."

Bev glanced at Powell whose hands were spread, palms-up.

"No problem."

"I'm glad to hear it. We've wasted enough time here. You all know what's needed. The teacher interviews need finishing. The gaps on the house-to-house have to be plugged. Mike and I still have a few people from the CUTS campaign to track down. And Bev, I want you to look for Cassie Swain."

A phone rang. He ignored it. "It's twenty-four hours since the murder and unless anyone has any better ideas..."

"Guv." D C Newman had his hand over the mouthpiece. "No need for a search party. Cassie Swain's turned up. It's the General. She's in Intensive Care."

"You can't see her. And she won't be talking. Not to anyone. Not for a long time."

Bev's palms tingled. She wanted to slap the smirk off the bloody woman's face. The badge on her seriously white coat said Dr Thorne. And she was – in Bev's side.

She and young Ozzie had been kept waiting in a room the size of a soap dish so long that Bev had gone through enough coffee to keep the Brazilian economy afloat. Oz didn't touch the stuff. He'd only been in CID a few weeks, hadn't had time to pick up too many bad habits. Bev was supposed to be keeping an eye on him. DC Khan was the tastiest bloke at Highgate, it was no hardship. Thorne, on the other hand, was a pain.

"Can you be more specific?" Bev's tone was polite.

The response was not. "The girl's jaw's smashed. A fair number of her teeth have been knocked out. And if the swelling in her skull doesn't go down – we'll be lucky to save her. So. No. I can't."

Bev had no problem with a woman five years younger, fifteen kilos lighter, who bore more than a passing resemblance to Kate Moss. It was the doctor's attitude that was the pisser. From the second the woman had swept in, she'd looked down. She did it so well, Bev reckoned she practised. Bev moved closer. She'd had a bad night; kept awake by vague worries she couldn't pin down. Sleep – when it came – had been fitful and filled with gory images of Michelle and other girls she'd known. This Bright Young Thing crap she could do without.

"What's your problem, love?" Even to her own ears, it was a threat. She felt Ozzie's gaze on her.

Doctor Thorne had an uncertain smile on her face. "I beg your pardon?"

Bev was standing, feet apart, arms folded. "I'm not asking you to beg my pardon. I'm asking for a bit of respect."

"I don't know what you mean."

"Yes you do. I've been hanging round so long someone wanted to plant flowers." She jabbed a finger in the air. "When you eventually get your act together – it's a one-liner saying sweet FA."

"I don't have time for this. I'm a busy person." She was fondling a stethoscope slung casually round her neck. Bev wasn't impressed by the prop; she'd seen enough episodes of *ER* to bluff her way into medical school.

"And I'm not?" She felt Ozzie's hand on her arm. Another time, she'd have left it there. You could file nails on his graduate cheekbones. She kept her gaze on the doctor who was finding it increasingly difficult to maintain eye contact.

"I didn't say that."

"That's exactly what you're saying. Your attitude? It sucks."

"Sarge?"

Bev looked at Oz. He was tapping his watch. She glanced at

the time. "Okay, okay. I'm out of here." She turned to the doctor. "Let's hope, Ms Thorne, that I get to the mad bastard out there, before some other kid gets a taste for hospital food. Not that you can eat a lot when your jaw's wired and your teeth have gone AWOL."

The woman ran her hands through her hair. Bev watched as it fell perfectly into place.

"Look, I'm sorry. I'm dead on my feet." The voice hadn't got much life either. Bev examined the doctor's face. Faint mauve smudges were just perceptible beneath the immaculate make-up under the eyes; she'd probably been on call for ages without so much as a Kit Kat.

But Bev was fresh out of compassion. "And Michelle Lucas is dead. Full stop."

Dr Thorne looked set to argue but capitulated quietly. "Point taken."

Bev capitalised by pushing another. "Cassie Swain? We really need to speak to her."

The doctor shook her head. "I really don't know. I'm concerned about the head injury. The next few hours are crucial."

What about the hours Cassie had already lost? Beaten and kicked within an inch, then tossed onto a skip. Not hidden. Not buried. Half way down Thread Street. It was a message. A bloody message. And what if old Bert hadn't been on the trawl? Thank God for insomniac winos. Bev shivered. She picked up her bag; they'd get nothing here. There was a clock on the wall. It had been bugging her all morning. She pointed. "That needs a new battery."

"Don't we all?" the doctor said.

Bev smiled. Superwoman might be human after all. She glanced at Ozzie. "We'd best be off." They were almost through the door when the woman relented and called them back. Bloody hell, Bev realised, Thorne looked even better when she let down the barriers, stopped trying to put on her official face.

"Leave me your number. If there's any change. Anything at all. I'll let you know."

"You're on." Bev took a card from her bag, scribbled on the back. It was only a few hours since she'd done the same for Vicki. Which reminded her… why hadn't the girl been in touch?

"Don't want mine as well, do you?" The voice had hope rather than conviction.

"No, DC Khan." Bev shook her head, smiling. "She does not."

"Let me get this clear, Mr Leigh. You saw nothing, heard nothing and if you'd seen Lord Lucan waiting for a 35 bus you'd say nothing."

Ronnie Leigh wiped lager from rubbery lips and burped. It was 11am and this was a house call that was going no further than the front step. "Bright for a cop. Aren't you?" His right hand transferred the excess alcohol to denims that had once been blue.

Powell moved forward but Byford put out a restraining hand.

"Perhaps we could talk about your involvement in CUTS, Mr Leigh."

Byford had verbal and visual evidence that put Ronnie in the campaigners' frame but Ronnie refused to be drawn; he scratched his groin with thick hairy fingers. "And perhaps we couldn't."

Byford sighed. "This isn't getting us very far."

Ronnie made to close the door. "You do your job, copper. I'll do mine."

Byford put a foot in the jamb. "What exactly is your line of business these days, Ronnie?" This was not small talk. He knew Ronnie's history so well he'd pass the exam.

"I'm on the sick."

"Nothing trivial, I hope?" Powell's bright smile confused the man.

"Nah. Bit of back trouble."

"Have to watch what you lift, do you, Ronnie?" Byford was at it now.

"You bein' funny?"

"I'm being serious. Dead serious. That break-in at The Eagle? Your name's all over it, Ronnie." Byford was busking; he had no particular incident in mind, but the pub had seen more raids than a kid's piggy bank. Keeping track of Ronnie's record was difficult. Even for Ronnie.

Byford's surmise struck gold. He watched as the man's alcohol-induced flush drained, leaving his face whiter than his T-shirt.

"That was nothing to do with me, you bastard."

"That's not what my man says." Byford looked at his watch. "Come on, Mike. Let's get back. That warrant should be about ready."

"Hold on, hold on." Ronnie was rubbing his chin. Byford didn't think the man was considering a shave. "I can't help with the girl. I didn't see nothin'."

"Save it." Byford gave a mock salute. "See you in an hour. Don't go walkabout, Ronnie." He stepped back as the man reached to grab his arm. Byford wasn't overly fastidious but Ronnie's personal hygiene left everything to be desired.

"There's no need for that, Mr Byford. I haven't been near The Eagle for months. Honest."

Powell put his hand to the door. "Won't mind us taking a look round then, will you?"

Panic crossed Ronnie's irregular features. He clearly didn't want them in the house and it wasn't because he hadn't got round to the hoovering. Byford made a mental note: The Eagle might be a non-starter but Ronnie Leigh had been up to something.

"How 'bout if I keep my ear to the ground. Let you know if I hear anything?"

Given Ronnie's shady network, it wasn't a bad offer.

Byford shook his head. "Not good enough."

Ronnie's glance darted between the two men. Byford noticed a line of sweat where the lager had been. "One thing I do know…"

Byford raised his eyebrows, waited.

"Tonight. Thread Street. There's gonna be a show of force." He leaned forward, dropped his voice. "And I'm not talking police force."

"Problem?" Ozzie asked.

Bev replaced the phone. "I'll get over it." She sat back, tried to relax. World's worst passenger, Bev. Ordinarily, she'd be behind the wheel but there'd been a couple of calls she needed to make. Recalling them brought back the concern. Vicki still hadn't turned up. There'd been no word left at the desk and no message on Bev's answerphone. What to make of it? She'd thought they were beginning to make a connection. She didn't want to think Vicki had done a bunk. But what did she know? She wanted to believe her but Vicki could have been lying through her lip piercing. She was a free agent, wasn't she? The outside chance that she might not be was another thing Bev didn't want to think about. There wasn't time.

"We stopping for a bite after this?"

She glanced at Ozzie's profile. Talk about tasty; he was Darcy with a suntan. She found herself musing about pleasing countenances, gentle dispositions and Ozzie wading out of the nearest lake. She was miles away.

"Sarge?"

"Sorry, Oz. Things on my mind."

"Must be good," he said. "I've never seen you smile like that."

Boy. He'd been looking at her. "Keep your eyes on the road, Constable." Shit. Why had she said that? She sounded like a sodding driving instructor.

"Anyway, Sarge, we stopping or what?"

Yeah, tongue sandwich. Stop it, Beverley! "Best not. There's too much to get through, Oz."

"Fair enough."

They drove in silence for a while. Bev was calculating whether she'd have a chance to pop home before Byford's Thread Street briefing. There'd obviously be a plod presence but the boss wanted a few of his own people out as well.

Oz was clearly thinking along the same battle lines. "Reckon there'll be trouble tonight?"

She shrugged. "Depends on the turnout. If the girls get wind of it and stay home, the johns won't hang around. Could be a damp squib." She yawned.

"Hope so. I could do with an early night." Oz turned left into a wide, tree-lined street. "What number we after?"

"Twenty-two." She spotted it. "Just passed it. Go to the end and turn round."

"Posh 'ere, innit?"

She was coming to the same conclusion. The Cedars estate was the sort of place estate agents tell the truth about. Half-beamed, black and whites. Mock Tudor, real money. Some of the garages were bigger than Bev's last bedsit. So were the cars, come to that.

She sniffed, put a pound of plums in her mouth. "Very Edge-bar-ston, dahling."

He grinned. "Ooh, don't."

"What?"

"I love it when you talk clean."

"Daft sod." She smiled: not just a pretty face, Oz.

They pulled up. He gave a low whistle. "How much are teachers on these days?"

"Dunno. Reckon we're in the wrong game?" She consulted a hastily scribbled note. "Anyway. This bloke's a Head of Year. The ones kids are supposed to go to if there's a problem."

"Must have seen a lot of Michelle then."

A sign told them to Beware of the Dog. She reckoned there should have been another warning callers about the bell; it played Greensleeves.

"Mr Brand? Henry Brand?"

She was looking at a small, portly man, probably mid-fifties. Half-moon glasses were perched on a high domed forehead, kept in position by ear flaps she reckoned he could land a plane with. He didn't look at her and addressed his remarks to Ozzie. "I'm not buying anything. I'm an agnostic. And I contribute every month to a charity of my choice." He was about to close the door.

Bev held out ID. "I'm Detective Sergeant Morriss. This is DC Khan. We need to speak to you about Michelle Lucas."

He glanced at the card then back to Oz. "This isn't very convenient. Can't it wait until tomorrow? I'll be on school premises from 7.30 onwards." Ozzie didn't move a muscle. Bev waited till the unspoken message finally got through. When she had the man's undivided attention, she made a point of looking down. He had the *Sunday Times* business supplement in his left hand, the index finger keeping his place.

"Sorry it's inconvenient, Mr Brand. I'm afraid it can't wait at all, let alone another day."

A sigh was followed by a resigned shake of the head. "You'd better come in."

As they filed through, she stuck out her tongue. It was childish but what the hell? She glanced back at Ozzie with a conspiratorial grin. He was looking straight ahead – into a huge, gilt-framed mirror on the far wall. She licked her lips a few times hoping to pass off the tongue business as a nervous habit. She looked round the hall: oak-panelling, stained-glass windows, a couple of ancient settles. Judging by the smells there'd been serious housework going on and not far away serious coffee was on the go. It soon became clear they were to go no further.

Brand was dashing round closing doors. He came to a halt in front of Bev, arms folded, newspaper still in place. "My wife. She's unwell. I don't want her disturbed."

Bev's sympathy was in short supply. "What can you tell us about Michelle?"

"That you haven't already learned? I doubt very much whether I can add anything at all."

She took out a notebook, gave her pencil an ostentatious lick. "Go on then."

"What?"

"Have a go."

He took off his glasses, scratched his head. "Michelle Lucas was fifteen years old. An average student. Certainly not stupid. Had she shown more inclination, she might have achieved a GCSE or two. I did not anticipate that she would be applying for Oxbridge."

Supercilious git. "What did you anticipate, Mr Brand?"

"The question is meaningless. You should attempt to be more precise."

"Go and stand in the corner, shall I?" She smiled, hoping for a latent sense of humour.

"Is that meant to be funny?"

She took a deep breath. "What I'm trying to say is this: from what you know of Michelle, what sort of girl was she? Did she have any problems, ever ask for advice? Is there anything you can tell us about her or her friends, that might help us find who killed her?"

"There are at least four questions there. Do you have an order of preference?"

Bev tapped a foot: never a good sign. "I prefer interviewees to help."

He sighed again. "Michelle Lucas was a typical by-product of a broken home and abusive parents."

By-product? Sounded like industrial waste.

"She had no respect for authority, lacked any sort of discipline. She was an insolent and attention-seeking adolescent."

Bev glanced at Ozzie. This went against all the reports back so far. Most people had drawn a picture of a pleasant girl, eager to please and seemingly undamaged by a less than promising early childhood.

"Attention-seeking?"

"Short skirts, tight blouses, loud mouthed."

"Typical teenager then?"

"She was a trouble-maker." He was scratching his head again, obviously ill at ease.

"In what way?"

"She just was." For a man who valued precision, the reply was woollier than a herd of sheep.

Bev made a note and looked up. "Was there trouble at school?"

"The girl's dead. What's the point..?"

"That is the point."

She watched him weighing up what to say. "Look. You'll probably find out sooner or later... There were allegations..."

"Allegations?"

"Michelle Lucas made certain accusations against a number of members of staff." He halted as if what he'd said was sufficient. The silence suggested otherwise. "It was absolute nonsense of course. And I wasn't the only one."

"Michelle accused you?"

"As I've already made clear – she constantly sought attention. It was me, me, me all the time with Miss Lucas."

"What was the nature of the allegations?"

"She claimed I tried to touch her."

"And did you?"

He widened his eyes, sharpened his voice. "That is a highly offensive remark, young woman."

"No more offensive than a schoolgirl being assaulted."

"Are you suggesting..?"

"I'm suggesting nothing. What did the inquiry find?"

"What inquiry? There was no inquiry. There was nothing to inquire into unless you count the delusions of an hysterical teenager."

"When were these allegations made?"

He waved a hand. "Sometime last month, I think. She went to the head. Mrs Sharpe."

"And?"

"Elizabeth soon had the truth out of her. Cock and bull from start to finish. I only mention it to prove my point about Michelle's propensity for the spotlight."

Bev nodded. "And the others? You said you weren't the only one she made accusations against."

"She never mentioned names. Well, she couldn't, could she?"

"She mentioned yours."

He pursed thin lips. "Look. I've done my best to help. If there's nothing else…" His body language was screaming at them to go. Bev considered: there was obviously a lot more, but maybe not yet. She looked at Ozzie. He shook his head. She smiled. "That's all. Mr Brand. For the moment."

"What you make of him, then?"

Ozzie was talking through a mouthful of tuna baguette. Bev was licking sugar off her fingers. Two cups of cappuccino were cooling on the dashboard. Esso's finest and a parking space just off the forecourt.

"Pompous git," she said. "Why do jerks like Brand go in for teaching?"

He brushed a couple of crumbs on to the floor. "To buy a house like that for one thing."

"Reckon?" She paused. "I wonder. I think we'll have a closer look at Henry Brand. And not just the size of his wallet."

"That stuff about Michelle?"

She nodded. "He was up-front but he had to be. Like he said…

we were bound to find out. He thought he was being smart."

Oz wiped his lips with a napkin from Bev's doughnut. "I suppose it's possible. She might have made up a story just to drop him in it."

"Anything's possible, Ozzie. It's possible Mike Powell will buy a round of drinks in the club one night."

He grinned. She liked working with this bloke, he laughed at her jokes. What's more it meant she saw very little of Powell these days, in or out of the bar. She took a sip of coffee. "I just don't see why Brand was so keen to shitbag the girl. Speaking ill of the dead, and all that."

She warmed her hands on the cup, swirled the liquid round, watching the patterns, thinking her thoughts. Why had he been such a bastard? He clearly hadn't wanted them in the house. He could barely look at Bev. And he hadn't shown the slightest sign of sorrow or regret at the waste of Michelle Lucas's young life. Then again – who had? Apart from the caretaker who'd found Michelle's body, the only tears Bev had seen shed were Vicki's. The only decent lead had come from Vicki. The only promise of help, Vicki. Bev crumpled the empty cup in the palm of her hand. And where the hell was Vicki Flinn now?

7

Across the city, the girls were gathering in Big Val's place: end terrace, back street, front room. The weekend's events had forced a camaraderie of sorts on women who normally wouldn't give each other the time of day. Out on the patch, they circled round like big cats staking territory. Now they were sitting round sharing six-packs, trying to look cool. Except Val.

Val was the oldest, admitted to forty; the meet had been her idea. She'd put the word out: only the kids at this stage. Six had shown – just one face missing.

Big Val had moved down from Leeds in the late seventies. She'd worked the streets longer than the Royal Mail. She was pinning a mass of unruly red hair into a beehive. "I'll tell you something for nothing. If we don't look out for each other, no bugger else will."

She was perched on a bed shared with a herd of stuffed pigs. Any size, any shade; if it had trotters and a curly tail, she went for it. Apart from a lumpy bean-bag, there was nowhere else to sit, so the girls were lying on the floor propped on an elbow or two. It was a wet Sunday, half past two, nothing else on.

Jo leaned across and took a cigarette from one of several packs lying open on an ash-grey carpet, the colour as much accident as design. The fifteen-year-old had given up but might as well have been on twenty a day given the blue haze hovering overhead. She was nearly six feet in her wedgies. "Come on, Val. It's not Ripper country, is it?"

"One kid dead. Another on life support. It's not Disneyland either."

A painfully thin girl called Jules took a swig from a can of

Red Stripe. The purple in her hair matched a massive bruise on one of her arms. "If I'd wanted a row, I'd have stayed at home." The fingers clutching the can had more rings than a Samuel's window. "What we gonna do about it? That's what you got us round for, innit? Or are you just trying to scare us shitless?"

Val was beginning to wonder. Maybe she'd over-reacted. The kids weren't fazed. Shell's murder hadn't touched them, nor Cassie's beating. Then again, they hadn't been on the game long; it was still a bit of a giggle. Apart from the odd swinging fist and flying fuck, they were virtually unmarked if not untouched. Not Val. There was an old scar the width of her belly: and it sure wasn't down to a dodgy appendix. She was lucky. Her best mate had lost an eye to the same crazy. She looked round, shook her head. These kids were more scared of their pimps than the perverts. They still believed they'd make a fortune, buy a cottage in the country and live happily ever. Yeah. And frogs still turn into princes. Jesus H. The pigs were the only things in the house she didn't owe money on.

"I know!" A girl who looked about twelve shot a hand in the air.

Jo looked over, sniggered. "S'not fuckin' school, Kylie."

"You're so funny, ain't you?" Kylie's mother had been a hooker. Only part-time. She went out when the gas or electricity came in. Known as Bill, she was, till she keeled over one night in front of a bus. Dead drunk. Then just dead. "Anyway, listen." Kylie was beaming, "We can work in pairs, can't we? Go out together, like."

Val sniffed; they'd tried that in Chapeltown. "Sure. Charge double then can't you?"

"Y'know what I mean," Kylie whinged.

"What happens when you're doin' the business, Kyle? Your mate gonna stand round hummin' *Strangers in the Night*?" Val countered.

"Keep an eye out, can't she?"'

Val said nothing; it didn't work like that.

"I reckon we should stick to our regulars. Better the dick y'know..." Marj was seriously large: dress size twenty; same as her age. She was also the best looking woman in the room and had the most punters.

"Could be right," Val agreed. "Least till we know the way the wind's blowin'."

"All right for you lot. Blokes only come to me once." Patty was stoned out of her head so often, she barely recognised her own reflection.

"Wonder why?" asked Jo.

"Fuck off."

"Cut it out." Val slung a pig at Jo: day-glo pink with one eye missing. Jo caught it with one hand. "That's a point. What's the filth doin' about it? Where's the bleedin' Bill when you need 'em?"

"Had one at my place."

The others looked round. Smithy had spoken her first words. They called her The Librarian. Always had her nose in a book. Even on the beat: had her own street lamp so she could read in the dark. Should have had shares in Mills and Boon.

"Go on then."

"What?" She was pushing huge red-framed glasses back into place.

"What they want? What'd they say?"

"Asked if I'd seen anythin'. Friday. When Shell bought it," she sniffed. "Course I flippin' hadn't."

"Tasty, were they?" Marj was licking glossy magenta lips; the shade looked great against her dark skin. "There's a couple of crackers down at Highgate."

"Sod off. There was only one. Some bird. Thought she was from the Social, first off."

That rang a distant bell. "All in blue? Dark hair? Mouthie?" asked Val.

"Spot on." Smithy yawned. She'd been up all night with Barbara Cartland. "Know her?"

Val nodded; the beehive sagged. "Bev Morriss. I know her a bit. She's all right."

"She wants to watch herself." A girl with hair as short as it gets rose to her Doc Martens. The fuzz on her skull was like a dusting of icing sugar. The thick black eyebrows could have been applied with a trowel. There was menace in the voice – unusual for Chloë.

"Why's that, then?" Val prompted.

"Goin' round askin' stupid questions."

"Her job, innit?"

"It's her job to nick Shell's killer. Not to go round getting' up Charlie Hawes's nostrils."

Just hearing the guy's name was enough. The girls sat up, listened, let Val do the talking.

"What you goin' on about, Chloë?"

"They're after Mad Charlie, ain't they?"

Everyone knew Charlie's way. He kept a lower profile than the invisible man. As far as cops were concerned, he didn't exist, let alone have a name.

"How'd they get on to him?" This was bad news.

Chloë folded her arms, glared at Val. "Your pal Bev? She had a little helper durin' her night on the town. Pointed her in all the right directions. Know what I mean?"

Val put a hand to her mouth. This was very bad news. "Cassie?"

"Don't be stupid. She was gettin' her face re-arranged."

"Who then..?"

Chloë looked at each girl in turn, then back at Val.

"You tell me, ma. Who's missin'?"

"Photo doesn't do her justice, does it, Victoria? Real goer was young Michelle."

Vicki would have agreed. Was keen to agree. Would have gone out of her way to agree. Except she couldn't move and couldn't see: Charlie's back was in the way. He was kneeling on the bed, staring at the front of the *Star.* The Sunday papers were strewn all over the floor but Shell's picture had only made the local rag. Charlie had been in the same position for ages; she was wondering how much his tan had cost. Where'd he been to get an all-over job? And where the hell had he put her clothes? They weren't within eyeshot and she had no way of extending that. Couldn't lift a finger, let alone her head.

Yet, he hadn't touched her. Well of course he had. He'd shagged her all night but he hadn't hurt her. He was good in the sack, but then she'd always known that. He hadn't said much so far. Didn't need to. The knife on the bedside table spoke volumes.

He stood, stretched, looked down and smiled. Lovely teeth. Gorgeous face. Looked even better with long hair. No wonder he charged his own tarts.

She wished he'd loosen the belts though: the leather was cutting into her skin. Maybe she could get him to take her to the loo again. Bet he slipped something in that Coke. It was getting dark; must be half-four, five-ish. Pissing down, she could hear it on the window.

"Now. What are we gonna do with you?"

Funny really; his voice was quite nice. Take the gag off me, dickhead.

"I'm gonna take this off in a minute. If you start anything, it goes back. Right?" She tried a nod but it hurt. He raised her head, started untying the knots.

The scarf had been Shell's. Lifted it at Debenham's. Then they'd wandered over to the smellies. Spraying stuff everywhere; having a right laugh. Stuck-up cows behind the counter hadn't liked that. Shell had taken a fancy to the Ralph Lauren. Smell was still there.

"You remind me of her, know that?"

She opened her mouth, didn't know what to say.

"Not looks. Not that. Just something…" He turned away, clenching his fists. "Shit. I don't know."

What was his game? It was a bit late for the sorry card. She still didn't know what to say. One word out of place and she'd be talking through gaps in her teeth. She darted a few glances round the room. Didn't stint himself. Not Charlie. Everything brand new. Leather sofas at one end. Thick cream carpet. Mirrors everywhere. Caught her looking.

"Having a good nose?" He turned. Christ. She wished he'd put something on. "Won't do you any good. You'll not be coming back."

Shit. She was going the same way as Shell. "How d'you mean, Charlie?" He laughed. Must have been the tremor in her voice. Her knees'd be playing *My Way*, if he hadn't splayed her legs.

"I'm not happy, Victoria. You've been a very naughty girl. And what happens to naughty girls?"

She closed her eyes. Not that. Please. Not that. Last year, a girl had fleeced Charlie. She'd kept a few quid back; just the once. He said it was the same as putting her hand in the till. She only had one hand now. Everyone said he'd taken a hacksaw to her.

She opened her eyes. He was just standing there, smiling. She watched as he sauntered over to a mirror on the far wall; slid it back to reveal a vast array of suits and shirts. He ran a finger along a line of shoulder pads, stopped halfway along.

"Black for mourning isn't it, Victoria?"

She shrugged.

"I didn't hear you Victoria?"

"Yes, Charlie." She'd say black was white, if that's what he wanted. He hummed to himself as he dressed slowly, admiring himself in the mirror. She stiffened as he wandered back, sat on the edge of the bed.

"Now, listen carefully, Victoria, while I tell you exactly what's going to happen."

"I'm sorry. Can you say that again?"

Byford had the phone in one hand and a bottle of Glenmorangie in the other. It was traditional. Sunday evening. Single malt. He'd stick at one tonight. Just in case. Tradition too for the boys to ring. They were punctilious about that, especially since their mother's death. Even now, he sometimes took out two glasses. He'd taken the call in the kitchen, expecting Richard or Chris. Richard, probably. It was just after seven.

It was neither. "I said, it ill behoves one of your officers to behave in a manner more suited to that of a schoolchild."

Byford poured. How the hell did the old dragon get hold of his number? Maybe he'd make it a double after all.

"Were you there, Mrs Sharpe? Did you witness the incident?" He could imagine the woman pursing her lips, tutting.

"No. I did not. But I have every faith in my staff, Superintendent. If Henry Brand says your Sergeant was making jokes and pulling faces, then she most certainly was."

Byford was pulling a few of his own. He'd already heard Bev's account of the Henry Brand interview. Okay, so she hadn't mentioned any wisecracks or messing around but she'd spelt out Michelle's accusations of assault. She'd brought him up to speed just before the evening briefing. Of all the statements she or anyone else had taken that day, it was the most interesting. And the most promising.

"As much as anything, Mr Brand made it quite clear that the timing was most inconvenient. Mrs Brand suffers with her nerves, you know. Surely it could have waited until tomorrow when we'll all be at school?"

Byford was still at the stage when every time he closed his eyes, he saw Michelle's face. He was unmoved by considerations of convenience.

"I shall be making a point of seeing you both. I want to know, for instance, why you, madam, didn't see fit to mention the allegations Michelle was making against Henry Brand in the weeks before her murder. And why – in the light of those claims – a proper inquiry wasn't held."

He was waiting for another tirade but all he could hear was the sound of his fingers drumming on the table.

Eventually she spoke. Her voice was calm and had ice in it. "What are you suggesting?"

"I'm suggesting nothing. I only found out about this a couple of hours ago."

"There was nothing to find out."

Byford ignored the remark. "I'll see you first. And bring the notes I assume you made during your conversations with Michelle. After that, you'll be able to send Henry Brand in. I want to talk to him personally."

He resisted the temptation to slam down the phone, replying in kind to her stiffly polite, "Good evening, Superintendent."

He took a sip of Scotch, slowly running it over his teeth, under his tongue.

So Brand had been telling tales out of school. And Elizabeth Sharpe had come gunning. And he thought it was only kids who snitched.

The sitting room had a chill in the air despite Margaret's warm reds and browns. He placed his glass on the mantelshelf. The coal was ersatz but the heat was real enough; so was the twinge in his back when he straightened. He still missed her. Not surprising: empty house, early night.

He wondered what time Bev and the others would clock off. He could have joined them but Powell was more than capable. The curtains needed drawing. He strolled across, put hands to glass, peered out and grimaced. He doubted anyone would be making waves on Thread Street, tonight. Plenty of puddles. It was still tipping down out there: big cats and Dobermans.

8

The fuzzy red lettering had run in the rain. The word TART, painted on placards three feet high, now looked more like an exhortation to break wind. The message had been strung up on every lamp-post in Thread Street. If Bev hadn't been dying for a pee, she'd have been in stitches.

Ozzie yawned, glanced at his watch. "What was it you said about a damp squib?"

"That, DC Khan, would be a megablast compared with this little lot."

This little lot was seven pillars of the community listing over a glowing brazier at the top end of the road. Half a dozen others were parading around with hoisted banners proclaiming what had read CUTS and TARTS but, after an hour's relentless downpour, could get them arrested. They'd given up chanting when an elderly man at number 30 had thrown a bucket of something from an upstairs window. Ronnie Leigh's threat of Armageddon wasn't holding up.

"How much longer we giving it?" Ozzie asked.

"Chucking out time, Powell said." It was just after nine.

"Good of him."

She laughed, started the engine. "We'll do another turn."

Most of the uniforms had already been stood down. A pair were still in position at either end of the street, a couple of others were stationed near the school and patrol cars were in easy call. Bev wouldn't like to be in Ronnie's counterfeit Nikes when Byford nicked him.

"Should have seen it coming, when you think about it." She flicked the wipers on, checked the mirror and pulled out.

"How d'you mean?"

"The girls aren't stupid. Why come out on a night like this? Specially with that for a welcoming committee." She flashed them a bright smile as she sailed past.

The brazier bunch looked glum but determined. As far as she could tell there was only one woman; they'd exchanged a few words earlier. The rest she didn't know from Adam: a couple of anoraks in their twenties; an elderly bloke with either a dog collar or a white polo and three middle aged men with sodden shalwars clinging to skinny calves, sharing an umbrella covered in huge sunflowers.

The woman had a plastic carrier from KwikSave over her blue rinse. Bev had every confidence it was a cheap means of protection rather than a measure of desperation. Indeed Blue Rinse gave every indication of relishing every moment. She was wielding a clipboard, conscientiously taking down every car number in sight. Bev had already urged the removal of one registration: an unmarked police motor being driven by DI Powell.

She turned right into the High Street. Lil's kiosk had been battened down for the night. Bev made a mental note to have a word with her. Not a lot escaped the old darling. She glanced along the row of shops. The Taj Mahal was having a good night: windows steamed up, outer door open, eau de Balti drifting out. Further down, outside Lloyds, a woman was using the hole in the wall, a friend keeping watch for mug-and-runs. A wino was sheltering in the offie doorway. A ghetto blaster on wheels whizzed past doing forty-five and God knows how many decibels.

"Ever regretted it?" she asked.

"What?"

"Not going in for something quiet. Y'know, regular hours. No nights. No weekends. Bosses who don't bugger off for a swift half."

"My old man wanted me in the family business."

"Yeah?"

"He's a taxidermist."

She laughed, wished she was. She could put a bit of work his way. "Taxi driver more like."

The lights were on red. She tapped fingers on the wheel. Far as she recalled, Khan senior had a burgeoning chain of small-ish shops; the sort that make Eight to Lates look indolent. Which reminded her; she hadn't been to Tesco. Again. Ho-hum. The lights changed and she turned right into Hogarth Road, running parallel now with Thread Street. The houses were big; redbrick, mostly bedsits, the odd sign advertising acupuncture, chiropractic and the like. It was quieter here. Not much traffic. A couple of dogs taking out owners.

"Do you get fed up with it, Sarge?"

She was set to trot out some flip remark, but Ozzie's voice had an edge she hadn't heard him use before. She glanced over. He was peering through rain trails on his window. "Sure. We deal with the crap. Treated like it too most of the time." She sensed his eyes on her now. "I'm not gonna come out with a load of bollocks, Oz. The old 'it's a tough job but someone's gotta do it' line. It's a bastard and you've really got to want to do it. You've got to wake up every day and want to get out and do it more than anything else you can think of."

"You do that?"

"Sure I do." She smiled. "Sad git, aren't I?"

"You're not. But there's no shortage."

She paused, picking her words carefully. He wouldn't be saying any of this if a) she was a bloke and b) Highgate's hard men hadn't been giving him a bad time. On the other hand, if it was true what they say about heat and kitchens, the police canteen was a blast furnace.

"Look, Ozzie. You just have to get on with it. I do. All day. Every day. Don't let them get to you."

They were subtler now; had to be. Even so, that sticks-and-stones stuff was bullshit. She could imagine the names Ozzie had to contend with. A pretty boy with a law degree and a mother from Lahore.

"Yeah. You're right."

So why did he sound as though she wasn't?

A second later, it didn't matter.

She was turning into Nelson Drive, another quiet, tree-lined road that would lead them back to Thread Street. The lamp-post halfway down on the left? There was something wrong. She narrowed her eyes, cropping everything else from the picture.

"Holy Mother. What have they done?"

A rope, nylon cord, whatever, had been strung over the top of the metal. A girl, head lolling awkwardly across her chest, arms hanging limply at her sides, was gently swaying. Her skirt had been hiked up, or was obscenely short. Long, stick-thin legs dangled, but even with four-inch platforms her feet were never going to reach the ground.

Val was slipping a foot into a fluffy pink mule. The shade clashed with the chiffon nightdress slipping off a well-rounded shoulder but in a room with a twenty-watt bulb – what the hell? Banjo wouldn't notice. And if he did, he wouldn't care. What with the rain and a patch full of pillocks, she'd been in the market for an early night – until Banjo phoned.

"Eh, Val. What's going on? There's more fuzz in Thread Street than on a pound of peaches."

She'd laughed out loud, told him he could call round. More men had been in Big Val's knickers than through her front door, but Banjo Hay was an exception. More of a mate really; they always had a good laugh. She even closed her eyes during the biz. Not many punters you can afford to do that with. Shame in a way, cause Banjo was one of the few worth looking at.

She yawned, stretching both arms over her head. Best put

your face on, girl. There was a well-worn tallboy against the wall. She'd picked it up for a fiver at Kev's junk shop. He'd chucked in a three-sided mirror as well. She peered in, pulled a face. Blimey. One was bad enough. After the full works and a dab of dodgy Chanel, she was ready for anything.

She pulled on a wrap and went downstairs to wait. Not even Banjo was allowed further than the front room. She looked round, fancied a joint, had to make do with a Marlboro. Banjo'd have some wacky baccy. Should have asked him to bring a few cans as well; the girls had drunk the place dry. She shoved a few toy pigs to the wall and lay on the bed. The kids would be well pissed off with the aggro in Thread Street; a bunch of do-gooders was no good for trade. She took a deep drag and closed her eyes. Maybe it was no bad thing. Least till the cops caught Shell's killer.

There was a tap on the window. She smiled: set your watch by Banjo. She hauled herself up, threw the butt into the empty fireplace, ran her tongue along her teeth then licked her lips. She was smiling when she opened the door. She'd have put it on the chain if she hadn't been expecting Banjo. Talk about stables and bolting horses.

"What do you want?"

"Valerie, Valerie. That's no way to talk to an old friend."

"None of your friends reach old age, do they?"

"Let's talk about that inside."

"Let's not."

"It's not a request, Valerie."

The kick was fast and would probably leave a dent in the door. She didn't see it coming; the edge of the wood caught her on the side of the face. Charlie Hawes was in the room before she was off the floor.

He strolled round, hands in the pockets of an expensive-looking black coat. "Banjo sends his apologies. Got held up by a couple of mates. My mates."

I bet he did, she thought. "What do you want, Charlie?"

"Me? I just want a quiet life. You know that, Valerie."

"Join a monastery."

He walked towards her slowly. She tensed when he lifted a hand but all he did was stroke a finger gently down her cheek.

"I'd put something on that if I were you. You'll have a nasty bruise if you don't look out."

"What do you want, Charlie?"

"Sit down."

"I'm okay."

"Sit down."

She perched on the bed.

"Michelle's murder is not good news."

Val looked down at her hands, clasped them tightly to stop the tremor.

He sat next to her, put an arm round her shoulder. "It's giving me a lot of grief. Know what I mean?"

"Yes, Charlie."

"See, the police want to talk to me and I don't like that. I don't like that at all. It's not good for business. You can see that, can't you, Valerie?"

"Yes, Charlie."

"So I want your help."

"Me?"

"You." He tightened the grip. "There's a cop sniffing round. Asking questions. Too many questions."

"I don't talk to cops. You know that, Charlie."

He took his arm away, turned her face towards his. "Thing is, lady, I want you to talk to this one. I want you to supply a few answers."

"I don't know anything."

"That's right. I'm going to fill you in."

She bit her lip.

"You cold, Valerie?"

"No. I'm okay."

"You're shaking."

"I'm okay."

He stood, strolled over to the fireplace. "This cop. She's at Highgate. CID. Name's Morriss. I want you to get in touch." He smiled. "Woman to woman, tart to tart. Put her right on a few things."

"Come on, Charlie, she ain't gonna listen to me."

He waved a hand. "Oh, I think so. See, a little bird told me you and Beverley go back a long way."

"Shouldn't listen to little birds. She's pulled me in a few times, that's all."

"You're not hearing me, are you? It's not negotiable. And if that little bird's been telling lies – I'll just have to wring its neck, won't I?"

His voice was steady but Val's heart was racing. She had a feeling the little bird might go by the name of Vicki Flinn.

"What do you want me to do?"

"That's better, Valerie. Much better."

Spelling it out didn't take long. She listened in silence, nodding now and again.

"Hope it's all clear. Don't want you fucking up, do we?"

She shook her head. He smiled. "Any questions before I leave, Valerie?"

She had to ask, needed to know, kept her voice casual. "Haven't seen Shell's mate, Vicki, for ages. Any ideas, Charlie?"

He laughed, walked to the bed, patted her head, Labrador style. "Don't you worry, Auntie Valerie. I'm taking good care of young Victoria. Matter of fact, she's hanging around outside now – waiting for her Uncle Charles."

Ozzie released the belts before Bev hit the brakes. Blood was whooshing in her ears and her scalp was doing its hedgehog impersonation.

She flung open the door, gulped cold air. Ozzie's heels rang in the silence. She knew she had to get up, had to join him, had to take control. She just needed a second.

He reached the body, looked back. "Don't bother, Sarge."

It was too late: she was already bent double, gazing into the gutter. She didn't hear him walk back but turned her head when he tapped her shoulder. He was holding something in his hand. "Nutters, or what?"

She swore as her eyes focused. The visual clarity did nothing for her vocabulary.

"Arseholes."

"Sarge, it's a joke. A sick joke. That's all."

The short black wig was askew now, obscuring the eyes but revealing a fibreglass skull. The head must have worked loose from the neck as the rest of the dummy swung in the breeze.

"Sarge, you all right?"

Her cheeks were moist, glistening. She dashed at them with the heel of her hand. "Get the bloody thing down. Now."

It was easier demanded than done. She stood at his side, arms folded, barking orders while he lowered the cord and mock cadaver. The clothing was barely damp, obviously hadn't been there more than a few minutes. She scanned the street; there were no house lights on nearby and no one was about. She'd get the local radios to put out a witness appeal. Someone must have seen something. A car was approaching. She'd been watching as it turned in from Thread Street.

"Come on," she said. "We'd best get back. I'll give you a hand."

He grinned. "I'll give you the head."

"Balls!" It wasn't an anatomical admonition; she'd just clocked the driver of the car. Her heart hit her DMs. Powell, Mike bloody Powell. It did not look good. The Rover slewed across the pavement, doors gaping. Her and Ozzie man-handling a headless, half-naked, female form.

Powell sauntered over, smirking. "Look Morriss, whatever

you pair get up to in private's fine by me, but not in the street and not on police time."

"Ha, ha." She paused. He waited. "Sir."

"What's going on, then?"

How could she tell Powell when she had little idea herself? At best, it was a vicious wind-up. At worst, a graphic warning. Either way, the bloody thing had been dressed like Vicki Flinn. She outlined the barest of bones and watched as he stroked his chin – in most people an indication of thought.

"So your little friend's a two-faced tart?"

She shook her head, genuinely bemused. "Sorry?"

"Been stringing you along, hasn't she?" Stringing? Was the man serious? "Making out she's a mate when all the while she's laughing up her sleeve." He was glaring at her now, jabbing the air between them. "Let me tell you something, Morriss. She was never going to take you to Mad Charlie. Pound to a penny she's one of Hawes's whores."

She sighed. Charlie jokes had been banned from day one and, more to the point, what was Powell going on about? "How do you work that lot out?"

"Stands to reason. He doesn't want you poking your nose in. He's saying back off, big time. They'll have staged this charming little tableau between them, be laughing themselves stupid."

She shook her head.

"Don't shake your head at me, girl."

"Even if Hawes is behind it – and there's nothing pointing that way – you can't possibly know the girl's in on it as well."

"She's a treacle. She'll do as she's told."

"Precisely. He could be holding her…"

"Oh, I'll bet he's doing that."

"…against her will."

"Little slag should be done for wasting police time."

Ozzie cleared his throat. "I think, perhaps, we should be getting back to Thread Street. Sir."

Bev had forgotten Ozzie was there; Powell probably hadn't even noticed.

"Don't bother, laddie. Ronnie Leigh got his wires crossed. Thought I knew where I might find him. And there he was. Down the Royal Oak. The big one's not tonight. It's Tuesday. Everyone else has buggered off and I suggest you pair do the same."

Bev watched him leave then had to transform two fingers into a mock salute as he did a sudden about-turn. "By the way, Morriss. I was on the blower with Byford earlier. He wants a word with you. First thing. His office." He shook his head, tutting loudly. "Shove something hard down my knickers if I were you."

It was the lure of mushy peas that did it. That, and the hunger-making exertion of grappling with an over-sized Barbie back at the nick. She shook her head, glanced in the driving mirror and gave a wry smile. The sight of Bev Morriss giving a fireman's lift to a dubious-looking dummy had inspired the wits of Highgate to a new low. Whatever. She'd been heading for home with nothing more than a mug of Horlicks in mind when the culinary vision struck. A mere street away and it was now accompanied by haddock and chips. She was wavering but the tempting smells drifting from Your Plaice or Mine tipped the balance.

"Hello stranger. Thought you'd turned Vulcan."

She smiled. "Don't you mean vegan? Wotcha, Sid. How goes it?"

He lifted a sizzling basket. "Swimmingly."

She rolled her eyes. Nothing changed. Sid Gounaris ran the best chippie in town but threw in the worst jokes. It was just round the corner from Bev's but she hadn't been near the place since the New Year and her week on a health farm.

"Y'all right, bab? You lookin' a bit peaky."

Dear Sid. He peppered the thickest Greek accent this side of Athens with the occasional dash of Brummie. Everyone was 'bab' – even the blokes. As for 'peaky' – she was sylph, not sick. Six kilos she'd lost since Christmas. On the other hand, coming across a Vicki Flinn look-alike dangling from a lamp-post probably wasn't conducive to a healthy glow.

"Top of the world, Sid."

"Usual?"

"Twist my arm."

Sid's arms were covered in curly black hair. At his temples there was a dusting of grey.

"Funny you comin' in tonight."

She sneaked a chip. "Oh?"

"Yeah, had some bloke in earlier askin' 'bout you."

She waved a hand furiously in front of her mouth, blowing hard. Sid looked up from salt scattering and grinned. "Serves you right."

The chip was still too hot to swallow but Sid was a dab hand at working out the garbled utterances of the impatient.

"Said he was friend of a friend."

"And what did you say?"

"Said, yeah, and I'm Jamie Oliver. C'mon, bab, this bloke's got dreadlocks down to his elbows and you can smell the jazz woodbines a mile away."

She grabbed another chip before he wrapped them, blew on it before taking a bite.

"What time was this, Sid?"

"I'd not long opened. 'bout seven?"

"What did he want? Exactly?"

"Says he had a message. He knew you lived round here but he'd lost the number or something. I said it was news to me."

"Ta, Sid." She was delving into her shoulder-bag, coming across the odd kitchen sink and fluffy Polo. She only had a tenner. She'd try to get to a cashpoint on her way into work.

He handed her the packet, voice becoming suddenly serious. "Look out for yourself, bab. There's a load of crazies out there."

By the time, she was parking, her only concern was whether Sid's finest would still be piping hot after she'd buttered bread and opened chilled Frascati.

No one was into stupid risks, but the day the bogeyman lurked in every bush was the day to hang up the ID. The guy in Sid's – given the two-bit description – could have been anyone. She locked up, looked round.

The car park was a piece of open ground at the back of the maisonettes. Apart from residents, it was used by drivers nipping into the shops. At 10.30 on a Sunday night, it was almost deserted. She frowned. The light by the staircase was out. Again. The local yobs used it for target practice.

Yes. She could see it now. There was broken glass on the concrete. Bloody nuisance, and nasty, given the number of little kids who played round the stairs. All those scabby knees and Germolene. She kicked away the worst of it; gave herself a pat on the back. The sudden, sharp, sickening whack to the small of her back was down to someone else.

She tried swirling round, but the impact was forcing her forward and she lost her balance. Her glass clearing had not been entirely successful. Her brain was trying to work out the site of the worst pain given the conflicting but equally pressing messages from both sources. It was no time for cerebral exercise; this was up close and physical. She was face down and pinned down; his knees were clamped at her sides, pressing on her arms. Something brushed across her eyes. It felt soft; might have been a scarf. Whatever it was, it was now tightly tied. Come on, Morriss, think: you can't move, you can't see. Maybe you can talk your way out of this.

"Why don't we —"

"Shut the fuck up."

Chatting was out, then. What was he doing? What did he want? Was he the guy who'd been quizzing Sid? Was he linked to the Lucas inquiry? There had to be a connection, didn't there? Otherwise it was too much of a coincidence. And Bev didn't do coincidence.

On the other hand, it was mugsville round these parts. Anyone walking alone, after dark, was seen as a mobile cash dispenser. It was bad news for the crime figures but it had never bothered Bev personally. Self-defence was second nature. This was hurting her pride almost as much as her spine.

"Look —"

She stiffened. Everything had changed. He had a blade. The metal was cold and hard against her neck. As her fear rocketed, so did her anger. She'd always loathed being pushed around, couldn't abide bullies and the thought that the mad bugger squatting on her back could possibly be Michelle Lucas's killer acted as a spur. The only problem was that she couldn't move an eyebrow let alone a muscle.

"What do —?"

"Fuckin' shut it, bitch."

Whatever he was up to, he'd have to get a move on. The place was quiet on a Sunday night, but it wasn't ghost town. Someone could pass by any time.

The knife was the sticking point; made her think twice about trying a swift kick or a fast buck. Several unidentified flying objects hit the ground not far from her head. A few others she recognised: loose change, a box of matches. The smell gave it away. It even permeated the scents clinging to the blindfold. Leather and mints meant only one thing: he'd up-ended her shoulder-bag. The blade was now pressing – no, resting – against her cheek. He hadn't cut her; not yet.

"Follow me, you're dead."

In a flash, the pressure on both face and back was gone; so had her attacker. She shot up, immediately regretted it. It hurt, badly. She snatched at the blindfold. What was the expression? Clean away. She didn't even catch a pair of fleeing heels.

Call it in, Bev. Come on, girl. Get a grip. On what? The phone had gone. Her purse had gone. She'd only just held on to her bladder.

She started collecting the rest of her possessions. Her hands were shaking. She slowly got to her feet. Her legs were shaking. She took stock. Her whole body was bloody shaking. So, this was shock. Deep breaths, Bev, come on. She had to get home; concentrate, focus, get down the details.

Her head spun, stomach churning. The thought of food made her want to throw up. Which was lucky. Sid's finest had all but disappeared. The fish had landed at the bottom of the stairs and the local wild life was out in force. A brindled dog with a touch of mange was amiably sharing the spoils with a scrawny, boss-eyed black tom. Three eyes locked on to hers. It was a low-life *Lady and the Tramp.*

It was strangely funny, but she wasn't laughing. And the tears burning her cheek had nothing to do with the lost supper.

9

"Good weekend, Beverley?"

Bev looked up sheepishly from a plate that held the better part of a small farm. She hadn't expected anyone else to be in so early; hadn't expected PC Sumitra Ghosh at all. Mouth full, she nodded and flapped a hand at the chair opposite.

Sumitra sat, eyes wide, mouth open. "What happened to The Diet? The Running? The New Woman?"

Bev swallowed a fork load of mixed grill and wondered if she'd ever looked so cute in uniform. Sumitra had the face of an angel and legs up to her epaulettes.

"Had what you might call a run-in last night," Bev told her enigmatically. "With Neanderthal Man. Gave me a bit of an appetite."

"Sounds intriguing."

"You should get out more. What you up to anyway, Summi?"

"Playing catch-up. I've been off since Wednesday."

"You still on porn?"

She nodded. "DOMS."

Bev thought for a moment. The only DOMS springing to mind were her post-run variety: Delayed Onset Muscular Soreness. Hurt just thinking about it.

Sumitra enlightened her. "Dirty Old Men Syndrome."

Bev smiled as she caught sight of someone coming in. "Talking of which."

Sumitra bowed her head, blushing on Bev's behalf. "Morning, Sir."

Mike Powell strode to the counter barely acknowledging Bev's over-bright salutation. Not that she'd lose any sleep.

"Not all old are they?" Bev picked up where they'd left off. "It's not all dirty macs and liver spots." Given some of the stuff Bev had seen on vice, neither age – nor rainwear – came into it.

She looked down. Two sausages and a slice of black pudding were swimming in a pool of tomatoes and egg yolk. She pushed the plate aside. She had a vague feeling of unease and was trying to work out whether it was more than the usual post-pig-out craving for a fag. "Can I have a look at the paperwork, Summi?"

"Don't see why not. Clear it with Wiseman first."

"Sure."

"Why do you want it?"

"Just curious."

"Not keeping you busy downstairs?" Sumitra smiled.

Bev held out her hands. "Rushed off me feet, mate."

Sumitra frowned, gently took hold of Bev's wrist, scrutinised a palm that resembled a road map. "That looks nasty, Beverley. Have you put anything on it?"

Bev winced; tried to hide it with a smile. "Double Savlon. Honest."

"You read tea leaves as well, Ghoshie?"

They looked up to find Powell looming, a take-out coffee and a couple of doughnuts on a tray.

"Sir?" The query was Sumitra's; Bev had already caught the drift.

He nodded at the women's hands. "If that's not just a harmless bit of palmistry – you want to watch out. People'll talk. They'll have you snogging in the rape suite before you know it."

Sumitra snatched her hand away. Bev studied her fingernails. "You should hear what they say about you." She noticed that the smile didn't reach his eyes, didn't get anywhere near his voice.

"Y'know, Morriss, I wouldn't have thought you had time to sit on your backside talking crap." He jabbed a thumb at Sumitra. "And if she was any good at telling the future she'd have told you about the old man. He's in his office. Popped my head round already. Can't see him for steam. Makes Raging Bull look like Ronnie Corbett.'

"It's just not on." Byford was at the window, his back to Bev. The rain had cleared but a leaden sky was making no promises. Bev was sitting in front of his desk, trying to work out what, exactly, was off. It was either her handling of the Henry Brand interview or the fact that some plonker on the front desk had given the headteacher from hell Byford's home number. Come to think of it, probably both. Byford turned, perched on the sill.

"Just because he'd met the woman at a parents' evening and she insists it's crucial to the case, he assumes it'll be okay."

"Maybe she threatened extra homework."

"And that's another thing." He moved to his own chair, sat facing her. "There are enough jokers round here without you going into a stand-up routine at the drop of a hat."

"Sir." For a man whose office walls were plastered in old *Private Eye* covers, she reckoned he had little room to talk. But when on thin ice – keep shtum. His mood wasn't entirely down to Elizabeth Sharpe's out-of-hours call. Bev knew he was pissed off with last night's débacle. Water wasn't the only commodity that had gone down the drain: it had cost a packet to police Thread Street.

"You know what this place is like. It's full of comedians. Everyone's going round humming 'Swinging in the Rain' and Vince Hanlon's running a limerick competition."

"Shame they've got nothing better to do." She folded her arms and crossed her legs, mentally working on a first line.

"We've all got something better to do." The reminder was unnecessary; everyone knew it was forty-eight hours since the discovery of Michelle's body. He sighed. There were smudges under his eyes. She wondered how much sleep he'd had. Probably as little as she'd had.

"Is there a link, Bev? Is Hawes playing sick games?"

She had no answers. She'd lain awake, running through the night's highlights but reaching few conclusions. The dummy had to be a warning and it had to be Charlie Hawes. But was there a connection with Michelle's murder? And did it have anything to do with her own attacker? The guy could have kicked the shit out of her. So why hadn't he? She was still smarting and not just from the cuts, but she couldn't put it off any longer.

"Talking of games, I got roped in to a spot of footie last night."

A raised eyebrow asked for more. Bev passed him the statement she'd worked on in the early hours. She'd underplayed it but as she watched him read, she thought the pen in his hand was about to snap. She'd felt the same as she'd written it. She'd gone over the incident again and again, but it was like trying to catch bubbles. She'd come up with snatched impressions, vague smells and a voice as featureless as the face she hadn't seen. Stale tobacco, heady scent and a rustling sensation weren't going to make *Crimewatch*. In the witness stakes she was a non-starter and her anger added to the humiliation she still felt. At home, after a medicinal brandy or three, she'd even toyed, briefly, with the crazy idea of not reporting it at all. Ridiculous, of course. Apart from anything else, there was the missing mobile and ID to report. The stolen ID had come as a bit of a shock.

"This is bad news, Bev."

She shrugged. "Wrong time, wrong place."

"Wrong answer." He jabbed the pen at her. "You can't possibly imagine this is unconnected to the inquiry." He gave her what Bev's mum would call an old-fashioned look. "This was down to Hawes. It has to be."

"I don't see it, guv."

"Get an eye test, then." He threw the pen on the desk. It seemed a touch over the top. "Within hours of getting out there, looking for the man, you're attacked in the street and threatened at knife-point. Strikes me he had more luck tracking you down than —"

The look on her face stopped him in his tracks. She rearranged it into something less incredulous but still regarded his outburst as unbelievably unfair. It was one thing to get pinned down by some unknown assailant, but then to get it in the neck from the old man… True, there were a few seconds last night when she'd thought Hawes was the joker playing piggy-back, but on reflection, Charlie'd never get his own hands dirty. Equally true, the man had a whole herd of heavies for the crap, but on balance she'd convinced herself it was a run-of-the-mill-mugging. Or maybe, she didn't want to believe that Hawes had been so close, so very close, and she hadn't done a fucking thing about it. She'd been there, *so* didn't like it.

"I kinda think I'd be on a hospital trolley by now if Charlie'd had a hand in it."

"It's not funny." He reread the notes, shaking his head.

No, really, I'm fine, guv. Don't fuss. She'd have balled her fists but the palms still stung.

"Forensics?" he asked without looking up.

"In hand." The scarf and her coat were on their way to the labs. They'd get the full treatment but she didn't hold out much hope. The replacement phone and ID were already in her bag and putting a stop on her credit cards had taken one phone call. As for her purse, she couldn't see bag-man getting much joy out of a library card, vid membership, or last week's lottery ticket. The few quid in cash certainly wasn't going to change his life.

"We'll wait and see what comes up, then."

Sounded like a dismissal. She stood. Thanks for asking, guv. It hardly hurts at all.

"I haven't finished yet." Byford said.

She felt like tugging her gymslip. What was his problem?

"We've got to pull Hawes in. The man can't just disappear. Someone must know where he is."

Bev said nothing. She'd checked with the hospital already

that morning. Cassie Swain was still unconscious. The next best bet – Vicki – could be anywhere, could even be with Charlie. Bev hadn't entirely dismissed Powell's jibe about her being one of Hawes's girls. She had to accept that she didn't know Vicki well; didn't really know her at all.

"Mike Powell reckons the Flinn girl's been leading you a merry dance."

She looked up, surprised. The mind-reading was pretty selective. She shrugged. "It's one conclusion to jump to."

"But you don't think so?"

"I don't know." It was the truth. Thoughts of Vicki Flinn had been among all the others keeping Bev awake last night. She'd run through their conversation in the canteen; recalled how easily the girl had already lied. A mother who'd died of cancer. Christ. Bev had been close to tears. Even being caught out only meant she laughed it off, changed the subject. How many other quick changes had there been?

"Look, Bev." Byford said. "She's not a minor. She's not been reported missing. There's not a lot we can do."

She nodded, didn't need telling. It didn't make her feel any better. "If that's all, sir, I've got a lot on this morning." She stood again.

"No. It isn't all." She waited as he rose and walked round the desk. "Are you sure you should be in at all, Bev? Your hands are a mess. God knows what state the rest of you is in, but that muck on your face certainly isn't working. He marked you, didn't he?" The voice was gentle at last, and it was giving Bev a hard time.

"Muck? This is Max Factor's finest. Cost a fortune, mate." She hoped the verbal light touch was doing a better concealing job than the ton of slap. "Honest. I'm fine. It only hurts when I laugh."

"Must hurt like hell then."

She smiled. He was still looking concerned. "Have you had a doctor look at you?"

"No treatment for injured pride, guv."

"I'm serious, Bev. You could have been killed last night."

She thought for a minute he was going to touch her. He was obviously worried sick; no wonder he'd been such a grumpy old sod. She was the same way herself. In fact, next time she laid eyes on Vicki Flinn, the girl was in line for some serious verbals.

"Don't worry, guv. I can take care of myself." Despite the night's events, she still believed it; had to believe it. She hoped Vicki Flinn could as well. As Byford had said, the girl wasn't a minor and hadn't been reported missing. Until they had something to go on Vicki Flinn was on her own. At least, given what little Bev knew about Charlie Hawes, she hoped so.

Vicki shook violently. She was on her own, in the middle of a room without a window. She must have slept. It must be morning. She hugged her knees. The heat was stifling, but she shivered remembering the night's bedfellows.

The fat ones were the worst: slabs of pasty flesh slapping about. The stink of their bodies and booze was still on her skin. Get it up, get it over, get the hell out, was her usual style. Except she couldn't get out, couldn't escape. And even if she could, now she knew what she knew, she wouldn't. Anyway, there was a minder the size of a planet on the landing. She'd only caught a glimpse when Charlie had hustled her in but she'd had further snatches every time Pluto opened up for another punter.

Looking back, she'd been stupid. Charlie had followed her in, sat her on the bed and gently removed her clothes and shoes. He had an overnight bag with him, and at that stage she'd actually believed he wanted to stay with her. She shook her head; should have known by the state of the room. She'd seen better furniture on a skip and the paper with its faded climbing roses was falling off the walls. Not Charlie's scene at all. She remembered his silence: it was spooky – he just sat there, stroking her all over with his fingertips. Then without warning, he'd stood in front of her and cupped her chin in his hands.

"You've been a naughty girl, Victoria. I've told you before. Someone in your position has to be very careful about the company she keeps." He wrenched her head back. "Who knows what secrets you've been giving away? No, Victoria, I'm afraid there'll be no more nights out with the girls. You'll be working from home from now on." He'd glanced round. "This home."

She wondered if the panic had reached her eyes.

He released her, kissed the top of her head then wandered to the chair where he'd left the bag. She watched his every move. He never hurried, always seemed to operate in slow motion. It must have given her a false sense of security; she'd run to the door, screaming and ranting, hurling threats and throwing fists. Where was the filth now? Where the fuck was Bev Morriss? She wished she'd never laid eyes on the bloody woman.

He'd come up behind, forced her elbows back, steered her to the bed. "Calm down. No one will hear. And if they do – no one gives a stuff."

She watched as he collected her clothes, folded them neatly and placed them in his bag. She bit the inside of her cheek, tasted blood. "Charlie. I never said nothing to her. Honest. Please, don't do this. I'll go away. Somewhere they won't find me."

"Oh, I don't think they'll find you here, Victoria."

He walked to the door, then turned and put a hand in his coat pocket. "I almost forgot." He threw a bundle on to her lap. "Just in case you get any silly ideas."

It was a small, soft, pink rabbit. Brand new. She'd bought it a couple of weeks earlier, a present for Lucie. Forgotten she still had it.

"Cute, that," he said, snatching it back. "Kid'll love that. Maybe I'll go round and deliver it in person. Know what I mean?"

She gasped.

"Yeah," he said, turning it over and over in his hands. "Maybe I will. Real soon."

She watched him leave, unable to speak, her vision blurred by tears.

Seven hundred and sixty-two kids attended Thread Street Comprehensive on Monday morning. It was an all time record. They knew about Michelle Lucas's murder and they watched *The Bill.*

Unsuppressed excitement pervaded the hall, making for much shuffling of feet and shifting of eyes. Bev stood at the back, kicking her heels, trying to look inconspicuous. Byford was on the platform, aiming for an affable approachability. A face that said: Come and talk to Uncle William. She smiled, knowing it concealed gritted teeth due to his belief that he'd been outflanked by the woman standing centre stage.

They'd arrived for the interview with Elizabeth Sharpe only to be warded off by the school secretary. The Head was busy, she said; finalising a form of words for the morning's special assembly. A placatory offer had been thrown in: Byford could address the children after.

Bev stifled a yawn. The Sharpe woman obviously liked the sound of her own voice, which was more than the kids did. She'd already witnessed the confiscation of three Gameboys and the dishing out of half a dozen detentions. Bev switched off after the Head's references to Michelle. It was all a bit damning with faint praise. She cast her eyes along the kids in the last row. Clearly the guidelines on school uniform didn't stretch this far back. Blimey. Bev's vests were longer than most of the skirts on show and she'd swear a few of the lads were wearing mascara. One girl had more rings on her fingers than a pair of curtains. Hell's bells. One of the little buggers had farted. That's right. Innocent looks all round. Blame it on the class anorak. Been there. Done that.

She dipped into Sharpe's oratory but the head was banging on about mock SATS. Bev wondered where the other teachers were, especially the delightful Henry. Hopefully, Ozzie might shed a little light; he was back at the ranch doing some digging on a file marked Brand H.

She heard Byford's name mentioned and tuned in again.

"... other officers will be on school premises from time to time during the course of the investigation. I expect everyone in this hall to extend the same level of courtesy and co-operation to the police as you do to members of staff."

"Fuckin' doddle then." The voice emanated from a few feet away: the girl with the rings. Bev edged sideways to get a better look. The movement caught Little Miss Public Speaking's attention and she turned. In a tentative, hand-of-friendship gesture, Bev smiled and winked. The girl smiled back but the obscene hand gesture accompanying it had nothing to with winking – she was a letter out. Cheeky little cow. Bev came the heavy with a look practised in the bath. The girl stuck out a tongue: pierced. And pulled a face: ugly. Unattractive as it was, there was something vaguely familiar. Bev was trying to place it when a booming voice broke the train of thought.

"Joanna Rigby. I do not appreciate talking to the back of your head."

The girl faced the front and Elizabeth Sharpe finally got her act together and called Byford to take the floor.

Bev filed it away then concentrated on the governor. She was impressed. The old man was good with kids. Had two of his own of course. Even so. Most of this lot probably thought Family Values was a cheap supermarket.

"...I never knew Michelle," Byford was saying. "But some of you did. And I want you to really think. It's the little things you saw. The little things you heard. Things you might not even think are important. In my experience they often make all the difference..."

He was injecting a touch of mild Brummie. There was no use talking posh to kids like this; it was an instant turn off.

"We'll be wanting to speak to some of you. Specially anyone close to Michelle. But if anyone else wants to have a word with me or Sergeant Morriss who's standing at the back of the hall…"

Seven hundred plus heads turned. Thanks, guv.

"…or any of my officers, then come and make yourself known. In the meantime, if any of you have any questions – don't be afraid to ask."

A hand shot up at the front and a little boy with a loud voice asked Byford for his autograph.

"What's it like being a celebrity, guv?"

Bev handed Byford a coffee, resisting the urge to shove an imaginary microphone in his face. He glanced up, detecting a cheekful of tongue. "Little sod still thinks I'm Inspector Morse."

She tutted, head shaking. "They don't teach them anything these days."

He gave a weary smile then returned to the notes on his desk. Bev lowered herself gingerly into a chrome and canvas chair. They were killing time in the school's first-aid room, waiting – again – for Elizabeth Sharpe. Shame there were no dishy doctors about; Bev's back was playing up, not to mention her feet. The DMs had been ten quid off in the sale but she was paying for it now. She took a sip from a mug that proclaimed a love of New York and took a closer look round. She'd been in cosier morgues. The only colour in the place was the cross on a medicine cabinet. They could have used the room next to Sharpe's. It was up and running as a temporary incident unit but – when the woman finally graced them with her presence – the guv didn't want any interruptions.

Bev had popped her head round to touch base and cadge the caffeine.

"Where is the damn woman?"

Byford was beginning to lose it. Bev was glad she wasn't in Sharpe's shoes. The sound of footsteps pre-empted an answer.

She sat up straight and was amused to see the guv straightening his tie. The gestures were wasted. The next thing they heard was a glass-shattering: "Young! This is not a race track!"

There was a squeak of rubber on wood as Young's skid came to an abrupt halt just outside the door. They heard a mollifying shout of: "Sir," followed by a more muted: "Dickhead."

Dickhead bestowed a detention on Boy Racer and quiet, if not calm, was restored.

Byford sighed. "And they say they're the best days of your life…"

"Only one answer to that."

"Enlighten me."

"Get another life."

She gave a wry smile; it was easier said than done. For a lot of the kids, Thread Street was as good as it would get. She'd interviewed girls round these parts who saw pregnancy as a career move. One of her mates had a daughter at junior school half a mile away. Nadir was the only kid in the class with married parents who still lived under the same roof.

"So sorry to have kept you waiting. There are always a million things to do on Monday mornings."

Bev looked round and caught a glimpse of Sharpe. The woman was already halfway across the floor; a stealth bomber would have made more noise. Bev was registering a navy blue suit: classy, costly and a cut above anything in her own wardrobe. The impeccable double rows of silver buttons added a vaguely military air to the authority exuding from every pore. Bev didn't know whether to curtsey or salute. In the event – and after a nod from Byford – she relinquished her seat, eschewed perching on the plastic covered couch and made for the nearest wall.

Byford didn't get up, didn't smile. "First thing I want to do is establish why you failed to mention the allegations Michelle Lucas was making in the days leading to her death."

Come on boss; don't mince your words. Bev kept her face blank but it spoke volumes compared with Elizabeth Sharpe's. The woman was giving nothing away, neither was her voice.

"There was no failure on my part. I had already dealt with Michelle's so-called claims. As far as I was concerned, the matter was closed." She crossed her legs at the knee and held her hands together loosely in her lap.

This was Bev's first opportunity to observe the woman at close quarters. She'd met the type before but was too wise to write her off on the basis of an initial assessment. Still, what the hell: bossy, patronising, pushy.

"And how did you deal with it?" Byford asked.

"I invited Michelle to substantiate what she'd been saying. She could not do so. In my opinion the entire episode was based on nothing more than malice and mischief-making. When I pointed out to her the consequences of slander against a senior member of staff, she withdrew every word."

"What exactly was she accusing Henry Brand of?" Bev's voice was deceptively casual.

Mrs Sharpe glanced over, and Bev had the satisfaction of catching a hint of irritation flash across her face.

"I believe you've already questioned him." She paused. "Or maybe harassed would be a better word."

Bev shrugged, stayed silent.

Mrs Sharpe pulled her skirt over her knees, then made great show of brushing off a speck of dust near the hem. Bev had no intention of getting the same treatment. "Mr Brand? What was he up to?" She made direct eye contact with the headmistress. "Only according to Michelle, of course?"

The flash of irritation had given way to a sustained glare. She appealed to Byford. "Do we really have to drag all this up again?"

"The girl's dead, Mrs Sharpe. I'll drag the canal system if I have to." He sat back, waiting.

The woman took a deep breath and folded her arms.

"Perhaps you'll find it easier if you consult your notes?" he asked.

"What?"

"A serious complaint against a member of staff? Obviously, you'll have a record of everything said."

"I saw no reason for that." She shifted slightly in the chair. "Anyway, I have total recall."

"Shame we can't say the same for Michelle." Bev couldn't resist it; the woman was acting as if she deserved a medal.

"You have a very unfortunate manner, Sergeant Morriss."

"Thanks," Bev smiled. "Now perhaps you can summon up your amazing powers of recall to put us in the picture as well. What – exactly – was Henry Brand accused of?"

"Michelle said he'd touched her breasts and tried to put his hand up her skirt."

"He groped her, then?" Bev asked. "According to Michelle, of course."

Mrs Sharpe pursed her lips. She glanced at Byford but if it was a plea for intervention, it was ignored. Bev had already been given the nod to carry on.

"This assault? Where did it take place? Allegedly?"

The woman glanced round, uneasily. Bev followed her gaze: the sick-bed? Never.

"Mrs Sharpe?" The poise had gone. "Here?" Bev pushed. "It happened here?"

An impatient sigh preceded the answer. "She'd complained of nausea and was sent to lie down."

"Who by?"

"Mr Brand."

"And?"

"She said he came in during break and asked how she was feeling. She told him she had stomach ache. She said he told her to close her eyes and lie still. She claimed he then assaulted her. Untrue, of course. Mr Brand says —"

"Don't worry about what Henry Brand says," Byford interrupted.

She shrugged. The woman's complacency was infuriating. Bev wanted to shake her. "So what did you do?"

"I questioned her closely, of course. It soon became clear she had a particularly sharp little axe to grind against Henry and was quite prepared to do so."

"And why would she want to do that?"

"You'll have to ask him, won't you?"

"Don't worry. We will."

"Not today you won't." She closed her eyes, traced the left eyebrow with her index finger. "Not here at any rate. Henry's not coming in. He's not well."

Bev glanced at Byford. "What's the problem?"

"A migraine, I believe. He spoke to the secretary first thing."

"Takes a lot of time off, does he?" Bev asked.

Mrs Sharpe folded her arms, took a deep breath. "No, Sergeant, I can't recall any other occasion."

She bit back a remark about total recall. "Funny, that."

"I beg your pardon?" Mrs Sharpe sounded as if it was the last thing she'd beg.

Bev held out her hands, inviting the others to share the joke. "The one day we want to question him and he's on a sickie."

"Your attitude leaves a great deal to be desired. I'm not sure what you're trying to imply but I don't care for it." Bev widened her eyes. She'd always been taught it was rude to point. "Let me make one thing absolutely clear, Sergeant: whatever you may think, I have every faith in my staff —"

"How much do you have in your kids, Mrs Sharpe?"

Byford got to his feet. The exchange had gone on long enough and wasn't going anywhere. "We'll leave it there for now but I'll want to speak with you again, Mrs Sharpe. In future, don't take it upon yourself to withhold information because you don't happen to see its relevance. I should have been told about this at our first meeting."

Mrs Sharpe rose as well. "I fully intended to mention it then. I have nothing to hide, Superintendent. As I recall it – you were the one in a hurry. Now if you'll excuse me…"

Her departure was as smooth as her dismissal. Bev watched the woman disappear, looked at Byford and slapped the back of her wrist. "How come I'm the one who feels naughty?"

"Years of practice."

She nodded blithely, then realised what he'd said.

10

"Come on, Sarge. You can't be in two places at once."

Bev gave one of her snorts. The governor was on his way to Brand's house with Powell, and she was still smarting. Ozzie sensed something, but wasn't in on the details. His solicitude was touching but she reckoned he was too sensitive for his own good. If the tables were turned she'd tell him not to be such a moody. "Yeah. And I'd rather be any where but here."

'Here' was walking along a rundown row of shops in one of Balsall Heath's sleazier back streets. They'd just passed a butcher's where a crowd of flies was window-shopping. Bev paused to read the ads in the next-door newsagent's. Gemma – who clearly had difficulties with English – was offering advanced lessons in French. So were Sonia, Sasha and Suzie.

Ozzie was looking over her shoulder. "Oo la la."

She grinned. "Come on. It's just round the corner."

They waited while a couple of guys in dusty overalls struggled across the pavement with a heavy pane of glass. She glanced at the shopfronts, decided it was for the video store, unless its owner was into the hardboard look.

The business they were seeking was over a second hand bookshop and entrance was through a side door. She rang the bell but there was no response. Ozzie hammered on the wood, dislodging a few flakes of grimy green paint.

A sash window was raised and a woman's head appeared. The stiff blonde hair looked bleached as well as starched, except for the roots that were as dark as the mascara-caked eyelashes through which she was peering.

"What bleedin' time do you call this?"

Bev glanced at her watch. "Quarter past eleven."

"Christ almighty. Sod off. Anyway, it's men only – unless you're after work."

"Okay, Marlene. Cut the crap. Get down here and open up."

"All right, all right. Keep your hair on, Sarge."

The face disappeared and a wide-eyed Ozzie turned to Bev. "You know her?"

"Everyone knows Marlene. More bookings than the Odeon when she worked the streets. All the cash that didn't go on fines went into this."

'This' was massage work. Thousands of Marlenes and the odd Marlon ran parlours all over the city. Every last one would be getting a police visit. Byford wanted Charlie Hawes's head on a plate.

When the face appeared next, it had a cigarette in its mouth. Marlene was puffing so furiously, Bev wondered if she was sending smoke signals. 'Piss off' probably.

There was ash on her skimpy pink nightie and at least another inch about to join it. "Gorra warrant?"

"Gorran ash tray?"

The inevitable happened and Bev watched, fascinated, as it fell into a cleavage of Grand Canyon proportions.

"Shit." Marlene swatted energetically but ineffectually, oblivious of the effect on a pair of 42 FFs.

Bev grinned as Ozzie took a step back, concerned that he might be knocked off his feet by the swell.

"You wanna watch it, Marl," she said. "You'll set yourself on fire one of these days."

The woman winked lasciviously at Ozzie. "Set everyone on fire, me." She yawned, stood back and opened the door wider. "You comin', or what?"

Ozzie didn't look over-keen but Bev shooed him in first then nipped in quickly, before Marlene's hands had a chance to wander.

"Down me passage, lad, then straight up."

Bev would have given a day's pay to see his face. They mounted the stairs in silence. The light was so low, she nearly asked if there was a power cut. Competing smells of dope and incense made her nose twitch.

Ozzie halted on the top step, a tentative hand on the nearest door knob. "This one, Mrs..?"

"Any one you like, lover boy." She was clinging to the bannister, catching her breath. "And it's Marlene to you." The voice was deep and husky and down to forty a day as much as the flirting.

The room was small, the bed vast. A clash of lilac and fake fur struck Bev first, then the distinct lack of chairs. "Okay, Marlene, that's enough."

Without a word, Marlene turned and led them into the office: the business end of the massage market. A market Marlene knew like the palm of her hand. If there was a degree in Giving The Punters What They Want, Marlene had a Masters. A wardrobe full of low-cut tops and skin-tight leather was as much a part of her service as an accent out of the Bull Ring and a script out of a *Carry On* film.

She sank into a beaten-up leather armchair, crossing her legs on top of a battered old desk. It was no mean feat and Bev was only thankful that Marlene slept in her knickers. Ozzie grabbed the seat furthest away and showed a sudden, intense interest in his notebook.

Bev strolled to the window, leaned against the sill and glanced round: cheap lino, no frills, every expense spared. Marlene was keeping the overheads down, in line with her retirement plan. She intended going for the golden handshake soon as she hit forty. Bev had heard it all before, but in Marlene's case… who knew?

"What can I do you for?" She recrossed her legs, giving Ozzie the eye, but he still hadn't come up for air. Bev wiped the smile off her face and considered her approach. She plumped for in-your-face. "I'm after a pimp."

Marlene's mouth made an exaggerated O. "Aren't they payin' you enough?"

Bev tapped a foot, slowly. Marlene lowered her legs and made for a drawer in the desk. A brief fantasy that Charlie Hawes might be hiding in it vanished when a half-bottle of Gordon's made an appearance.

Marlene smacked her lips. "Want to join me? Got a mouth like a desert, I have."

"That'd be the Gobi, would it?" said Bev.

"Cheeky cow. Sling us a glass, lover."

Ozzie lifted his head from a still virginal sheet of paper.

"In that cupboard on your left, you lovely boy."

Ozzie held a tumbler at arm's length but Marlene's scarlet-tipped fingers still managed to linger a tad longer than strictly necessary. Bev shook her head. Marlene made Mae West look like the girl next door. Thirty-two-years old and she'd had more men than the Russian Army. "If I didn't know better, Marlene, I'd say you were trying to change the subject."

She poured a finger of gin. "What subject's that?"

"Pimps in general. Charlie Hawes in particular."

Bev watched the liquid disappear. Marlene ran a finger along her top lip.

"Nothing particular about Charlie. He's got fingers in more pies than Mr Kipling."

"You know him then?"

"Kipling? Yeah. Gives good cake."

"Marlene!"

"Got a fag?"

Bev shook her head.

"Back in a min. Must have a fag. Helps me think."

Bev sauntered over to Ozzie, who still had his head down. He jumped when she tapped him lightly on the shoulder. "She won't bite, you know."

He didn't look too sure.

"Come on. She likes you. She might open up if you talk to her."

"That's what scares me," Oz said.

Marlene returned wreathed in smoke and carrying a pack of Marlboro.

"Anyway," Bev said, "about Charlie Hawes."

"He's a mad bugger. Bad for your health, is Charlie."

"So's baccy but I know where to get hold of it." Bev moved towards the desk. "We have to find him, Marlene. A girl's dead, one's in hospital, a third's missing."

Marlene ground the half-smoked cigarette into a tin ashtray, then reached for another. "I'm sorry about that. But I can't help."

"Can't or won't?"

"Do you have any idea what the man's like? Charlie Hawes doesn't make idle threats. If he says jump, you make for the nearest window."

The accent had all but disappeared. Bev wondered what else was false or laid on thick.

"How many have you been through, Marlene?"

"Don't be stupid. I just listen to what people say."

The denial was too fast. Bev jabbed a finger in the space between them. "You're right there, Marlene. Everyone says he's a vicious bastard. Everyone says he beats up on his girls. Everyone says he's a pile of steaming shit. But you know what? No one wants to do a sodding thing about it."

She took a deep drag, then talked through the smoke. "Ever wondered why?"

Ozzie cleared his throat. "Thing is, Marlene, if he gets away with it, he'll just carry on. If you were to point us in the right direction, he's no way of knowing we got the steer from you. If you're worried, we could arrange protection."

Bev closed her gaping mouth and returned her gaze to Marlene, who was sitting with one arm across her chest, the other hand cupping her chin. There was a lengthy silence while she weighed Ozzie's words. "A babysitting copper? 'Bout as much use as a crocheted condom."

"That's a no, is it?" Bev asked.

Marlene gave a deep sigh. "I'll think about it. I can't say fairer than that. Thing is, Charlie's got mates all over the place. If he found out I'd opened my gob, it'd be dead meat time, know what I mean?"

Bev recalled the butcher's window. She gave a reluctant nod. "Okay, Marlene." She handed her a card. "You can get me on this number. Anytime. Just don't leave it too long." Bev gave Ozzie a nod. They were at the door when the woman spoke again.

"The girl that's missing? What's her name?"

Bev turned. "Vicki. Vicki Flinn. You know her?"

"Tall bird. Skinny. Shacks down in some squat by the park?"

"That's the one."

"Yeah. Haven't seen her lately. Can't see Charlie Hawes being interested though. He's more into kids."

"Christ, Marlene. She's only seventeen."

She lit another cigarette, releasing twin streams of smoke through flared nostrils. "Exactly."

Bev narrowed her eyes. The way Marlene was talking didn't tally with a woman who claimed to know Charlie Hawes only by repute.

"She knows a damn sight more than she's letting on."

Bev paused, sandwich midway to mouth. Ozzie wasn't usually so categorical, or so judgmental. She agreed, but was curious to hear his thinking. She took a bite out of a cheese bap. "Go on."

He glanced round, as if Charlie Hawes might be lurking behind a Busy Lizzie or a bottle of sauce. There were only a dozen tables and Bev couldn't picture Pimp King or any of his coterie in a place that boasted red gingham cloths. Anyway, there was no alcohol, no smoking and definitely no lap dancing. It was pensioners' happy hour in the Kozee Korner on a Monday lunchtime. Added to which, the hairdresser's next door, Curl Up and Dye, was another magnet for the local wrinklies. Going by the scattering of white hair and pink scalps it was a case of shampoo and set, followed by soup of the day all round. Either way, the place wasn't a million miles from Thread Street and as for decent sarnies it was streets ahead of the police canteen.

"I wouldn't trust her as far as I could throw her," Ozzie confided.

Bev grinned. "You're just peeved cause she was giving you a hard time."

"I beg your pardon." His face was going as red as his tomato juice.

She lifted a placatory hand. "Sorry. I meant, winding you up." She wished he wouldn't purse his lips like that. "Anyway, you know what I mean."

"You're simple enough. It's women like her I can't follow. All that nudge-nudge wink-wink stuff."

Bev shovelled sugar into her tea, then remembered she'd given it up.

"You're not going all prudy on me, are you, Oz? She's a hooker. She's not going to spout Shakespeare, is she?"

He shrugged. "S'pose not. Anyway her tactic's pretty subtle, isn't it?"

It certainly was. "What tactic?"

"Obfuscation. And not just at my expense. She hid behind it from the word go. All those gags about you looking for work and Kipling's cakes." He wiped a bread roll round his soup dish. "While she's cracking dubious jokes, she's not exactly giving anything away."

Obfuscation? Must be a legal term. She'd never seen him so heated, but was it anger at what he saw as Marlene's wool-pulling or was he pissed off because she'd flashed her knickers at him?

"What makes you think the lady's got any goodies worth sharing?"

"Methinks the lady dith protest too much."

"Doth."

"Whatever." He shrugged and there was a peal of laughter from four old dears at the nearest table. Oz flashed them a smile. Bev wondered if he went for the older woman and quickly calculated how many years she could give him.

He was still waiting for her response.

"I hear what you're saying, Oz. All that stuff about jumping from windows. And liking them young."

"And how come she only asked about Vicki Flinn? You told her a girl was dead."

"And another was in hospital." Bev chewed her bottom lip. "She might have seen it in the paper. Michelle's murder was all over the front page on Saturday. And Cassie's attack made a few lines in the *Star* this morning."

"Could be. You'd think she'd have mentioned it though."

"Then again she could be genuinely scared. One toe out of line and, with Charlie Hawes, you've lost your legs."

"That's the trouble, Sarge. If people don't talk – how the hell are we going to find out anything?"

"Let's go and have a word with old Lil. Nothing fazes her. She's seen off three husbands and number four didn't look too good last time I saw him. If that doesn't work –" she brushed stray crumbs off her skirt – "I'll have to come up with something else."

She waited outside while he settled the bill. She'd said nothing to Oz, but Marlene had already given her an idea. She just needed a little time to think it through.

"Coupla packs of Polos, please, Lil."

"They'll rot your teeth, y'know."

Bev laughed; judging by the state of Lil's pearlies, she spoke from bittersweet experience. Seen it all, had Lil. The old girl had been a fixture on the corner of Thread Street as long as anyone could remember. Back in Bev's days on the beat, the kiosk had been a regular port of call for many a clandestine smoke. Sucked mints then, as well. She handed Ozzie a tube and pocketed the other. "Anyhow, Lil. How's it going?"

"Damn sight better than it's goin' for you lot." The cackle was straight off a blasted heath. Like a streak of lightning, Lil's hand shot out, clutching a folded copy of *The Mirror*. "Shift yourself, girl." Bev stepped aside. Without breaking stride, a puce-faced jogger ran past, snatched the paper and shoved it down his vest. He disappeared before Bev drew breath.

Lil smiled. "Don't worry. He'll settle up on Sat'day." She jabbed a none-too-clean finger in the air. "And you haven't paid for them mints."

Bev tried her pockets, then tried it on. "Got any change, Oz?"

Lil slipped the coins into a bum bag round her middle, slapped hands on hips, and cast an appraising eye. "Who's your young fella then, Bev?"

They exchanged bemused glances as Lil emerged from her cubby hole for a more formal introduction. She'd come over all coquettish, gently rocking on her grubby trainers like a Spice Girl's granny. With difficulty, Bev kept a straight face. "Lilian Higgs. This is DC Ossama Khan. Ozzie. This is…"

He bowed his head, extended a hand. "Mrs Higgs. Or may I call you Lil?"

Bev observed agog. Talk about putty. The old darling was drooling.

"Eh, Bev! You'll stick like that if the wind changes." Lil laughed and removed a nub end from behind her ear. "Got a light?" She shuffled nearer while Bev ferreted in her bag for matches.

"Ta, duck." She blew the smoke through the side of her mouth, which probably accounted for the odd tobacco highlight among the grey strands. "Any road. You aren't here to talk about the weather. What's up?"

Bev held out empty hands. "I'll be honest with you Lil. We're up shit creek without a teaspoon."

"That young tart?"

"Did you know her?" Bev asked.

She waited while Lil picked and flicked a fleck of tobacco from her top lip. "Bit. Seen her round. And her mate."

"Vicki Flinn?"

"Nah. Whatsername? Cassie somethin'. Shared a room up at Fair Oaks, they did. She was shittin' herself about Shell."

"When was this?"

"Sat'day. Late afternoon. Didn't know a thing till she seen it in the paper. She was standin' right where you are now. I told her she ought to talk to your lot."

"And?"

"'I ain't talkin' to no cops,' she says. She was shakin' like a leaf, poor cow."

Bev considered this. "What else did she say?"

"Said she didn't know anything. Didn't believe her though, and I was right an' all."

"How do you mean?"

"She's in hospital, isn't she?"

Talking to no one, thought Bev. "When did you last see Michelle?"

Lil stuck her bottom lip out. "Must have been Friday. Day she copped it."

Bev felt a stir of excitement. "What time would that be?"

"Nine. Half nine."

"Wagging, was she?"

"Not unless she was at night school."

Bev's eyes widened. She almost grabbed the old woman's scrawny arm but several unidentified objects lurked in the creases of her greatcoat. "You saw Michelle Lucas the night she died?"

"That's what I said, innit?"

The eyes were blazing now. "For Christ's sake, Lil. Why the hell didn't you say something, come forward, pick up the phone?" The old woman shrugged. "No point. She's dead, isn't she?"

"She was murdered, Lil. Whoever killed her is still out there."

"Exactly. But the bloke I seen her with isn't a killer. He wouldn't hurt a fly. He's a right gent."

11

"What do *you* want?"

The woman's door was barely open but he still caught a whiff of cooking fat and cooped-up cats. A skinny tortoiseshell sidled through the gap and marked its freedom by depositing white hairs on black trousers. He bent to stroke it, but the cat hissed and bared its teeth. The woman looked as if she'd like to do the same.

He straightened up, gave a lazy smile. "What do I want? That's no way to greet an old friend of the family." Smile still in place, he pulled an envelope from his coat pocket. "Especially when he comes bearing gifts."

Her eyes narrowed and she made a grab, but he swung it out of reach.

"First things first, Mrs Flinn. Where are your manners? Shouldn't you be inviting me in?"

She folded thin white arms across a scrawny chest. "I should be phoning the Bill, that's what I should be doing. And if that fool daughter of mine had anything decent between her ears, she'd be telling you to sod off."

His mouth tightened. "But she hasn't. And she isn't." He put a foot in the doorway and a finger on her cheek. "And you want to watch your mouth."

She stepped back and rubbed a hand across her face, distorting lines already etched too deep. Her belligerence gave way to resignation.

"What do you want, Charlie?"

"A little chat. That's all."

She hesitated, knowing he wouldn't give up without a fight.

She couldn't believe Vicki had gone off with him. Not after all she'd said. Stupid cow couldn't even say it face to face. Reluctantly she opened the door wider. "Five minutes. That's all."

He took a deep breath and followed her through a dark passageway. He had to squeeze past an upturned bike without a chain and a cardboard box full of sleeping kittens. The kitchen was filthy. Hairs and grease everywhere. There was something sticky on the soles of his shoes but he had no desire to investigate. He hovered in the doorway, careful not to touch anything.

"See you sold your shares in Proctor and Gamble then."

"What?"

"Never mind."

There was a carry-cot on the floor near the cooker. A baby was crying: face red, fists clenched, tufts of dark hair sticking out from her tiny head.

"Little Lucie doesn't sound too happy."

The woman had positioned herself against the sink, aiming for the laid-back look. "Keep away from her. She's too young even for you."

He didn't say anything, just slowly – very slowly – looked her up and down. Everything about her was faded: ill-fitting denims, sloppy sweater, mouse-coloured hair. Taking his time, he walked towards her, shaking his head, tutting. "Didn't get the message, did you?"

"What message?" Had Vicki sent another note?

The expression 'didn't know what hit her' made sense now. She saw the hand, subconsciously admired the long, manicured nails, but the blow didn't register for several seconds. Then, tentatively, she ran her tongue along her teeth; the loose one at the front was hanging by a thread. She knew he was watching her, waiting for a reaction, but she was too busy bracing herself for the next strike.

He lifted his hand but only to reach for a greying dishcloth festering on the draining board. He held it between thumb and index finger and flung it in her face. "Told you to watch your mouth, didn't I?"

The blood tasted vile. She could feel it oozing down her chin. Her lip was probably split as well. He was close enough for her to count the tiny flecks of hazel in his eyes. She was shaking so much only the sink was keeping her upright. She used every ounce of effort to keep her voice level. "You don't scare me, you little shit."

He stroked a finger along his jawbone then tapped it slowly several times on his chin. The silence was awful. She broke it without thinking. "Soon as you're out of here, I'm on to the cops."

He sighed. "I don't think so."

Steeling himself to touch her, he grabbed a handful of hair and yanked her head back. The cold water was a shock. It was splashing into her eyes, running into her mouth and nose. Struggling made it worse. She couldn't catch her breath. The panic accelerated when she realised his hand wasn't on the cold tap.

His eyes were searching the window sill behind her. "Watch it. Wash it. It's all the same to me, Annie."

She stiffened as he reached across her for a spray gun, held it in front of her eyes.

"Don't worry. I'll save you a bit. You'll be able to give the place a good scrubbing when I'm gone. I'm surprised at you, Annie. You could age trees with the rings on that top over there. Get a grip, girl. The social wouldn't like it. Not with young Lucie around."

The baby was transfixed: staring, wide-eyed.

He held the container aloft, apparently studying the label. "It's good stuff, this, Annie. Anti-bacterial. Just the job."

She screwed her eyes, tried not to scream as the liquid hit her lip. It tasted worse than the blood. When she spat, he rammed it into her mouth. She started to gag and her knees gave way. He held on for a few seconds, then let her drop. There was a hank of hair in his fist. He leaned over her, rinsed it off his hands. He curled his lip as the hairs joined tea-leaves and eggshells clinging to the bottom of the sink.

The woman was on the floor, slumped against a cupboard, her sweater soaked and blood-stained. He nudged her with his foot. "Accidents in the home, huh?" He tutted. "Who'd have thought it? Sooner you get that seen to, the better." He looked round for a cloth to dry his hands. A tea towel had dropped from a hook on to a dish of dried-up cat food. He left it, shook his head, knelt beside her. "Look, Annie. You're a busy woman. I only came to get a few things straight, then I'll get out of your hair. Okay?" He gently lifted her face towards him. "Okay?"

She didn't react so he moved her head up and down in an exaggerated nod. "Thing is, we don't want Mr Policeman round asking tricky questions, do we?" Now a heavy-handed shake. "Lost your tongue, have you?"

She tried to speak but her lips were swollen, her mouth on fire.

"What did you say, Annie?" He paused. "Did you say you swear on Lucie's pathetic little life you won't talk to the police?"

She nodded.

"And did you say you'd rather eat shit than breathe a word against me?"

Another nod.

"And did you say you'll be only too delighted to let them know Vicki's with a friend, in Brighton, you think. You'd like to help more of course, but you don't know the friend's name, let alone her address."

"Shore."

He laughed. "That's right. Sea shore. Now. Just to show there are no hard feelings." He reached into an inside pocket and handed her the envelope. "There's a few quid in here. Don't spend it down the boozer. It's from me and Vicki, for you.

Right?"

She nodded again, followed him with her eyes as he got to his feet and walked to the carry-cot. He bent down and chucked the baby's chin. Lucie's bottom lip quivered but then she grinned revealing two perfect white teeth. Charlie turned his head to the woman. "Got your eyes, hasn't she, Annie?" He stroked the child's hair, reached into his pocket and laid a small furry bundle by the child. "And that's something for the kid. Just from Vicki. Special delivery."

He was back across the room in seconds, grin like a Cheshire cat on cream. "That seems to be everything… for now. Make sure you have got it right, won't you, Annie? Next time, it'll be bleach. And I'll bring my own shooter."

12

Bev jabbed Byford's number into the car phone. There was a slim chance he'd still be at Henry Brand's place. The way Ozzie was driving, they'd find out soon enough anyway.

"Come on. Dammit."

"Can't go any faster, Sarge."

She stopped drumming the dashboard. "Not you. Where's the guv? Why isn't he answering?"

"Search me." It was an enticing prospect but not one to dwell on. If Lil Higgs was right, the last man to have been seen with Michelle Lucas was currently entertaining the governor and the DI. Lil had seen it all from the steamed-up window of a number 50. Friday night was bingo night and she'd been on her way to meet a mate out of the Essoldo. She'd spotted two figures arguing near a car parked on double yellows just up from the Taj Mahal. She'd clocked Brand straight off and – curious – had swivelled round to see the girl's face. Lil had been in no doubt: "Michelle Lucas or I'm a monkey's uncle."

Bev shook her head. "Amazing, isn't it?"

Ozzie, who was taking a corner on two wheels and a prayer, beamed. "Thanks, Sarge. Reckon I should go in for the advanced course?"

"What?"

"Driving, the —"

"Yeah, yeah." She swatted the words away. "I mean, as a rule, Lil's as canny as a barn full of owls. But 'cause it's Henry Brand she didn't even think about it."

"She did. Just didn't think it worth mentioning."

"'Cause he wears dark suits and talks posh?"

"Because he taught her kids and her grandkids and she's known him for years."

"That's okay, then. Proper gent, isn't he?"

"I'm only trying to see it from Lil's point of view, Sarge. Women of her generation still look up to men like that: teachers, doctors, vicars. You know what I mean."

Bev closed her gaping mouth. "Well done, Khan. That's a clean sweep. Ageist, sexist and élitist."

She saw his hands tighten on the wheel. "Doesn't make me wrong."

They drove in silence. Ozzie slowed at one point to allow an ambulance to overtake, blue lights flashing. She tried Byford again; this time the number was engaged. A couple of times, she caught Ozzie glancing at her, something obviously on his mind. They were almost at Brand's before he decided to share it. "You know, even if Lil did see Brand with Michelle – it doesn't follow that he killed her."

"It follows that she was dead not long after. It follows that he's a lying toe-rag. And it follows that he's got a stack of questions to answer."

She folded her arms, waiting for a response.

"What the fuck —?"

She followed his gaze. The F-word from Ozzie was a shock; so was the scene outside Brand's house. Byford's motor was all but hidden by a bank of police patrol cars, estates emblazoned with media logos and an ambulance with its lights still flashing.

Big Val was feeling small. She stood in the middle of the pavement looking up at Highgate nick. She'd never gone in through the front door before. Come to think of it, she'd never been near the place without a police escort. She'd been hauled in more times than a fishing net but always accompanied by a couple of vice boys. They'd drive round the back and drop her off in the custody suite where she was on first-name terms with everyone and even more familiar with the routine: form-filling followed by cash and condom-counting. As long as a girl wasn't pissed or stoned, she could be processed and back on the patch within an hour. Being brought in was one thing, to turn up voluntarily something else. She caught a glimpse of herself in the huge glass edifice: black boots, white leggings, chequered blouson. She looked like a nun on a zebra crossing. Christ, if she didn't stop dithering, she'd get taken in anyway. She sucked a last drag on her fag and slung it in the gutter.

Loins girded and resolve firmed, she swept through the revolving doors as though she owned the place. She misjudged her momentum and had to make a pretty sharp exit or she'd have found herself back on the street. As it was she staggered in, hoping not to be mistaken for a drunk. Not that a bit of Dutch courage wouldn't go amiss.

There was time to perfect the spiel. Two old dears and a suit were already in a queue, behind a nice young man giving details of the aliens who'd abducted him from New Street Station in 1602. Vince Hanlon was on the desk and did not look convinced. Val winked in commiseration. She was glad it was Vincey; he was a good bloke. She grabbed a seat against a wall that was livened up with posters of the 'Have You Seen This Man?' variety. She'd shagged two of them but her eyes had been closed at the time. They were wide open now as she sat back and had a good look round.

Front of house was well plush compared with what the girls knew as the dungeon. Actually, Patty the crackhead always called it custody but only because some clever dick had told her it was named after the paintwork. There was no flaky yellow out here, it was all executive greys and aristo blues, and so much greenery she wondered if there was work going as a gardener.

She listened as the Elizabethan space traveller filed a complaint of police negligence and watched him head happily back into the community. The suit had long since left. The old biddies were now banging on about a flasher at the bottom of the garden. Val couldn't work out whether they were reporting or requesting one. Vince listened patiently, said he'd see what he could do, and sent them on their way. She waited while he quaffed half a mug of tepid tea then wiped his lips with the back of a hand.

"God almighty. It's no wonder I'm going grey. Y'need to be a Freud to work in this place."

Val sniffed. "That'd be Clement, would it?"

The face was deadpan but he wasn't fooled. "Daft sod. Anyroad. To what do I owe the pleasure..?"

Thirty quid sprang to mind but she was meant to be acting sombre. She leaned closer, looked round and dropped her voice. "I'm scared, Sarge. I've been getting these death threats."

"Death threats?"

She nodded vigorously. "And I'm not the only one. Most of the girls are saying the same."

Given the nature of the girls' game vilification was par for the course, but in the light of Michelle's murder Val was betting the claim would be taken seriously.

Vince poised pen on paper. "What sort of threats? Tell me about them."

"Look, Sarge. No offence. I've been hanging round out here long enough. It's like a bloody shop window. Know what I mean."

"Don't worry, love. If you're not safe here…"

"I'm not gonna be here, am I? I'll be out as soon's I've said me piece. Anyway, Sarge, like I say, no offence, but I'd rather talk to a woman. This business has put the wind up me. Another woman'd know where I'm coming from."

There was a tremble in her hands and a catch in her throat.

"Okay, love. I'll see who's in."

"Not some kid just out of nappies, Sarge." He reached a hand to the phone. "And not one of them stuck-up cows that treat you like shit."

Vince saluted with a smile. "Does madam have anyone in mind?"

"Nah." She dismissed the remark with a wave of her hand and made towards the chair but turned before he'd finished punching the numbers. "Actually, Sarge, if you're serious – there is someone I wouldn't mind having a word with. Can't remember her name. Dark hair. Bit shorter than me. Nice smile. Got a real gob on her."

Vince's frown gave way to a smile. He lifted a finger to halt the flow. "I'll just see if she's in."

"May as well get back." Byford turned to Bev. "Not a lot we can do here."

She could think of a few things but none of them legal. She moved away from the window as the ambulance disappeared down the street, Henry Brand's last words still ringing in her ears. The final glimpse through gaping doors had been Brand hovering solicitously as a paramedic worked on his wife.

"Convenient, isn't it?" Byford was in key-jangling mode, and despite what he'd said, was obviously in no great rush. He had thoughts and wanted to sound her out. She could always tell.

"What's that, then?"

"Just as we learn he was with Michelle on the night she was murdered, wife takes an overdose, and he starts screaming police harassment."

"You saying he helped her?"

"No."

Bev picked up the hesitation. "But..."

He shrugged. "It helps him no end, doesn't it? Wouldn't look too good if I pulled a man in for questioning when his wife's at death's door. Specially with the press gang outside."

Bev's face suggested she wouldn't have the same dilemma. But much as she disliked Brand, the theory didn't hold.

"He couldn't have known he'd been seen by Lil – it's less than an hour since we found out ourselves."

"True. But he was well aware I wanted to question him. Neither me or Mike got a word in edgeways with this lot going on."

She looked round. "Where is Superman?"

Byford gave an exaggerated sigh. "Inspector Powell's handling the media."

"He'll like that." The smile faded. "How the hell did they –"

"You tell me. They were all over the place when we got here. And there's Brand shouting his mouth off about the police hounding innocent people in their own home."

Sounded familiar. "Been there. Had that."

Byford rubbed a hand over his face. "Yes. He mentioned you."

"I aim to please." She smiled, then was serious. "A bloke like Brand wouldn't risk topping his wife just to avoid us, would he?"

He shrugged. "Nothing amazes me any more, Bev."

"Hold on." She paused trying to recall what Brand had said. "She was in bed last time I came. Migraine or nerves or something. I got the impression she was a bit fragile."

"She is now."

"What's she supposed to have popped then?"

"Don't know. Brand was in no state to help. He was running round like a headless chicken. He thought she was shopping, turns out she never got up. He found her in bed. Unconscious."

"What time was that?"

He looked at his watch. "Half an hour ago?"

She was trying to work it out but the timing was all wrong.

"I know, I know," Byford said. "I'm asking the same questions, Bev. Trouble is... no one's got any of the answers."

"I can help you there." Powell was striding across the room looking pretty pleased with himself. "The press boys got an anonymous tip. Well, Matt Snow did. He was the only one giving anything away."

"Big help, that." The smile suggested she meant it. "But it can't be that anonymous when you think about it."

Byford obviously was. "Course not." He looked at Bev. "Who else but Brand could have known what was going on?"

"Unless he made the call himself." Bev was interrupted by Powell who'd lost his earlier perkiness.

"No way, Morriss. He'd only just found her. He was gutted."

Byford didn't share the view. "If you're so concerned, you can get yourself up to the hospital and hold the old boy's hand till he's ready to answer a few questions."

"Me?"

"Problem with that, Mike?"

"No, it's just —"

Byford wasn't interested. "Brand's the closest we've got to a break in this case. He was seen with Michelle on the night she died. At the very least he's a witness. I don't know what's been going on here but it takes second place to that girl's death. I want answers, and whatever Brand has – or hasn't – been up to, he's going to supply them."

The ensuing silence was broken by footsteps in the hall. Ozzie popped his head round the door. "Sarge? There's a call. Vince Hanlon. Says one of the girls has turned up at Highgate. Wants to talk to you. Something about death threats?"

13

It had to be the big redhead in the corner. Bev grabbed a couple of coffees on the way over. "Wotcha."

The woman looked up from the stars in *The Sun* and mirrored Bev's smile.

"Val, isn't it? Val Masters?"

Any hesitation was down to the current Titian beehive, jostling with the black raffia bouffant in Bev's memory bank. Uncertainty vanished the minute the woman opened her mouth. "Lend us a couple of quid, Sarge. Me belly thinks me throat's cut."

Bev already had her hand in her pocket. "I'll get it. What d'you fancy?"

"I could murder a plate of chips."

She'd got death on the brain; must be the threats. "Two secs."

"Maybe a couple of eggs on the side?"

"No prob."

"That geezer's sausages look a bit of all right."

Bev glanced at the next table, relieved to see someone tucking into bangers and mash.

"Okay, sausages."

Val was still scanning the horoscopes when Bev staggered back with a tray.

"Got you a few slices of bread and butter, Val."

"Better be low-fat." Then, with barely a pause, "Joke."

She waited while Val built a chip buttie the size of a house brick.

"Let's have a look at these threats then."

"I've only got the one. I bunged the rest in the bin." She

licked grease from her fingers, burrowed in a black shoulder-bag and eventually retrieved a crumpled, none-too-clean sheet of cheap, lined notepaper. Bev bet there'd be dabs all over it, and not a single whorl the writer's. She skimmed the words; read them again. The author had clearly not had the benefit of a grammar school education.

FUCK OFF SLAG
NO MORE WARNINGS
YOUR NEXT WHORE

She waited until Val's mouth was more or less empty. "Fill me in, love. How many have you had? When did it start?"

Val pursed her lips, which by now had lost at least one layer of scarlet. "Must be a good six, seven weeks since the first. It come by hand, though. Not in the post."

A nod from Bev. "'bout Christmas, then?"

Val winked. "Made a change from all the cards."

Bev watched, fascinated, as Val pensively ran a sausage along her lips then sank suspiciously-white teeth into the meat. Her mastication was attracting quite an audience.

Bev cleared her throat. "Er, Val, you were saying..? 'Bout the letters?"

"Sorry, chuck, I was miles away. Let's see, now. There's been four, definite, mebbe five. Tell you the truth, Sarge, I didn't reckon much to it at first. Not till young Shell, like. You get used to the abuse and that. People shouting filth, shoving shit through the letterbox. Know what I mean?"

Another nod. "What did the others say?"

"Same sort of crap. Slag, whore, tart."

Bev pointed at the note. "It says no more warnings. Tell me about the earlier ones.'

Val shrugged. "Sorry, chuck, can't remember. As I say, I got rid of the buggers straight away."

Bev was distracted by raucous laughter from a group of blokes at the next table. Bet they weren't discussing needlework.

"So you can't remember anything?"

The headshake was loosening the beehive's foundations. "One of the others might."

"Go on."

"After Shell, a few of us got together. Started chatting like, and it turns out I'm not the only one on his mailing list."

"His?"

"Do me a favour, Sarge." Bev shrugged; a lesser woman would have quailed under so much contempt.

"You obviously don't recognise the writing, but any ideas who might be sending them?"

"Don't be soft. I'd tell you if I knew. Or I'd send the boys round."

"I'll pretend I didn't hear that." Bev put her elbows on the table and leaned closer. "Talking of boys, what do you know about a big boy called Charlie Hawes? Word is, he was Michelle Lucas's pimp."

"Name rings a bell…"

Hallelujah. "They call him Mad Charlie," Bev said. "Mind, that's unfair to psychos."

Val turned her mouth down. "Nah. Can't place it. But you know me, Sarge. I keep well away from pimps. Can't be doin' with the bastards."

Bev hid her disappointment; someone had to know him, didn't they?

"Tell me about the meeting."

"What?"

"The girls. You said you got together." Intriguing, that was. She knew about the national groups; the more vociferous women had been joining voices for years but she couldn't see the likes of Val and Vicki becoming card-carrying members of the Collective.

"It was just me and the kids really."

Curiouser and curiouser. "Oh?"

"Some of them are still at school, Sarge. Someone's gotta look out for them."

"Gonna be a regular thing is it?" Could be useful, that.

"What do you think we are? The Women's Institute?"

"Just wondered." She couldn't see Val filling jars – not with jam anyway. Shame, though.

"As it happens, they're coming over to my place tomorrow. There's another protest on the patch. Usual load of God-botherers and do-gooders. They're a bloody nuisance. It don't half piss the punters off. Me and the girls are gonna crack a few cans, get a vid."

"Can I come?"

Val choked on her sausage. "You what?"

Bev sneaked a chip. "I mean it. I'd really like to."

"I dunno…"

"Go on, Val. It'd be great. Could be dead useful. Captive audience and all that." She bit back a line about two birds with one stone. There must be worse ways of putting it, but offhand she couldn't think of one. And anyway, she'd have to clear the idea she was working on with Byford before sharing it with anyone else. Val was clearly still considering the request.

"Dunno if they'll buy it. You being the Bill."

"If anyone can swing it, you can. Go on, Val. Put a word in. Tell them I haven't got two heads."

Val was chewing her bottom lip.

"Look, Val, you said yourself, you're not the only one getting these threats. Those girls are easy meat, standing targets. I'm not looking to give them a hard time. Nothing I say's gonna get them off the game. I just don't want to see anyone else hurt."

The big woman made up her mind. "Okay, I'll do it."

"Brill."

"Can't guarantee how many'll turn out though. One of the kids has already legged it."

"Who's that then?" Bev tried to keep her voice casual.

"Don't know if you'd know her." Val wiped vestiges of yolk with the last of the bread. "Dead pally with Shell, she was. Girl called Vicki."

"Vicki Flinn?" Bev frowned: Vick had done a runner?

"Yeah. She give me a bell last night."

"Where from?"

Val closed her eyes. "Hold on. It's on the tip of me tongue. Somethin' with a B." Eyes wide and finger in the air, it finally emerged. "Bognor. No. Wait a min. Brighton. That's it. Brighton."

"Big place, Brighton. Did she say where she's staying? Who she's with?"

"Nah. Cheeky little cow. Only rings cause she wants me to tell her ma she's all right. I says, 'Who'd you think I am? Your social worker?' I mean, it's a couple a buses to Annie Flinn's place and I hardly know the woman."

"Want me to go?"

"Nah. I'll get round to it. Don't bother."

"I'll nip round this evening. Best she knows. She'll be worried if she doesn't hear."

Val snorted. "Worried? About Vicki? Pigs'll fly jumbos. I'll go at the weekend. Put her out of her misery."

"No!" It came out sharper than she'd intended. "Really, Val. I'd like a word with her anyway."

She shrugged. "Suit yourself."

"Got the address?" May as well get it from Val. Bev could have dropped Vicki anywhere the other night. The girl had lied about her mother's death. There was no guarantee she'd been on the level about where her mother lived.

"Got a pen?" Val ripped a corner off the newspaper, scribbled a few lines and passed it across.

Good. Bev looked back at the big woman. "If you get any more of these letters, hang on to them. And tell the girls the same. The more we have, the more there is to go on. I'll be straight with you, Val. At the mo, there's not a whole bunch we can do. The nutters who go in for this kind of thing are sick but they aren't stupid. They know not to leave fingerprints, not to lick envelopes. We've more or less got to catch them red-handed. Or hope they cock up. Big time."

"Reckon it's the bastard who killed Shell?"

Bev hunched her shoulders, held out her hands. The gesture was eloquent enough. "What time are the girls coming round, then, Val?"

"Eight, half eight?"

Bev pushed her chair back and got to her feet. "Great."

"Thank your stars then."

"You what?"

Val shoved *The Sun* across the desk, pointed out a horoscope.

Bev leaned over and read aloud. "Do not be afraid to let new people into your life. With your instincts at their most reliable, you would do well to trust them. Remember, a little friction is not always a bad thing."

Val was nodding sagely; knew all about friction, did Val. Bev grinned; didn't know it was yesterday's paper, though, did she?

14

Byford was on the phone when Bev popped her head round his door. He beckoned and she took a seat, waiting as patiently as she could for him to finish. She'd been doing some calculations and if the Lucas case was a bank account, they were in deep red shit. After her chat with Val, she'd checked their deposits with both incident rooms. Getting on for four hundred statements had been taken; twice as many doors knocked; visits were ongoing to massage parlours, adult cinemas and dodgy vid shops. In the eighty hours since they'd gathered round Michelle's body in the park, there was next to nothing in credit. Apart from Lil, no one had had a sniff, and Charlie Hawes made the Scarlet Pimpernel look like the ubiquitous bad penny. It was time to speed things up.

Byford replaced the receiver. "There've been a couple of sightings of a BMW on the cruise, Friday night, about the right time." He nodded at the phone. "I'm sending Kent and Newman, see if they can flesh it out."

Gazza and Dazza. They'd love that. Three-day-old sightings of a motor.

"Anything on the reg?" she asked.

"What reg?" He shook his head. "No. We've got two different partials from two different sources. They're both iffy, anyway."

"Nothing on Charlie at Swansea?"

Byford rolled his eyes. "What do you think?"

"Not so much as a push-bike." It figured; a man whose business was so shady it was subterranean was hardly likely to leave a paper trail. Charlie'd know as well as her, that as long as the DVLA had an address, he could register his motors in any name he liked. It was illegal, but it wasn't exactly up there with pimping, murder or the odd spot of mayhem.

Sending Gaz and Daz out was all a bit drowning men and clutching straws. She was about to grab at one herself. She studied the guv's face. It was difficult to gauge how he'd react.

"What would you say to me doing a bit of moonlighting?"

"What?" His eyebrows were heading for his hairline.

"With the girls."

"What!"

"Look, guv, we're getting nowhere, we're talking to blind Trappists. We're not even close."

She gave him edited highlights of her interview with Val, including the news about Vicki. It had pissed Bev off, the thought that the girl had done a bunk without so much as a goodbye. She noticed he didn't say much; probably didn't want to rub it in.

"Thing is, guv, if I can get the girls' trust, go out on the streets, it could give us the break. I'm bound to pick something up. Might even flush Charlie Hawes out of his sewer. At the very least they need a minder."

"No. No. Absolutely no." The table bang was superfluous. The message was loud, clear and too quick.

"Is that an 'I'll think about it'?" The voice had an edge he was meant to catch. She wasn't talking off the top of her head; she'd given it a lot of thought. She wasn't some kid who watched too much telly and – as he well knew – she'd passed every self defence course going.

"Is this down to Sunday? Look, guv, I was jumped from behind. There was nothing I – or anyone – could've done about it. This'd be different. Apart from anything else, I'd be prepared."

"Prepared for what? Round two? For Christ's sake, Bev, the man had a knife. It wasn't for carving your initials in a tree."

She held her arms out. "Look, I'm fine. I made too much of it. No one's even mentioned it." That was a porkie but needs must. “Come on, guv, at least say you’ll consider it?”

“What’s to consider? Apart from anything else, you can’t possibly expect me to agree to one of my detectives getting tarted up and hanging round street corners?”

She appeared to give it some thought. “Well… maybe not Mike Powell or Oz Khan.” She smiled; he didn’t.

“Not funny, Sergeant.”

“Come on, guv. Think of it as a fact-finding mission. I’m not talking turning tricks.”

“I should bloody well hope not.”

She couldn’t recall the last time she’d heard him swear. She leaned closer.

“If I can’t win the girls over, it’s a non-starter anyway. But it’s got to be worth a try. Won’t you even have a think?”

She was asking a lot, but the stakes were high. One girl dead, another under armed guard in hospital , and Vicki Flinn holed-up in Brighton. The phone rang, pre-empting Byford’s answer.

She watched as the colour drained from his face, tried to read upside down the notes he was making. The phone back in place, he laid the pen on top of the paper and looked up slowly. “I can’t give you official backing.”

“But?”

He rose, walked to the window, perched on the sill. “Apart from any risk to yourself – there’s a host of pitfalls. We’re talking entrapment, inadmissible evidence, endangering witnesses. Never mind the egg on faces all round if it fails or gets thrown out of court.”

Sound arguments but there was still something about his voice. It was almost as though he was thinking aloud. She waited a few seconds then gave a gentle prompt.

“But..?”

He seemed reluctant to meet her gaze; he was reluctant. “That was Harry Gough on the phone. She’d been cut. I’m not referring to the neck wound.”

Bev closed her eyes; there'd been no other knife marks on Michelle's body. She took a deep breath, afraid of what was coming.

"Internal injuries. Serrated blade. Knife. Hacksaw. Something like that. Post mortem. Thank God."

Eyes still closed; image still there. Come on, Bev, blank it out, concentrate on the killer. She looked down at her hands. The right palm was warm and sticky. Her nails had opened up the cuts.

"Was she raped?"

"She'd had sex."

"What's that supposed to mean?"

"She was a prostitute, Bev. She'd had intercourse several times. It's impossible to say whether the killer raped her. She was too badly damaged."

She closed her eyes again, spoke softly through teeth clenched tightly. "I want this bastard."

Byford spun round. 'No, Sergeant. We'll get him. This is police business, not personal. Get that straight. If you're not clear on that score, there's no way you're going out there."

She watched as he moved back to his desk, sat down.

"I can do it? You're letting me go?"

He rested chin on hands for a few seconds. "I can't sanction it officially. You know that, Bev. I'm talking blind eyes, unpaid overtime. And…" He paused. "If the shit hits the fan, you're on your own. At the same time, you tell me everything. Every time you go out, I want to know where you are, where you're going, who you're with, what you're doing."

"You sure about the last bit?"

"Shut up before I change my mind. I'll have a word with Mike Powell, maybe mention it to a couple of the others but the less people who know the better. Okay?"

It was the best she'd get and more than she'd hoped. Better than taking leave and going out on a limb which was what she'd intended.

"I'll be at Val Masters's place tomorrow. Eightish. Drinking. Smoking. Watching porn.'

She kept a straight face. So did he.

"Be able to keep an eye on the protest as well then, won't you?"

"What?"

He lifted a hand. "Joke! Don't panic. We'll look after that, you stick to the girls."

"Like glue. Y'know, according to Val, the first threat arrived about Christmas."

"Same time the CUTS lot started up. I had realised."

She got to her feet. "Thought so. Just keeping you on your toes." She smiled, headed for the door.

"And, Bev," Byford said, "make sure you stay on yours."

"Always said you were a tart, Morriss."

"Ho, ho." Pause, pause. "Sir."

Bev was about to swap insults with Mike Powell, whom she'd bumped into on the wide, stone staircase of the City General.

He gave her arm a supposedly playful punch. "It'll give the lads a good laugh. They'll all be wanting a look at your charge sheet."

"How long you been working on that, then?"

The grin vanished. "Trouble with you, Morriss. No sense of humour."

Apart from finding Powell as amusing as a war zone, she wasn't in the mood for laughter.

She was on the way to see Cassie Swain; *see* was all she'd be doing. She'd phoned ahead. The girl was still unconscious. Bev would have been hard pushed to explain the visit, apart from a vague feeling that Cassie and the girls was what the case was all about. And, sadly, it was too late to do anything to help Michelle. "I take it the governor's had a word?"

"Just." He gestured at the hospital. "I've been called off, thank God. Back first thing."

"Get anything out of Brand?"

"Sod all. He won't leave the wife's bedside. They won't let me near him."

She watched as he pulled on a glove. "Must be off his head," Powell said.

His train of thought was never easy to follow. "Brand?"

"No, dummy. Byford." Now she knew where it was going. "What's it going to achieve, Morriss? Apart from you making a bit on the side?"

"Jealous?"

"Incredulous." There was real venom in his voice. Bev reckoned it was down to the boil festering on the side of his neck. "The margin for cock-ups beggars belief."

Not bad. But he wasn't punning. "Good to know I have your support on this one. Sir."

"You don't. I wouldn't let you loose in a convent. God knows how you managed to swing it with Byford."

"He's always had a soft spot for a pretty face."

Judging by his four-letter snort, irony wasn't Powell's forte. Bev hoisted her shoulder-bag higher. "By the way. If the guv's had a word, he'll also have told you to keep it quiet. So if I hear any smut going round the station about my charge list – you can bet your ass, I'll put your name under deposits." She smiled sweetly. "Night. Sir."

Monday evening. Half seven. The General was fairly quiet. Bev waved her ID at reception, nodded at the security guard and headed for IC. Hated hospitals, always had. Post mortems were a doddle compared with visiting the sick. Enervating heat and nauseating smells didn't help, but it was more than that.

"Sergeant Morriss." A smiling Dr Thorne was coming down the stairs, still managing to look like something off the cover of *Vogue*. Me, thought Bev, I'm more of a *Beano* babe.

"How's it going, doc?"

"It's gone." She grinned, glancing at her watch. "I've been off duty for precisely one hundred and thirty-three seconds. I'm off home to change then I'm going for an Italian."

"We're talking food here, aren't we?' Bet the damn woman could eat like a pig without gaining a gram. Was there no end to the injustice?

"I've no energy for anything else."

"It's Bev, by the way."

"Bev?"

"Bev Morriss."

The doctor held out a hand. "Ursula. But my friends call me Lal."

"I didn't realise you shouldn't be here," Bev said. "You should have mentioned it on the phone."

She shrugged. "No problem. I'm glad you wanted to come."

That was a bit of a turn-up given her attitude last time. Bev's eyes widened. "Cassie hasn't come round, has she?"

"'Fraid not." She propped open a heavy fire door with her backside, then they were on the corridor leading to the unit. "Sounds stupid, I know. It's just kind of nice to think someone cares."

"No one's been to see her?"

She turned her mouth down. "Flying visit from her social worker. Your officers pop their head round the door from time to time. That's about it."

"They're not getting under your feet, I hope." The twenty-four-hour police guard was being split between three PCs. It sounded heady stuff but in reality it meant sitting round for hours at a time with nothing to do.

The doctor shook her head. "You'd hardly know they were here."

Bev scanned the empty corridor. "You can say that again."

"Don't worry, she'll be in with Cassie. The woman officer often sits by the bed for a while. The men tend to stay outside more."

Bev nodded. It figured. Alison Granger was in her forties, had teenage daughters of her own.

The doctor paused at the entrance to the unit. "One thing I meant to mention – a huge bouquet of white lilies arrived this morning for Cassie."

Bev suddenly shivered. "Can I see the card?"

"I'll get one of the nurses to chase it. I'm just going to get out of this coat, grab my bits and pieces. You only want a few minutes, yes?"

"Sure."

"I'll leave you to it, then. She's at the end, on the right."

Bev crept in, strangely cowed by the life-or-death battles being waged in the still silence. She tried not to think, but it was bringing it all back. The daily, sometimes twice daily, visits to her dad. She and her mum sitting either side of the bed as the invisible cancer carved deadly inroads. The three of them talking about anything but: banal chit-chat about ready-pasted wallpaper or West Bromwich Albion. As a good little Catholic girl, and with the unshakeable faith of a twelve-year-old, she knew he'd get better. Even now, the anger and unfairness could reduce her to tears.

She nodded at an intense-looking blonde woman stationed behind a console in the middle of the room. Her eyes were scanning a bank of monitors, and judging by the look on her face, Bev reckoned that viewing vital signs was a lot more demanding than watching *This Is Your Life*. She moved on, aware that her presence had barely been registered.

Bev was wrong about the silence. There was a constant low-level hum from countless hi-tech machines fulfilling functions that failing organs could no longer perform. Human sounds were what was missing. All eight beds were occupied but there was no noise, no movement, nothing. She thought of dust sheets and still lives, wondered why she was creeping around on tiptoe. Bev smiled. "All quiet?"

She watched as Alison pushed a hand through a mousy fringe, surprised to see grey roots along the hairline.

"As the gra —" She stopped herself. "As the proverbial."

Bev put a finger to her lips. "I get the picture."

Alison lowered her voice. "I'd rather you get the bastard who did that." She was pointing behind her. "Know what, Bev?"

She shook her head, had a feeling she was about to find out.

"Hanging's too good for some people."

The woman was halfway to the door, trying to hide tears that Bev had already spotted. She covered the short distance to Cassie's bedside.

It was the first time she'd laid eyes on the girl. Her head was swathed in bandages and she was on a ventilator with a drip in the back of each bony wrist. A stiff white sheet was covering most of her body but just about every visible part was badly bruised. The damage to the girl's face was obvious; God alone knew what was going on in her head.

She moved closer, gently stroked Cassie's hand. She was what? Fifteen, almost sixteen.

She'd been in care for two years and on the game for eighteen months. In care! Some bloody care. Children's homes were cash-and-carries to the likes of Charlie Hawes. All a pimp had to do was flash a few wads and a show of affection and a vulnerable kid like Cassie was carted off to vice-land.

Bev had seen it time and again. A cycle of abuse. Broken home, parental abuse, children's home, pimp abuse. Not at first, of course. Pimps weren't stupid. They made the girl feel good: bought her a few clothes, bits of jewellery, talked about love. By the time she realised she was destined for red lights not bright lights, it was too late. She'd be hooked on booze, drugs or – more often than not – the bloke himself. They genuinely loved the bastards. And when it was eventually beaten out of them, they were trapped: shit-scared and totally dependent.

Bev could count on the fingers of one hand how many girls

she knew who'd stood up in court to give evidence that would send a pimp down. There was a gentle tap on her shoulder.

"You okay?" It was Doctor Thorne.

Bev rubbed her eyes with finger and thumb. "Fine. Bit tired."

The doctor looked but said nothing.

"Thanks for arranging this." Bev glanced at her watch. "I'd best get off now." She paused. "Will she..?"

Dr Thorne shook her head. "I don't know. There's been no real change since she was admitted."

They were in the corridor when the doctor spoke again. "I checked, but there was no name."

Bev looked puzzled.

"The flowers?" Dr Thorne prompted. "You wanted to see the card?"

"Right."

"The nurse remembered it well. She threw the card away, but it said: Cassie. My Girl. Forever."

Bev frowned. "Why did she throw it away?"

"She thought they'd made a mistake at the florists's. It was black-edged. They're for mourning. She didn't want Cassie to be upset. When she comes round."

Bev nodded, comforted the word 'if' hadn't been used. She made a mental note to check flower shops. "Talking of coming round – d'you know anything about an Enid Brand? Brought in this afternoon with an overdose?"

They started the walk to reception. "Yeah. A&E gets first crack at anything like that. She should be okay. She swallowed a stack of paracetamol but we almost certainly got to her in time."

"Did you come across her old man by any chance?"

"Certainly did. If I was married to him, I'd swallow acid." She put a hand to her mouth. "Forget I said that. Very unprofessional."

Bev smiled. "Go on."

"The man was impossible. A walking ego. Making demands.

Insulting everyone. I threatened to call security if he didn't back off." She paused, stunned at herself. "What am I saying? I shouldn't be telling you this."

"It's my charm."

"It's your cheek."

They'd reached the front desk by now and Bev watched as Dr Thorne casually applied a perfect coat of lipstick. She was well impressed. Without a mirror, Bev ended up looking like a refugee from Chipperfield's or as if she'd been smacked in the mouth.

"Why'd you ask?"

"What?" Bev was still trying to work out the secret.

"The Brands?"

"Oh. Right. Need to ask them a few questions, that's all."

"She should be out tomorrow. She's only in for observation. The old man was walking across the car park when I came down to meet you."

"Out the back?"

"Yes. There's a bird's-eye view from the staircase."

"Interesting." She smiled but didn't elaborate. Doctor Thorne wasn't to know that Henry Brand was supposedly glued to his wife's side or that he'd arrived at the hospital in the back of an ambulance. "Anyway, enjoy your fettucine or whatever."

"Fear not. After a carafe or three of Chianti – I'd enjoy a wet flannel." She half-turned, looked back. "Fancy joining me?"

It was the best offer she'd had all year: not-so-fast food; a cheeky little vino; the start of what could be a good friendship. Work encroached enough as it was and she wasn't even on shift. "I'd really like to. But…"

"No worries. Some other time." The voice was brisk and Bev was already regretting the refusal as she watched the doctor stride towards the double doors. The woman was strikingly attractive, held down a top job and probably earned megabucks. And the invitation was as close to admitting she was lonely as she was ever likely to go.

Bev sighed, put Doctor Thorne on her mental back-burner and headed for the security guard. Five minutes after that she was on her way to see Annie Flinn.

15

The woman looked as if she'd had an argument with a food blender.

"Mrs Flinn?" Bev was unsure; there was a hint of Vicki round the eyes, but not in the hostility.

"What do you want?"

Nice to see you too. "I'm Bev Morriss. Detective Sergeant Morriss. West Midlands police."

"I'm very happy for you. Now sod off."

She'd have slammed the door if Bev's foot hadn't got in first.

"I have a message from your daughter."

There was a barely perceptible pause in the flow of bile but it didn't last long. "Which one?"

It was half eight. It was brass monkeys. Tesco was closed. "Okay, missus. Up yours. I'm out of here."

The woman reached out an arm, milk-white and twig-thin. "Hold on. There's no call for that."

She looked closer. Annie Flinn's eyes were more than bloodshot; the whites were pinks and leaking like rusty taps. They looked sore, or Bev's words had stung more than she'd intended. The woman sniffed and ran the back of her hand under her nose. "You comin' in or what?" It wasn't an apology but it was close.

The kitchen was at the end of a narrow hall. There was no bulb and Bev almost tripped over an empty cardboard box taking up half the floor. Annie already had a hand on the kettle.

"Tea?"

Bev took a quick glance round and crossed her fingers. "No, ta. Never touch the stuff. Prick me, I'd bleed Nescaff."

The woman reached for a jar of instant. "No skin off my

nose. All tastes the same to me. Milk? Sugar?"

Bev's smile was as weak as she knew the coffee was going to be. "As it comes." There were no chairs; she leaned against the least filthy wall.

"What happened to your face, Mrs Flinn?"

Annie reached a hand to her cheek but it was way too late for concealment. "Thought you'd come to talk about our Vicki."

"That's right."

The woman grabbed a dubious-looking dishcloth and started swatting the draining board. Bev asked again, keeping her voice gentle. Annie replied without turning round. "Oven cleaner. Me own fault. Should have read the instructions. Talk about Mr Muscle."

Bev was dying to talk to Mr Muscle: the muscleman who'd split Annie's lip and put a shed-load of work her dentist's way. She went on instinct with the next question. "This Mr Muscle wouldn't go by the name of Charlie Hawes, would he?"

For a split second Annie Flinn froze, then spun round, eyes blazing. Bev kicked herself for not having waited till the woman was facing her.

"Are you deaf? It was an accident. Got the stuff all over my hands, then rubbed my face."

"Let's have a look."

Balled fists were whisked under her armpits. "Nothing to see. I had gloves on."

"Right." She sauntered over to the cooker, gingerly opened the oven door; there was enough grease for an oil spill. She looked at Annie, said nothing. The woman was lying, but was she lying about Charlie Hawes?

Annie jerked a spoon round a couple of mugs then chucked it in the sink where it joined a bike chain soaking in six inches of black water.

"D'you want this or what?" Her hand was shaking and hot liquid sloshed over the sides on to a formica top.

The woman was on a knife-edge; Bev pushed. "You didn't answer the question."

"I don't know any Charlies. Right?"

But she hadn't forgotten it. Her body language was tighter than a shoal of clams. If Bev didn't change tack, she'd get nowhere.

"How many daughters you got then, Mrs Flinn?"

"What is this? Family Fortunes?"

Bev shrugged. "Suit yourself."

They swallowed a few sips in synch. Bev took a closer look round to take her mind off the taste. It occurred to her that Charlie Hawes had probably been here in the last few hours, standing where she was now, drinking from the self-same mug. She took another mouthful: maybe not. By rights, the man should have left tangible signs. She chided herself for the thought. What was she expecting? Cloven hoof marks and a whiff of brimstone?

The silence was broken by a wail from above. Annie stiffened but her voice was calm. "That's the bab. It's time for her feed."

Bev smiled. "That'd be Lucie, would it?"

The aggression was back. "What do you know about Lucie?"

What? not *how?* And why the look? "Vicki mentioned her."

Bev's smile was infectious but Annie's was shortlived. She dropped it, then jammed hands in jean pockets. "Best say what you come for. She'll just get worse till I sort her."

"Bring her down. I'd like to see her."

The woman shook her head. "She'll not get back to sleep if I get her up."

Bev handed the mug back, grateful for the early out. "Right. I'll leave you to it then. Just wanted to let you know Vicki's in Brighton. Staying with a friend. She doesn't want you to worry."

"Yeah. She sent a postcard."

"What?"

"Told you. I got a card."

The baby sounded as if she hadn't touched food for a month. Other noises followed: a creaking bed spring, a slamming door, footsteps across the ceiling.

Annie was edging out of the kitchen. "Thanks for comin'."

"Hold on. When did you get this card?"

"Can't remember. Saturday, was it?"

"I dropped her outside here on Friday night, Mrs Flinn."

"Yeah. That's right. It come this morning. Anyway. She's okay."

Bev stood her ground. "So what did it say? Wish you were here?" Her smile wasn't returned.

"I haven't got time for this now." The woman was increasingly agitated, her eyes willing Bev to leave.

"I'll just take a quick look then I'll get out of your way." Bev held a hand out.

"What?" She looked as if she'd been hit.

"The card. I'd like to see it."

"For fuck's sake, I don't know where the soddin' thing is." The woman ran a hand through her hair.

Bev slowly fastened the buttons on her coat. Had Vicki really been in touch? Or was Annie lying? Or am I just pissed off at not being on the mailing-list? She tried reading the woman's face but she was on a different page. "I need to speak to Vicki urgently, Mrs Flinn. If she gets in touch again, I want to know about it. Get an address, a number, or tell her to call me."

The woman was listening, but not to Bev. She was concentrating on the footsteps coming down the stairs. Her voice was louder than necessary.

"I've asked you to go."

A man appeared in the doorway, holding a screaming baby under his arm.

"Yeah. Sod off. Now."

Annie made to take the child but he pushed her aside, headed straight for Bev.

She shouted over Lucie's screams. "She's a cop. CID."

He was a hand's span from Bev's face. "I don't care if she's CIA. You've been told to fuck off. Twice. You deaf or stupid?"

Bev didn't flinch despite the olfactory onslaught of second-hand halitosis and the baby's stinking nappy.

"Hello, Steve."

It was a lucky guess, based on Vicki's toy-boy tag. The man invading her space oozed sex and was twenty if he was a day. He took a step back, but was still too close. "What you been saying?"

He wasn't addressing Bev but she answered anyway. "Mrs Flinn's said nothing."

He narrowed piercing blue eyes, pupils like pinheads. "Lying slag."

He held the baby at arm's length; there were puncture marks from his wrists to the inside of the elbow. "You're supposed to keep this quiet. I won't tell you again."

Annie took the child, held her close, cooed soothing sounds.

He swaggered to the fridge, pulled the tab on a can of Red Stripe, swigged half the contents. He enjoyed an audience. He had a neat body, set off by a tight white T-shirt and black combats. He was a looker, despite the shaven head and dark stubble. Bev yawned. She'd seen it all before. Cocky little geezers who keep their brain cell in their Calvin Kleins. Think they're real hard cause they only hit on soft targets. Give this bloke a few years and he'd be banged up or burnt out. He turned, can halfway to mouth. "You still here?"

"I'm going. But I'll be back."

He burped beer fumes across the kitchen. "Don't bust a gut."

She strolled over, studied the piercings around his ear. "It's not guts I bust."

He smirked but was first to drop his gaze. Bev turned slowly and walked across to Annie. "If you want to talk to me, at any time, you'll get me at Highgate nick."

"She don't talk to the filth."

"Talks to you, doesn't she?" She spoke without turning.

"You wanna watch your lip."

This time she turned her head. "I've been watching Mrs Flinn's, as it happens. And I don't like the look of it."

"I can't help it if the clumsy cow —"

Annie shrieked. "Steve. Enough. She's going. Aren't you?"

"Walks into a door, Annie?" Bev's voice was low but insistent. "Is that what he was going to say?"

The woman shook her head. The movement disturbed Lucie who'd cried herself into a fitful sleep. The baby turned, fixing Bev with large, blue eyes. A tiny sob escaped on the deepest of sighs. Bev stroked a finger along the curve of a soft, warm cheek. Poor little love. It wasn't so long since Vicki had been like this. She handed Annie a card.

"Don't forget, Mrs Flinn, if you hear from Vicki, tell her I need to talk. Call me any time. If there's anything else – anything at all – I'll be on this number. If not for yourself, think of Lucie."

Blotting it out was the only way. Vicki covered her eyes with the tips of her fingers, as if it would help, knowing it didn't. The tears, warm at first, cooled as they ran down her cheeks, were cold by the time they reached the insides of her wrists. She was hunched on the edge of the bed, bony elbows sticking into her knees, listening out for the next tosser. It wouldn't be long before she lost count. Thirteen so far. Wham. Bam. Up yours ma'am. Christ. They'd be getting discounts next; buy one, get one free. Charlie wasn't in this for the cash, this was about control. She'd seen it in some mag at the clap clinic; control freaks they were called, blokes like Charlie. Too effin' right they were. Forcing her to open her legs to his mates made him look well hard. No one messes with Charlie Hawes. That was the message. Great way to ram it home. None of his other girls'd be in any doubt. She was the one with the questions: who knew where she was? Was anyone looking for her? And how the hell did she get out?

She uncurled her legs, balled her fists and started pacing. She couldn't even have a pee without a minder breathing down her neck. Pluto, the man planet, took turn and turn about with a little sleazeball, acne on legs and more meat on a toothpick. First time she'd clocked him, she'd mistaken his squint for a glass eye. Talk about cold; he was a threat to shipping. No. If either of them was her passport out of this black hole, it wouldn't be The Spot. If she'd worked it out right, Pluto would be on again in the morning. She'd have another go then. Sweet talk him? By the time she'd finished, he'd have honey trickling out of his arse.

She halted where she imagined the window had been. A real drag, it being bricked over. Not that she'd jump. This was a top floor flat and she wouldn't get far with a limp. She just wanted a glimpse of the sky, a butcher's at normal people going about everyday biz. Her norm now was the bed, the bog and a quick bath between johns.

She wandered over to the door. Locked. Natch. At least when the Bill banged her up, it was only for a night. She wondered again about Bev Morriss, their hours together, searching for Cassie. If it hadn't got back to Charlie, she wouldn't be in this mess. She'd stopped blaming Bev; she'd only been doing her job. Vicki hoped she was doing it now and was searching for her.

There were footsteps on the stairs. She drifted back to the bed, wiped the dampness from her cheeks with the heel of her hand. She'd have used the sheet, but she knew where it had been.

16

The twin hollows in the squashy velvet were a dead giveaway: it was the comfiest seat in the house and Bev was a gnat's eyelash from taking it. The sage-green and gold piping didn't sit easy among the Ikea minimalism, but the chair was an Emmy Morriss hand-me-down and Bev had never been one to look a gift horse in the mouth. Her own mouth was watering, thanks to the Easy Spice takeaway and *Interview with a Vampire* – her favourite movie of all time. She'd taped it off the telly and watched it at least once a month. She balanced and braced; Chicken Madras and Pinot Noir were on the tray, Brad Pitt and blood donor on the screen, posterior a nano-second from soft furnishing when some inconsiderate sod rang the bell.

She couldn't stop the groan; regretted its ear-shattering volume; feigning death or even deep sleep was no longer an option.

"Okay, okay. This had better be good." She parked her dinner on top of the telly and paused the vid.

A quick glance at the clock confirmed a growing suspicion. There was only one person who'd come knocking, uninvited, at this time of night.

"Mavis!" The bellow was an advance warning. "If you're on the scrounge, I won't be responsible for my actions."

The woman had borrowed so much sugar, she could open a sweet shop. It was a ruse, all she wanted was a goss. "It's late and I'm knackered." Bev tightened her mouth, narrowed her eyes and snatched at the door. "What the — ?"

Ozzie lifted a hand in defence. "Sorry, Sarge, I didn't... Maybe I shouldn't have come."

She saw his eyes take in her Black Watch jimmies and Garfield slippers. Bit of a couture shock after the blue suits and Doc Martens. She ran a hand through her hair: nerves rather than necessity. "I was just..."

"Yeah. I can see. Look, no worries. I'll catch you later."

"No. It's okay." It wasn't every night Ozzie Khan came calling. It wasn't any night, come to think of it. She held the door open. "Grab a pew. I'll just slip into..."

"Something less comfortable?"

She heard a girlish giggle, realised it was her own, turned it into a cough. Oriental aromas pervaded the sitting room, reminder of an unconsumed feast. She gave the tray a lingering look, hoping he'd catch on fast.

"Don't bother on my account, Sarge. Shame to let it get cold. Anyway, I'm used to seeing women with no clothes on."

There was a wide grin on his face till he clocked the look on hers. He tripped in the rush to explain. "Not women... I didn't... just my sisters."

Her look was now a glare. He tried again. "Forever slopping about the place in their nighties. Mum's always on at them."

She was intrigued, filing facts: Ozzie lived at home, then, surrounded by women. "How many sisters you got, Oz?"

"Three." His face softened. "Youngest's sixteen. Oldest's twenty-two."

"So you're Big Brother?" She didn't wait for a reply, but mulled it over in the kitchen, where she grabbed an extra plate and fork. He was kneeling down, browsing through a stack of videos when she came back. She retrieved the tray and took the weight off her feet.

"Gonna get stuck in?"

He looked up, puzzled, then saw what was on offer.

"You have it, Sarge. I've eaten."

"It's great, this. Chicken Madras. Have a bite of my naan if you play your cards right."

He shook his head. "It's a bit coals to Newcastle."

Quick shrug. "Suit yourself."

He took a closer look. "Do you really like that stuff?"

She paused, fork halfway to mouth. "No. Horrible. Can't stand it." Sarcasm dripped with the sauce.

"Come on, Sarge, it's vile. Now if we're talking my Madras…"

She laid the fork down; savoured the words. "Your Madras?"

He gave an ostentatious sniff. "Legendary, mate."

She looked at him, looked at the tray. Wondered what the hell they were doing, in her place, ten at night, sounding like a couple of foodies? He surely hadn't come to swap recipes? "Let's do Delia another other time, Oz." She waved a hand at the settee. "What's it all about?"

He sat, legs crossed, and stroked his chin, presumably recalling the reason for his visit.

She nibbled naan while he arranged thoughts.

"Are you watching that?"

She glanced at the screen; Mr Pitt up to his neck – well, someone's neck – in gore. "I was."

He took a tape from his coat pocket. "I want you to have a look at this." It wasn't a holiday video. His voice told her that.

"There's no need to see it all."

She watched, curious, as he headed for the VCR and inserted the tape. It was unlabelled, or more accurately, there was nothing on the label. He certainly hadn't called in at Blockbusters. But he had cued it. He sat cross-legged on the shagpile and hit play.

Spielberg it wasn't. Hand-held, ill-focused and grainy it was. She sipped wine as the camera panned along a brick wall to a naked body. The figure was face down and spread-eagled on a mattress. She leaned further forward. The lads on vice were always seizing crap like this, then it was standing room only in the viewing suite at Highgate. She'd seen it all before; bare bum on bed was pretty tame. She only got queasy when foreign bodies or German shepherds were sniffing round.

Then the camera zoomed in.

There were marks across the buttocks. Red ribbons, were they? Laces? A couple more appeared. The body arced in mute protest, but was restrained by leather straps tethering wrists and ankles to the iron bedstead. She put the glass down. Whoever had the whip was just out of shot; all she could see were macabre tendrils, flashing in and out of frame as they made contact with flesh. Another pan. Whip handler. Shot from the waist down revealing a pasty paunch, bowed legs and a stiffy the size of a lighthouse.

Ozzie pressed pause.

She swallowed the last of the wine.

"You never see the guy's face. When he's finished with the whip, he has sex then it fades to black."

Sex? Not the term she'd use. Rape. Sodomy. Assault. She didn't speak. She was trying to pin down a niggle at the back of her mind.

"God knows who she is. Or what state she's in," Oz said.

Bev laid the tray on the floor and hunched forward on the chair. "Rewind it, Oz. Back to where we came in."

Wide shot, side-on: wall, bed, body, slim, pale skin, shiny dark bob.

"Freeze it on the arc." She sensed his eyes on her but she was staring at the screen.

He missed it a couple of times, had to rewind, slow forward, rewind, before hitting the spot. The image was flickering but not enough to obscure what they'd almost missed.

"That's not a girl, Oz."

She watched as he peered at the screen, slowly shaking his head. "I must have seen it half a dozen times…"

Bev sat back, reached for a cigarette, remembered yet again she'd given up. "Where'd you get it?"

He turned to face her, kneeling now. "That's why I wanted to see you."

She narrowed her eyes, hadn't a clue what was coming. "Go on."

He opened his mouth, searching for words, eyes anywhere but on Bev. "This afternoon?" he said. "You went back to the nick with the governor? Left me at the Brand place, to get rid of the press?"

"Yes?" She was trying to keep track of his Adam's apple.

"I went round the back. Just to check the place was secure?"

Her mind was racing. "And?"

"The door was on the latch."

"And?"

"I went in; found the tape upstairs."

Bloody, buggery bollocks. No wonder he'd been rambling on about Chicken Madras. Anything was more palatable than this. Her mind was racing, repercussions as well as questions darting like silverfish. The sixty-four thousand dollar big one was: how old was the boy on the bed? For only one dollar less: what the hell was Ozzie playing at?

"You found it?" She wasn't sure she wanted the answer. The tape was proof of only one thing: that he'd broken every rule in the book. Entering and pocketing property was stealing. And even if it turned out to be evidence, it was inadmissible evidence. Instead of landing Brand in the dock, it would drop Ozzie in the shit. And as it was currently parked in her player, she'd be floundering in it as well.

"I was looking for the loo."

"Course you were." She rolled her eyes. "Cut the crap, Khan. You can try that line on the governor but don't bullshit me."

"I did take a leak."

"You can say that again." She wandered over to a wall cupboard, took down a bottle of Leapfrog. She poured two shots, vaguely aware even while doing it that he didn't touch alcohol. The sharper thinking was focused elsewhere.

At the very least, Henry Brand's image as a respectable suit had taken a hammering. There'd been a barrel-load of changes in education but there was no way bondage and buggery were on the national curriculum. Brand apparently had both on his CV – so just how qualified was he? Was he a looker or a toucher? Watching was no big deal – a caution maybe. But these home movies were usually hands-on. Produced and passed round personally. She drained her glass, readied the second; double Dutch courage was required for the next notion. What if Brand had been pointing the camera – or even wielding the whip? Corporal punishment for big boys. And exactly how big were the boys? Consenting adults might get away with filth like that on the tape but if the boy on the bed was a minor…

She glanced at Oz, didn't know what to say. He'd taken a risk coming here. By rights, she should be on the phone to Byford. "What the hell were you thinking?"

He ran his hands through his hair. "I know I was out of order."

"Your mind – that's what you were out of." She drained the second glass, debated whether to have a refill, realised a clear head was off the cards anyway and went for the hat trick. "Where was it?"

"In a drawer."

"Kitchen drawer? His old lady's knicker drawer? C'mon Oz, I'm trying to think of a way out of this mess."

"It was in a desk. Upstairs. I needed the loo; didn't know where it was…"

"So you tried every door?"

"The one at the end of the corridor was locked."

She closed her eyes. "And you opened it?"

"There was a bunch of keys on a hook in the kitchen. Anyway, I get in. Place is like a library: books everywhere, desks, filing cabinets, computer set-up, sound system, leather chesterfield, drinks cabinet, coffee maker."

"Help yourself to a cup of Kenyan, did you?"

He shook his head. "It's just that it looked like he spends a lot of time holed up in there."

"I dare say he does. I can't see Enid sharing his taste in movies. Anyway… you opened the drawer?"

"Yeah." He cupped his head in his hands. She waited till he was ready to share. "The tape was under a couple of magazines. I didn't even think about it. Played it there and then."

She sighed, couldn't believe how a bright bloke could be so stupid. Oz's fast-track career was in serious danger of derailment. What justification was there? Every copper was force-fed the Police and Criminal Evidence Act. Ozzie was a law graduate, for fuck's sake – he'd have had seconds.

"I wasn't thinking straight. I mean, at the time, I thought I'd hit pay dirt. There's this pompous little git, holier than thou-ing all over the place, making out Michelle's an hysterical tramp, when all the while he's into hardcore S and M."

Bev shook her head. The girl's murder was priority one. But did the tape make Brand more or less likely to be her killer? Right now, whatever the answer, it was academic.

"We can't use it, Oz. You entered the place without permission. You searched without a warrant. We can't even plead 'just cause'."

He shrugged. "We can now."

Disingenuous, naive or barking? Either way she lost it. "It's a bit bloody late now, isn't it?" Bev, who rarely raised her voice, was shouting. "If this gets out, you're looking at a disciplinary hearing at the very least."

He was staring at the floor. She sighed, could just about understand how initial excitement had overcome professional integrity. Not just coppers believed the cards were stacked in favour of the criminal, but coppers especially had to play with a clean deck.

"Look, Oz. I won't report this, but you and me are the only ones who can know about it, right? Brand's a pervie little toe-rag but we have to get evidence that can go before a court."

He was looking at her now, speaking quickly, enthusiasm

back. "You bet, Sarge. I owe you one."

She flapped a hand, thoughts elsewhere. "What concerns me most at the moment is how we get you out of the doo-doo. That tape's got to go back. And before he misses it. Assuming he hasn't already."

"Don't worry about that."

"You just don't get it, do you? Have you any idea how big a stink Brand'll kick up if he finds out we've got it? We haven't got a legal leg to stand on and Brand's got enough nous to know that."

Khan tapped the side of his nose. "Not as much as me, though."

"What?"

He hit the eject button, held up the tape. "This is a copy. A friend of a friend's got his own edit suite in Selly Oak. He owes me a favour. I made a duplicate. The original's back in Brand's desk, all locked up and nowhere to go." Ozzie rose, tucked the tape in his pocket. "I might be stupid, Bev, but I'm not crazy."

Bev? Now Oz really was pushing his luck.

17

As good nights' sleep go, Bev's had been a bummer. The 7am alarm ring was almost a relief. She dragged herself out of bed, drifted into the kitchen and went through tea and toast-making manoeuvres.

Her stomach's movements were probably down to eating too late and drinking too much, but Ozzie's news wasn't helping. She felt sick just thinking about him ferreting around in Henry Brand's house; couldn't believe he'd actually lifted the tape. As for the guv's reaction if he found out? She didn't want to go there. Ozzie's offer to do her a balti one night was nothing short of buttering-up. On which thought, she plumped for dry toast.

Six bites in she hiked a corner of the blind. The sky was gun-metal grey, again.

Shame. Might have gone for a run had it been perkier. She smiled. "Yeah. And frogs might play cricket."

Fact was, since Frankie's ankle sprain, she'd lost impetus. Pounding pavements, even dodging dog turds in the park, was tedious without her mate's running commentary. Frankie was tall and dark; half-Italian and full of dolce vita. Bev hadn't set eyes on her in a week, hadn't even put in a call since Michelle's murder. Mental note: ring Frankie. Mental note two: blitz Tesco. Mental note three: catch killer.

"Just like that!" The Tommy Cooper impersonation was not her best. She headed for the shower, wondered why she bothered with the radio when cascading water drowned every sound. Towelling between her toes, she realised why. There was a phone-in on Brum Beat's breakfast show. She perched on the edge of the bath, concentrating. Jerry Springer was Jeremy Paxman compared with this twaddle. Birmingham's very own Garth Savage was in full fight, supplementing a grating nasal whinge with an obligatory transatlantic twang.

"The oldest profession? Is it time for retirement? In the wake of the tragic killing of one young girl, this morning we probe prostitution. And I make no apologies. Night or day, women are openly selling sex on the streets of our fair city. Is it a private service or a public nuisance? Is it time for the red light district to get the red card?"

Who wrote this stuff? If it wasn't so serious, she'd be laughing. She shook her head, moved to the radiator where knickers and bra were warming. Mr Savage was in danger of overheating, his delivery growing more demented.

"We thought long and hard before going ahead with this controversial debate but in the final analysis we came down on the side of public interest. Already people are taking to the streets in large numbers to air their side of the argument. CUTS campaigners… have they got a point? I want to know what you think."

Bev thought he'd be looking at an incitement charge if he didn't curb it.

"With me is one of the leaders of that campaign who, at this moment in time, would prefer to remain anonymous. We'll call him Kenny. My name's Garth Savage. We're waiting for your call. On the line now we have Wayne."

"'lo, Garth." Troglodyte Man. Garth did his unctuous best to inject life.

"Wayne. What's your take on this?"

"You what?"

"Never mind. What do you want to say, Wayne?"

"Them birds are great. If you're short of readies, there's one –"

"Thanks for the call, Wayne. Who do we have on line two?"

"My name's Vera. Vera Woods. I've lived in Thread Street all my life. Born there, I was. It's a disgrace. You can't go out your own front door these days."

"And what do you want done about it, Vera?"

"Castration."

"What?"

"Castrate the buggers. I blame the men. Some of the tarts are nice girls. Pick me pension up for me they do, get me a bit of shopping in."

"Thank you Vera. Kenny, if I can turn to you? What is the aim of the CUTS campaign?"

"Exactly what it says. We want to clean up our streets. Reclaim them for decent folk. We want respectable women to be able to go out without being hassled by kerb crawlers. We don't want our kids coming across used condoms and dirty syringes on their way home from school..."

"Sounds like a tall order, Kenny. How are you going to achieve all this?"

"Peaceful protest, Garth. It's time for ordinary people to stand up and be counted. As of now, we're intensifying our presence on the streets. The silent majority has found its voice."

Yeah, yeah, yeah. Predictable tripe.

"And let's face it, Garth, if the women had the sense they were born with, they'd get out while they still could, wouldn't they?"

"What do you mean by that, Kenny?"

Yes. What do you mean? Bev's hand stilled, as she lifted brush to hair.

"One of the girls is dead. Seems to me, there's a message in there somewhere."

"Not sure what you're saying, Kenny."

"I'm not going to spell it out. I will say this though: we won't rest until the streets are free of sex and vermin. We're looking for a big turn out in Thread Street tonight. If any of your listeners want to..."

Bev was out of the room and on the phone before he'd finished the sentence.

"I'm getting a transcript, guv, but they won't give me the bloke's real name." Bev was sitting on the stairs, phone glued to her ear. It was still red hot from the conversation before with a snooty bint purporting to be Garth Savage's producer. Tamsin Winner, M A in stonewalling, had taken condescension to new heights.

Bev had nearly sunk to a slanging match but contented herself with a sotto voce: shit for brains and an audible "Thank you so much."

She'd counted to ten and taken several deep breaths before ringing Byford. The guv was a Radio Four man and had listened in silence as she'd talked him through the phone-in and her subsequent attempts to reach 'Kenny'.

"We should have sent someone round. Collared him on the way out of the studios."

The criticism was unspoken but she heard it anyway, tried keeping her voice level.

"I thought of that. There was no point. He never set foot in the place. The producer says it's normal practice. They always give the impression the main players are in the studio. The listeners like it. It's good for figures. This joker was on the end of a line somewhere."

"They'll have a number, then?"

She'd already asked. "They claim he called them. And even if they had it, they wouldn't give it out. Some crap about protecting sources." She snorted. "Protecting arses, more like."

He wasn't amused. "Get a recording as well as the transcript. There might be something in the voice. See you at work."

"Sir." She was talking to the dialling tone. "And thank you too."

Not a happy Byford this morning then. Perhaps she'd caught him mid-shave. She wasn't sure why she'd called him at home anyway. Maybe it was a subconscious bid for Brownie points. Trying to earn a few credits in case the Ozzie-induced crap hit the air conditioning. "Yes, sir, you've got me bang to rights but I'm a fair cop really."

She shook her head, rose to her feet. The Brand tape business was the first serious step out of line in her career. She didn't intend taking any more.

18

Bev's VDU looked like a promo drive for Post-its. She sat down, blew out her cheeks; it'd be quicker to work out who hadn't left a message.

The Brum Beat recording and transcript were ready for collection; good. Security at the City General had lined up last night's CCTV tape; great. Sumitra's boss had okayed Bev having a shufti through the files; brill. Things were looking up. She despatched a rider, jotted DOMS on her desk pad, returned to the notes still littering the screen.

A nutter had responded to the witness appeal; apparently the Nelson Drive dummy was a Mrs Cherie Blair. The informant a Mr George Bush. It was filed in the bin; more missives peeled off. She made a sucking noise through her teeth as she scanned her screen. The loony call had clearly prompted further entries in Vince's limerick competition. She'd forgotten about that, but if the feeble efforts in front of her were anything to go by she should walk it.

She despatched them in Bush's direction and was still smiling when she took the last Post-it. The smile dropped. *Dawn Lucas rang. Not urgent. Calling again.*

Not urgent? Not urgent? Who the… No name, time, date, not even an initial. It had to have been taken by some bozo on nights. She glanced at her watch. Just after 8.30. The shift change was well past. The bin took the brunt of her fury.

She was on her hands and knees, retrieving litter, when Powell popped his head round the door.

"A humble curtsey'll do, Morriss."

"I'm not in the mood. Right?"

He leaned in the jamb, arms and ankles crossed. "Neither's the governor. Wondered why you hadn't graced us with your presence at the briefing."

"Shit!"

"Precisely. Up to your neck."

She rose to her feet, brushing specks off her skirt. "I'll have a word."

"He's buggered off. Got a call from Henry Brand. Man's ready to talk but only the boss is good enough. You weren't around, so he grabbed Khan. Probably thinks the lad needs a lesson from an old pro."

She curled her lip.

"By the way, Morriss, when are you making your début?"

It had always been an act. She could see that now. How else could she have opened her thighs to a load of wankers? It was a good little earner, of course. Cash in hand as well as cocks. But it wasn't the real Vicki Flinn out there. It was obvious now she'd had time to think about it. She'd closed her eyes and sent a stand-in. No one had even come close.

'Course that was BC – Before Charlie. Under Charlie Hawes's malevolent wing, she was out on her own, playing for more than a fistful of fivers. AD wasn't something she dwelt on.

She swung her legs over the side of the bed. If there'd been a carpet, her pacing would have worn a trail. She'd bunked off loads of times, in her head: gone bopping down Broad Street with the girls; had a drink or two in the Jug; polished off a few Big Macs. Had to do something or she'd crack.

She kept going back to the first time, the very first punter. Saw herself tottering out the front door in Annie's huge heels; red strappy little numbers, they were. She got a leathering for that, later. A Friday, it was. Good Friday. Not last year, the year before. Just hit fifteen; same age as Shell. She'd needed a few bob for the flicks. It was a damn sight easier than a paper round. Anyway, Annie had turned more tricks than the Magic Circle – it was no big deal.

But it was.

Hanging round street corners, trying to look cool, when any minute she thought she'd throw up or shit herself. Locking eyes with some bloke, having a split second to work out whether he was straight or a sicko. Touching up his wallet before his dick, but feeling nothing.

Easier said than done.

She'd soaked for hours, thought she'd never get out of the bath. Couldn't get rid of the stink: sweat and booze and greasy cooking. Swore she'd never do it again. Five weeks later, she needed a pair of boots. Like everything, it got easier. Easy come, easy dough. Big joke, wannit? Regular stand-up comedian, she was.

She sighed, wrapped thin arms round her body. Hadn't had a bundle of laughs of late. There'd been five blokes last night. All pushing sixty. Where was Charlie getting the buggers? Must have added a senior citizen's shag-scam to his other rackets. And what else had he planned for her? She shuddered at the possibilities.

He kept his cards close, but she'd heard the odd whisper out on the landing: one-sided calls on a mobile. She'd listened intently, memorising bits and pieces. Never knew when that sort of info'd come in handy. There were gonna be changes when she got out of this place… *if* she could get out of this place. A proper job for one thing; police snout, maybe.

"You decent?"

She recognised the voice. It was man-planet's idea of a joke. Question was: had Pluto got it in him to be her straight man?

19

Bev's blood pressure was hitting six figures; not unlike the sum Dawn Lucas was bandying about.

"Lost my little girl, haven't I?"

Bev watched her knuckles turn white. It was lucky Earth Mother was on the end of a phone.

"And you're inquiring about..?"

"Compensation. Criminal injuries. It said in the paper, she was…"

Bev's pencil snapped. The woman was a dog turd. The Bet Lynch voice had uttered barely a syllable of sorrow, let alone regret or curiosity. On the other hand, they'd had no joy tracking her down. Bev needed to keep her sweet.

"Where are you calling from, Mrs Lucas?" She retrieved the business end of the pencil.

"Phone box."

"Give us the number. I'll call you straight back."

There was silence for a few seconds; she might have been weighing up the pros and cons. "I can't make it out. I ain't got me glasses."

Good excuse, if it was the truth; either way Bev was none the wiser to the woman's whereabouts. "Glad you rang anyway, Mrs Lucas. As Michelle's next of kin there are one or two things –"

"I'm not identifyin' her. I just couldn't do it."

She'd done sod all else; why spoil the habits of a lifetime? In the absence of relatives, they'd had to call on the superintendent at the children's home. The woman had passed out.

"It's been done already. So it's not strictly necessary for you to go through the procedure again."

"Good. I'd rather remember her like she was."

Like she was three years ago? The sentiment stank of hypocrisy. Bev kept her voice neutral; she still had to get the woman to Birmingham. "There are Michelle's belongings, of course."

Another pause. "Oh yeah?"

Michelle's entire legacy, as Bev was painfully aware, was stuffed in a couple of black bin liners, currently under lock and key at the kids' home. She didn't think Lucas would go a bundle on a few clothes and a hairbrush. She took a deep breath, wishing she'd done a season at RADA as well as her time at police college.

"Thing is, Mrs Lucas, you'll have to collect them. Sign for them, you know?"

"Difficult, that. Gettin' time off and everythin'."

Don't put yourself out. "There's a few bits of jewellery. A gold watch."

"Is there any…" There was a slight hesitation. "… money?"

Bev recoiled at the avarice. "There is a bit, yes." Four grimy tenners stashed in a shoe.

"I'll think about it."

Bev started doodling a fat juicy carrot. "We could discuss the compensation claim as well… if you were passing, like."

"I hate that place. Gives me the creeps."

Much like you give me the creeps, Bev thought. The woman had done a bunk with a bloke who'd been playing round with her daughter. "Where are you living now, Mrs Lucas?"

"Manchester."

"Big place, that."

"Yeah. Yeah." Small talk wasn't on Dawn Lucas's agenda. "What you reckon then? Is there a claim in it, or what?"

"Could well be. Thing is, Dawn – mind if I call you Dawn? – thing is: we will need to talk in person. See, when it's a big pay-out, the bean counters have to make sure there's no monkey business. Know what I mean?" Much as it grieved her, a claim would be considered. Bev shook her head; shame Michelle's death hadn't caused a bit more grief.

"How big?"

If she got anything, it'd be the standard £11,000. Fatal tariff, they called it; blood money, Bev called it. "Phwor. You got me there. I'd have to have more to go on, before I can give you a steer on that."

"Fire away."

Pass the excocet. "Sorry, love. Not on the blower. More than my job's worth. Know what I mean?"

Silence. Bev held her breath. Could go either way. And if Lucas hung up, guess who'd get it in the neck?

A response came reluctantly, but it came. "I'll meet you."

I'd rather eat shit. "Good thinking."

"I ain't comin' there, and I ain't going to no cop shop neither."

"Could be a problem, that."

"Why?"

"The CICA boys won't buy it. Not with big claims like this…"

The pips sounded. Bev mouthed a prayer which was answered by the clink of coins being fed into the slot.

"What were you sayin' 'bout big claims?"

That's my girl. "The criminal injuries lot. They'll want it all done proper. Full interview, name on the dotted line. Have to be done here, see. Can't dish out a load of readies in a Little Chef, can they?" There was another pause then Bev came up with the cherry on the carrot cake. "'Course, there could be a reward in it as well. I'll be honest with you, love. We need all the help we can get. More we know about Michelle, more chance we have of catching the killer. We've spoken to all her mates and teachers and stuff but everyone paints a different picture. We still haven't got a proper handle on her, know what I mean?"

"Yeah. I'd need to think about that." You sure would. "This compensation stuff? Give it out straight away, do they?"

"All the time, Dawnie." Seven months, if you're lucky.

Another silence; more held breath.

"You can bring someone with you for a bit of moral support." Bev curled her lip; propping up Lucas's morals'd be a struggle for the Archbishop of Canterbury. "Shell's dad perhaps?"

"Don't talk wet. The man's never laid eyes on her."

Bollocks. "Must've got our wires crossed. We were told there was a Mr Lucas at Gorse Street with you and Michelle."

"Was there 'ell. That was Ginger Riley."

Yes! A name. Bev's fist hit the air, her voice stayed level. "Perhaps Mr Riley would like to come with you?"

"Bet he'd love to. He's been dead two year."

Double bollocks.

"I ain't gonna get any crap from you lot, am I?"

Unfortunately not; not without evidence. "How do you mean?"

"I know what them dozy morons round there were sayin' 'bout me."

Who didn't? According to neighbours, Dawn Lucas had the maternal instincts of a cuckoo.

"Slaggin' me off, sayin' I dumped Shell."

That wasn't all they were saying. She listened with half an ear while scrolling through witness statements on the computer. She paused at Jack Goddard's, the caretaker at Michelle's school: ...Lucas shacked up with some bloke known as Sicknote... blah blah... place like a branch of the social... blah blah... bruises... neglect... underage sex... Bev sighed. They'd heard the same story time and again, but street talk and hearsay wasn't going to convict Lucas. It wouldn't even get her in court.

Bev tuned in properly. The woman had stopped talking but only to light a baccy. "Honest to God, I begged her to come but she dint want to leave her mate. Said she was gonna stay with her. Arranged it with the girl's mum and everythin'."

"You did?" Bev hoped her incredulity wasn't showing but there was no cause for concern.

"Nah. Shell done all that."

"What was the family called?"

"Come on. It were three year ago."

"Does the name Flinn mean anything to you? Vicki Flinn? Annie Flinn?"

"No. Never heard of 'em." The answer was quick. Too quick? "Anyway it weren't just that. There was her schooling. Loved Thread Street, she did. She were dead settled there."

According to records, Michelle was as settled as a vegan in an abattoir. "Kids?" Bev said. "Who'd have 'em, eh? Always think they know best, don't they?"

"Tell me about it. Mind, our Shell weren't thick. Sharp as a knife, she was. Told her many a time, she'd cut herself if she weren't careful."

Bev closed her eyes. "Chip off the old block, eh, Dawn?"

"Will I get me expenses? Train fare. Stuff like that?"

The woman had a one-track mind. "Don't see why not. How soon can you get here?"

"Tuesday, innit?" Bev waited as the woman worked it out. "Next Wednesday. A week tomorrow."

"Can you make it a bit sooner?"

"What's the rush?"

A sloth on mogadon had more urgency. "Just that the authority meets on Friday. If I had the gen by then…"

"Tomorrow. I'll give you a bell from New Street. I'll have a good old think 'bout things – see what I can come up with."

"You do that, Dawn…"

The pips hadn't gone; Lucas had hung up.

Deep in thought, Bev replaced the receiver. On the face of it, Lucas knew diddly. Point was: the end of a phone wasn't on the face of anything. A good cop needed eye contact for all those little giveaways. She could have been lying through her teeth.

Bev was under no illusions. Dawn Lucas wasn't going to waltz in with the killer's identity. But she was the girl's mother. She might – conceivably – give them an insight into Michelle's.

Either way, she had to admit it: the appalling woman intrigued her. She'd met loads of low-lifes before, but Dawn Lucas was in an under-class of her own. Sod all the psycho-crap about social deprivation and dysfunctional families; she wanted to know what made the woman tick. At the same time, it might shed light on why her fifteen-year-old daughter was lying in the mortuary.

Bev tilted her head back, tried stroking away the tension in her neck. Her eyes were closed. In the darkness, all she could see was Michelle.

20

She was like a corpse, naked, flat on her back, one arm hanging over the side of the bed.

Lying doggo: that's what they called it. It was an act and she was bracing herself for her big scene. She'd run it through her head a dozen times, had no idea how it would pan out. Even so, when the key turned, her body stiffened. She was better prepared for the sudden shaft of light from the landing, she didn't move a muscle.

"I said, are you decent?"

Pluto was framed in the doorway. She sensed him hovering, wondering what the problem was. Ordinarily, she'd be up and about, dying for a pee. His face was hardly friendly, but it was becoming familiar, and lately she'd taken to babbling on, in vain attempts to get him to talk. Seeing her like this, she was hoping the fear factor would get him over the threshold. If anything bad had happened, Pluto'd be in a whole world of trouble.

"Get your arse off that bed."

Was there uncertainty in the voice? Difficult to tell, when she only had a series of grunts to judge by. She had to get him to open up, had to get him closer, and not just feet and inches. The longer he treated her like a piece of meat, the likelier she'd end up a carcass.

"Come on, you lazy cow. It's gone nine."

She didn't need telling. The toast and coffee combination coming up the stairs was alarm call enough. She was ravenous but if her stomach rumbled, so would Pluto. Once he was in, she'd busk it; play on his weak spot, assuming she could find it. She'd be working to her strength. As far as she knew, she only had one.

She counted the silence: ten seconds, fifteen, twenty, then she heard the key being taken out of the lock and the door closing. She held her breath, heard his footfall. He was inside, getting nearer, she could smell him now, smoke and soap. She'd already calculated where he was likely to touch her and didn't flinch when he tapped her arm.

Her legs were slightly apart and she'd bet a week's takings his eyes were opened wide. Up to now, Pluto's ogling had been done on the sly. She'd clocked him gawking through the crack in the bathroom door and sneaking glances every time he dropped off a tray. He'd have to be gay or carved out of granite not to be getting an eyeful. There was no rush. A bloke with a hard-on had to be easier to manipulate. And this was the tricky bit. Soon as he realised she wasn't sick, the second she moved, it might all go pear-shaped.

She kept her eyes closed, although something told her his peepers wouldn't be glued to her face. She eased her thighs apart, lifted her haunches a tad and moaned. Her left hand was lying at her side. She inched it over her hips and let it lie between her legs. He didn't make a murmur. She stroked her fingers through her pubes then slowly drew the tips up her body; over her belly and between her breasts. He hadn't given her a slapping; she hoped it was a good sign, hoped he was gagging for it.

She ran her tongue along her lips and lifted her hand to her mouth, moistening each finger with exaggerated licks, then gently slid her leg over the side of the bed where he was standing. There was definitely a bit of heavy breathing now. She'd better open her eyes, in case he figured the whole palaver was a wet dream.

He was looking at her fanny. Looming over her, he seemed even bigger. What was he? Six foot two, more than twice her weight, old enough to be her dad. She wondered if he had kids; bet he wouldn't want his daughter holed up in a place like this.

Up close, he wasn't as gross as she'd thought: dark chocolate eyes, long lashes. He was wearing black again: combats and a cotton shirt, open at the neck, a pack of Silk Cut in the breast pocket. But what was going on inside?

She was only going to get one crack at this. If she said the wrong thing, hit the wrong button, it'd be back to square one. Coming on strong had got him in, but talking sweet – if anything – was going to get her out. She waited till he was looking at her face then flashed her brightest smile. "It gets lonely in here."

He shrugged but didn't move away. She sat up, hugged her knees, watched as his eyes roamed down. "Hate sleeping on me own. Always have. Ever since I was a kid. Hated it when me ma turned the light out. Always thought there was a bogeyman under the bed."

She shivered, hunched narrow shoulders. "Seems like nowadays, they're all in it."

She looked down at her feet, put a catch in her voice. "They make me skin creep. All them old geezers, pawing and slobbering all over the place." She sniffed loudly, ran the back of her hand across her nose.

She knew he was looking at her now, she lifted her head and met his gaze. "Know what I do when they're trying to get it up?" She paused but there was no reaction. "I think about you. Imagine you're in here with me. Pretend you're my feller."

He was frowning. She made a space on the bed but he stayed where he was.

"I've got this favourite one, see. You've taken me to the pictures. Something mushy, romantic. We're holding hands in the back row and all that. Popcorn, cokes, choc-ices, the lot. Then you take me to that posh Indian place down Broad Street. Some geezer comes in selling flowers and you buy me a red rose. Then we go back to our place and we take each others' clothes off and have a bath." She paused. "And all that."

He perched on the edge of the bed. "All that what?"

She wasn't brilliant at coy; hadn't had a lot of practice. She bowed her head. "You know."

"Tell me. What do we do? When we've had this bath?"

She looked up; he had a lovely voice, like something off the radio. She lifted her hand to brush an imaginary eyelash from his cheek, well pleased when he didn't back off. He wouldn't have let her touch his boots ten minutes ago. Her smile was genuine, the first for days. "Not what you think. It's different with you."

"How do you mean?"

"We have a good snog and everything. But in bed, we just have a cuddle and hold each other tight all night. You whispering my name and..." Her bottom lip quivered, then she swallowed hard.

He put a hand on her shoulder. "What is it? What's up?"

"I can't call you anything. I don't know your name. You know I'm Vicki and I don't know what to call you. Spoils it, doesn't it?"

He took the cigarettes from his pocket. "Smoke?"

She nodded, like a child who'd been offered ice cream. "Yes, please."

He lit hers as well, handed it over. "You can call me Dan."

"Dan." She tried it a few times. "I like that. Thanks, Dan. Tonight'll be even better. I'll be able to call —"

"You said the film one was your favourite?"

"That's right. There's loads, though." She took a deep drag, spoke through the smoke. "The thought of you's the only thing that gets me through." She was swinging her legs. "Don't suppose you'd..?"

"What?"

"Nah. Doesn't matter."

"Go on."

She laid a hand on his knee. "We wouldn't have to do anything, like. But one night, when everyone's gone, and I've had a bath and everything, could you just come in and lie with me, just for a couple of minutes or something, just till I get off to sleep, like?"

He moved her hand a few inches higher. "Maybe. Who knows?"

She left her hand where he'd placed it, started circling her forefinger. "It'd be lovely. Just the two of us. It'd give me something to look forward to." She dropped her glance, realised how true it was.

He inched his thighs open. "Have to see, won't we?"

21

"What you got there, Sarge?"

Bev glanced over her shoulder. She was in the viewing suite at Highgate, so engrossed she'd only just noticed Vince at her elbow.

She curled a lip. "Not a lot, mate." The footage was from the CCTV at the General. It had landed on her desk, minutes after the Lucas phone call had left her reeling. It was not going to win any Oscars.

"Looks like a Yeti in a snow storm." Vince said.

"It's not that good."

Either the hospital's camera needed major surgery or this was a duff tape. It amounted to the same thing: it was not going to prove that Henry Brand had surreptitiously left his wife's bedside. The obnoxious little snot rag was in the clear. The blur was so impenetrable, Bev couldn't have picked out her own mother. Shame. The enlightening call she'd envisaged putting through to Byford was a no-go now. She rubbed her eyes, everything looked as bad – and not just on the screen. The boss and Ozzie were still at Brand's place. She hadn't heard a peep and they'd been gone more than two hours.

She stood, removed the tape, held it aloft. "I was hoping this was going to nail someone, Vince, but it's about as much use as a glass hammer."

"Can't win 'em all."

"Every now and then'd do." She smiled. "Still, you never know, one of the techies might be able to tweak a few knobs."

She grabbed her bag, made for the door. "Who's out tonight, Vince?"

"Thread Street?" He fell into step with her. Uniform had asked for extra bods from CID to police the protest, especially after the provocation on the airwaves that morning.

"Three-line whip, isn't it?" Vince said. "You going, Bev?"

"Nah. I've got something on." It was the first meet with Val and the girls. They were at the lift door. "By the way, Vince, did you want something?"

"Sod it. Sorry, Bev. The guv wants a word. In his office. Like yesterday."

"I couldn't budge him. He gave a categorical denial. Says the girl withdrew the allegation. According to Brand, Michelle Lucas backed down completely."

"Yeah, well." Bev shrugged, sniffing. "In the words of what-sername, he would say that, wouldn't he?"

"Mandy Rice-Davies." Byford turned from the window, put his hands in his pockets. "Wasn't she a bit before your time?"

"So was Attila the Hun. But I've heard of him."

The quip was her first since entering Byford's office. She'd found him sitting at his desk, going through papers, no more and no less affable than normal. She'd listened without interruptions to a run through of Brand's interview. It was a case of Henry 'Brickwall' Brand. He denied seeing – let alone talking to – Michelle on the night of the murder. As for Cyanide Lil, he offered to pay for an eye test; his own wife had perfect vision and would be only too pleased to confirm his presence in the home throughout the hours in question. Or she would, as soon as she'd recovered from the accidental overdose. The final brick in the façade had been Brand's assertion that a tearful Michelle had taken back the sexual assault allegations. There'd not been a single syllable about official complaints or bent coppers. Bev sat back and started to relax.

"We've only got Brand's word for it, guv."

He nodded, walked back to his seat. "And in the absence of

any evidence, that's all we will have. As for the assault claims, even if Michelle was alive, it would still be her word against his."

"Yeah. And who's going to listen to a trainee tart?"

He lifted an eyebrow.

"I'm not having a pop at you, guv, but you know as well I do, there are blokes in this place who wouldn't piss on a prostitute if she was on fire."

He was rolling a pencil between his fingers. The movement stopped but he didn't pick up on the remark. "Brand could be lying through his teeth, but without proof..."

Bev recalled Brand's idiosyncratic notion of home entertainment. "Must be something, somewhere. Have to take a closer look."

"You could have had a bird's-eye view this morning. I wanted you with me. Why weren't you at the briefing?" Most people shouted when they were angry; Byford didn't.

Her bum was prickling. She tried not to shuffle. "I'm really sorry, guv. There was a stack of things on my desk when I got in. I lost track of time."

"It's vital everyone's there. In future – make time."

She nodded. Great word that: future. Maybe she could consign Ozzie's light-fingered fuck-up to the past.

"If you can't cope with what's on, the undercover stuff will have to go."

She narrowed her eyes. Was he having misgivings? Already? Either way, he was deadly serious. So was she. "There's no question of my not coping, sir. Several matters needed immediate action. I thought I was prioritizing."

"And my briefing was last on the list?"

She was saved from another foot in mouth by Byford's secretary who came in with a tray of coffee.

"Helen. Thank you." He glanced at Bev. "An extra cup, please."

She smiled; it looked as if the worst was over.

"I mean it, Bev. You can go ahead with the meeting tonight

then we'll take another look."

It wasn't the time to argue. "Okay."

"Right." He was rubbing his hands; he'd said his piece and it was time to move on. "You'd better fill me in with what was so pressing this morning."

She returned his smile, told him about the CCTV tape, the slight chance that it could be enhanced and mentioned the check – blank so far – with city florists and black-edged cards.

"What about the stuff from the local radio?"

"There's a goodie bag on my desk: transcript and recording. I've had another listen, but..." Empty hands held out made the point.

"Get someone to drop it in. I'd like to hear it myself." He tried the coffee, added more sugar. "Is that it?"

"Saving the best bit till last, guv." She saved it a few seconds longer while Helen deposited another cup.

He sat back, hands on head, as Bev brought him up to speed on the Dawn Lucas phone call, omitting her own enhancement of the woman's chances of hitting immediate paydirt.

He listened carefully, nodding here and there. "Think she knows anything?"

"Difficult to say. She was cagey as a zoo when I spoke to her."

"And she's calling from New Street tomorrow?"

She nodded, knew what was coming.

"Shame we couldn't get an address."

"Tell me about it." The dig was unwarranted and she refused to rise. She leaned across and took undue delight in nabbing the last chocolate hobnob. It would have to keep her going till lunch with Frankie. She took a bite and brushed the inevitable crumbs off her skirt. "Like Brand in a way, isn't it?"

"It is?"

"Well, what did you get from him? How long were you there? An hour? Two hours? What's he said? Naff all. Just enough to get us off his back. He's never going to give anything away, is he?"

His eyes were searching her face. "You think he's got something to give?"

She looked down, couldn't meet his gaze. She hated the deception. It wasn't the way they worked. "I'm just saying people only tell us what they want us to know. We can't actually force them to say anything. Certainly not the truth."

"You don't like Brand, do you?"

She shrugged. "What was he like with you?"

He opened a drawer to his right, helped himself to four Jaffa cakes. "Hospitable. Apologetic. Keen to help."

"Regular little Uriah Heep."

He leaned forward, held up a finger. "I've told you before, Sergeant. Don't let personal likes and dislikes get in the way of your professional judgement. You and Brand obviously didn't hit it off. Maybe the man has a problem with women in positions of authority."

Women in any position. She let it go. "Point taken."

"How's young Khan shaping up?"

The sudden change of tack nearly threw her. She reached for her coffee and a few seconds thinking-time. "Fine. He can chew gum and walk in a straight line."

"He's not running for president. And you're not answering the question."

"Really, guv. He's a good bloke and I think he's got the makings of a decent cop. He's enthusiastic, alert, keeps his eyes and ears open."

"What about his mouth? He hardly said a word when we were at Brand's. Seemed on edge as well."

She placed the cup back in its saucer. "Might have been a bit nervous with you around, guv. He's never like that with me."

"It sends the wrong signals. Keep an eye, Bev. A lot of people round here are dying to see him fall flat on his face."

"Wouldn't be all those geezers with the tart-resistant fire extinguishers, would it?"

"Put it away! You'll get us arrested."

Bev flapped her hands, not that anyone noticed the semaphore. Prêt à Manger was enjoying the floor show. Bev groaned; the place was packed. Trust Frankie to make an entrance. Five minutes late, she'd raced over like a thoroughbred filly, class on legs, despite the fake fur, fishnets and a quiet little number in fire-engine red. As if the wardrobe wasn't loud enough, she was also brandishing a black lace basque like some sort of demented matador.

"It's for you. Thought it'd give you a bit of street cred." She tapped the side of her nose. "Know what I mean?"

Bev shuddered; she had a good idea. Maybe she should've kept mum about the girls. She watched, aghast, as Frankie held the thing up to the light.

"What do you think?"

"I think you should sit down." The hiss was through clenched teeth. "Now!"

"Don't get your teddy in a twist."

Bev lunged forward, stuffed the offending article in her coat pocket. "It already is."

Frankie shrugged, then eased her five-ten frame on to the sort of stool that challenged the less vertically blessed. Amid an expanse of gleaming chrome and sparkling glass, she shone like a bird of paradise in a sackful of sparrows. A gentle ripple of applause emanated from a set of suits at the nearest table. She inclined her head with the nonchalance of a diva, then leaned forward to ask Bev if she thought they were bankers.

"Don't, Frankie. Just don't."

She laughed, tossed her head, clouds of blue-black hair billowing. Bev sighed; if she ever tried that, they'd come and take her away.

"Come on, my friend. Chill out."

"Chill out? If I got into that I'd be effin' hypothermic."

"No chance." Frankie was casually rifling through the goodies

Bev had bought for lunch. "It only just fits me." She winked. "Unless you want to take it along tonight. Show you're game. Break the ice."

Bev smiled, shook her head. The girl was a nutter. They'd been mates since infant school and there was nothing they didn't talk about. It was cheaper than therapy and any confidences were as safe as state secrets. Safer, come to think about it.

"This for me, Bevvie?" She'd commandeered the BLT. "Good girl. This fat's no good for you."

Bev pursed her lips. The girl could eat for Europe and still get into a size eight. And she made the pre-Raphaelite lot look like a bunch of losers with alopecia. "It's a good job I like you. Otherwise, I'd really hate you. Know what I mean?"

Frankie fluttered her eyelashes and flashed a smile. Then, suddenly serious, she said, "Only trying to cheer you up, my friend. Sounded like you were having a bad day."

"I've had better. But no shop talk. I whinged enough on the phone. What've you been up to? How's your pa?"

Frankie grimaced, held crossed index fingers aloft. "Don't mention the P-word."

Bev grinned. Far from being the embodiment of evil, Giovanni Perlagio worshipped the ground his only daughter walked on. Trouble was, he covered it in cotton wool as well. He approved of Bev; lady cop, wasn't she? Mature? Responsible?

"When you gonna get a proper job? he says. When you gonna get a good man? he says. When you gonna have bambinos? he says." The accent was so heavy it needed subtitles.

Bev laughed. "Nothing new there, then?" How she was going to find a fellow who'd even approach Gio's wish-list was anybody's guess. Bev reckoned the Pope would be borderline.

"If only! He's getting worse. Says he'll double what I'm on if I'll join him in the business."

He ran a restaurant and wanted to run Frankie's life as well. She was holding out; making ends meet with flexi-hours in

Music Zone while struggling as a semi-pro session singer.

"Tell him you're on five grand a week."

"I wish."

Bev winced as Frankie used her teeth to tear open the last of the sandwich packs. "You will. One day. Then I'll be able to tell everyone: I knew her when she was just a shy, retiring little nobody." Frankie crossed her eyes and stuck her tongue out. Bev laughed. "Maybe not."

"I'm doing the Fighting Cocks Saturday. You coming?" Frankie asked.

"You know me, mate. I'll be propping up the bar… if I can get away."

"Yeah. Sure. That means you'll be working."

Bev grinned. "You sound just like my dear old mum."

They halved the low calorie chicken club and chatted about books, blokes and when they'd start running again. Bev realised she'd switched off for the first time since Michelle's murder.

"Another coffee?" Frankie asked, getting up.

Bev glanced at her watch. "Yeah, why not?" Lunch breaks were like blue moons; might as well savour it. Anyway, the nick knew where she was and there was always the mobile. She moved the stool nearer the window. She always sat upstairs, best place for a spot of people-watching. Talking of which, the rain was getting worse. Multi-coloured umbrellas were sprouting like giant mushrooms all over New Street. Probably why the bloke wearing the serious shades just across the way caught her eye. That and the fact the rest of his gear looked like a job lot from the Mafia shop: long black coat, pristine shirt, shoelace tie. Most people in a similar get-up would look ludicrous. So how come he didn't?

She glanced round as Frankie arrived with refills. "Eh. Frank. Get a load of that. Fit or what?"

Frankie pressed her face against the glass, screwed her eyes, turned her mouth down. "Bit short for me. Anyway, you know what I think about blokes with pony tails."

"Hadn't spotted that."

"Sherlock would've." Bev groaned then brightened at the sight of a double-chocolate-chip cookie. Frankie was looking out of the window again. "Reckon you're on a loser anyway, Bevvie. Ponytail Man's already got a little friend. Coming on a bit strong, isn't he? Talk about frightening the horses."

Bev wasn't listening. She was looking at the girl. She'd seen her before. Thread Street.

Yesterday. Same class Michelle Lucas had been in.

"Bev! Where you going?"

"Won't be a min."

The man didn't have to be Charlie Hawes. It could be anyone. Gut feeling, instinct, whatever, was telling her different. Her heart was racing and it had nothing to do with the speed she was taking the stairs. A contretemps with a tray full of sushi slowed the pace. She almost missed her footing. She did miss the action over the way. The birds had flown. She couldn't believe it; stepped out into the road, scanned the street; turned and looked up. Frankie was miming a steering wheel and pointing in the direction of Victoria Square. Shit. The street was supposed to be pedestrianised.

She was aware of furtive glances as she made her way back; must have cut quite a dash tearing out like that. "Didn't get the number, did you?"

"Chassis? Ignition? Engine? 'Course I didn't."

In as far as it's possible to slump on a stool the height of Blackpool Tower, Bev slumped.

Frankie sighed. "I haven't got my lenses in. I'm sorry. Is it important?"

"Dunno. Could be."

"Tell you what, Bev. It was a black BMW. And the driver was a woman."

"Sure?"

"Sure I saw lots of hair."

"Dreadlocks, maybe? Could it have been a bloke?" Bev could see the answer on her face. "No worries. Should be able to get a steer through the girl." She took a sip of lukewarm cappuccino. "Frankie? Can I ask you something?"

"'Course you can, my friend."

She leaned closer. "Do I look like a cop? Is it so obvious?"

Frankie smirked.

"It's just that people keep staring. Have been ever since I came back."

Bev sighed as her friend ran through an exaggerated once-over routine. It didn't last long, Frankie's eyes soon widened and she threw a hand up to her mouth. Bev looked down. A basque dangling from your coat pocket did nothing for your social standing.

"Thank God you're not carrying cuffs, Bevvie." Frankie was biting her bottom lip. Bev, dignity shot, felt herself blush. Both women were laughing when Ozzie Khan appeared. Bev spotted him first. He was walking up the stairs, obviously looking for someone. His frown lessened only a little when he saw her.

"Sarge. It's the Swain girl. She's conscious."

"Who was the friend?"

Bev glanced at Ozzie. He was all studied casualness.

"Frankie? Mate from school. Six kids. Old man's an all-in wrestler."

"You're winding me u–"

"Eyes on the road, Constable."

She turned to hide a grin. Frankie'd given Oz the full monty: prolonged eye contact, power-smiles, multilingual body language.

"Seemed like a nice girl."

"And your mind on the job. Talking of which, what happened at Brand's?" A scrawny cat shot out from under a parked car and

Bev hit a phantom brake as Ozzie went for the real thing. The cat put its paw down and escaped intact. Bev glanced in the mirror. "Nice one, Oz. Anyway, you were saying..."

He ran a hand through his hair. "Don't remind me. I kept thinking: any minute now the old boy's gonna say something. Tell the guv somebody'd been sniffing round, know what I mean? Then I reckon: how'd he know anyway? I'd put the tape back, left the keys where I found them. He's not gonna open his mouth if he thinks his sordid little secret's safe, is he?"

The argument was solid; she'd been clinging to it herself.

"Still felt as though I had 'guilty' stamped on my forehead though. Having the chief there didn't help either."

She resisted a crack about Indians; settled for a sage nod.

"Tell you what, Sarge, Brand was real edgy; something was bugging him. He'd dropped the outraged-from-Edgbaston card completely. Offered coffee. Keen to help. Sucking up to the guv. Mind, he wanted us out of that place. Kept banging on about the wife; saying he was expecting a call any time. He'd have to pick her up straight away."

"No one's spoken to her yet have they?" Bev made a mental note, didn't wait for a reply. "What about the accidental overdose lark? You buy that?"

He shook his head. "Naw, he was giving it the hard sell. If he mentioned it once, he said it half a dozen times."

They drove in silence for a while; wipers dealing with rain and spray. Bev switched to thinking about Cassie Swain, wondering what the girl might know; and more to the point, what she'd be willing to share. Ozzie was still on the Brand track.

"The sleazeball's sitting there as if butter wouldn't melt in his armpit and all the time I'm thinking —"

"Did a lot of thinking, did you?"

She saw his head turn towards her. "Not with you."

"The guv reckoned you never opened your mouth. Must have been all the activity in your brain."

His mouth was open now. Wide. "Said you were on edge as well," Bev said. "Don't worry. I put him right."

The smile was weak. "Cheers."

"Don't mensh." She was studying her nails. "Thing is, Oz, that sort of set-up – it's not good if you're all uptight. You need to chill out more."

His left eyebrow looked unconvinced.

"I'm serious. Relax. What you doing Saturday?"

"Noth–" She smiled as he hedged his bets. "Dunno. Why?"

"Fighting Cocks?"

"Illegal, innit?"

"The Fighting Cocks. Pub in Kings Heath. There's live music at the weekends. They've got a blues singer who's so laid back she thinks meditation's a stimulant. It'd do you good, Oz. Take you out of yourself."

The turning for the General was coming up on the right.

"Who's going?"

"Just me."

"Can I let you know?"

"Frankie'll be there already."

"What time?"

She smiled, shook her head. Worked wonders every time, the F-word.

"Not a word. I'm really sorry." Doctor Thorne slid a slim gold pen into a holder on her white coat.

"It's okay. Not your fault." Bev tried to hide her disappointment. Whatever secrets Cassie Swain might hold, they weren't up for grabs. Not yet, anyway. Bev's two-minute detour en route for Intensive Care had made no difference. According to the doctor, Cassie had barely opened her eyes, let alone her mouth.

"She was beginning to respond. I'm almost certain she could hear me. And there was movement in her fingers."

"Positive signs," said Bev.

Doctor Thorne's wavering hand signal was less sure. "There can be a series of false starts. You think they're coming out of it, then..." she looked at Cassie. "And there's no guarantee the brain hasn't suffered permanent damage. Given that she does pull through, she may not remember anything."

Cassie was in the same position as the night before. The bed was huge and accentuated her slight, fragile frame. She was fifteen but looked about twelve. There was a dark eyelash on the bridge of her nose. Bev moved closer, smoothed the lash away then gently ran a finger along the outline of her face. She looked up to find the doctor staring.

"Did you know her before all this, Sergeant?"

The soft voice was hard to take. Bev shook her head, looked away and carefully cradled Cassie's hand.

"I'm sorry I got your hopes up," the doctor said. "I should have waited."

"No, I'm glad you called. And thanks for going through Highgate. The mobile's sorted now." Bev smiled. It sounded so much better than "the mobile's switched on now."

The doctor slipped a hand in her skirt pocket. "I'd better get off. If there's nothing else... Sergeant?"

"I'll hang on a minute, if that's okay. And I told you, the name's Bev."

She smiled, was about to say something when her bleeper sounded. "I'd better get that. Catch you later."

Bev turned back to the bed. The girl was surrounded by people and medical paraphernalia, so how come she looked so vulnerable? Bev sighed. What she really wanted was to give Cassie a cuddle, stroke her hair, tell her someone cared. She lifted the flap on her shoulder-bag, fumbled around till her fingers felt the soft fur. She hoped Paddington'd be happy here. He'd gathered a bit of dust during his sojourn in the hospital shop so she flicked it off and popped him on the pillow close to

Cassie. She stood back, smiling. The red coat and shiny black boots were quite a fashion statement. As for the message on the label round his neck, well he couldn't have been in safer hands. Bev read the words again: Please look after this bear. Thank you.

She looked back at the girl's pale face. "And please look after Cassie," she mouthed.

22

"What a night!"

Bev was dripping all over Big Val's doormat. Puddles were forming at her feet, rivulets trickling down her neck.

"Still tippin' it down?"

Bev widened her eyes. "Nah. I always look like this." Val, on the other hand, looked different. What was it?

"You comin' or what?"

"Yeah. Cheers." Val pressed against the wall as Bev slipped through sideways. The woman wasn't called Big for nothing.

"First on the left, chuck."

Bev ran a hand through sodden hair. "It's foul out there. You'd think everyone'd be tucked up by the fireside, but Thread Street's buzzing. Must be a hundred or more on the protest already." She'd left the MG outside, but done a quick recce on foot. Ozzie had been keeping a low profile with Mike Powell. The guv's was even lower; she hadn't spotted him at all. The uniforms were all over the place. Noisy but not nasty was the general verdict.

Val yawned. "Tell me about it. I've been on all day. Have to make hay while the sun shines."

Make something, thought Bev. "It's the hair!" She pointed. "What've you done?"

Val's red beehive had been supplanted by an unruly haystack.

"This?" She lifted a hand. "It's me Lily Savage. I've got a mate in the rug trade. Ever need sortin' you know where to come."

"I'll bear it in mind."

"Ditch the coat. Take the weight off your pins. I'm gonna put me face on. Shove that lot on the floor." Her arm gave a wide sweep of the room. Bev peered round; the subdued lighting was crying out for a torch. Where exactly was she meant to sit? As far as she could see, there were no chairs. She eventually made out a bed, covered by a tartan throwover and what looked like several herds of stuffed pigs. She moved closer. There was a huge mountain of fluffy porkers, and barely room to perch a buttock. God knew what made her look up, but there was a matching tableau in the massive mirror above the bed. She grinned: pigs could fly, then.

She decided not to join the farmyard action and gravitated towards the fake log fire. There was another mirror on the wall. She pulled a face and smoothed a few damp tendrils into place; looked down and pulled another. The dress wasn't right. She'd scoured her wardrobe but it didn't do police tart. She'd changed her mind – and gear – several times, eventually plumping for an above-the-knee, little aubergine number in crushed velvet. Compared with Val's jade silk kimono – it didn't work. Still, at least it wasn't blue and no one would ask her to read the meter.

Val had left the door open, and judging by the smell of dope was having a crafty drag. What was the nasal equivalent of a blind eye? The girls could get as stoned as a rockery as far as Bev was concerned.

"Wanna drink, chuck?" Val was still in make-up but the forty-a-day voice was loud and clear.

Bev dithered, then plunged. "Sure. What you got?"

"Red Stripe, Red Stripe or Red Stripe."

She grinned and shouted back. "Cuppa char, then. Not!"

She glanced at her watch. Twenty past eight. Where were the girls? Cold feet? Toe-nail cutting?

"'ere y'are."

Bev turned, expecting to take ownership of a can of lager, but Val had a bean-bag in each hand.

"Chuck one over there, Bev. There's a couple more next door. Whether we're gonna need 'em or not…" She shrugged and floated out on a wave of Lou Lou and Imperial Leather.

Bev bagged a bag and watched as her dress rapidly turned from above-the-knee to below-the-knickers. Thank God she'd eschewed Frankie's basque for M&S briefs. She grabbed the hem and gave a few tugs. It was one thing to enter into the spirit of the occasion but a girl had to draw the line somewhere.

Val returned, cans in hands. "Cheers, chuck."

Bev had a couple of sips, regretted not bringing a bottle of wine or Scotch. "What time did you tell the others, Val?" The casual tone was supposed to conceal her growing concern.

Val shoved the pigs over and flopped across the bed, back against the wall. "Eight."

There was an uneasy silence. It was beginning to feel like one of those parties where no one turns up.

Val lit a Marlboro. "They know the score, Bev. It's down to them whether they play ball."

Bev watched as she picked a fleck of tobacco from the tip of her tongue. The big woman obviously had something on her mind as well. Bev waited, hoping she'd share.

"I have to say Bev, none of them was delirious at the prospect of meeting you, but only Marj told me to fuck off." She paused. "Actually, she told me to tell you to fuck off."

"Marj?" Bev matched the name with a face; came up with black. "She hates cops." The words 'white' and 'woman' went unspoken but both knew they were there. She looked round for an easier topic while she grappled with harder thoughts. "What's with the pigs?"

It was quite a collection, sixty-plus. Everything from a two-inch piglet to a two-foot porker, Barbie pink through pillar-box red and every lurid shade in between.

Val opened her mouth then appeared to change her mind, settled for a wide grin and a vague: "Dunno, really. Just sort of grew, like."

"Nice." It sounded pathetic even to Bev's ears. She took

another drink, wondered what she was doing, discussing cuddly toys with a middle-aged prostitute when a stone's throw away her mates were trying to keep order on the streets. She cocked her head on one side. The crowd was beginning to chant and though the words were inaudible the message was pretty clear: tarts were not flavour of the month.

"Don't worry about that lot, Bev. It won't stop the others. Not if they want to come."

She nodded. But did they?

She took another swig. "Hey, Val, you heard any more from Vicki?" She was making conversation; nothing more.

The hand with the cigarette halted, half-way to Val's mouth. Bev asked herself why? And why was Val suddenly spouting on like there was no tomorrow?

"Nah. She must still be down south. Lucky cow. I wouldn't say no to a few days in Brighton." She winked as she took a drag on her fag. "Could do with a bit of sea air. I love all that stuff, don't you? A bit of a paddle; a few sticks of rock; fish and chips on the front. They always taste better outside, somehow, don't they? You goin' somewhere nice this year, Bev?"

Bev tried not to narrow her eyes. One mention of Vicki, and the woman was babbling like a swollen brook. "Dunno. I haven't thought about it, yet."

She studied the big woman's face; stayed silent, hoping it would force the talk. While Val made a great play of sorting out the pigs, Bev flicked through her mental file on Vicki. Was she missing something, apart from the girl herself? She waited a while longer, but Val's flow of words had apparently dried up.

"Val?" She wasn't even sure why she was asking; it was just another niggling doubt among all the unknowns and half-truths that seemed to make up the Lucas inquiry. "You did get a call from Vicki, didn't you, love?"

"You calling me a liar?"

The response was fast, but it wasn't an answer. But why

would Val lie? And why were Bev's bullshit antennae suddenly twitching? She was on dangerous ground; she stepped lightly. "'Course not, love, but anyone can make a mistake."

She watched as Val ground the butt into a glass ashtray. The woman was either working on a reply or ignoring the remark. After twenty seconds or so of silence Bev added softly. "It's just that if we're wrong about Vicki, the error could be fatal."

"I got a call. Right?" The big woman turned her face to Bev; it had 'final answer' all over it.

"Sure." If she pushed further, she'd likely be shown the door. She put a question mark over Brighton and lifted her can. "Absent friends."

Val nodded. "Absent friends."

Another uneasy silence was broken by a tap on the window.

Val hauled herself off the bed. "That'll be Patty. She's got a thing about knocking on doors. She got chucked through one once. I won't be a tick." Judging by the smile and her manner, Val wasn't going to dwell on the Vicki thing. Neither was Bev; it was time for action.

She tried standing; wondered if anyone had ever come up with a dignified way of getting out of a bean-bag. Given the expanse of thighs she was showing and the gap in between, she decided not. A final push and she was on her feet, so how come she still felt like a sitting duck? She smoothed her skirt, sweaty palms leaving damp smudges. She swallowed, took a few deep breaths. Most of these girls, she'd be seeing for the first time. She felt like some bimbo on *Blind Date.*

There were a few giggles and shushes then Val returned with not one girl but two. "Bev. This here's Patty. This is Smithy."

Bev ran through a mental list drawn up by Val: Smithy the librarian; Patty the smackhead. Apart from their temporary resemblance to drowned rats, it checked out. Smithy's pale face was swamped by huge red-framed specs. Patty's looked as if it should be; poor girl blinked a lot and appeared to have trouble focusing.

Bev smiled, bit back some inane drivel about the weather and held out a hand. "Good to see you."

Smithy growled, "Wotcha," and made straight for the bed. Patty didn't appear to notice. "Gorra smoke, Val?"

Val chucked the pack and a box of matches but it was too much for the girl's spatial skills. Bev retrieved both from the floor and handed them over.

"Ta." She studied Bev's face. "I ain't seen you before. Eh, Val, she new round 'ere?"

Bev looked at Val, who rolled her eyes and tapped the side of her head. "Sit down, Pats."

Bev sighed; bright girl, then. She glanced at Smithy who had her nose in a book with a pink cover. Talk about hope over experience.

"Jules'll be here in a min. And Chloë." Smithy imparted the information without looking up. "They're doing the offie run."

"We had a whip round," Val explained.

Bev was working on a quip along the lines of "Lucky you." It was never cracked owing to a hammering on the front door, backed up by a quasi-police rap through the letterbox.

"Spread your legs and kiss the floor. Officer Dibble's at the door."

Bev's eyebrows were up to her hairline, till she caught sight of Val's downturned mouth. She watched as the big woman strolled towards the door muttering something about bloody comedians.

"Come on, ma, it's pissin' down out here."

Bev heard the door open, feet being stamped and a rustle of coats being hung up; all interspersed by banter and belly laughs. Two girls eventually swanned in, wearing hats fashioned out of plastic carriers from Oddbins. They'd already made a dent in the Lambrusco and were passing the bottle round like a microphone. The skinny one put Bev in mind of Vicki until she whipped off her hat, revealing hair the same shade as Bev's dress.

"That was for you, cop. Make you feel at home. Know what I mean?"

Bev had an idea. The girl moved closer. "Wanna drink?" The offer was friendly but the distance between Bev's face and the bottle was a touch too intimate. Purple Locks didn't wait for an answer. "We bin watchin' *The Bill.* Do a lot of door-smashin', don't they? You into all that?"

Bev stared, stood her ground, bit back several retorts including a novel technique for recycling glass.

"Jules." The caution was from Val and accompanied by a shake of the head. The others were silent, watching.

The girl burped and stood back, if not down. "What you doin' 'ere, anyway? A slinky frock and a bit of slap don' mean nothin'. Still Miss Piggy, ain't you?"

Great start, thought Bev. Real sisterhood stuff. If she didn't play this right, she'd lost them. She took a few sips of lager, kept her voice casual. "When was the last time you saw Michelle Lucas?"

Wrong-footed, the girl hesitated. The room was silent as the others waited, each aware of the muffled sounds of the crowd a couple of streets away. Jules was kicking her feet, staring at the floor.

"Can't remember."

"Try hard, Jules. Try very hard. Hang on to that image. Remember Shell when she was alive; having a laugh, a good time. Me?" Bev paused, aware everyone was looking. "Me? I saw her two days ago, on a slab, in the morgue. And you know what? I wish to God I hadn't. I can't get rid of it: the sight; the stink; the fuckin' waste."

Bev stared; it was clear the others would take their cue from Jules. Talk about hearing a pin drop. The girl held Bev's gaze, then turned to Val.

"What you standin' round for, ma? She needs a glass."

Bev nodded. Smithy went back to her book and Patty used Val's absence to sneak another fag. The dumpy girl who'd arrived with Jules approached Bev.

"Met before, ain't we?"

The girl's shaven head and dark brows didn't ring any bells.

"Remind me."

"Chloë Davenport. You ran me in a coupla years back." Bev ran it through her memory; couldn't place the girl.

"Put on a bit of meat since then, I have. And I had hair down to my bum."

Bev pointed, recognition finally dawning. "Blondie!" It was coming back to her. The girl was unusual in that she came from an apparently loving home, had both parents on the scene and wanted for nothing, yet she repeatedly absconded and went on the game. The father particularly was beside himself with grief. Turned out he was jealous. He'd been abusing her for ten years. Chloë reckoned she'd been giving it away so long, she might as well make a few bob. It had taken Bev hours and hours of gentle coaxing to get the story. Chloë's old man died in a car crash two weeks before his court date.

"Why the..?" Bev made chopping motions with her fingers.

Chloë shrugged her shoulders. "Just grew out of it."

She'd be sixteen now. Sixteen or seventeen. What was it her father called her? Angel. My little angel. Bev smiled. "It suits you, Chloë."

"Here y'are, girls. Come and get it."

Val placed a tray in the middle of the floor. Cans, bottles, a couple of glasses and a few mugs. She delved into the pockets of her kimono and pulled out packets of dry roasted nuts and Bombay mix. A packet of prawn cocktail crisps had been nestling in the region of her boobs; this she slung at Smithy.

"She likes the colour," Val mouthed at Bev.

"What's this?" Patty was trickling the mix through her fingers.

"Told you before, girl. It's to eat." Val lowered her voice and looked at Bev. "Caught her tryin' to smoke it once."

The girls grabbed a drink each. Chloë and Jules shared a bean-bag, Bev took the other and looked round. The turn-out was better than nothing but it was a bit disappointing. Part of her had been hoping that the girl she'd spotted in town at lunchtime would put in an appearance. She'd had no joy tracing her through the school.

Smithy finally put the book away. Her glasses had slipped and she pushed them up with a finger. "Oh, yeah. Kylie's not comin'."

"Why's that?" Jules asked. "Too much homework?"

Bev waited for the laughter to subside. "Who's Kylie?"

"Kylie O'Reilly."

"You winding me up?"

"No. It's Kylie O'Reilly. Really."

There was a lot of giggling going on until Val intervened. "Don't be so bloody daft." She looked at Bev. "Straight up. It's her name. She's a nice kid. She was at Fair Oaks but she's on a trial foster now. Hasn't stopped her waggin' though. She's prob'ly been grounded."

Bev made a mental note. The girl would have to be chased up in the morning. She ran through the list again; looked as if there was only one no-show.

"What about Jo? She coming or what?" Val asked.

"It's her ma's bingo night," Jules drawled. "She's doing a spot of baby sittin'."

"'Bout bloody time."

Bev lifted an eyebrow at the venom in Val's voice.

"It's Jo's kid, innit?" Val said. "She expects her ma to do everythin'. Selfish little cow. I wouldn't trust her with a pair of gerbils."

"How old's Jo?" Bev asked.

"Fifteen. Had the kid a coupla years back."

Bev turned her mouth down; at thirteen, the only thing she'd delivered was a newspaper.

"What about the father?"

"God knows. Jo don't." Val shook her head. "She ain't the first and she sure won't be the last."

Bev wanted to ask more but Jules dismissed the subject with a flap of her hand. "Yeah yeah. Borin'." She looked at Bev. "Come on. We've wasted enough time. Sooner we get this over with, sooner we can get down to the vid."

"Yeah. What d'you get, ma?" Patty asked.

Val kept a straight face. "The Sound of Music."

Smithy jabbed a fist in the air and shouted. "Yo!"

The big woman shook her head. "Soft sod. Nah. I got the new Bruce Willis. We can have a group drool."

"Yuk," Patty spat. "He's a right old wrinklie."

"You lot quite finished?" Jules lit a spliff, stared at Bev. "The lady's waitin'."

Bev took a deep breath, dived in. "I don't know how much Val's said, but the idea's dead simple really."

"Patty'll appreciate that," Jules muttered.

Bev ignored the interruption. "I need to get out on the patch. Michelle's killer's still out there, and he's almost certainly the same nut who's put Cassie on life support. I'll be straight with you, girls: the leads we're following are getting us nowhere."

"Nothin' new there, then." Jules's contempt came wreathed in smoke.

"Precisely," Bev hit back. "That's why we've got to try something different."

"So how's you gettin' tarted up and hangin' round street corners gonna do any good?"

Jules was asking all the questions, but it was plain to Bev everyone was hanging on the answers. She looked at each girl in turn, wanting them all to be clear about the significance of what she was about to say.

"There's no reason to suppose the killings have stopped." She lifted a hand to quell a chorus of protest. "I'm not saying there's another Ripper on the loose, but until we find a motive, until we have a better idea what's going on – then the risk is there. If –" she stressed the word – "*if* this guy's targeting prostitutes, the closer I work with you the better. Apart from anything else I'll be keeping an eye out for you."

Again, the only noise was a muffled chanting from Thread Street. Each girl was working on her own thoughts.

"You sayin' it's a mad punter?" Jules was trying hard to sound as if she didn't care.

Bev shook her head. "I've told you – we just don't know."

Val nodded towards the door. "What about that lot out there? Not exactly fans of ours, are they?"

"Fuckin' hypocrites," Chloë hissed.

"Fuckin' what?" asked Patty.

"Never mind, Pats," Jules reached across and dropped ash in an empty can. "Ma's got a point though. What you doin' about rent-a-mob?"

"All we can." Known members of the campaign had been traced and interviewed and tonight's protest was being recorded on stills and video. But Bev couldn't see the killer posing for happy snaps. "Same with the death threats. You name it, forensic have done it. We're still no nearer."

"What death –?" Patty reached for the pack of Marlboro Val was thrusting at her. "Ta, ma."

"What were you saying, Pats?" The girl was lighting up. Bev waited, but whatever it was it had gone. The blank look was accompanied by a vague, "You what?"

"Pats is pleased to get anything in the post." Jules sneered. "Me? I use 'em to wipe me arse. We all do, don't we, girls?" The crude mime that went with the graphic language had most of them bent double. "The wankers who send 'em are all shit-for-brains."

Bev cleared her throat; the lavatory humour wasn't going

anywhere. "One angle we haven't mentioned." She paused, wary of snakes and baskets. "What about the pimps?"

"What about 'em?" Jules asked.

"You tell me."

"Don't know any, do we, girls?"

It was a lie. Bev knew it. They knew it. She reeled off half a dozen names; big players in the vice market. "We've questioned all of them over the last few days. They're keen to help. Shell's death's bad for business they reckon."

"There y'are then," said Jules. "What more do you want?" The cocky smirk lasted just two words.

"Charlie Hawes."

The chanting from the street sounded louder in the silence of the room. Bev looked round but none of the girls met her gaze. "Hawes as in Mad Charlie. Mad Charlie as in Michelle's pimp."

"Thought you were tryin' to help us?" Patty said plaintively.

"I am, Patty. I am. I don't want any of you to end up like Shell."

Val lit another Marlboro and spoke through the smoke. "I can't see it'll do any harm. I think we should give it a whirl."

Bev looked at the big woman; was that a deliberate change of subject, or what?

If it was, Jules caught on quickly. "How's it gonna work?"

Bev hesitated. She wanted to pursue the Hawes line but didn't want to alienate Val further, or the girls at all. She ran through how she'd join them on the streets, as and when she could; that it'd be a case of keeping her eyes and ears open. There was a half-hearted joke about legs but Bev ignored it. When she wasn't around, Bev said, she wanted them to keep tabs on the punters; take registrations; jot down descriptions; look out for anything or anyone in the slightest way suspect. She'd organize personal alarms and ask about extra police patrols.

She caught a few glances being exchanged, then Jules answered for them all. "You're on."

Bev smiled, circled her can at the girls. "Cheers."

Val hoisted hers. "Bottoms up."

Jules hadn't taken her eyes off Bev. "Up yours, an' all."

Bev joined the general mirth but with a lot less force.

"Seriously, cop-lady," asked Jules. "What you gonna do when you get a punter?"

The girls were all ears. Bev went for breezy. "No worries. I'll know how to handle it."

"I bet you will," Jules grinned.

"'ere, if she's turning tricks…" All eyes turned to Patty. "We oughta get a cut. It's our patch, innit?"

Bev shook her head; what could you say? Looking on the bright side, the subsequent piss-taking of Patty, took everyone's mind off Jules's poser about punters. Bev had it all worked out; she just wasn't ready to share.

"Okay, you lot." Val broke up the action. "We've done the biz. Let's get down to the important stuff." Pizza the Action was doing some sort of promo deal. Val took orders and wandered through to the kitchen, mobile phone in hand.

"What's it like bein' a cop, then?" Patty asked.

"Why?" Jules laughed. "You gonna sign up?"

"Sign on, more like," said Chloë.

Patty scooped a handful of pigs and aimed at the girls' bean-bag. Jules and Chloë dived to the carpet, giggling and screaming.

"Wass goin' on in there?" Val shouted. "I can't hear myself speak."

Jules wagged a finger at Patty. "You're in big trouble now, girl. Better pick 'em up or she'll have you."

Patty wagged two fingers. "Sod off."

Bev knelt and started gathering the animals.

"Very attached to her piggies is our Val," Jules said. "She's given 'em names and everythin'. She can tell you where she got 'em, and when. Loves 'em, she does. They're like kids to her."

Bev returned them reverently to the bed. Then, out of the corner of her eye, she caught Jules clutching her sides.

"What's so funny?"

"You should see your face."

"They mean a lot to her," Bev protested. Child substitute had briefly crossed her mind.

"They sure do." Jules pointed. "That one's Kev. He was a DC in Leeds. That's Frank, he's a sergeant now, moved to Wolverhampton last year. That's Joey, he was an inspector in Digbeth but he's some big cheese at Lloyd House these days."

Patty picked up a pig with one eye and no tail. "This bugger had me an' all. Billy Nelson's his name."

Bev knew her dental work was on display but this made notches on the bedpost look pretty tame. "What are you saying? That when Val –" she searched for a suitable verb – "services a cop, she gets a pig?"

It was Jules's turn to look nonplussed, then she beamed. "No, you daft sod. They're not punters. They're collars. She buys one every time she gets fined. Well, she used to. She can't afford it no more."

"Can't afford what?" Val breezed in with a roll of kitchen towel and a bottle of ketchup, which she handed straight to Patty.

"Ta, ma. You remembered."

Val curled her lip. "Tomato sauce on pizza? How could I forget?"

Bev smiled, beginning to relax. The girls were good company. It made her think again about Vicki. Maybe she'd over-reacted. Why shouldn't the girl be in Brighton? Val had probably just been on edge, what with the girls coming round and the protest and everything. She yawned, sank back into the bean-bag, stretched her legs. It hadn't been a bad night's work. An understanding had been reached, and though there was nothing new to go on she'd be well placed in the days ahead.

"How long's the pizza gonna be?" Smithy asked.

"'Bout eight inches," Jules smirked.

"You should be so lucky." Val accompanied her quip with a slack-lipped pout of panto-dame dimensions. It sparked a session of note-swapping on well-hung punters. There were one or two well-known men in town that Bev would never look in the face again. The girls were rolling around in hysterics on the carpet. Bev was the only one to hear the door. The others had bought the booze so she grabbed her bag and crept out. The laughter was infectious and Bev was grinning from ear to ear when she pulled the door open. The pizza delivery bloke bore a striking resemblance to Ozzie. It only took a second to work out why.

"Oz, what are you doing here?" She registered how the street light was simultaneously shining and casting shadows in the rain on his face. She noted how the girls' laughter had reached a new peak, knew instinctively the timing was all wrong.

"You're wanted, Sarge. We've got another body."

23

The fastest way back was on foot. Thread Street had been cordoned off anyway, because of the protest. They ran through stinging rain, Ozzie ahead, Bev close by, coat mis-buttoned, dress clinging to her thighs. Terraced houses and parked cars flashed past peripherally as every step took them closer. The only sound was the slap of soles on wet pavement. Bev had a host of questions, breath for just one. "Any ID?"

"Not yet."

One name was beating in her head, keeping time with her pounding footsteps. How could she have been so stupid? If Vicki Flinn was in Brighton, Bev was The Queen. She'd been sold a line, and bought it wholesale.

As they rounded the corner the crowd, mostly silent now, turned to stare. Bev slowed up and scanned faces as she made for the park's iron gates. People were congregated in small groups, sharing umbrellas; others were clustered along the railings, sheltering under the sparse overhang of trees. Anti-whore placards lay in the gutter, others were propped between the metal spikes. Strange, she thought, how no one was claiming ownership now – or authorship. She nodded at a uniform, one of many, circulating with notebooks and questions.

There was a ripple of excitement as several people pointed up the road. Bev turned and recognised a blonde off the local TV news. The girl must have flashed something to get past the police tapes. She was stumbling towards the action as fast as four-inch heels allowed. A camera crew was right behind, the first of many, once the news really broke. Bev tightened her mouth. The media were going to love this. Enough cops around to police a state funeral and still there'd been another murder. The crowd was already loving it. The drongos were wetting their knickers at the thought of getting on the box. In her mind, all Bev could see was a body. She shook her head. "Let's get on with it."

Ozzie held the gate open. "Watch your footing. It'll be slippy." He handed her a torch. "The governor said you'd know where to head." She frowned, then recalled that Ozzie hadn't actually visited the scene. She led them down a path through the trees to Bogart's pool. She was shivering, didn't know whether it was down to the cold, or shock, or something else. Bare branches overhead provided little protection from the rain; naked roots were a hazard underfoot.

"Shit!"

"You okay?" Oz asked.

I'm alive, aren't I? She said nothing; realised she was too angry to speak. They were close now. She could see torch beams playing through tree trunks, raindrops dancing in the flares. She gasped as a wider tableau suddenly appeared. She should have realised immediately that the police floodlighting had kicked in, but she was jumpy, on edge. It took time to get used to the glare; she used it for steadying breaths, aware there were worse sights ahead. Everything was bathed in shades of black and white and silver. It reminded her of a Hitchcock movie. She realised simultaneously, that the impression had been reinforced because she'd glimpsed the silhouette of a man standing near the water. It was Byford's; maybe she'd tell him, one day. Now was not the time for small talk. She looked again, his head was down, hands deep in his pockets. There must have been others around – the crew that had rigged the lighting for instance – but he appeared a forlorn and lonely figure. It was as she moved further in, and he turned at the sound, that she saw the body. She froze for several seconds then forced herself to continue, focusing exclusively on the girl.

She was young: early to mid teens; long limbs. The bobbed

hair appeared black. The face couldn't be seen from this angle. Bev was ninety per cent sure she knew whose it was. She concentrated on breath control and continued the visual examination. The girl's arms were flung out as if she'd fallen, although there were no obvious injuries. She was wearing a short denim jacket and a denim skirt that was now round her waist. Bev itched to pull it down, straighten it, restore a little dignity. Given the greater degradation to come, the act would have been pointless, except in putting off the inevitable question. Byford voiced it anyway. "Do you know her?"

Bev didn't answer. Keeping her glance on the girl, she inched forward, anxious not to contaminate the scene or slip in the sodden earth. She was silently chanting prayers to a God she'd never forgotten but thought she'd long ago renounced.

The girl's head was facing the water. Bev had to work her way carefully around the body. There were noises: SOCOs gearing up; the bark of a police dog. All Bev remembered later was Byford's whispered warning.

"Prepare yourself, Bev. She's a mess."

Bev knelt and gently lifted strands of hair obscuring the girl's features. Her eyes were drawn not to the face, but to a gaping wound in the slender, white neck. She registered two thoughts. First: Byford was right, the body was a mess. Second: whoever it was, it wasn't Vicki Flinn. She released a breath she hadn't realised she'd been holding and knew without doubt she was about to throw up.

"It can happen to anyone. Don't be so hard on yourself."

Bev's eyes – and pride – were smarting. She gave a wan smile, aware Byford was only trying to make her feel better. She was still trembling, perched on an ancient tree stump, didn't yet trust her legs to take her full weight. She could still smell blood and piss and decay but it wasn't just that. She'd convinced herself the victim was Vicki and when she'd seen the dead eyes of a stranger, the shock had given way to a sick relief, followed by spasms of guilt, then a gut-wrenching anger. Literally.

She'd never take the piss again when some other poor sod puked at the sight of a body. The only saving grace was that she'd made it to the water. The contents of her alimentary canal had sunk into the murky depths of Bogart's Pool. Pity the poor bloody divers if they had to drag it. And they might. They hadn't found an ID yet and it looked as if several items of clothing were missing. SOCOs were on the case, but a proper search needed daylight.

"Why don't you go home?" Byford suggested. "DC Khan can give you a lift." He nodded at Ozzie, who was hovering at a discreet distance. "Get some rest, Bev. You'll need all your energy tomorrow."

She looked up and a sharp pain shot through her head. "I can't. There's loads to do."

"It may have escaped your attention," Byford drawled, "but half the bloody force is out here already."

Sarcasm and swearing; as bad as that. She was dying to know how the unthinkable had happened.

"Don't ask," he sighed. "A body. Under our ruddy noses." He nodded as a dog handler signalled to ask whether it was okay to go past. "Christ, I could do with a cigarette."

"Thought you'd never smoked."

"Exactly." He rubbed a hand down the side of his face. "The doctor thought she may have been here several hours. She might even have been killed somewhere else and dumped later."

Bev nodded. At least the girl hadn't been dragged off the street in full view of the local constabulary. "Couldn't have been much before four, surely?" she asked. "It's still light before then." Even the most ardent dog walker or fun runner would break off pursuits to report a body in the park.

"Your guess is as good as mine. That's all we are doing till the post mortem." He pushed up a coat sleeve, glanced at his watch.

"Harry'll be here any time. I'm happy to hang round. I still think you should get off."

"Who found her?"

"Some bloke who says he nipped in here to take a leak."

She supposed it was possible. "One of the protesters?"

He nodded. "Mike Powell's talking to him now."

She closed her eyes, saw the girl's gaping wound again, swallowed hard, tasted bile.

"It's the same killer, isn't it?"

Byford didn't answer. He was staring into space, an expression on his face she hadn't seen there before. It was an appalling crime. He seemed somehow diminished by it. She sighed. They'd all be diminished by it once the hacks got going.

"The media circus'll be setting up tent."

He shrugged. "We might need them if we don't get a name soon. I thought you might know who she was." He paused. "For a minute back there you did too, didn't you?"

She didn't say anything. He pushed. "Vicki Flinn?"

She gave a quick nod. "Sick, isn't it? I was actually relieved for a second."

"You like the girl. It's only natural."

"Natural? Somebody loves that girl." Bev nodded towards the body. "She was somebody's baby once. There's a mother somewhere out there, waiting for her to come home." She looked down at her hands. "And for a few seconds, I was actually pleased that it wasn't someone I know."

"You're all in, Bev. Go home."

"Hold on." She narrowed her eyes. "The meeting tonight? A couple of girls didn't show."

"Bev." He kept his voice low. "She could be anyone. There's no reason to suppose..."

The mobile was in her hand before he'd finished. "It's worth a check."

She guessed Val had been waiting by the phone. It was

answered at the first ring. Bev dodged a few questions then put several of her own. It soon became clear the victim wasn't Jo; the girl had turned up minutes after Bev's sharp exit. Val's description of Kylie was too close not to call. She hung on impatiently while Val searched for a number for the girl's foster parents.

Bev glanced round uneasily. Byford had wandered off to have a word with one of the crime-scene team. A dog barked, made her jump. She shivered; the place was giving her the creeps. She hated the shadows and the smells, the creaking of branches and snapping of twigs. She only had to turn her head to see the dead girl.

It was a relief when Val came back with the goods. In return, the woman wanted details Bev didn't know and reassurances she couldn't give. She evaded another volley of questions and rang off promising to be in touch. She glanced at her watch: just after ten. It took less than a minute to establish that Kylie was safe at home. Bev shoved the phone back in her pocket, rubbed her face with her hands. Now what?

"Sarge?" It was Ozzie, running towards her. "The dog. It's found something."

She glanced over at Byford, who was already rushing back.

"Just through here." Ozzie was in front. "It was nosing round one of the bins."

They reached a small clearing. Bev knew the handler by sight, couldn't remember his name. At his side, a massive long-haired Alsatian was yanking frantically at its lead. "It wasn't hidden, sir," the man said. "It was just shoved on top of all the rubbish."

Byford was pulling on surgical gloves as he peered into the bin. "Looks like a bag or something."

Bev moved nearer, hair rising on the back of her neck. It was about time they had a break. She watched as Byford delved in. It put her in mind of a lucky dip at a church fete. But what he brought out was of no use to a middle-aged male cop. It was a tasselled hat, royal blue, with a silver trim. And it was part of the uniform for one of the best girls' schools in the city. Bev recognised it immediately. And the name that had been embroidered so neatly on the tag inside.

She must have gasped. There was a sharp edge to Byford's voice. "What is it?"

"I think it's one of ours, sir." There was silence as she struggled to make sense of what she was seeing. The dog barked, irritating an already impatient Byford. It acted as a prompt even though her thoughts were still unclear. "It's the name. You don't come across it very often." Bev met Byford's gaze. "I know a Louella Kent. And I know she goes to the Holy Child School."

"And?" Byford asked.

"The Louella Kent I know is DS Kent's daughter."

24

"No. It can't be."

The conviction was absolute. Not just in a voice clipped with authority but in the woman's face. The regular features and blue eyes were unremarkable except for being fixed in total and utter disbelief. Until now, Bev had only encountered Louise Kent in court. The woman was a partner in a big city law firm. She didn't suffer fools gladly; didn't suffer them at all.

"You've got it all wrong."

Louise sounded so convinced that for a moment Bev's certainty wavered. Then she remembered the school books, the passport pictures sellotaped onto a *Friends* pencil tin.

Louella and classmate: grinning and pouting, monkeying around. What kid hadn't giggled through a session in a Woolie's photo-booth?

Bev swallowed hard. She hated the job, hated herself, hated the whole goddamn fucking mess. "There is no mistake. I'm so sorry."

Louise ran a hand through her hair. "It's Tuesday. She's with Gary on Tuesdays."

Bev shook her head. Louella wasn't with Gary; she was en route to the city morgue. God alone knew where Gary was. Why the hell else was she doing this? Telling Gary would have been bad enough, but at least he could have broken the appalling news to his wife. That was going by the book. Trouble was the Kents didn't have the book, and Bev was making it up as she went along. As soon as she realised Gary wasn't at home, Bev had tried backing out, but Louise Kent wasn't a woman who could be fobbed off. The solicitor knew damn well that a post-midnight police call wasn't a social visit. Bev kept telling herself she'd had no choice. In an ideal world it shouldn't be happening like this.

"He hasn't told you, has he?" Louise was fiddling with a bowl of potpourri on the hall table. She wouldn't look at Bev, didn't wait for a reply. "No. He wouldn't want anyone at work to know."

Bev had no idea what the woman was talking about. "Know?"

"You'd better come through."

Bev didn't want to go through; didn't want to discuss Gary Kent's messy domestic arrangements. She'd just told the woman her daughter was dead. Either Louise Kent was in denial or the solicitor in her genuinely believed it was a police cock-up. Bev followed her into a room at the end of the hall. Louise had obviously been working. There was a dictaphone on a desk and a couple of pens were marking a place in a brief. A black tailored jacket was slung over the back of a swivel chair; soft leather pumps lay on the deep carpet.

Bev tugged at her dress. She felt like something the cat wouldn't deign to drag anywhere. Damp velvet still clung to her thighs and her hair was plastered like a cap to her skull. She cursed herself. Why hadn't she brought a WPC? Why hadn't she listened to the guv? Byford would've handled this nightmare a damn sight better. But, oh no. She was Gary's mate, she'd argued, and shit job though it was, she'd do the decent thing. Some mate Gary was turning out to be.

"Gary's not here," Louise said. "I threw him out. Two weeks ago."

What was she meant to say? And what the fuck was Gary playing at? How long did he think he could keep something like this quiet? "Mrs Kent. We... I..."

"He has Lou one night a week and every other weekend." She paused, honing the sarcasm. "Work permitting. Naturally."

No, he doesn't. Not now. Not ever again. "Mrs Kent..."

Louise Kent was perched on the edge of the desk, arms folded. There was a poster on the wall behind her, a tourist board promo: suntanned couple, toothy smiles, blue sea, bluer sky. But it wasn't a poster. Bev looked again. It was a holiday snap blown-up. Louise and Louella posing on a cliff top, each with an arm round the other's waist. They could almost have been sisters; the same dark hair, the same heart-shaped face. They looked so happy, it was impossible not to smile back. Bev realised Louise was watching. The woman had slipped her shoes back on and was swinging a leg. The body language was telling Bev to get a move on.

Bev wanted to run. She wanted a drink so stiff she could carve it; more than anything she wanted to wake up and find it was a bad dream. She cleared her throat. "Mrs Kent. We found Louella's..." She was searching for words; didn't have the phrase book.

"What? What did you find?" The woman's hand went for the crucifix round her neck.

Bev could smell her own sweat. "Your daughter's school hat. Some of her books." She could see them now. They'd been dumped in the same bin, their pristine covers spattered with fag ash and lager dregs.

"It must be a prank. No!" The woman was desperately searching for the acceptable. "Bullies. It'll be the bullies. The girls are soft targets for the thugs from Thread Street. They get jeered at in the street. They're always having dinner money stolen. And their mobiles. One girl had her face slapped. Lou's always saying how the Holy Child girls have to go round in groups. I've told her a million times not to cut through that park. Some lout will have snatched her bag and she's been too afraid to say anything. I wondered why she hadn't phoned. Then again, I was back late. That's what it'll be, won't it?"

She was babbling, trying to convince herself; pleading for

reassurance.

Bev took a few steps closer. "Mrs Kent. Is there anyone I can call?"

"Of course!" She snatched up the phone at her side. "Gary'll sort it. You'll see. What time is it? Gone twelve. She'll be in bed."

Bev waited as Louise hit buttons then tried to take the receiver from her.

"No." The courtroom voice was calm. "I'll do it."

Bev watched as the colour drained from the woman's face. The knuckles of the hand clutching the phone were white, the fingers of her other, still twisted the gold cross. Louise tried several times to replace the receiver but her eyes were unfocused, swimming with unshed tears. Bev took it gently from her, laid it in the rest.

"Is he coming?"

Louise nodded dully. "Half an hour."

"Can I get you anything? Tea? Brandy?"

Bev needed a shot of something. She was thinking the un-thinkable. Every cop knew random killings were rare. Murderers almost always know their victim and the nearer the relationship the closer the odds. Gary was Louella's father. He was also an insider. He knew details about Michelle Lucas's murder that hadn't been revealed to anyone outside the team. Position of the body; location of the wound; likely weapon. Details that appeared to have been duplicated in the latest killing. She told herself not to be stupid. Gary was a decent bloke. For God's sake, his kid was lying on a slab. Either way, when a cop was in-volved in any crime, in any capacity, it was bad news. Bev was beginning to feel out of her depth. She brought her mind back to basics. "Want to show me where everything is?" Louise looked blank. Bev prompted. "The kitchen?"

The room was a clash of pine and primary colours. An un-finished game of Cluedo was still spread out on the table. A Mickey Mouse bookmark peeped from the pages of

Wuthering Heights. It was more of a family room, she thought, then realised how inapt the description was. Gary was shacked up across town. Louella was dead.

"Why don't you sit down? I'm sure I'll be able to find things." Bev busied herself while Louise sat slumped, staring into space. The woman was falling apart. "While we're waiting, I'm going to put a call through to my boss. Just to let him know what's going on."

It was possible she hadn't heard; she certainly gave no indication. Bev stood just outside the door, half an eye trained on Louise. The woman noticed nothing – not even Bev's return.

"That's fine. He'll be along shortly." He was still at the scene, but it was only ten minutes in a car.

"I want to see her." Louise shot up and was making for the hall. "I want to go to her. Now."

Bev laid a hand on her arm, spoke softly. "It's not possible. Not yet."

Louise stiffened, jerked away. Bev read the signs, braced herself. The woman was on a knife-edge, panic rising, her glance darting about in a frantic search for escape routes, a bolt-hole. Hands clenched into hard, tight fists, she struck out at the nearest target. If the blow had been more than glancing, it could have dislocated Bev's jaw, but she dived to one side and grabbed the woman's wrists. The tears in Bev's eyes were not for her own pain, but they acted as a catalyst. Louise covered her face with her hands and sobbed. Bev laid her arm around the woman's shoulder and steered her back to her chair. She pulled up a seat for herself and just stayed close. Words weren't going to help at this stage. Questions – a mountain of questions – would come soon enough.

25

"Did you not think it odd when Louella didn't turn up?" There was no hostility in Byford's voice.

Bev saw Gary Kent struggling to keep it out of his. "No. I told you. I got a call."

It was well past one in the morning. They were in the governor's office back at Highgate and she was sitting in at Byford's request. The interview wasn't going on tape and there'd been no caution. They were the only concessions Byford was making to Gary's position as a police officer.

"Yes." Byford consulted his notes. "You said she rang around four to tell you she was spending the night at a friend's."

Kent nodded, barely able to speak even though the bizarre session was at his own request. He'd insisted on getting the questions out of the way. Bev saw his point. He was sharp enough to realise he'd be under suspicion. He wanted any doubts and rumours cleared up fast, so the inquiry didn't lose pace. They all did. But it didn't make the ordeal any easier.

He could also, though Bev didn't want to believe it, be lying through his teeth.

"Was that normal?" Byford persisted. "Did Louella often stay out?"

She saw Gary's fists clench; she'd winced too at the implication. He took a deep breath.

"She's fifteen-years-old. It's what teenagers do. She revises with her friends, watches videos, has sleepovers."

Had, thought Bev. The reality hadn't sunk in even though he'd identified the body. According to Byford, Gary had said nothing, just nodded once, then turned on his heel. His motor had been collected ready for forensics, and his alibi was being checked.

Eliminating him as a suspect – assuming they would – was a priority. They'd all seen TV interviews with grieving relatives who'd turned out guilty as sin. He was hiding it, but Bev reckoned Gary was going through hell.

"Did you check?" Byford was showing no emotion either but she couldn't believe it wasn't there. Kent was a CID officer with seventeen years in the service. Whichever way this scene panned out, it was personal. And painful. For all three.

"We've been through all this." Gary ran a hand over his face. Bev reckoned he'd aged ten years in an hour. His redhead's pale, freckled complexion now resembled mottled parchment. A comb and a shave might have gone some way to restoring his normally groomed appearance, but somehow she doubted it.

"Let's go through it again," Byford said.

Gary sighed. "She's stayed with this girl – Becky, Rebecca Adams – a few times." There was a pause. "Especially since Louise and I…"

Byford helped out. "Split up?"

"Stopped living together. Look, our marriage has nothing to do with this."

Byford shrugged.

"It hasn't," Gary insisted. "Neither of us has ever stopped loving Lou. She always knew we were both there for her."

Bev looked down at her hands. No one spoke for a while.

"Anyway." Byford broke the silence. "It now emerges that Rebecca knew nothing of this arrangement."

Gary nodded, worrying a piece of loose skin at the side of his thumb.

"How did Louella sound?" Byford asked. "On the phone?"

"Bit rushed. Said she was in a hurry."

"Could there have been someone with her?"

He rubbed his eyes. "I don't know. The line was breaking up. I'm always on at her to make sure the battery's charged. You know what kids are."

Bev made a note. Far as she knew, they hadn't found a mobile.

"Did you ring your wife? To confirm the story?" Byford asked.

Gary stared at Byford for a few seconds. His voice was calm at first. "I tried ringing Louise. She was in court. I was going to leave a message at the house but the answerphone wasn't on."

Bev closed her eyes. The woman would blame herself; was already. Guilt and grief had been etched on her face. It was yet another image Bev would want to forget.

"As for checking Lou's story..." Gary paused, beginning to lose it. "It wasn't a story. Lou doesn't make up stories. She's never lied to us. She's young for her age, never been in any trouble. She's a good girl, an A star pupil. We never let her out on her own. We always know where she is, who she's with, what time she'll be back. She's not some little slag on a street corner."

"Like Michelle Lucas?" They were Bev's first words and could have been chipped from ice.

"I didn't mean it like that." He rushed to apologise but Bev's face said it wasn't enough.

"I really didn't." There was a catch in his voice. "Lou's never harmed anyone in her life. She didn't deserve to die like that."

"No one deserves to die like that, Gary."

"'Course not. It goes without saying."

Not necessarily, thought Bev. Shell and Vicki might not have the benefits of a private education and professional parents, but they were as good as anyone.

"Honest, Bev," he said. "I hear what you're saying. What do you think I've been doing the last few days? I want the bastard behind bars as much as you do."

She leaned forward. "What have you been doing? The last few days? Who've you spoken to? Where've you been?"

Gary shook his head, turned his mouth. "It's been routine, mostly. Chasing up interviews, alibi checks, you know the sort of stuff."

"What about the Beemer?" Bev asked. "You and Daz have been on that, haven't you?"

"Yeah. That as well. Cruising round. Asking questions."

"Any trouble?"

"Bit of verbal. Can't think of anything out of the ordinary."

Byford slipped his pen into a pocket, pushed back the chair. "We'll look at it again in the morning. Right now you're too knackered to think straight about anything. Get home. You need sleep." He glanced at Bev. "We all do."

Sleep would be a long time coming, she knew that. "D'you want a lift, Gary?" It was a rapprochement of sorts, though she hadn't forgotten his remarks.

He shook his head. "I'll walk. I need the air." He reached the door, looked back. "I'm telling the truth, boss. I've killed no one. But when we catch the bastard, make sure I'm not around."

"You can't stay on the case, Gary," Byford said. "Not now. You know that."

Gary opened his mouth. Bev thought he was about to argue, but he left without another word. She'd caught the look in his eye; silence didn't necessarily mean acceptance.

26

"This is not acceptable, Victoria."

She was cradling the left side of her face, unsure whether the wetness between her fingers was blood or tears. She was definitely crying. It hurt. A lot. He'd snatched the phone from her hand, whacked her twice. She was so scared she could hardly breathe. Charlie was white-faced, furious.

"Who were you speaking to?"

"No one. Honest." She lifted a hand to fend another blow. The phone smashed across her knuckles.

"You!" He hurled the mobile at Dan. "Outside."

She peeped through her lashes, didn't want to meet the contempt in Dan's eyes. The poor sod had fallen fuck, line and sinker and now they were both in it. Up to the neck.

Dan had come to her bed, as she knew he would. There'd been a bit of word play, bit of foreplay then a serious shag or three. What bloke didn't turn over and crash out? She'd watched the rise and fall of his chest, waited for deep-sleep breathing, then rifled his pockets. She'd eased herself off the bed, crept to the furthest corner, prayed to any passing god to give her a break. She already had a plan. She reckoned it would be one call at the most. And Bev Morriss was her best bet. According to Sleeping Beauty's fake Rollie it was ten to two in the morning; bit early for an alarm call, but tough tits. Except it wasn't. 'Cause the old bag hadn't picked up; the naffin' answer phone was on.

She'd been dithering around, wondering what the hell to do next, when any choice disappeared. Charlie had burst in and was now calling the shots. "I've asked nicely. Now I'm asking again. Who were you speaking to?"

She met his glance. His colour was coming back, if anything his face was flushed. She'd never seen his hair loose before. How could anyone so scary look so good? "No one, honest, Charlie." He took a step closer. She hoped she'd kept the panic out of her eyes. "Me mum. I tried me mum. Just to let her know I was all right, like."

He gave her an incredulous stare.

"Straight up, Charlie. Cross me heart and —"

He grabbed her hair, yanked her head back. "Don't tempt me." He kicked her legs from under her. Then he pinned her to the floor, his knees under her armpits. "Want to know what happened to the last girl who fucked with me?"

"Went clubbin', did you?" She didn't care any more. There was nothing she could do, and Charlie could do anything he fucking fancied.

"In a manner of speaking, Victoria. Yes. You could say that."

"Makes a change from cuttin' them."

He narrowed his eyes. There was an emotion in his voice she couldn't identify: sorrow? pity? shame?

"You're a stupid, stupid little slut." He released her wrists, rose to his feet. "Get up. Put something on. I can't stand the sight of you."

There were red finger marks on her wrists, broken skin on her knuckles, angry bruises already coming out on her legs, God knew what her face looked like. It all hurt like shit. And she didn't give a toss. She felt bad about Dan though. He'd been quite nice to her really, given her an Aero and a can of Coke. God knew what he'd be getting from Charlie.

"Me and him dint do nothin', you know."

Charlie was miles away; lucky sod. He scowled. "You what?"

"Dan. He was just bein' friendly, like. We were only talkin'."

She watched in alarm as he threw his head back, then recognised the strange sound as laughter. "Oh, Victoria, that's good. That's very good."

She snatched the sheet off the bed, threw it round her shoulders, glared at him. "It's true. We were just snugglin' up, keepin' warm. Looks on me as a daughter, Dan does."

He was laughing so much, the tears were running down his cheeks. "He's an old perv, then. You were shagging for Europe."

She gulped. He stopped laughing, stared, asked the question for her. "How do I know that? How do you think I know, Victoria?"

Her gaze flicked to the condoms by the side of the bed. Charlie shook his head. "Don't be silly. They could be anybody's." She watched as he made great play of peering at the ceiling above her head, then keeping his gaze up, strolled a circuit of the room. He spun round, with a wide beam on his face. "Smile, Victoria. You're on Candid fucking Camera."

She felt sick. "You sad bastard. Is that how you get your rocks off?"

He tutted softly. "Come, come Victoria. You know me better than that. Let's just say it doesn't come naturally for everyone. A lot of guys need a little help; visual aids, shall we say?"

She sat on the edge of the bed, sank her head in her hands. "You been makin' dirty vids of me and all them wankers?"

"You're just one of the extras, Victoria. My clients are the stars. They like to see themselves in action. Most of them ask for it, of course. They want their bit on the side and are happy to pay for a little memento. And there are those who don't. They generally end up shelling out more. A lot more. Rates vary, of course: starting from straight sex and going, well, there's only one way really, isn't there?"

"You're sick, you are."

"Not me, babe. But my oh my, you should hear what some of my clients want. Make your hair curl it would, Victoria."

"And you lay it all on?"

"I provide a service, Victoria. With extras."

"And if they ain't buyin' – you blackmail the buggers." She

studied his face. It was as if someone had lit a candle behind his eyes. Telling her all this was turning him on.

"Who's a clever girl, then?" He patted her head. "And, of course, the higher they are, Victoria, the harder they fall. Judges, teachers, doctors. The odd dishonourable member's a bit like hitting oil."

She'd heard enough; too much. Charlie Hawes was a man who kept his business cards so close they were glued to his chest. If he was shooting his mouth off it meant she wouldn't be opening hers.

"What you gonna do with me, Charlie?"

"Well, Victoria, I had got a nice little job lined up. Round at Marlene's –"

"Massage Marl?" Her eyes widened.

"That's right. Dab hand, is Marlene. She runs one of my most successful establishments. She'd have been only too happy to show you the ropes."

She clutched the sheet so tightly it was like a second skin.

"Shame, really. I thought you'd be ready by now. But I want my girls to be happy in their work."

She couldn't hold back the snort. "Like Shell?"

"That should never have happened."

"Accident was it, Charlie? Tripped over a razor, did she?"

"Shut the fuck up." She recoiled, ready for another smacking but he regained control quickly. He clearly had other things on his mind. She watched as his hands moved to his crotch. "Thing is, Victoria: what am I going to do with you now? I thought you'd fit the bill but I don't think I can trust you out there. Not after tonight."

Out there? Out there! She saw a life-line, met his gaze. "Course you can, Charlie. I only fibbed cause I didn't want Dan to get in the shit."

"I don't give a monkey's about Danny boy, but that phone call, Victoria. That was very ill-advised."

"No harm done, Charlie. Like I say, she wasn't there." She hoped she didn't sound too eager.

He sighed, moved closer; stroking the bulge in his trousers. "I'm just not sure anymore. I'll have to give it some very serious thought."

"You do that Charlie. You'll see. I'll do anything you want." She dropped the sheet and opened her thighs.

"There's never been any doubt about that, Victoria." Casually he knocked her legs together with his knee. "But I'm not going in there. Not after Dirty Dan and God knows who else has been sniffing round."

It was as bad as a smack in the mouth. She blinked hard but tears were pricking her eyes.

He ran a finger along her lips. "Still. I'm sure we can come up with an alternative. What do you think, Victoria?"

27

"What do you reckon, guv?" There was no need to ask; Byford's face said it all.

"There's nothing to go on. She doesn't even say where she is."

Bev sighed; tell me something I don't know. She was sitting at her desk. Byford hadn't bothered to pull up a chair. She'd played the message twice for him now but any number of encores wasn't going to make it any clearer.

Even Bev had put it down to a heavy breather at first; a breather with attitude. "Where the fuck are you? You've got to get me out of this hole." There was a slight pause on the tape, then, as if Bev was besieged daily by anonymous abductees: "It's Vick."

Bev had known better starts to a morning. A wrong number had woken her just after seven and then she'd spotted the flashing red light of the answer phone. She'd hit the button and Vicki's voice had floated from the speaker. Bev's first thought was, thank God, she's alive.

Alive, even though she sounded scared to death.

She'd played the tape again and again, against a video-wall of snatched images still running in her head: the pounding along wet pavements; the ghouls in Thread Street; Byford's lonely figure by the water's edge; a body in the mud. She'd been wrong about the victim being Vicki, but she was right about the girl not being in Brighton. So where was she? Why hadn't she said? And why had the call ended so abruptly? Bev had an idea about that and didn't want to go there.

All the way to Highgate she'd been asking herself if it would have made a difference if she'd been in to take the call. She still didn't know the answer. Maybe she'd hoped for reassurance from Byford, but the boss was looking as shattered as she felt. They'd had a late night and the day ahead was going to be long. It could explain his indifference.

She watched as he tossed the newspaper he'd been holding onto her desk. A picture of Louella Kent, smiling and smart, in school uniform, took up most of the front page. "At least Vicki Flinn's alive," he said.

It was an echo of her own initial reaction, but it rang hollow. "Yes. But for how long?"

"Come on." He was heading for the door. "We haven't got all day."

"Hold on. What are you saying? That we just give up on her?"

"I'm saying there are priorities."

She opened her mouth but he was clearly in no mood for argument. "Look, Bev. You've done everything you can. The number's not traceable. And, even if it was, there's no saying it would lead back to Hawes."

But something had to. Or someone. She ran a couple of recent conversations through her memory. Neither Val nor Annie Flinn had told the truth about Vicki, but did they know they'd been lying? And who had enough clout to put words into mouths? "Guv. Charlie could —"

"It's not a priority. We've got enough on as it is." He pointed to the paper. "I shouldn't have to spell it out."

She watched him leave, then scanned the headlines.

GIRL KILLED AT VICE DEMO
POLICE OUT IN FORCE

Bev mouthed a "Whoops." No wonder he was in such a good mood. Just wait till the media found out who she was.

"Can you confirm that the murdered girl was the daughter of a serving police officer? Superintendent?"

Matt Snow, Crime Correspondent of the *Star*, was front row but centre stage. Bev glanced at Byford. He was good, she'd give him that. She doubted anyone else had spotted the tell-tale jaw-clench. On the subject of telling tales, as Bev well knew Louella's name hadn't been released, let alone her parentage. More than that, both were being deliberately withheld. Though Gary's elimination as a suspect looked imminent, the Kents were under enough pressure without a posse of hacks stalking their every move.

Bev turned her attention to Snow. His fringe was in its customary Tintin tuft. The ubiquitous brown suit had mud splatters up the legs. No prizes for guessing where he'd been earlier. Snow and the rest of the media had been scavenging in the park, until the action switched to Highgate and a 10am news conference. Three dozen hacks and hackettes had filed in, filling the room with cheap scent and expensive aftershave, moaning about newsdesks and banging on about deadlines. Snow had certainly bided his time. The proceedings had been gradually winding down after what Bev considered a masterly damage-limitation exercise by the guv. Then Snow had lobbed his bomb. He could barely conceal his glee. Not just at outmanoeuvring the police but at getting one over on the broadcast boys. There were more cameras around than in a branch of Dixon's, but Snow had sniffed out the biggie.

Bev was taking it all in from the platform. Mike Powell and a couple of press officers were also in attendance but the safety-in-numbers theory was looking pretty shaky. Byford laid his pen on the table, then met the reporter's gaze. "I'm not yet in a position to release the victim's identity."

Bev had heard the tone before; it was designed to quash further inquiry. This time there was a design fault.

"But you do know it?" Snow persisted.

"I have that information. It's not for release."

"I'm not asking for identification. I'm asking for confirmation."

Bev shuffled in her chair, watching Byford's discomfort increase as Snow's peers sat back to enjoy the show.

"You're splitting hairs, Mr Snow."

"I'm doing my job, Superintendent, which –" He paused, glanced at his notebook – "according to the people I've been speaking to, is more than you are."

Bev kept her face blank but was shocked at the attack. God knew what it was doing to the governor. The case was getting to him anyway without trial by tabloid. Snow didn't hang around for a reply. "People are scared, Superintendent. Two teenage girls have been found dead, virtually in the same place, within the space of six days. One of the victims was a known prostitute. And you're sitting there saying there's no link?"

"I'm saying it's too early to draw that sort of conclusion."

"And will it be too late when another girl's found with her throat cut?"

"How do you know that?" Bev felt herself flush. She was meant to be observing, now all eyes were on her. "The cause of death. Who told you that?"

Snow's pause was a second too long. "I assumed it was the same as the Lucas girl."

"Assumed?" She glared at him. "And did you also assume her father's identity?"

She was pleased to see his unease but it only lasted a couple of seconds.

"If you must know, I got a tip-off. And as you're well aware, I can't reveal my source.

"Anyway – " He returned his attention to Byford. "The real question is, did the killer assume last night's victim was a street girl. In which case, shouldn't you be issuing a warning to women about a serial killer?" He paused. "Or did he know exactly what he was doing? Did he kill the girl because her father's a copper?"

Either option was a minefield. Bev could see the headlines

now. There'd either be a rash of 'New Ripper' scare stories or Gary Kent would find himself splashed across every front page in the country. She glanced round the room; in effect they had no option. The pack was licking its pencils and sharpening its claws.

Byford folded his arms, leaned forward. "At this stage in the inquiry, speculation of any kind is unhelpful and could be damaging. We should all be dealing in known facts. What we know – as opposed to what you're conjecturing – is that two girls are dead and the killer or killers are still at large. What we need are witnesses —"

"Witnesses!" Snow was on his feet, his rise so sudden the chair toppled back. "There must have been two hundred people in Thread Street last night and a good many of them were your officers. I'd have thought you had witnesses coming out of your ears."

Bev glanced at Byford. He was doing the jaw thing again. It was difficult not to notice this time.

"Your figures are as overblown as your theories, Mr Snow. We are in the process of interviewing everyone who was involved in last night's protest. The numbers are nowhere near what you claim. And as you well know, our interest begins much earlier in the day. We are anxious to speak to anyone who was in the area from around 3pm onwards."

Snow was smirking. The point had been made and would appear in bold print later, no doubt.

"What lines of inquiry are you following, Superintendent?"

"We're anxious to trace anyone who may have seen either girl during the relevant times. We're checking backgrounds, family, friends, anyone who knew either of the victims. As in any major investigation, we are asking people with information to come forward."

"The people I've been talking to want information from you. They want to know whether their streets are safe to walk in. They want to know what steps you're taking to catch this man.

People are scared, Mr Byford. They're scared and they want to know what you're doing about it."

Bev watched as Byford gathered his papers and got to his feet. "Nothing. Absolutely nothing." He stared at Snow. "Not while I'm wasting time talking to you."

Bev was beginning to think it was a waste of time. Twenty eight and a half minutes kicking your heels on a draughty concourse at New Street Station was enough for anyone, especially when you were downwind of a burger bar. Eau d'onion and hot fat was clinging to her hair.

Dawn Lucas had suggested the spot; it beat wearing a red carnation and carrying a copy of *Bella* which had been her other bright idea for mutual recognition in a sea of strange faces. She'd phoned from a call box just before boarding a train at Manchester Piccadilly; a train that had pulled in – Bev checked her watch for the umpteenth time – half an hour ago. She was keeping her eyes peeled for a twenty-something female with blonde hair and blue eyes: Dawn's lavish, and fairly useless, self-portrait.

So far, Bev had been accosted by a less than fragrant bag lady and serenaded by a tone-deaf busker whose repertoire was limited to *Tiptoe Through The Tulips* and *Abide With Me.* The man's whippet was in better voice. Bev had handed over a pound on the understanding he'd tiptoe off.

She needn't have bust a gut to get here, though anything was preferable to the news conference from hell. Byford was going round like a bear with a migraine and the fall-out had filtered down the ranks. Everyone was under pressure to get a result but no one knew where the goalposts were. The plods were on witness interviews; Ozzie and a few teams were still trawling the massage parlours; others were tracking down known kerb crawlers. Byford and Powell – poor sods – were at the post mortem. It was all routine stuff, deadly dull but more often than not it cracked cases. Either that or a killer got cocky or careless; hopefully both.

For Bev's part, she was going on the patch tonight. She'd fixed it on the phone with Val. The girls were reeling over the latest killing, so how many would show was anyone's guess. At the very least, it would give Bev an opening to pursue the Brighton line, face-to-face; she hadn't told Val about the message from Vicki on her answer phone. The only decent bit of news was that Gary Kent's alibi checked out. Not that his wife would be too pleased to learn where he'd been, or who with. Gary had even turned up for work, said it was the only way he was going to get through the next few days. Louise didn't need him; she had her sister with her. The guv had eventually relented and sent him off to the General to interview a GBH: some bloke found in a Balsall Heath alleyway with both legs broken and a face in desperate need of a nose.

"'ere, are you Bev Morriss?

It was a voice that could grate hard cheese. Bev turned to see who owned it. She was a short, skinny, blonde with more slap than Boots and a red Lycra skirt that could have doubled as a headband. Her smile revealed a gap in her teeth that was navigable.

"Wotcha." Bev held a hand out in greeting. "Thought you'd got lost."

"Nah. I got chattin' to this bloke on the train. We went for a swift half. There's a bar just round there. Then I needed a pee." She smiled. "Bin waitin' long?"

Sarcasm was too cerebral. Bev shook her head. "Let's go, shall we?"

"Go? Go where?"

"We need to talk, Dawn. That's why you're here."

"It's dinner time. I 'aven't eaten yet. I'm starvin'."

Two Happy Meals and a bag of chicken nuggets it took. Bev paid, then chauffeured Dawn to Highgate. It was like having a hyperactive stick insect in the passenger seat. The woman never shut up: *EastEnders*, the Royals, Birmingham drivers. Not a word about Michelle. The loquacity lasted till they were ensconced in an interview room at Highgate, then Dawn ran out of steam.

"You okay?" Bev asked.

"'ot in 'ere, innit?" She shrugged off a sky-blue fleece and stretched her little sparrow legs. "Could do with a drink."

"I could probably rustle up a cup of tea."

Dawn curled a lip as if it had been an offer of paraquat. "Aw, go on then."

She returned to find Dawn crashed out, lolling and snoring like a rag doll with dodgy adenoids. She moved nearer and looked closer. Dawn's crop top had ridden up to her bra. This doll also had heavy bruising and cigarette burns. The marks were unmistakeable when you'd seen them before. Bev stood and stared for a while then shook Dawn gently on the shoulder. The woman shot up, saw Bev and relaxed. "Must've dropped off. Sorry 'bout that." She realised where her top was and why Bev was silent. She tugged it down with both hands. "Had a nasty fall."

"On an ashtray?"

"That the tea? Ta. Pass us a spoon." Subject closed. Bev sighed. If a man ever lifted a finger to her, he'd walk with a limp for the rest of his life. For all Dawn's hard-woman posturing, she was some bastard's punch bag. And like so many women, she was letting the thug off the hook. Bev took a seat across the table and opened a file.

"Them the papers I gotta sign, then?" Dawn's face was creased in an effort to read upside down.

"All in good time. I need a statement first."

"But I don't know nothin'."

"Michelle was your daughter, Dawn. Tell me about her."

Dawn Lucas's story, in some respects, was like so many Bev had heard.

"Fell for Shell at fourteen, I did. We told her she was me sister. Only found out like when she were six or seven."

"So Michelle was close to your mother?"

"Well, she were till me mam died. She got cancer." Dawn closed her eyes for a second or two. "Bloody doctors. It should have been picked up on one of them smears. Forty-seven, she was. Anyroad, our Shell came to live with me and Kev. But he didn't have no time for kids so he buggered off. I was stuck in a poxy bedsit all day, couldn't get a job, couldn't see a way out. Did a bit of street work to make ends meet. You know how it is."

And so did Michelle, Bev thought.

"Anyroad, I met this bloke and me and Shell moved in with him. She were ten, eleven, summat like that. She were growin' up fast. Had her own friends. Always out, always up to tricks, know what I mean?"

Bev had a good idea. "Who were her friends? Can you give me any names?'

She pulled a face. "Never bin no good with names. Sorry. Anyway, this bloke gets offered a job up in Manchester, good money, movin' expenses, the lot, and he asks me to go."

"And Michelle? Was she included in the deal?"

Dawn's eyes flashed in anger. "I told you before. She could've come if she'd wanted."

Bev said nothing, her expression asked for more.

Dawn looked away, then down at her hands. "To tell you the truth, she dint have much time for Ginger. Reckoned he was a dirty old sod."

"And was he?"

"Nah. He were a good laugh. He were a good bit older than me. But I still miss him. Treated me okay. Know what I mean?"

Her eyes were too bright. She was on the verge of tears. Bev found herself almost feeling sorry for the woman. "Anyway. Michelle didn't go. And as far as you were aware, she'd arranged to stay with the family of a schoolfriend?"

"That's right. Next thing I know she's in care."

Bev pushed Dawn for more details. They went over the same ground again and again but they were getting nowhere. Bev put her pen down and rubbed her face.

"That it, then?" asked Dawn. "Shall I sign the papers now?"

The woman was getting well excited over a release form and a witness statement. Bev nodded. "Yes. Sure. You'll be wanting Michelle's things. Then I'll get you a cab."

"Hold on! What about the compensation? You said I had to sign a load of stuff. I was thinkin' like, if it was a good bit I might stick round. There's not much to keep me up north. I 'aven't got a job or nothin'. Thought, mebbe I could make a fresh start. A mate of mine down the market reckons it could be hundreds and hundreds of thousands."

Bev looked down, already regretted talking-up the woman's hopes. She reached into a drawer. "I've got the paperwork here for you, Dawn. You'll have to fill it in and wait and see."

Dark eyebrows were drawn together. "What about the big payout, and the meeting on Friday?"

"I'm sorry, Dawn." Bev pushed an application form across the desk. "They will look at your claim but it'll be eleven grand, max. It'll take a few months."

"But you said…" Her voice was like a kid's who'd just been told there's no Father Christmas.

Bev felt like the wicked fairy. "I'm really sorry, Dawn. I had to get you here to talk about Michelle. I shouldn't have lied. It was wrong of me." She'd have felt less of a heel, if Dawn had thrown a wobbly or called her a lying cow, but the woman just sat back, resigned to yet another kick in the teeth. "Nah. It's okay. Had a day out, ain't I?" Consciously or not, her bony hand was stroking her bruised flesh. She sighed, then retrieved a cheap, white bag from the floor. "I'd best be off, then."

Bev laid her hand over Dawn's. "I can give you a number. In Manchester. Someone to talk to. A place to go if things get really bad."

"Women's refuge?"

Bev nodded.

"Been there, done that." She rubbed the dark skin under her eye. "'e always fetches me back. It's only when 'e's on the juice..." There was no need to explain. "Anyroad." She scraped the chair back. "No worries. Summat'll turn up."

Bev doubted that. Dawn was nearly thirty and so far, nothing even halfway decent had appeared. The woman wasn't a monster, just another victim. "I've had Michelle's bits and pieces brought over." Bev got to her feet. "I'll just go and get them."

"No." Dawn shook her head. "I don't want nothin'. I don't need anythin' to remember our Shell. I've got a nice picture. That'll do me."

Bev froze. "What did you say?"

"I've got a picture. Sent it me she did. Not long after I left."

Bev swallowed. "Got it with you?"

Michelle was on the left, long hair like blonde curtains, either side of a cheeky grin. A taller, skinny girl had an arm round her shoulders. She was as dark as Shell was fair. Bev didn't need to ask who it was. The photograph was a couple of years old and she hadn't seen her for nearly a week but she'd know Vicki Flinn anywhere. Question was: who was the figure in the background?

"I was asking the wrong questions, guv." Byford was holding a photograph between his fingers. Bev was hovering the other side of his desk. "When I went to Annie Flinn's, it was to find out what she knows about Vicki. Turns out, I should have been asking about Michelle."

Byford nodded. "Worth another visit, at least."

She sniffed; a bit of enthusiasm would be nice. The snap didn't prove anything but it raised a few queries. Dawn had been loath to leave it but changed her mind when Bev handed over travelling expenses and slipped the woman a few quid from her own pocket. Talk about pound of flesh – she'd then persuaded Bev to help her with the CICA application. She said she'd lost her glasses, but Bev reckoned a pair of binoculars wouldn't have helped much. Dawn knew her ABC but had trouble with anything after D.

Byford was still looking at the picture. "Who's the other girl, Bev?"

"Don't know yet." Bev had already spent ages poring over the blurred outline mostly hidden by the trunk of a sprawling horse chestnut. Either the girl just happened to be walking past or she was deliberately ducking out of shot. There was a lot of hair and not much else.

"I'll get back to the Flinn place, then, shall I?"

He shrugged. "May as well."

She reached for the print but Byford held onto it for a few seconds. "Beautiful, wasn't she? Michelle."

Bev glanced at his face; wistful like the voice. "You okay, guv?"

"I've just spent two hours watching Harry Gough carve up Gary Kent's girl." He glared at her. "What do you think?"

She stared back. "I think it's the pits. It comes with the territory."

He lifted a hand. "Sorry. It's not your fault. Anyway…" He gave a rueful smile. "If you read the press, it's all down to me."

She had. Vince Hanlon always kept a *Star* on the front desk. She'd seen the latest edition. It couldn't get any worse in the final. Not with words like police, chief, clueless, all over the front page. "Come on, guv, they'd blame their own granny if it sold more papers."

"Maybe."

She watched as he rearranged bulging files and piles of clutter on his normally pristine desk. He looked tired, gaunt, and though he was dismissing her, she didn't want to go.

"I take it Goughie didn't have much to add?"

He pursed his lips. "Not a lot. Looks like the same MO. He reckons she was attacked from behind. There are no defence marks, but there were fibres of some sort under her fingernails. They're on the way to the lab."

"Better than nothing, guv."

"If we ever get anything to match them with."

"When, not if." She sounded more confident than she felt.

He dismissed the sentiment with a flap of his hand. "What have we got to go on? We've had a couple of sightings of a BMW. Apart from that, no one's seen anything, heard anything or saying anything. I'm getting flak from upstairs and flak from the press. And you know what's worse?" He paused. "It could easily happen again."

He was right. They had no motive; didn't know what they were dealing with.

"The attack on Louella wasn't sexual. She wasn't touched," Byford said.

"Thank God." Gary and Louise would be spared that agony.

"But why was she killed, Bev? Was it to get at us? Is there a pattern here or was it a random attack?"

She shook her head, sighed. "What about releasing details on Charlie Hawes? You know the sort of thing. We're anxious to trace blah-de-blah."

He folded his arms and leaned forward. "I think you're developing a fixation about this man, Bev. We know he's a pimp. That's all we know. There's nothing to link him to the murders."

She opened her mouth to argue but Byford wouldn't take kindly to a slanging match. She kept her voice level. "Hawes was grooming Michelle Lucas. He scares the shit out of the girls. I think he could be holding Vicki Flinn against her will. At the very least, it would be useful to talk to him."

"And where's the photograph? Or E-fit?"

It was a valid point. Without a visual of some sort, the appeal wasn't likely to get anywhere. All Vicki had told her was that Charlie was fit, dark and a bit of a looker. "I could try to persuade one of the girls to work with a police artist. We might come up with a decent likeness."

"We still haven't got anything on him."

She was impatient and didn't hide it. "I think it's worth a shot – unless you've got a better idea."

He sighed meaningfully. It was an opportunity to apologise. She didn't take it.

"What's that?" She'd just noticed an evidence bag partially covered by a couple of files.

"Crime scenes must have left it while I was at the morgue." He scanned the handwritten tag. "Yes. It turned up this morning, not far from the girl's body." He was frowning. "What do they call these things, Bev?"

She took the bag for a closer look. Inside was a soft ball of stretchy black fabric. "Scrunchies."

He'd never heard of them.

"For hair," she explained. "Plaits, ponytails."

He nodded, but his attention was now on a note he was reading.

"Anything there?" she asked.

"Scene of crimes report. Just a few edited highlights till later. Lots of prints and tracks but not much good. The place was a quagmire with all that rain. They've turned up the usual stuff. That," he pointed to the bag Bev was still holding, "was about the only thing that stood out. The hairs that were on it are at the lab." He tossed the paper on the desk. "No guarantee it's hers of course. And even if it is, I can't see where it'll take us." She was lost in thought; puzzled. "Something on your mind, Bev?"

"I don't see how it can be Louella's. I can barely get my hair in a ponytail, and Louella's was much shorter."

"Doesn't have to be Louella's," Byford said. "Lots of girls use the park. I'll get on to forensic though, tell them to rush it through."

It wasn't much to go on. They still had to find the killer. Even then, it might be unconnected. On the other hand, it could be evidence that would help secure a conviction.

The phone rang as he was reaching for it. He grabbed a pen and scribbled on a lined pad. The call was over in seconds. "Thanks, Vince. Hang on to him. I'll send her down."

She pulled a face, had intended getting straight off to Annie Flinn's.

"Best put the Flinn interview on the back burner. Chap downstairs reckons we've been looking for him. Says his name's Charlie Hawes."

28

The lawyer looked more like the pimp. That was Bev's initial impression. She was observing through reception's one-way mirror and guessed, rightly, that the older bloke was a brief. Charlie had come prepared: quite the little boy scout. They were waiting stiff-backed near the front desk, standing out like designer gear on a market stall. Rumpole's broken nose was floundering in a sea of acne scars and his hairline hadn't so much receded as done a runner. Alongside him was the elusive Mr Hawes.

Bev cast a long, lingering look. They'd been trying to flush him out for days and there he was. She stared, trying to match up the Armani-clad man in front of her with the glimpsed figure in New Street. Had it been him?

She half expected Hawes to sport a pair of horns or have 'mad git' stamped across his forehead. But no. Vicki was right. He was well fit. Mind, a tan like that would work wonders for an anaemic anorexic. Not that he was skinny; he had the profile and proportions of some Greek statue; she just hoped he'd have a damn sight more to say. She used her fingers as a comb, checked her skirt wasn't stuck up her knickers and went to find out. Vince was embroiled in paperwork; the *Telegraph* crossword, probably. She let him get on with it.

"Mr Hawes?" Both men turned: the only reaction. "I'm Detective Sergeant Morriss." There were no smiles or social niceties on either side.

Charlie nodded, then gestured at his sidekick. "This is Max Viner. My legal representative."

She tilted her head quizzically: as good a way as any of asking why he thought one was needed.

"Mr Hawes is here because it has come to his attention that the police are anxious to speak with him in connection with the recent tragic deaths of two young women."

Despite the lawyerspeak, and a face like an over-cooked pizza, he could do voiceovers for silk. Bet he gave good phone. Best place for him, as far as Bev was concerned. "Yeah. You could say that. Let's go and have a little chat, shall we?"

Viner wagged a short stubby finger. "Before we go anywhere, let me make it quite clear that my client is here in order to help the police with their inquiries. It is also his intention to illustrate his innocence of any allegation or involvement in either of these shocking crimes. And –" a final ferocious wag – "in order to prevent any further harassment by members of the West Midlands police force."

The voice had coarsened as the volume increased. Vince lifted his gaze from four down.

"Everything okay, Bev?"

"Never better." She smiled broadly. Viner could shove it. Whatever crap he spouted, Hawes was in it up to his neck. The man was either an arrogant fool or believed himself fireproof. They'd soon find out.

Byford was waiting in Interview One. Not a place in which to spend much time. Stale smoke and sweat hung round, despite a daily swabbing with a dose of Jeyes. A grey metal desk matched the grey walls and floor. A tinfoil ashtray was the only accoutrement.

He looked up but stayed seated as she ran through the introductions. She could tell by a tightening of the guv's mouth, that Viner was as welcome as a sweet-toothed wasp. A lawyer in the equation played hell with their strategy: Byford was going to take the lead but encourage Hawes to do the talking; give him enough rope, etcetera. Bev would sit quietly, smile disarmingly and trip him the second he cocked up. Seemed like a good idea at the time.

Charlie flourished a virginal handkerchief and wiped a chair before sitting. Viner stayed on his feet while opening a slim attaché case and taking out several sheets of typed A4.

"My client has prepared a written statement, detailing his whereabouts and activities from the day of the first murder to –" he glanced at a chunky gold wristwatch – "a little over an hour ago. No doubt you will want to check everything. Indeed, my client is anxious that you should do so. You'll see that there are names, addresses and telephone numbers of colleagues, acquaintances and friends who will verify Mr Hawes's presence and vouch for his good behaviour at all relevant times. I can personally guarantee the integrity of most of these people."

Bev had no doubt he could. She had no doubt the story would check out in every detail and that every one of the characters would lie through their dental-work to save Charlie's flawless skin.

Byford accepted a copy and tossed it on the desk. "Perhaps I could ask why your client has gone to so much effort to put his case across?"

Viner was making great play of smoothing his tie. "It's not so much putting the case across, Superintendent, as setting the record straight."

Byford inclined his head.

"We have heard on excellent authority that your police officers have been paying visits to various establishments across the city asking questions which can only cast doubt on Mr Hawes's good name and reputation."

"What reputation?" The question slipped through Bev's credibility gap.

Viner glanced disparagingly, concentrated on Byford. "My client is a respected businessman. He has no criminal record and has never had dealings with the police."

Bev noticed a thin line of moisture above the lawyer's

rubbery lips, dreaded to think what was oozing from his armpits. She glanced at Charlie, realised he'd been looking at her. He still was. More than that, he was studying her, appraising her, probably marking her out of ten. Knowing she was watching, he continued the appraisal. She crossed her legs, managed to stop herself folding her arms. He'd be expert in body language; she refused to talk it. He looked her in the eyes and flicked his tongue along his top lip; the movement so fleeting, she might have imagined it. But not the smile. His mouth was creased at the corners, as he looked down at his smooth hands with their perfect pink nails. She forced herself not to shift in the seat.

"My client is concerned that erroneously pursuing him will have a detrimental effect on the inquiry. Mr Hawes is anxious that you do not waste further time." He allowed himself a tight smile. "Particularly after reading press reports of your progress so far."

"That's decent of him," Byford said, leaning back, hands crossed behind his head.

"And what exactly is your client's line of business?" The question was directed at the brief but Bev was looking at Charlie.

"Though it has no relevance to your investigation, Mr Hawes is a freelance leisure consultant. His services are used by several of our leading citizens."

"That posh for pimp is it, Charlie?" Bev was hoping for a reaction. "Was Michelle Lucas one of your services, Charlie?"

A flustered Viner darted a glance at Hawes. "My client is here at his own volition. I see no — "

Hawes silenced the lawyer with a single raised finger. "That's all right, Mr Viner. Sergeant Morriss has every right to ask her tacky little questions."

He smiled as if at a naughty child, then turned to Byford. "As far as I can recall, I never even met the girl. As for my business dealings, you're welcome to go through my books, look round my premises. My vehicles are at your disposal should you wish to carry out forensic tests. My home is available for you to search, should you think it necessary. Like you, Superintendent, I want these dreadful crimes solved." He glanced at Bev. "And I want her off my back."

Viner gave a discreet cough, started collecting his belongings. "I hope this little meeting has been useful, Mr Byford. I'm sure we all want this investigation brought to a successful and speedy conclusion." He laid his case on the desk. "There is one other small matter..."

Bev exchanged glances with Byford. The brief was doing casual, very carefully. Her crapometer was off the scale.

"My client is concerned that your diligence in pursuing him might be down to deliberately misleading information."

Bev snorted. And you're on which planet?

"Let me make myself clear. We are concerned that a business rival, indeed someone who may bear ill-feeling towards Mr Hawes, may be misdirecting the course of your inquiry in order to incriminate my client."

The penny plunged. "Stitch him up?" Bev asked. "Is that what you're trying to say?"

Viner held out fleshy hands. "Who can say? It's a point to bear in mind. The corollary would be, of course, that if someone is trying to implicate Char... my client... then it begs the question: why?" He paused, then supplied the answer. "Are they, for instance, eager to shift the blame from themselves?"

So that was Hawes's little game. Play the innocent and drop some unsuspecting sod in the excrement. She almost admired the cheek.

Both men stood. Her eyes widened. There was cheek, but this was taking the piss. They thought they could just swan out. Charlie gave an ostentatious bow in Bev's direction. She spotted a flash of white flesh at the nape of his neck; his expensive tan had sold him well short.

"Going somewhere, gentlemen?" Good on you, guv. Byford

wasn't in the habit of being dismissed. "You haven't finished your tea yet."

Bev blinked. What was he playing at? Even Viner had lost his air of insouciance. He sounded almost as bewildered as he looked. "What tea? There isn't any."

"No," Byford agreed. "But there will be. Answering questions is thirsty work. And by the time your client's finished, he'll be parched. Won't you, Mr Hawes?"

Bev almost missed the flash of anger across Charlie's face. The smile that followed was more lingering, and probably just as lethal. "It's a funny thing, Mr Byford, I never touch the stuff. It's the caffeine, you know. Bad for the health."

"Not the only thing, is it, Charlie?" She expected to be ignored; she was.

Hawes sat, pointed at the empty chair and nodded at his brief. Viner took his cue and lowered himself into the seat. "I really don't see what further —"

"Michelle Lucas, Mr Hawes. What can you tell me about her?" Byford was holding a pen, looking expectantly.

Hawes held out empty palms.

"Cassie Swain, Mr Hawes. What can you tell me about her?"

They were still empty.

"How many girls are you grooming, Mr Hawes?"

"I don't do hair, Mr Byford."

"Do a lot of make-up, though, don't you, Charlie?" Bev couldn't even fake a smile. She lifted his statement. "How much of this little lot is fantasy?"

"Shut the — "

"My client has nothing further to add." Viner put a restraining hand on Charlie's arm.

"Everything you need is in there, including Mr Hawes's home address and business premises. There are also several telephone numbers where he can be contacted again." He added doubtfully, "Should the need arise."

Bev glanced at the guv. He was furious. "Sergeant, get that tea sorted."

"My pleasure, guv." It was anything but. She was just beginning to needle Charlie; more prodding might reveal him as the little prick he was.

Byford held up the man's statement. "We'll need this checked, Sergeant. Give it to DC Newman."

"No prob."

It obviously was for the brief. "How much long —"

Byford looked at Viner. "As long as it takes."

Charlie was leaning back in the chair, a gentle smile on his lips. Bev sauntered past, dropped a casual, "How's Vicki, Charlie?"

"Fine."

Gotcha! She spun round. Apart from profanities, it was the only spontaneous remark he'd uttered during the entire charade. Her broad smirk was short-lived.

"At least as far as I know."

She wanted to wipe the yawn off his face. "And how far's that, Charlie?"

He was casually picking sleep out of the corner of an eye. "I vaguely recall the name. She came to me for a job once."

Lying bastard. "As what?"

"Part-time scrubber." He smiled. "I had an opening for a cleaner."

"Oh yeah."

"I couldn't take her on, of course."

"Why's that?"

"Didn't like the look of her." He was eyeing Bev again; bopping him would be a joy.

"Too old for you, Charlie? Schoolgirls are more your line, aren't they?"

"My client –" Viner was on his feet.

"Shut it, Max. Sit down."

"So when did you last see her?"

"Months ago."
"I don't believe you."
"I don't give a shit."
"You're lying."
"Prove it, bint."
Bev smiled. The veneer of civility was cracking. Viner tried for damage-limitation in the shape of distraction. "Are you arresting my client, Mr Byford?"
"No."
"In that case —"
"...not yet."
Charlie was tapping his fingers on the table. It was the only sound. Bev glanced at each man in turn. They all knew that until there was evidence, Charlie could walk whenever he wanted. Viner stated the obvious. "Unless you're arresting Mr Hawes, he is free to leave. I remind you, Superintendent, that my client is here to further your inquiries, not as a target for hostility and offensive comment."
"Chill, Max. Let them run their little checks. I'm in no hurry. Make sure you're recording it all for the case, though."
Bev glanced at the brief. He clearly wasn't up to speed. "Case?"
Charlie outlined it, slowly. "Police harassment. Defamation. Perverting the course of justice."
She snorted. That was rich. That was rolling in it. Byford obviously agreed.
"Tell DC Newman to start with Mr Hawes's car, Bev."
"Cars, Superintendent. I have several. For business, of course."
"Of course," Byford murmured.
Bev opened the door, but she didn't want to leave; didn't want to stop pushing the bastard about Vicki. But she knew she had to play it clever. She couldn't reveal she'd heard from the girl. If Charlie did have her holed up, there was still a chance he didn't know about the message. Finding out could be bad news: the worst. Bev glanced back to find Hawes's gaze on her legs.

"Eh, Charlie, I hear Vicki's gone to Brighton. Know anything about that, do you?"

He re-ran the empty palms routine. "Search me." Her eyes narrowed, as his blank look turned into a fake frown. The voice was mock-concern. "That can't be right. She's a friend of yours. She'd have sent you a card." There was menace in the pause; she felt it even more when he spoke again. "Surely you'd have heard from her by now? Beverley?"

There was a sharp intake of breath from Ozzie. "Slow down, Sarge. That was a red light."

Bev glared at him.

"D'you want me to drive?" he asked.

She tightened her grip on the wheel, left her foot where it was. "Do I look as if I want you to drive?"

"You look gutted to me."

Ozzie had borne the brunt of Bev's anti-Hawes tirade. The guv had eventually assigned half a dozen officers to crack the man's alibi. Checks so far suggested that only a Trident sub would be more watertight.

She hit the horn, till a two-mile-a-fortnight banger pulled over to let them pass. "He's fireproof, bombproof and bloody waterproof."

"Have you ever thought he might not have done it?"

Never. Not once. And it was too late to start now. "He's as guilty as sin. He's just never been caught."

She heard a sigh, was aware he'd turned to look through the window. Not that he'd see much. It was beans-on-toast-in front-of-the-telly time where Annie Flinn lived; more *Neighbours* than Neighbourhood Watch. The Robin Hood estate was all single mothers and double buggies. Family values were Australian and about as remote. Ozzie was doing her a favour tagging along.

"Sorry, Oz. But if we don't come up with something rock hard, he's gonna get away with it. He's got witnesses sewn up like patchwork. How the hell does he do it?"

"Threats, I suppose," he answered, but the voice had little interest.

"Yes, but what with? It's not just the girls. He's got all sorts of people backing him up. Councillors, a vicar, a couple of footballers. They're queuing to throw him a line."

"What road's this woman's place on?"

"Sherwood Street."

"You just passed it."

"Shit."

She jammed the anchors on and a woman cyclist very nearly went into the back bumper. Bev mouthed an apology but the woman gave her the finger and a mouthful.

Ozzie's face was set in disapproval. He waited till she was halfway through a three-point turn. "You're letting the bloke get to you."

It was lucky she had to keep her hands on the wheel. "What are you saying? Exactly?"

He scratched his head, regretted saying anything. "Look. I can see you're upset…"

"You don't see anything. He's not getting to me. He's getting to them. His girls. His goons. A sudden shedload of character witnesses. The man thinks he can walk on water."

They were outside Annie's pebble-dash semi. Bev turned to face him. "The thing is –"

"Sarge." He tapped his watch. "It's nearly six. If you don't mind, I'd like to get this over with. I've got something on tonight."

She said nothing, released the seat belt, got out, knew her face would be flushed. He'd as good as told her to shut it. Was he right, did he have a point? Byford had as good as told her she was fixated on Hawes; now this. Coming from Ozzie, it was somehow more of a slight.

"Sorry, Sarge, it's just – " He had to lengthen his stride.

"Forget it."

Annie must have seen the car pull up; she was leaning against the door, arms folded across her scrawny chest. "I was just on me way out."

"Nice one, Annie." Bev lifted a foot. "Now try this. It's got bells on."

"I'm goin'– "

"It's February, it's brass monkeys and you're wearing slippers and a T-shirt."

"Smart arse."

Bev smiled, bowed her head. "Got a few questions for you, Annie."

"Know it all anyroad, don't you?"

"Gonna ask us in then?" Bev said. The woman seemed to notice Ozzie for the first time. "This is DC Khan. He's with me." As superfluous remarks go, it was a cracker.

Annie clearly liked what she saw. "Lucky you."

"Much as I'd like to stand here engaged in intellectual banter, we've got work to do."

"Yeah, well, it's not a good time."

"It's never a good time, Annie… "

The rest of the exchange was lost in a bellow from within. "You gonna stand there gassin' all night, woman? Shut the bloody door."

Annie hunched her shoulders in mute apology. Bev took it as an invitation and slipped past. "Quite right too. It's Arctic out here."

The narrow hall was more of an obstacle than ever; a clothes-horse and a bike had joined the general clutter since Bev's last visit. In the gloom, a shin made contact with a pedal and the subsequent trip sent her flying into a load of boxer shorts and babygros. "Remind me to fix you up with a couple of light bulbs, Annie."

"She don't need nothin' from you, cop." The Boy Wonder, all

mouth and muscles, had come to the kitchen door.

"Evening, Steve. Dash of milk and two sugars for me." He moved aside, incredulous not chivalrous. "Close your mouth, son. I can see your tonsils."

He was so intent on Bev he hadn't noticed Ozzie. Then he did. "'ere." He grabbed Ozzie's arm. "We don't want your sort in 'ere."

"My sort?" Ozzie asked softly, barely above a whisper. "Now, what exactly do we mean by that?"

Bev was watching like a hawk. Steve Bell's brain wasn't on the same planet as his brawn. If he was going to lash out, it wouldn't be verbally. Can't be right all the time.

"Coons. Coloureds." He sniffed loudly. "Specially Pakicops."

A tap dripped in the silence. No one moved, then Ozzie looked down at the man's hand, black fingernails still clutching the sleeve of his jacket. He didn't speak, but slowly lifted his glance to Steve Bell's face. Bev felt the hairs rise on the back of her neck. There was a glint in Ozzie's eyes she'd never seen before. She didn't like it. Neither did Bell. He released his grip and strutted back to the table and a half-eaten meal.

Annie was in the doorway, wringing her hands. "Let him have his tea in peace, we can talk out here."

Bev pulled out a chair. "Let's not." She nodded to Oz; they both sat. "I'm sure Steve'll be only too happy to help."

A mouth full of sausage and chips prevented a reply, but judging by the scowl her confidence was misplaced. "Had any more postcards recently?" Bev asked casually.

Annie strode to the sink, filled the kettle. "If that's all you're here for, you've had a wasted journey."

"That's okay. I enjoy the stimulating company." Aiming for casual, she continued, "Anyway, you'll be pleased to hear Vicki's fine." She waited while Annie absorbed that little snippet then threw out something for her to chew on. "Got it from the horse's mouth so to speak: Charlie Hawes told me." The woman's face gave nothing away. Steve's fork was more forthcoming. Bev was sure it had momentarily stopped shovelling food. "Heard of him, have you, Steve?"

He took a swig of lager, swilled it and swallowed before executing a slow shake of the head.

"Shit!" Annie's hands were trembling, which could explain the half a ton of sugar she'd spilled on a surface that already had enough stains for a poor man's Jackson Pollock. Clumsy or calculated? Bev was undecided.

Lover Boy had no doubt. "Clumsy cow."

"Shut it," Ozzie snapped. Bev couldn't have put it better herself. If looks could kill, they'd both be fertiliser. She went to Annie, took the cloth and started clearing the mess. Annie sank into the empty chair, stroking her cheek, which was still red and presumably painful. "I know Vick's fine. I told you that. I don't need no one comin' round here tellin' me what I already know."

"Charlie tell you, did he, Annie?"

"I don't know any Charlies. How many times I got to tell you?"

"Bright idea of his. Getting you to tell me she was in Brighton."

"For fuck's sake. She sent me a soddin' card."

Bev draped the cloth over a tap, looked through the window. Annie wasn't going to budge. She'd lie through her gums to protect herself from Hawes. Going by the state of her face, who could blame her? But who was protecting Vicki? Bev sighed; she was going to keep quiet about the phone call. Telling Annie wouldn't do any good and it could do a bunch of harm.

It was dark outside. Bev could see the tableau behind her reflected in the curtainless window. Steve was mopping up egg yolk with a slice of Mother's Pride. Ozzie was looking on in disbelief if not disgust. Annie had her head in her hands. Bev puzzled, whirled it round in her mind. Something was different but she couldn't place it. She turned round, it was time to get the show on the road. "Tell me about Michelle."

Annie looked up. "Who?"

"Michelle Lucas."

Steve let out a loud burp. "That bird in the paper, you soft cow."

"Oh yeah. The one that got murdered. On the game or somethin'."

"That's right. Tell me about her."

"Look, what is this?" Annie folded her arms. "I seen it in the paper same as everyone else."

"You sure about that? You sure there isn't anything I ought to know?"

She was talking to them both but all she could see of Bell was the back of his head. He'd had it shaved again; it was all pink, like a baby's bum with nappy rash. Did he really think it made him look hard? Or was he getting that from page three of *The Sun* which was now covering his empty plate.

"I seen it in the *Star*," Annie said. "End of story."

"I don't think so." Bev reached into an inside pocket. "Anyway, this story's got pictures." She covered the bimbo's boobs with the photograph: Vicki and Michelle. "Now think again, Annie. What is it you're not sharing with me?"

Bev gave the woman credit for thinking on her feet. "That don't prove nothin'. Vicki's got loads of mates. Don't mean I know 'em. She never brings nobody back here."

She also awarded Annie marks for major porkies. "That's not true, though, is it? Vicki didn't have to bring her back here. Michelle was living here when that was taken."

"You're mad, you are. I've never seen her before in my life."

Bad move. Hyperbole.

"How about that then, Annie? Ever seen that before?" She was pointing to the tree and she didn't wait for an answer. "Only every time you look out of the bloody kitchen window."

"Shove those in, Oz."

Ozzie curled his lip, lifted a pound of Lincolnshire pork

sausages and dropped them in Bev's trolley. They joined half a dozen deep-pan pizzas, a mega pack of frozen chips and enough burgers to stock a chest freezer.

"Your food's not fast. It's supersonic," he said.

She shrugged. "Unlike some, I don't have a doting mother and a million adoring sisters catering to my every whim."

"I do my share," he protested.

"Yeah, well, I do it all. And when I get home late, the last thing I want is to go prancing round in a pinny, rustling up a bit of haute cuisine."

"Please yourself."

She took a Black Forest gâteau from the freezer cabinet and gave him a sweet smile. "I do."

He shook his head. "You'll get fat."

"Not me, mate. Run it off, I do. I'm like a streak of lightning in the mornings. People stare in awe as I flash past all of a blur."

He wasn't impressed. Not surprising really. It didn't convince her. Tomorrow's run would be her first for weeks. Even now she was half hoping Frankie would cry off.

"Told you this'd be a good time to come, didn't I?" She reached across for a family pack of Neapolitan.

"There's never a good time for Tesco."

He was wrong there, even a couple of check-outs were empty. She made for the nearest.

"Yeah, well, my bread bin thinks I've emigrated. Still, it was good of you to keep me company. You're off out tonight, aren't you?" She was fishing but he wasn't biting.

He nodded, started unloading. "We hadn't finished, had we?"

She was puzzled for a moment, then remembered. "Ah! The Annie Flinn book of fairy tales."

"Our Annie wouldn't have it, would she? Not till you caught her out." He gestured for her to explain. "It was pitch black when we got there. How did you know there was a tree out back?"

She winked. "Lucky guess. Worked, though, didn't it?" Faced

with the irrefutable, Annie had no option but to come clean. Michelle had stayed with them for about three months. It had slipped her mind, she claimed. The girl was hardly ever there, always out or in her room. And anyway, it was ages ago. Couldn't remember why she left; some business over a bloke. Good riddance to bad rubbish as far as Annie was concerned. As for the figure in the background, looked more like a dab of grease to her.

Ozzie gave a low whistle. "You've got a nerve."

"Yeah. Not sure how far it takes us, though."

"Well, we now know truth is a difficult concept for Annie and that animal." Ozzie was holding the sausages: somewhat apt in the thought-association stakes.

"Bell was out of order. I thought you were gonna land one on him."

Ozzie sniffed. "Water off a duck's back, that in-your-face stuff."

He opened his mouth to go on, then thought better of it. She prompted. "As opposed to?"

He shook his head. "Doesn't matter."

As opposed to the racist literature in your locker, Paki-gags in the canteen, shit through the letterbox and faceless taunts on the phone. A cocky little thug like Bell wasn't the only sick git in need of treatment. Still, a few tests might help. "Run a check on him in the morning, Oz."

It was near freezing outside. She looked up. The sky was like black velvet with a sprinkling of silver glitter. No tea-cosy effect tonight; it was going to be pretty parky.

"I'll get a bus if you don't mind, Sarge. I'm running a bit late."

"Sure you don't want a lift?"

"No, my sister's just up the road from here. I'm babysitting." He flung a Blues scarf over his shoulder. "You got anything on?"

She was joining the girls soon, so long johns and a thermal vest if she had any sense. The guv had wanted her to knock it on the head. He couldn't see any mileage in it now they had

Charlie – if not in custody – at least on tap. Bev had stood firm; this was about the girls now. If they had the goods on Charlie – she'd be doing her best to get them to share. More than that. She'd told them she'd keep an eye on them and she would. She smiled picturing Jules and Patty and the others. "Same as you, really, Oz. Spot of babyminding."

29

"How'd you get into this lark, then, Jules?" Bev stamped her feet, puffed out a plume of white breath, wished it was smoke. She didn't have any baccies but reckoned she was the only girl in town with a thermos of Earl Grey down her waistband. The tea was to ward off the cold and the flask to warn off the fruitcakes: whipped out fast it would turn into a mean blunt instrument. Not that anyone was about. She'd seen more life in a cemetery.

"Took exams, dint I?"

"Yeah, yeah." Bev rolled her eyes and snuggled into the knee length fun fur, courtesy of Frankie. The fuchsia clashed something awful with Jules's aubergine pageboy.

"Well, don't ask dumb questions. I walked out the front door, opened me legs and put me hand out." She rubbed her thumb against her fingers and winked a kohl-rimmed eye. The girl made it sound natural, like a rite of passage.

Bev sighed to herself; from where she stood it was dehumanising, dangerous and could be deadly. "There's got to be easier ways of making a few bob."

"Who's talkin' a few bob? Know how much I make on a good night?"

Bev turned her mouth down. "Couple a hundred? Three?"

"Yeah, and that's for starters. Anythin' a bit kinky and you're talkin' twice that."

Bev recalled the grimy tenners stashed in Michelle's shoe: definitely nothing good about that night. "Don't you ever get scared?"

"Don't you ever shut up?"

She lifted her hands. "I'm curious, that's all."

Neither spoke for a while. Jules perked up when a Range Rover turned into the road but it cruised past. Bev noted the number anyway. A scruffy Jack Russell cross trotted along the pavement and christened the nearest lamp post before disappearing through the park railings. "Busy here, isn't it?" she mused.

"What you expect after the demos? Bloody do-gooders." Jules sniffed. "Ain't done me no naffin' good."

The protests had been suspended till the weekend but it looked as if the punters had been scared off anyway. So had Patty and co. Apart from Big Val, who was doing a bit of business, Jules was the only girl on the street.

"That geezer who picked up Val? Regular, is he?"

Jules nodded. "Yeah. Calls himself Sonny. He rings her up so's she knows to wear her Cher gear. She has to stand by that gatepost in her fuck-me shoes and a couple a bin liners: white."

Bev frowned. Jules shrugged. Silence reigned.

"I was scared once." There was something in the girl's voice that made Bev turn. Take away the slap and the silly hair, and Jules was just a skinny kid; sixteen at most. She should be at home watching the box, playing CDs or down the youth club having a giggle. "Not the first time." Jules was staring straight ahead. "With the first one, I was so pissed, he could have had two heads. He was all right as it happens. Hands me the cash and says, 'You shouldn't be doing this, love.' Give me a bit extra, so I'd go home."

"And did you?"

"I did actually. Then I needed the readies for somethin' else. Carn even remember what, now."

"Couldn't you have asked your mum?"

She threw her head back, laughed out loud. "You're kiddin', ain't you? It was 'er idea in the first place."

A tracksuited jogger ran down the pavement on the other side of the road. They watched till he turned the corner. "Mad or what?" Bev asked. It was so cold, frosted net curtains had formed on a couple of parked cars.

"He's harmless. Never gives you any grief. Not like most o' the miserable sods round 'ere. Spit at you, some of 'em." She jammed her hands in her coat pockets. "I always think the geezer what cut me was mad. You know. Mental."

"Yeah?"

"Only young, he was. Mind, I reckon they're the worst. They get what they're after then don't want to put their hand in their pocket. Always get the money first, Bev. Best tip I ever had."

"Right." She nodded sagely before remembering she was here to keep an eye on the girls not boost her bank balance.

"Yeah. This nutter had a blade. Cut me tits he did, then dumped me down some poxy country lane. Me own fault. Shouldn't have got in the car. 'Nother tip: never get in a motor with a strange john."

Bev felt she should be making notes in case there were questions later.

The girl pulled a pack of Embassy from her pocket, lit one and took a deep drag. Bev was relieved not to have been offered.

"In them days, I never looked a punter in the face. You have to, though. You can always tell by the eyes. It's true what they say. You get a sixth sense. And watch out for the good lookin' geezers. Cocky sods. Reckon they're doin' you a favour." She stifled a giggle. "There's one bloke so full of himself he reckons Patty ought to pay 'im. Says she owes 'im a fortune."

"What about when you leave school?"

"What? You mean..." She put on a posh voice that didn't quite fit. "When you gonna get a proper job?" She sniffed loudly. "Everyone asks that."

"Okay. When are you?"

She jabbed the air with her cigarette. "Listen, darlin'. My sister, Mand. She's eighteen. She works in an 'airdressers five days a week. Brings home fifty-five quid. I make twice that in an hour – and I ain't on me feet all day."

The attraction was obvious: city streets paved with punters' gold. The hidden costs seemed a high price for the easy money.

The girl missed nothing. "It's all right for you, innit?" She took another drag, let the smoke drift down her nostrils. "Bet you've got A-levels comin' out your arse. Bet you're a real daddy's girl. And I bet your ma ain't on the game."

The thought of Emmy Morriss playing anything more strenuous than a game of Scrabble almost brought on a coughing fit. But the poor little poor girl act was bollocks. It was as unattractive as it was unconvincing and needed knocking on the head. "Do me a favour, Jules. You'll be telling me next you live in a cardboard box in the middle of the road."

Jules tossed her head back with a furious "Fuck you."

"Well, come on." Bev was extricating the thermos. "Loads of kids have it tough; doesn't mean they all turn tricks."

Jules's flush almost matched her hair colour and her eyes flashed as she stamped an ankle-booted foot. "Yeah, well. Let's just say I... I..." She struggled to find the right words, then flung them out defiantly. "Let's just say I like it!" She raked her fingers through her hair. "And that's another thing all you nosy cows want to know: what's the sex like? Well, I'll tell you. The only diff between me havin' a quick shag and you havin' it off on a one-night stand is I get paid for it."

Bev said nothing: what could she say? She poured tea into the flask top, lifted it to her lips. She could have mentioned AIDS, unwanted kids, broken bones, but it was nothing the girl hadn't heard a million times before.

Jules took a final drag and flicked the cigarette over the road. "Birds like you'll never understand."

They both watched as the red end glowed then faded into the dark. Bev tried not to think of Shell's young life snuffed out too soon. She sighed. "You're selling yourself short, love."

"Oh yeah?" Jules grabbed the cup and gave a filthy laugh. "How do you know?"

Bev smiled, shook her head, then sprang back as Jules spat

out the tea.

"What the 'ell's this muck?"

"Earl Grey."

"You forgot the soddin' milk. It's like gnat's piss."

"It's not –" Bev got no further. She watched, open-mouthed, as Jules's hand shot down her knickers. A hip flask had never been so aptly named. The girl took a slug, wiped her mouth with her fingers. "Val give it me. Bit of Dutch courage." She lifted it to her lips again, winked at Bev. Shame you're on duty."

Bev snatched it away. "Shame you're under age."

"What for?"

They burst out laughing.

"Glad someone's happy in their work." They turned at the sound of Val's voice. She'd ditched the bin liners but still sported a Cher wig, and was tottering gingerly towards them on a pair of red stilettoes that put new meaning into hell for leather. Bev looked down smugly; thank God pumps had made a comeback.

"Me soddin' feet are killin' me." The big woman relieved Bev of the Scotch. "I wouldn't care but I have to sing *I Got You Babe* these days before he can get it up."

Jules sniffed. "Tell him to sod off."

"You're jokin'." Val fanned a fistful of notes. "I'm all right till the weekend now."

"Did you get anything out of him?" Bev asked.

Val's eyebrows met in the middle. "Oh! I see what you mean. Nah. He never had owt to do with Shell. He keeps away from the kids. Prefers his women with a few miles on the clock."

"Old bangers, you mean?" Jules asked, all innocence.

"Cheeky cow."

Bev joined the laughter and tried to keep it going, even though she'd just spotted something that wasn't funny. She looked again, screwing up her eyes. It could have been a trick of the light; except there was no light. There was something, someone, in the park. She kept her voice casual; alerting Jules and Val would be tantamount to putting it on Tannoy. "I'm just going to take a turn down the road. Stay together while I'm gone, right?"

"What's up, Bev? Need a pee?" Jules grinned.

"Something like that."

"Should've brought a bottle, chuck. You never get caught short, that way."

"She's got a flask, Val. Mind, I reckon it's full already."

Bev shoved the thermos back in her waistband and headed down the road. She'd recced the boundary earlier and as far as she could tell there was no gap. Soon as she was out of sight, she'd be going over the top. And given the height of the railings and the length of her skirt that was exactly what she'd be doing. Needs must when the devil blah-de-blah.

It wasn't the most elegant of sights: good job there was no one around. The landing was a tad more graceful. She stood and waited for a few seconds, listening; just listening. The muffled hum of traffic from the High Street was a constant, but apart from her own breathing, that was about it. Her eyes were used to the gloom now, and she scanned her surroundings. She was heading for a massive oak off to the left. It was her marker for whatever it was she'd seen. It had only been a blip on the edge of her vision, but it shouldn't have been there. The park was in near-darkness – and trees don't move.

An owl hooted overhead and she jumped. The need for back-up flashed through her mind, but only amid a jumble of thoughts. Uppermost was a picture of herself, Charlie Hawes and a pair of cuffs. She shook her head; stupid and not true. There was no point calling in a load of plods till she'd got a better handle on what was going on. Anyway, it was just as likely to be the neighbourhood flasher or a saddo gawping at Jules and Val. What's more, approaching from behind would give her the element of surprise. If it began to look iffy, she'd keep back, maintain surveillance and summon the troops.

She was inching forward, senses on full alert, when she heard it. A rustle. Ground level. Not far. She gently eased the flask out. Another scurrying. Even closer. She pressed herself against a tree: moss, slimy under her fingers. She strained her ears till she could hear her own pulse. It was there again. She widened her eyes. Shit a masonry block. It was a huge great rat. It was two sodding rats.

The hiss she emitted was loud enough for the rodents to think catfood, but not so loud as to alarm the two-legged variety.

She moved on slowly, soundlessly. The oak was in spitting distance. She waited, watched, listened. There was no movement; no sound. Then she saw it. A card. Pinned to the tree like a mini wanted poster. She held back, silently counted to sixty. She tightened her grasp on the flask, edged forward, looked closer. He must have been doing this when she'd glimpsed him from the street. She didn't need to take it down; it was easy to read. She didn't recognise the handwriting and there was no name, but she'd have staked her life on knowing who it was from. She read it again: *Wish you were here.* It was a postcard from Brighton.

Her heart hammered, palms damp despite the cold. She had to get back to the girls, but first she needed a minute to calm down. She took a deep breath, gave it thought. It was Hawes. It had to be. The bastard had been watching her, goading her. There'd be no prints, nothing to nail him, but this was a follow-up to his crack that afternoon in Interview One. It was a threat, and it wasn't even veiled. She gritted her teeth; a habit she thought she'd lost. They'd had to let the shit go, of course. His statement checked out.

She looked round carefully. Without knowing why, she was certain he'd gone. Equally sure the girls were safe. She'd been the target tonight, and she'd walked straight into his sights. It was a game of cat-and-mouse and she'd just played Jerry.

She glanced at the card again. She'd bag it later, maybe send a SOCO in the morning, but Hawes would be water-walking till hell froze over.

She sighed; best get back. Flask in knickers, she retraced her steps. The climb was easier this time round; she had a leg-up from a handy tree. As she rounded the bend, she spotted the girls.

Sweet Jesus. They weren't alone.

For a second, she thought it was Hawes, but this man was big; way too big. Oh, my God. Hawes had sent a heavy. She cursed her stupidity. She'd been duped by the side-show in the park. She broke into a run; saw him lift his arm. What the —?

Hold on. Val was doing the same. Now Jules. Bev slowed, tried to catch her breath. It was a round of high-fives.

"There you are. Where you been?" Jules asked.

"You all right, chuck? You look as if you've seen a ghost."

The heavy breathing prevented more than a slim smile and a gasped, "Never better, Val."

Now she was nearer, it was obvious the bloke wasn't Charlie Hawes. Christ, he was black for one thing.

"That's good." Val handed her the hip flask anyway.

Bev took the booze without thinking. "Why's that?"

"This gentleman here is asking for you."

The flask halted halfway to her lips. Bev studied him a little closer. "Really? What can I do for you, Mr..?"

Val nudged Bev's elbow. "It's more a question of what you can do for him, Bev."

The big woman's wink was superfluous. Bev swigged deep. She just stopped herself stammering, "Come again?" opted instead for, "How d'you mean?"

The man's broad smile would have lit a black hole, but he wasn't so hot on the verbals.

Jules was. "He wants a shag," she explained.

"Yeah, he clocked you just before you went walkies," Val said. "He liked the look of your ass, so he hung on."

Bev had another swig. "How nice."

"'Ow much you charge, little lady?"

Little lady? She'd have had another drink but she was driving. She reckoned the aggro in the park had gone to her head 'cause she surely wasn't thinking on her feet. "Well, actually, Mr… er…"

"I'm a bit short on cash, right now. I was wonderin' whether American Express..?"

The man was so incredibly polite, Bev almost agreed. Almost. She narrowed her eyes.

Jules had her head down and was clutching her sides. Val had her legs crossed in the fight to keep her face straight. The face lost. Bev watched as she wiped the tears from her cheeks. Jules was doubled up now. "I'm wettin' me knickers here. And it's your soddin' fault."

"My fault?" Bev was all righteous indignation. "That's good, that is."

"Not a patch on Banjo, though," Val crowed.

"Banjo?"

"Bev." Val slipped an arm round the man's waist. "Meet Banjo. Banjo Hay. He's my mate."

Bev held out a hand and Banjo beamed. "It's been a pleasure."

Val winked again. "Not yet it ain't."

Bev opened her mouth to remonstrate but Val was still revelling in the set-up she'd staged.

"Hate to break up the party," Banjo said, "but I gotta split."

Bev glanced at her watch. It was almost eleven, she had an early start and she had a gut feeling that Hawes wouldn't be back tonight.

"I'm gonna call it a day as well. Fancy a lift, you pair?"

"Banjo's droppin' me, aren't you, chuck?"

It looked like news to Banjo, and it was a bummer for Bev; she'd wanted to press Val about Charlie Hawes and the Brighton line. It would have to wait. "Jules? How 'bout you?"

The girl hid a yawn behind her hand. "The night is young. Anyway, it's chuckin' out time soon. Should make a bob or two then."

Bev shivered, felt someone walk over her grave, realised it was the prospect of some cheesy knee-trembler between Jules and a dirty old man with beery breath and clammy flesh. It shouldn't be happening. Not to any kid. Any night. Anywhere. "We could go via the chippie?"

The girl's face lit up. "You buyin'?"

"You bet."

"You're on."

She could murder Jules. She'd had Bev in stitches with her take on Val's version of *I Got You Babe*, but now she couldn't get the damn tune out of her head. It was half an hour since she'd dropped the girl at a run-down tower block on the wrong side of Edgbaston. If Jules had sung it once, she'd sung it half a dozen times, and now even Bev was doing a Cher in the bathroom mirror. It wasn't as though there weren't other thoughts churning round in the grey matter. The postcard, for instance. Bev had nipped back for it while Jules waited in the MG. It was bagged and tagged and ready to go, but she'd bet a pound to a penny it wouldn't take the case any further.

It wasn't just the card. There was something bugging her. It had been niggling away even before she went on the patch; lurking at the back of her mind. It would come tantalisingly close then dart away before taking shape. It might have been something she'd seen. It could just as easily have been a word or a phrase. It was getting to her, almost as much as that sodding tune.

"Sleep on it, our Bev." That's what her mum would say. It was Emmy Morriss's answer to everything. That, and a nice cup of char. Bev brushed her teeth, still tasted salt and vinegar, brushed again. "Dar-da-dar-da…" She tightened her mouth, grabbed a hot water bottle and flushed the loo. She checked the answer phone for the umpteenth time then reset the alarm.

Her running gear was laid out ready for the morning; she'd rescued it from the back of the wardrobe when she'd dropped off the Tesco goodies earlier.

Sometimes the place seemed more like a hotel, though the room service wasn't up to much. The laundry basket was overflowing in one corner and the shoe tidy wasn't living up to its name in another. She ignored both and, full of good intentions, headed for the cheval glass. Head on one side and hands on hips, she took an appraising look. The black silk jimmies added a certain oriental touch. She wondered if she could get away with them in class: decided they were more Bruce Lee than Tai Chi. Still, what the hell? There was no one around. Might even make her feel virtuous. She stood, eyes closed, feet apart, knees bent, resting her palms gently on the front of her thighs. She took a deep breath, tried focusing on her Chi then thought: sod it, can't be arsed.

She flung the duvet back, making a conscious effort to stifle yet another saccharine rendering of *I Got You Babe.* "Babe! Of course!" She perched on the side of the bed, ran the scene at the Flinn place through her head again. That was it. There'd been no sign of the baby. Lucie could have been asleep upstairs. But Annie hadn't even mentioned her. There were no bottles, no bibs over the radiator; none of the paraphernalia that had cluttered the kitchen on her earlier visit.

Where was Lucie? What did it mean? Bev had no idea. Yet. Just a feeling that it was important and a conviction that she had to find out.

30

Bev poked her head gingerly out of her front door. It was 6.30am and one degree above freezing. As if that wasn't bad enough, Mavis Holdsworth was out with her broom, giving the communal balcony a good going over. That's all I need, thought Bev, a nosy neighbour with altruistic insomnia. The idea of a dawn run was already losing what little attraction it had ever had, without a biting commentary from a woman whose idea of exercise was chewing gum.

"There y'are, our Bev." Mavis leaned on the broom handle. "Thought you'd be up with the worms."

"Larks."

"Yeah, them an' all."

Bev refused to ask how she'd acquired the insight; Mave would spill the beans anyway.

"I dropped your washing in last night. Saw you'd dragged the joggin' gear out of retirement."

There were advantages to leaving a spare key with a neighbour. Bev just couldn't think of one at the moment. "How's that mate of yours? Rita, is it? I haven't had a chance to have a word."

Mave sniffed. "You're too late. She's done a bunk."

"Oh?" Bev tried not to sound too relieved.

"Yeah. Phoned me up. Full of herself, she was. She's back on the game."

"What?"

Mave tapped the side of her nose. "Dark horse, that one, Bev. Never opened her mouth the whole time we work together, then she gives me a bell and I can't get a word in edgeways."

"That'd be a first."

Mave ignored the remark. "Knocked it on the 'ead, she said, when she got spliced, but the old man was goin' out every night, comin' back with a skinful, claimin' 'is conjugals and knockin' 'er about. Said she was back on the streets. Whorin' was a damn sight better paid."

"Licensed prostitution."

"You what?"

"Marriage."

Mave still looked blank.

"It's how some people see marriage," Bev said. "Licensed prostitution." She looked at Mave's uncomprehending features and shook her head. "Never mind. Anyway, I'll cross Rita off my list of things to do."

"Just as well, isn't it?"

Bev had turned to go but there was something in Mave's voice. "Why's that, then?"

"This new fella of yours." Mave leaned the broom against the wall, took a butt end from behind an ear and a box of matches from an overall pocket. "Kept quiet about 'im, didn't you?"

"New fella?"

"Yeah. He was round last night."

"Last night?"

"Is there an echo out 'ere?"

"What are you saying, Mave?"

She watched as concern replaced laughter and Mave put a hand to her mouth. "You 'aven't got a new bloke, 'ave you?"

Bev shook her head.

"'e was in your place. Said you wanted 'im to pick up a few things."

"What things?"

"I didn't like to ask."

"Since when?" Bev ran a few thoughts. "What time are we talking here, Mave?"

"Bout 'alf eight. 'E had a key. Knew 'is way round."

Bev pursed her lips. She'd have to go back in. She hadn't noticed anything odd; nothing obvious had been taken or deposited. Mind, given her housekeeping skills, the place usually looked as if it had been done over.

"I'm ever so sorry, Bev. I never thought, not with the flowers like. I mean, your bog-standard burglar doesn't usually come armed with a bouquet, does he?"

Bev tried to think, to picture. She couldn't recall seeing so much as a weed in the flat. "What did this bloke look like?" she pressed.

"Well that's why I thought you 'adn't said anythin'. I mean, 'e's not exactly your usual type, is 'e?"

Bev put her hand on her hips. "Enlighten me, Mave. What type are we talking here?"

Mavis finally lit her fag. "I just thought 'e was a bit young for you. That's all."

"And that's it? A young bloke with a bunch of flowers."

"And the 'air." Hollows appeared in Mave's cheeks as she took a drag. "I don't like deadlocks even on black blokes."

"Dreadlocks, Mave. Dreadlocks." Bev frowned. "So he was white?"

"As you and me."

Bev glanced at her watch. "Look, I'm doing this run if it kills me." Mave rolled her eyes. "When Frankie turns up, keep her talking. I'm just nipping back for a second. While I'm gone, have a think about last night. What time did he leave? Was he carrying anything else? Would you know him again? Remember everything you can. Close your eyes and imagine the whole scene as it happened."

"You could get me hypnotised," Mave offered eagerly.

"Lobotomised," muttered Bev.

"Pardon?"

"Nothing."

She considered doing the James Bond bit: back pressed against the wall, slow slide round the door and lightning-fast drop into the firing position. Then she thought again: a mobile phone wasn't particularly quick on the draw, and hardly likely to scare anyone.

More to the point, it was too late, far too late. Whoever had been in could have returned while she was asleep. She'd been dead to the world. Bad choice of phrase, Bev. It was true though. He could have come back and made it a permanent lying in state. So why hadn't he?

It was one of a stack of thoughts doing the rounds in her head as she checked the place over. The TV and vid hadn't been touched: literally. She'd have spotted prints a mile off in the dust. Her camera was still on the sideboard, she'd made a mental note last night because she'd need it for Frankie's gig on Saturday. As for her hundred quid emergency money, she'd hidden it so well, she hadn't a clue where it was.

It all appeared as she'd left it; nothing gained, nothing gone. In a weird way, that made it worse. Some bastard had been in here, invading her space, and she hadn't sensed a thing. Her only gut feeling last night had been a touch of heartburn cause she'd pigged out on fish and chips. So much for the famous Morriss intuition.

And where were the flowers? The only thing green and growing was a distinctly jaded Christmas cactus, skulking in a corner of the sitting room.

She searched the kitchen bin, glanced round, chewing her bottom lip. She didn't like it; didn't like it at all. Some lying toe-rag had smooth-talked his way around and presumably had a good nose. But why? If Mave hadn't opened her mouth, Bev would be none the wiser. So what was his game?

She shivered; tried telling herself it was cold, but it was more than that. It was a bit late in the day, but she was feeling spooked. She'd counselled Christ knew how many burglary victims in her time; now she knew what they meant. It wasn't that belongings were nicked, it was that a stranger had been prowling round.

Her gaze fell on the evidence bag. She moved closer, folded her arms. Charlie Hawes. Was it down to him? Was he trying to pull her strings? Not content with putting the wind up her in the park, had he organised a welcome-home party as well? She considered the timing. He could have done it himself; more likely he'd sent a gorilla to say it with flowers. So where were they?

No, no, no. She saw it now. They were a floral smokescreen for Mave's benefit. Worked a treat, hadn't it? The way Bev saw it, the flowers were never going to be left; the idea was to scare her shitless. She snorted; sod that. She squared her shoulders, made for the door. And stopped.

Think again, bird brain. How the hell could he have known that Mave was going to be around? Maybe the flowers were a prop, but as it turned out, he didn't need to leave them – mouthy Mave would get the message across better than a host of daffodils.

Bev pulled a face; she needed more time to think it through but Frankie had arrived a couple of mins back, and was clearly on good form going by Mave's cackles.

She took a last look round then dashed into the bedroom to grab some lip balm. She'd half-turned when it caught her eye. She did a double take. That was odd. She always left it in her bag; certainly couldn't recall taking it out last night. She flipped it over, took a steadying breath. Looking on the bright side, it was one less mystery to solve. She now knew where her stolen ID was.

It was less clear why the thief had cut out her eyes.

The cold was making Bev's eyes water: the cold and chilling thoughts about unlooked-for eye surgery. She ran harder; she'd soon warm up. She hadn't said anything to Frankie, didn't want her to fret. As for Mave, Bev would buttonhole her after the run. If she made it. She was puffing like an asthmatic whale. As for Frankie – the girl who was supposed to be recovering from injury – she was setting a cracking pace.

"What was all that about then, Bev?"

Bev aimed for casual. "I had a gentleman caller last night."

"Lucky you. Left a box of Milk Tray, did he?"

"You watch too much telly."

They ran in silence for a while, for which Bev was truly grateful. She concentrated on the run. It was amazing how the old fitness levels plummeted when you broke the exercise routine. Now that she was just about hitting her stride, she realised that in a masochistic sort of way she'd actually missed it.

The streets were deserted at this time in the morning, apart from a couple of milk floats and the occasional 35 bus. The red-brick houses had that sleepy appearance of dimmed lights behind drawn curtains. She caught the odd blast of John Humphrys drifting out of a window or two, Radio WM out of a few more. "Nothing changes, does it, Frankie?"

"How do you mean?"

"It's, what, nearly a month since the last run? But everything carries on as per usual." She pointed at a house coming up on the left. "They'll have breakfast telly on. We'll get a whiff of bacon from number 12 and any minute now, you'll get a whistle from Wolfie."

They didn't know his name but the guy at 17 left for work at the same time every morning. He invariably waited till they were a few doors along, but the two-tone greeting never altered.

"There you go." A few seconds later, he sailed past in a beat-up Beetle. Bev gave an ostentatious wave. "I rest my case."

"Creatures of habit, Bev. We all are. You should know that." Frankie slowed the pace. They were approaching the park and needed to cross the road.

"Sure we all have routines. But..."

The train of thought was lost as she waited while Frankie negotiated the narrow iron gate. The vast open space of Highbury Park was nothing like its gloomy dense equivalent at the back of Thread Street but Bev still found herself fighting flashbacks. Good job Frankie was alongside.

"Wolfie was a bit tardy this morning, anyway, Bevvie."

"Oh?"

"Yeah, we were late leaving your place. And you changed the subject brilliantly. You still haven't told me what was going on. Who exactly is Milk Tray man? And has he got a mate I can have?"

God forbid, thought Bev. "He didn't exactly leave a calling card, Frankie."

"Mave must have known him, surely?"

"Mystic Mave? 'Fraid not."

They ran past one of the park's regulars, an elderly woman with an adolescent Dalmatian. Bev was relieved to see the dog was on a lead. It had taken quite a shine to her in the past.

"This secret admirer of yours, then, Bev, what was he up to in your pad?"

She banished the new-look ID to the back of her mind. "Mave said he was dropping off flowers."

"Cool. Last man who gave me flowers was my dad. And that was only 'cause I was in hospital."

Hospital. The General. Waxen white lilies. And Cassie Swain. Bev pulled up sharp.

"What's up, my friend?" Frankie asked. "You got a stitch?"

"You all right, Sarge?" Ozzie had joined her in the breakfast queue. The canteen was chocka; even the air was thick with hot fat and singed toast. But Bev's three-mile run merited more than a bowl of Mave's warm porridge. Not that the offer hadn't been fulsome. Probably trying to bring the colour to Bev's cheeks. She'd felt it drain when Mave confirmed that Dreadlock

Man had been armed with white lilies. That and the fact that he had nice teeth was the sum of Mavis's wisdom on the intruder front. Another stunning success for her own personal Neighbourhood Watch.

Bev reached for a pat or four of butter and flashed Ozzie a smile. "I'm starving."

"I can see that."

She mentioned the run, then touched on the break-in. She kept it light but Ozzie's face dropped. "Jeez, Sarge, you should get the locks changed. Pronto."

She slammed her forehead with a palm. "Coo! Wish I'd thought of that." She rolled her eyes. "Course I'm getting them changed. There's a bloke sorting it now."

He ran a finger along his jawline. "Any idea who it could have been?"

Byford had asked the same question twenty minutes earlier. She'd had to mention Hawes, of course, but she'd held back and hedged. If the guv thought Hawes was going after her, he'd put the kibosh on the undercover stuff. Anyway, as Bev saw it, the closer Hawes got, the easier he was to collar. She gave Ozzie a similarly potted version as they shuffled along the counter, then changed tack. "Is that all you're having?"

He looked from his slice of toast and marmite to Bev's heaving plate. "I'm okay. Anyway, if I change my mind, there's enough there for two."

She drew herself up to her full height. "This is fuel, Ozzie. The body's a temple."

"Way you eat, it's a listed building."

"All right, our Bev?" Doreen on cash desk interrupted, saving Ozzie's life. Her eyes, like sultanas in a Peshawar naan, peered at Bev. "You look a bit peaky." She totted up sausages, eggs, tomatoes, beans and double fried slice. "Still, nowt wrong with your appetite, is there?"

Bev thought this a bit thick coming from a woman who wore

skirts you could camp in.

"'ave you done your limerick yet?" Doreen asked.

Bev pocketed the change, shaking her head. She'd forgotten Vince's venture into the literary world.

Doreen ploughed on. "They've got to be in by tomorrow. 'e's got a stack already."

"What's the prize?" Ozzie asked.

Doreen tapped the side of her nose. "It's a secret."

"Knowing Vince, it'll be edible." Bev looked round, then made for a table by the window. She nodded at Gary Kent, who was just leaving.

"If I were the boss," she told Ozzie, "I'd make him take time off. He looks as if he hasn't slept in a month."

He shrugged. "Coming in is his way of coping. I suppose the routine's important to him just now."

"Talking 'bout routine, have you run a check on Steve Bell yet?"

"First thing. Should hear back any time."

She nodded. They ate in silence. Bev ran through a mental list of things to do. She'd already checked with the General. There'd been no visitors for Cassie, or further floral tributes. Highest priority now was Lucie. Last night's conviction had not lessened. She glanced at Ozzie, who was stifling a yawn. "How was the babysitting?"

"Apart from being up half the night, it was brilliant." His eyes crinkled into a warm smile. "I'm now not only Number One Uncle but also the world's greatest living authority on Thomas the Tank Engine."

"I'm well impressed," she said. He was glowing with pride, you could hear it in the voice. She'd bet he was brilliant with kids. There weren't many blokes who'd show you that side of their character. She was trying to remember the last time someone had gone all gooey on her over a baby. She narrowed her eyes. Oh, shit.

"You all right, Sarge?" Oz's face was creased in concern.

She raked her fingers through her hair. "I should have seen it before."

"Seen what? What are you on about?"

She was still thinking it through. "How could I have been so blind?"

The chair tipped as she sprang to her feet. "Cover my back. I can't make the briefing."

"Where are you going?" Oz asked.

"To get some answers."

"You got built-in radar, Annie?"

"What the fuck's that supposed to mean?"

Bev leaned against the door jamb. "Just that every time I show my face round here, you're on your way out. Thought you might have a little device that tells you when I'm coming."

Bev watched the emotions flicker across Annie Flinn's face; her voice had none.

"Thought you were the cab."

"Yes. I bet you did." This time the woman's departure was more than wishful thinking. Annie Flinn was wearing full slap and a half-decent coat. Bev had little interest in what was on her back but a lot on what was in her hand. "What's with the suitcase, Annie?"

"I'm getting away for a few days."

Bev shook her head slowly. "No, you're not. Not till you've answered a few questions."

The woman tried closing the door but a size seven DM was in the way. Bev followed through with a firm hand on the peeling paintwork. They were so close she could smell lemon shampoo and see where Annie had missed a bit with the make-up.

"I'll give you a lift," she offered. "When we've had a little chat."

"I've got nothing to say."

"Fine by me. I'll do the talking." She pushed the door further open. "After you."

Annie shrugged her shoulders, trailed down the hall. The narrow passageway was just as gloomy but at least it wasn't full of junk. Bev's soles stuck on the grimy brown lino but a bit of oil was preferable to another whack on the shin. "Where you off to, then, Annie?"

The woman dumped the suitcase on the kitchen table, then walked to the sink. Bev hated talking to people's backs. Not that this one was saying anything. "Come on, Annie. Where are you going?"

A tap dripped and the fridge hummed. There was a stale emptiness about the place: old smoke and ancient cooking smells. She tried a new topic. "Where's Lucie?"

Annie's hand shook as she filled a glass from the tap and lifted it to her mouth. Bev waited till she finished drinking, then waited some more. It eventually became clear that an answer wasn't imminent. The woman had her hands on the edge of the sink and was staring through the window. Bev took a deep breath. "Okay, then. Where's lover boy?"

Not a murmur, not a movement. So that was the game. Keep your trap shut so you don't fall into one. Bev would have preferred a slanging match; silence was infinitely harder to play with. She let it hang for a while, then moved closer and laid a hand on Annie's bony shoulder. "Where's Lucie?"

Annie shook it off irritably, turned away.

"I know the truth, Annie." Well, a bit of it.

The woman took a crumpled pack of Silk Cut from her pocket, lit one from a gas ring, then resumed her place by the window. Bev tightened her mouth; there was more to all the stonewalling than just being arsey. But Annie's face had already unwittingly confirmed Bev's suspicions. She'd seen it in the woman's eyes; or rather she hadn't. The likeness between Annie and Lucie was missing. Maybe it was there in diluted form but it wasn't the real thing. Not the mirror image that Bev had finally seen. Not the same dark blue eyes. Not the same wide smile. Oz's unbridled delight had prompted the memory of a girl. A girl who'd lied about her mother. And a girl who'd lied about her daughter.

"She's Vicki's, isn't she?"

She didn't need Annie's confirmation. The picture had developed on the drive over. A prostitute getting pregnant? It was an occupational hazard. Look at Jo. Look at Dawn Lucas. Look at the effing statistics.

Annie flicked ash into the sink. Bev had to fight the urge to spin her round, force her to talk. "It's why she's gone AWOL, isn't it? She'll do anything to protect her baby. Where is she, Annie? Who's she with?"

The woman blew a column of smoke rings, watched them drift upwards. Bev unclenched her fists, brought down the volume. "Charlie's got her holed-up, hasn't he? Has he got Lucie as well? I can just about see how you'd stand by and abandon Vicki. Big girl now, isn't she? Made her bed and all that. But a baby? What sort of a woman are you?"

Annie spun round, eyes glaring. "You know sod all. Why don't you just fuck off and leave us alone?"

"I'll leave when I have answers."

"Me sister's lookin' after the bab. I'm not well. I need a break."

Bev lifted her arms, played an imaginary violin.

"It's your bloody fault," Annie screamed. "Police harassment, that's what this is. You're turning me into a nervous wreck."

"Where are you going?"

Annie closed her eyes gave a deep sigh but at least she answered. "Blackpool. Long weekend." She doused the butt end, threw it in the direction of the bin. "Not that it's any of your business."

There was a hammering at the front door. Bev could almost feel the woman's relief.

"That'll be the cab."

"Send it away. I'll take you to the station. When we've finished."

She was back within seconds, which was time enough. The suitcase was no longer on the table. Most of its contents were sprawled across the floor. Annie froze, silhouetted in the door-frame. Bev was kneeling, holding up baby clothes and a soft, pink blanket. "Clumsy cow, aren't I?"

The woman lifted a hand to her gaunt features.

"Can't say I think much of your holiday gear, love."

Annie's eyes were unnaturally bright. "You've no right…"

"Save it!" Bev rose to her feet. "Where were you taking it?"

"Oxfam."

The callousness was like a red rag. "Why not try looking out for your own kid, Annie?"

"That's exactly what I am doing. Now why don't you just bugger off? I don't have to tell you nothing."

Short of thumbscrews or a rack, she was right. A copper's instinct wasn't evidence, and proof of any crime was non-existent. Bev shook her head in disbelief. "How do you look at yourself in the mirror, Annie?"

Just for a second, it looked as if the woman was about to crack. Bev was so focused she barely heard the mobile. She swore under her breath as Annie turned away, then snatched the phone to her ear and barked a peremptory, "What?"

Byford was on the other end. Recognising the voice was no problem. The difficulty was taking in what he was saying. "I want you back. Now. We've got a confession. Both murders."

31

Highgate nick was buzzing with news of a result, the corridors full of high-fives and wide grins. Bev kept her head down, mind open, and made straight for Interview Three. A plod with bulging hair and big biceps was hovering at the door.

"Can't let you in, Sarge. The governor wants him to sweat."

She nodded. "Shove over, Andy. I just want a peep." Jack the Ripper could have been in there, it still wouldn't convince her they had the right man.

Couldn't be, could it? It wasn't Charlie Hawes.

She had to stretch to reach the eye hole. A thin bloke in his forties was perched on the edge of a metal chair. His knees were clamped, fingers cradled in his lap. He looked like a backroom bean-counter: a tad pompous but essentially anonymous. She took in the Burton's suit, the matching shiny grey shoes, the heavy eyebrows, the thin lips and the flecks of grey in the slicked black hair. She almost missed the tiny cross dangling from his left ear. Once spotted, she couldn't take her eyes off it. It was like a silverfish, darting and quivering. There was either a draught in the room or man at Burton's had the wind up him.

"He been charged?" Bev's nose was still on the door.

"Nah. He just walked in off the street. The governor was in with him earlier for an hour or so. Him and DI Powell. Didn't say a dicky bird to me. I'm just here to keep an eye."

"Can't see you having a problem." She turned to face him. "If he's the killer, I'm the Virgin Mary."

"He's a time-waster, guv. Got to be."

Byford's unwavering stare was adding to Bev's unease. She

was standing on the other side of his desk, shuffling her feet. She'd popped her head round the door, fully expecting that by now, Prime Suspect would be Prime Plonker and Byford would be banging on about eliminating yet another moron from the inquiry. It happened all the time. Every big case, every witness appeal, every *Crimewatch* reconstruction, the loonies came out like a rash and were generally let off with a slapped wrist. That was the usual scenario, only this time Byford had summoned her, was using a different script. This time the story appeared to stand up. The man's background was being checked and though the guv wasn't cracking open the Moët, there was a sparkle in his eyes. Bev's only conviction was that they were in danger of being distracted by a futile diversion. She wanted nothing to slow the inquiry.

"Have you spoken to him?" Byford asked, knowing she hadn't.

"No," she admitted, "but — "

"But nothing. Sit down." He took a tape from a drawer. "Keep still. And listen."

Given the tone, it was not the time to argue. "This is what he's told us so far."

She watched as he put the tape in the machine and pressed play. A soft voice, accentless and without inflexion, began to describe the final moments of Michelle Lucas's life. He told them where he'd picked her up, described her clothes and her wounds.

Bev could hear the whoosh of her heartbeat in her ears. She was straining to pick up a nuance, waiting to pounce on the slightest slip. She was trying to marry the narrative with the nerd downstairs. It was too pat, too prepped. It wasn't possible. Was it?

"He could have got it from the papers, guv." She hated the hint of pleading in her voice.

"Keep quiet!" he thundered, face flushed. "Concentrate on the voice."

She screwed up her face, listened less to the words, more to the way they were spoken. There was something familiar. When had she heard it before? Byford was watching, way ahead. It felt like a test but her mind was a blank.

He hit the pause button. "Kenny. Remember him?"

Of course. The nutter on the radio. The studio interview; all that rabble rousing. "And that proves what?"

"On its own, very little."

Obviously more to come. "So?"

"You recognised the voice. Eventually." He took a sip of coffee; he hadn't offered her a cup. "Mike recognised it immediately."

"What are you saying?"

"Kenny," he said, as if the name it had inverted commas, "also happens to be the man who discovered Louella Kent's body on Tuesday night. His real name is Duncan Ferguson. Mike interviewed him at the scene."

Golden Rule Number One: suspect the victim's nearest and dearest. Golden Rule Number Two: suspect the person who found the body. She'd always hated rules. She studied her nails. "He'll be blaming it on voices in his head next."

"He already is."

The attempted nonchalance failed. Her head shot up, eyes wide. "What?"

"He says he's acting under instructions from the devil. Voices tell him what to do. He's scared he'll kill again."

She shook her head and sighed. "Classic."

"For God's sake, Sergeant, he wouldn't be the first nutter to kill a hooker. It doesn't make the girls any less dead."

She felt the first faint stirring of doubt, wouldn't admit it even to herself.

"Come on, guv, if you were so sure you'd have charged him by now."

He banged the desk with his fist. "That's enough."

She'd seen him angrier, but never at her. He leaned across the polished wood, pointed a finger. "You can't accept the killer isn't Charlie Hawes, can you?"

She met his eyes, registered the deep lines and lilac shadows. The media were still giving him a hard time. She felt sorry for him. But not that sorry. "And what about you? Are you so desperate for a collar, you'll take the first one that comes along?"

The silence lasted for ten seconds. She looked away first.

"Get out." Only two words, but the delivery had more impact than a diatribe.

She held her hands out. "I just – "

"Now."

She halted at the door, hated leaving it like this. She had more time for Byford than any cop she'd ever worked with. But it didn't mean he was always right.

"Before you go," he said, "you need to bear two other factors in mind."

She turned, not sure she wanted to hear.

"Ferguson goes on to describe both murder scenes in detail. There's no way he could have picked it up from the press. A lot of it hasn't reached the papers." He paused, obviously wanting her to be quite clear on the point. "And he told us about the money in Michelle's shoe."

She pursed her lips. It could have been an inspired guess; most prostitutes hid their cash.

"And before you add anything," Byford said, "he knows how much and which shoe. And he knows because he says he put it there."

The shock must have shown in her face. However great the temptation, Ferguson could no longer just be written off.

Ozzie was sitting at her desk, scribbling a note. Bev plonked down a steaming cup of coffee and folded her arms. "You might be fast track but no one gets promoted that quick."

Ozzie glanced up and grinned, saw her face and shot up smartish. She flopped into the chair, stretched her legs. "Checking it out for size were you?"

"Bit big for me, Sarge."

He said it with a straight face, but Bev's was poker-like. "Thanks, mate."

"I didn't – "

She flapped a hand. "Forget it."

"You all right, Sarge?"

No, she bloody wasn't. "Fine."

She'd done a detour via the interview room, wanted another butcher's at Duncan Ferguson. He'd been on his knees, eyes closed, fingers steepled. Talk about God-bothering, he was certainly getting up her nose. She'd asked herself the same question over again. If Ferguson was in the frame, was Charlie Hawes still in the picture?

"Thought you'd be chuffed," Ozzie said. "What with the case being pretty well sewn up."

"Tacked round the edges, Oz. Tacked round the edges."

"Not what I've heard." He pulled up a seat. "Word is, DI Powell's found a stack of stuff at Ferguson's place."

"Powell couldn't find yeast in a brewery."

"Well, he's come up with enough for charges."

"Murder?"

"Not yet."

She shrugged.

"You don't buy it, do you?"

She put her elbows on the desk and her head in her hands. "I just don't know, Oz." When she closed her eyes, she still saw Charlie Hawes. Was her mind sealed as well? "It just doesn't feel right."

"Doesn't always come down to feelings, does it, Bev?"

There was a touch of concern in the voice. It was time to change the subject. "What's Powell come up with?"

"Scrapbook full of cuttings. Prostitute murders going back to the Ripper. Hate mail he hadn't got round to posting."

So Ferguson was the arse-wipe who'd sent the girls their loo paper. She recalled Jules's graphic demo during the meet at Val's place. Wouldn't do any harm to check; she made a mental note, reached for the coffee. The case against Ferguson was mounting. So how come she felt so low?

The concern was in his face now. "None of it makes Charlie Hawes a saint, Sarge. There was every reason to go after him. No one's gonna think any the less of you." He paused. "I certainly don't."

Were her feelings that obvious? "What did you want anyway, Oz?"

He pointed to a couple of print-outs on the desk. "Came through earlier. Makes interesting reading."

"Steve Bell?"

He nodded. "Bit academic now."

She sipped the coffee, skimmed the reports. "It's a soddin' crime wave, Oz. Christ, you could swim in it."

Stephen Joseph Bell was older than he looked and even more brain-dead than he appeared. He was twenty six and he'd been in and out of youth detention for years before getting to spend time with the big boys. Probably saw it as career progression. The list was impressive: taking without consent, criminal damage, assault, wounding. She looked at Oz. "One of life's givers, then?"

"He's been straight for three years."

"He's been lucky for three years." She threw the papers on the desk. "Losers like Bell don't do straight."

Ozzie was studying his fingernails. "Word is he does both."

"Oh? Swings both ways?"

He nodded. "Someone in the incident room remembered him from way back. Reckons he boosted his pocket money down the Queensway as a rent boy. Got into it while he was still at school."

"Let's do a bit of digging."

He looked questioningly. "Reckon it's still worth it?"

"Sure do. Ferguson might have confessed, but he hasn't been convicted. And you know what they say, Oz?" She tapped the side of her nose. "It ain't over till the fat lady sings."

"You said it, Sarge." He turned but she still caught the rider. "I wouldn't dare."

Lucky the phone rang; she was about to chuck it at his rapidly departing back.

"Thanks for the call. I got here soon as I could." Bev was struggling to keep up. Why did doctors always walk so fast? She blamed *ER*. Mind, Doctor Thorne looked very fetching in a flapping white coat. She smiled; Oz'd be sorry to miss it.

"I didn't ring till I was sure. She's definitely coming out of it. She's opening her eyes, trying to talk."

They stood to one side as a muscular porter raced past with an unconscious child on a trolley. A woman – presumably the mother – was running alongside. Bev caught a glimpse of her face and prayed the future didn't hold a similar fate for herself.

"You all right?" the doctor asked.

Bev nodded. "I take it Cassie hasn't had any flowers since I last checked?"

"Not that I know of. Why?"

"Just wondered."

They'd reached Intensive Care. "You'd be better off asking one of the nurses." Doctor Thorne smiled. "They know far more about what goes on round here than I do." She held the door open. "I'll catch you later."

Alison Granger was at the bedside again. Cassie was about the same age as one of Alison's daughters. Bev tiptoed down the ward, not that normal footsteps were likely to wake many of its occupants.

"Hi, Alison. How's the patient?" Bev's face fell; the patient looked as lively as a wet park bench.

"Not so bad, Sarge," she winked. "Bit tired, if you know what I mean." She rose and beckoned Bev towards the end of the bed. "She's trying it on."

"Not with you, Alison."

"She's as compos mentis as you and me, when she wants to be." She leaned closer. "I've caught her peeping every now and again. If anyone's around she doesn't like the look of, she pretends to be asleep."

Sounded reasonable to Bev. Bit like a one night-stand she'd once had. "She said anything yet?"

"About half an hour ago. Asked where she was. How long she'd been here."

Good signs. Bev nodded. "I'll sit with her. You grab a coffee and a bite to eat."

The seat was still warm; Bev pushed it nearer. The bear she'd bought earlier was at Cassie's feet. She rescued it, laid it on the pillow. She thought she caught a flicker in the girl's eyes but might have been mistaken.

Gently, she held Cassie's hand, willing her to respond. There was only the rise and fall of her breathing under the thin white sheet. Gradually Bev started to talk. She told her about Michelle, she told her about Vicki, she told her about the other girls and what they were trying to do. She held nothing back: she ran through her thoughts on Louella, Annie Flinn, Charlie Hawes, and the anorak who'd confessed. She kept her voice soft and confiding, as if Cassie was a good mate and as she spoke, she stroked the girl's hand. "Thing is, Cass, what if we've got the wrong man? What if he's a wally after the proverbial fifteen minutes? Anyway," she lowered her voice even further, "you can't tell me Charlie Hawes is Mr Clean. God, I'd like to pin something on him."

Bev felt a slight pressure under her fingers but Cassie's face remained a blank canvas. "I bet he did this to you, didn't he?

See, I reckon you and me, we could put him away, but I can't do it on my own."

Bev held her breath. Nothing. Short of a good shake, there was little more she could do. "I'm all talked out, Cass. Bore for England, me. I'll just sit a while if that's okay with you." She slumped back in the chair, still clutching Cassie's hand, and closed her eyes. She was knackered; knackered and racked off. She'd invested too many hopes. Cassie was as scared as the others; probably even more terrified. Unbidden, images sprang to Bev's mind. Michelle naked in the mortuary, Louella dead in the park, a laughing Vicki across the table in the police canteen. As if that wasn't enough, she recalled the little girl from the trolley, and her own father with as many drips in him as an umbrella stand.

She swallowed hard but knew it wouldn't stem the flow. Sodding hospitals; bloody places. She sniffed loudly and dashed her cheeks with the heel of her hand, the damp tears cooling her skin. She let go of Cassie, wrapped the girl's fingers round the bear, leaned over and pecked her forehead. "I'm off now, Cass. Ta for listening."

She straightened and gave the girl a last glance. Her eyes widened as one of Cassie's slowly opened.

"England?" said the girl. "You could bore for soddin' Europe."

Bev felt like shoving the bear in a bedpan, then she saw the girl's smile.

"You don't half talk a load of crap. D'you know that?"

"Give me the good stuff, then, Cass."

The girl's smile vanished. "I'm cream crackered, honest."

"I'll come back. Any time you're ready."

The girl looked down at the teddy bear, stroked its ear between thumb and forefinger. Bev could have kicked herself; she'd asked too much, pushed too far. She'd almost given up, was about to leave, when Cassie spoke again. Her voice was muffled but the message was clear. "I'll think about it.

Come back tomorrow."

"If you're tied up, I can come back."

Bev's eyes travelled from the fluffy pink towel turbanning Val's hair to a man's blue-striped shirt barely covering her boobs.

"Thursday, innit?" The big woman winked. "Don't do bondage Thursdays. Come in, chuck."

Bev followed Val's swaying rump as it sashayed into the front room. Frank Sinatra was doing the rounds on an old Fidelity. Bev's mouth twitched, but any irony in the lady being a tramp was lost on the big woman. She watched as Val swooped to retrieve a smoking ciggie from an overflowing ashtray.

"Don't make 'em like that any more, do they?"

The player? The records? Ol' Blue Eyes? Bev hedged her bets, uttered a noncommittal "Right."

"Grab a pew. I'm on maintenance."

"Maintenance?" Bev sank into a bean-bag. "You make more than me. What you doing on maintenance?"

Val rolled her eyes. "Body maintenance, you daft sod."

Bev was thinking grease guns and MOTs but looking round it was all moisturisers and CFCs. For someone whose make-up could fit in a matchbox, it was riveting.

"I've waxed me legs, masked me face, shaved me armpits and I was just about to do me nails," Val said.

"Don't let me stop you."

"As if."

Bev was keeping it light. There was a good chance it was going to get heavy later. "How's Banjo?"

Val wiggled her shoulders and arched an eyebrow. "Ooh, chuck. He can pluck my strings any day. Know what I mean?"

"Pluck?"

Val's laugh almost dislodged the turban. Bev watched as she ran a finger along a display of tiny bottles on top of the mantelpiece. Colours started at lurid and went through every shade of garish. The finger hovered between scarlet and fuchsia. Val finally plumped for fresh blood. She perched on the bed, and hoisted up a surprisingly slim, elegant foot. For a woman of such generous proportions it was a bold move, a rare sight. And not one on which Bev wished to dwell. She glanced round. "Thought you only collected pigs, Val."

There was a toy rabbit under the table. Bev leaned across to retrieve it but turned back as Val let rip a string of expletives. The bottle was on the floor, the nail polish seeping into the carpet. "I'm still sticky," Val said. "Grab a bit of cotton wool and get it up, will you, chuck?"

Bev soaked a pad in remover and worked out as much of the stain as she could. Frank was still crooning away in the corner. He'd just hit the bit about not dishing the dirt with the rest of the girls. Bev looked at Val and knew what he meant.

"Ta, kid. Chuck it in the bin, will you?" Bev looked round. Val smiled. "It's out the back. Pop the kettle on while you're at it."

The kitchen was obviously not a place in which Val spent much time. It was tiny, with a floor like a chessboard and walls in magenta. Even Bev felt a touch of claustrophobia. There was a packet of Yorkshire tea and a bag of sugar on the side. She made for the fridge, which was bare bar a carton of milk and a slab of Cadbury's. A quick scout round the cupboards unearthed a taste for baked beans, pickled onions and Horlicks. Could explain why Val was short on crockery.

"Do a lot of entertaining, do you?" Bev asked, placing a mug on the floor by Val's feet.

"Yes," she smirked. "But not in the kitchen." She was blowing her nails dry: finger not toe, thank God. "Anyway, Bev, what you doin' here?"

"Wanted you to have a decko at this." She reached into an inside pocket.

"You'll have to hold it for us, chuck. Don't want to smudge

me handiwork, do I?"

Bev held a plastic envelope in front of Val's face. The letter inside was composed of words cut from newspapers, though Bev reckoned Ferguson had dropped an 'L' and inserted an 'F.'

Fuck off slag. Go home Hooker scum

Val sniffed. "Charmed, I'm sure."

"What do you think, Val? Is it the same as the others?"

She screwed her eyes, chewed her bottom lip. "Not sure, chuck. To be honest, if you've seen one – "

"It's important. Have another look."

Val checked her nails then took the envelope from Bev, held it closer, squinting. "It could be." She shrugged. "That's the best I can do."

Bev nodded. It was better than nothing.

"Sorry, chuck. But they're all much of a muchness. There's only so many ways you can tell a tart to get lost. Know what I mean?"

"Sure." Bev took a sip of tea, wondered how long it would take Val to ask.

The big woman handed it back. "Where'd you get it, Bev?"

Was the tone a tad too cas? Bev made hers slow and deliberate. "From the bloke we're about to charge with Michelle's murder." She was watching closely but had to dodge half a mouthful of tea as it shot out of Val's mouth.

The big woman dabbed at her chin, glanced at Bev. "Sorry about that, chuck. It went the wrong way."

Wrong way; wrong man? Bev said nothing; waited again. Sinatra was the only one saying anything. Bev took another sip. Her eyes never left Val's face. Which was more important? What someone said, or what they didn't? Bev was itching to find out.

"You haven't asked who," she said.

Val shrugged, as if it didn't matter. "You'd have told me if you wanted me to know."

"Would I, Val? Is that what you do? Only tell people what you want them to know?"

The big woman's mouth was like a letterbox in a post strike.

"What would you say if I told you we had Charlie in?" Okay, I lied.

"I'd say a you were a bloody miracle worker." The sneer was genuine.

"Hallelujah," cheered Bev. "And I've just performed another."

"You what?"

Bev leaned back, hands crossed behind her head, surveying the latest. "You've miraculously got your memory back. Never heard of him before, had you?"

Val made an angry grab for a pack of Marlboro. "You bang on about him so much – it feels I've known him a lifetime."

There was real anger in the big woman's voice. Bev had misjudged the pace. Sod it; there was nothing to lose now. She leaned forward, dropped her voice. "He's gonna get away with it, Val. Charlie'll walk. How many more lives is he gonna fuck up before someone says enough?"

"I've got nothin' to say."

"You didn't get a phone call from Vicki, did you?"

She lit a cigarette. It wasn't much of an answer.

"When did Vick have the kid, Val?"

"What kid?" She was lying, but her eyes weren't. Bev saw it among the terror.

"Are you really so scared of the little shit?" she asked gently. "I really thought you were different, Val. I thought you cared." She leaned closer. "He preys on kids. He's a fuckin' monster."

Val jabbed the air with her cigarette. "If you're so sure he done it, get some soddin' evidence. That's what they pay you for, innit?"

Bev looked away. There was a truth in there that was difficult to face.

Val hadn't finished. "I don't do any bugger's dirty work. An' I'll tell you this straight, Bev. The way you go on about him?

It sounds personal."

She'd never got out of a bean-bag so fast. She towered over Val, who'd slid down in the seat.

"It is fuckin' personal. Hawes has made it personal. He was in the park the other night – left me some fan mail. He's been in my home. He's threatening me. He's trying to freak me out. But you know something, Val? I don't scare easy."

Bev was surprised to find a moistness in her eyes and put it down to rage.

There was concern in the big woman's voice. "Leave it be, Bev. Back off."

"I don't do back off. Oh, and Val…" She paused. "Next time you see Charlie, tell him that from me." She was winging it. Val knew more than she was letting on, but it was anyone's guess how much.

"I don't – "

Bev flapped a hand. "Save it."

At some point, Sinatra had segued into *Luck Be A Lady*. One letter out if you ask me, thought Bev. She reluctantly turned away.

"The girls'll be out tonight," Val said.

Bev didn't react. So?

"You comin', or what?"

It sounded like a spot of bridge-building. Bev was out of bricks.

"Thought you didn't do back off."

Bev glanced at the big woman. "Your point being?"

"Didn't last long, did it? Just a one-night stand for you, wasn't it? It ain't like that for me and the girls. On the game, they call it. Well, there's not a lot of fun in it." She flicked ash in her empty mug. "I thought you were supposed to be lookin' out for us out there. Got cold feet, did you?"

"Got cold everything." Bev gave a tepid smile. She had to admit Val had a point. "Okay, I'll try and make it."

Val's reply was lost in a piercing scream coming through the letterbox. "Ma! Val! Let us in."

"Jules?" asked Bev.

Val nodded, lifted her eyes to the ceiling. "Christ, if she hammers the bloody door any harder, there won't be anything to open."

Bev went with her, it was time to leave anyway. Jules was hidden by Val's bulk so Bev heard rather than saw. The words tumbled out in the girl's excitement.

"They've taken him in, ma! Right outside Woolie's. I've just seen it. Bundled into the back of a car, he was."

Val laid her hands on Jules's shoulders. "Hold your horses, kid. What you goin' on about? Who's taken who, where?"

"The Bill. They got Charlie Hawes. And I'm bleedin' sure they ain't takin' 'im home."

The station. That's where they'd taken Charlie Hawes.

Bev was heading back under her own steam, still fuming she hadn't been on the Highgate welcoming committee. She was driving as fast as she could, but the school run meant traffic was at a crawl. She'd left Val's place and got straight on the phone. Her joy at Charlie's detention was tempered by a childish churlishness that she'd been kept in the dark it was happening. Charlie was helping inquiries, Byford had told her. He'd been cautioned, was under arrest but not charged.

They'd had a call. A Mr Angry, from Ladywood, complaining about his lock-up. There was something squatting in it. A black BMW. A black BMW that hadn't appeared on Charlie's helpful little list. A glaring omission as it happened, because the motor had Charlie's name all over it. Okay, slight exaggeration. There was a phone bill made out to a Mr C Hawes. And there was more. There was evidence of a passenger. A girl with blonde hair. They had a Hawes–Lucas link, and forensics were working full pelt to see if they could pin down another with Louella Kent.

The breakthrough had added impetus and focus, and every scrap of evidence from both crime scenes was getting the works.

Bev listened to the details with a growing smile, a cross between smug satisfaction and incipient excitement. Quite what it meant as far as Ferguson's confession went, she neither knew nor for the moment cared. The spotlight was back on Charlie, and Byford wanted her in on the questioning. The only thing holding her back was a C-reg Volvo full of snotty-nosed kids pulling revolting faces out of the back window. She could do that. She did a quick Quasimodo then brought out the star turn; no kid could top a flashing blue light on the roof.

Talk about conjuring tricks. You had to give it to the guv. Bev was well impressed. In terms of the interview, she was taking a back seat. Mind, it had a great view and Byford hadn't ruled out the odd heckle. She'd have to watch her lip a bit; the tape was running this time.

Charlie, looking even tastier than before, was in the same chair that Ferguson had occupied only a few hours earlier. Rather than tight-arsed perch, Hawes was laid-back loll; legs stretched in front, hands crossed behind his head. The pose was in line with the look: expensive ivory chinos and baggy cotton shirt open at the neck. He was either feeling the heat or showing off his tan. Given the guv's fancy footwork, she hoped the heat.

"You can see my dilemma, can't you, Mr Hawes?"

Charlie shrugged, not even trying to conceal a yawn.

"You were quite clear on the point when we last met." Byford glanced down at a notebook. "'I never even knew the girl' is what you told us."

Charlie gave an exaggerated sigh. "What I actually said was as far as I know. And that's still the case. I don't recall meeting Michelle Lucas."

"Then how do you explain the fact that she was in your car?" Byford sounded awfully polite and reasonable. Bev would be putting the verbal boot in by now. Her glance went from Charlie to the evidence bags neatly lined up on the desk. Inside the first was a single hair which, though coiled, was blonde and very long. The tiny stain on the scrap of carpet in the second was less apparent to the naked eye. Not that it mattered, the tag was quite clear. There was more of the same at the lab. The findings in front of them were preliminary. Not so much a rush job as a rocket launch. Essential, with Ferguson still shouting his guilty mouth off. Charlie was saying nothing.

"Blood and hair. Both Michelle's. How did they get there, Mr Hawes?"

Bev looked back at Charlie, searching in vain for a sign of unease.

"I don't know."

Byford smiled. "I think you're going to have to do better than that."

"If I knew, I'd share it with you." Was that a wink? The oik had actually winked at her. Cocky little sod.

"Are you sure you wouldn't like us to contact Mr Viner?" Byford asked.

Charlie had already refused his solicitor. Bev reckoned he was about to change his mind.

"When I feel the need to call Max, I'll let you know, okay?"

Bluff? Bravado? Bullshit? Bev hadn't a clue, but anything that kept a brief at bay was fine by her.

"So let's get back to Michelle," Byford said.

Charlie pursed his lips, jabbed a thumb in Bev's direction. "Can't you send our Beverley to get coffee? I'm parched."

"I don't do skivvy," she snarled.

"Sergeant." Byford played peacemaker. "Just pop your head out."

PACE obliged them to feed and water sleazeballs like Charlie. At least if she could collar someone in the corridor, Byford wouldn't have to stop the interview. Andy was passing and she put in an order.

"I'm still looking for answers, Mr Hawes. At some stage Michelle Lucas was a passenger in your car."

Come on, guv, thought Bev, stop pussyfooting around.

"The girl was a prostitute." Byford's polite tone didn't waver. "What does that make you? Punter or pimp?"

Bev would like to have seen Charlie's reaction, but she was still by the door.

"Confused, Mr Byford, confused." He was doing a lot of heavy sighing, was Charlie. "I can only imagine it must have happened when the car was stolen."

"Stolen?" How Byford kept the incredulity out of his voice Bev would never know.

"Yeah. Two, or was it three weeks back?"

"And this theft," Byford paused, "was it reported?"

"Come on, Superintendent. As if I'd bother the police with something as trivial as a missing motor." He lifted his shoulders, turned to include Bev in the general bonhomie. "Not when you people have far weightier matters to keep you busy."

"This motor," Bev asked, "how come you never mentioned it before?"

Charlie was all innocence. "Didn't I?"

"Your little fairy story's there, Charlie. Take a look."

He reached eagerly for the papers he'd brought to their first interview. Bev watched incredulously as he traced every line with a finger, his lips moving to the words he was pretending to read. He looked up, shook his head. "Nope. It's not there." He smiled at Bev. "It must have slipped my mind."

"What mind?" Bev asked.

He paused, deep in thought, then hunched over the table, cradled his head in his hands. There was a shudder in his next breath and another in the subsequent sigh. She glanced at the guv. My God. Was the hard man cracking?

After what seemed like hours, he sat up, hands posed in

surrender. "Is it too late?"

She answered quickly, her breathing suspended. "Too late for what?"

"To report the theft of my car."

She wondered if he practised the smile in his mirror; imagined how it would look minus a few of those perfect white teeth. Thankfully, there was a knock on the door. Bev relieved Andy of the tray, managed to resist dumping it in Charlie's lap.

"No sugar for me. Everyone says I'm sweet enough. What do you think, Beverley?"

She gave him the finger.

"Should I describe the sergeant's gesture for the tape, Superintendent?"

He was enjoying it. She went back to the door, out of harm's way: his. Would nothing get under this scumbag's skin?

"Let's cut the crap, Charlie." Byford changed tack and tone. It had the desired effect on Bev; no effect on Charlie. He must have played cool guy so often, he no longer recognised the heat. Byford increased it.

"This story of yours about the motor. That's all it is, isn't it? A story. Once upon a time..." He leaned forward. "Only this time they didn't all live happily ever after. Michelle Lucas didn't live at all. What happened, Charlie? You were her pimp. What went wrong? Did she get greedy? Did she want a bigger cut?"

"Not the most appropriate choice of words, Superintendent." Charlie was scratching the back of his neck. Byford was dangerously close to wringing it. Bev had never seen the old man so close taking a pop.

"Just supposing the girl had ever worked for me." Charlie glanced at his watch. "And that's a very big supposition, Mr Byford. But let's just say she did. Why on earth would I kill her? Fifteen years old? Beautiful girl like that?" He was barking, if he thought they'd fall for that. "Not that I knew her, of course." He smiled. "I saw her picture in the papers. A pimp would have to be mad to get rid of a kid like Michelle. Talk about killing the goose."

"Profit and loss. That's what it comes down to, is it, Charlie?" Bev asked.

He ignored her, held out his hands. "I'm a businessman, Mr Byford. I make killings all the time. On the market or on paper. Not in real life."

"Tell me about Louella Kent. Where does she fit into this?"

"How the hell should I know?" A touch of impatience? Good. Bev folded her arms. "Look, I'm getting bored. How much longer is this going on?"

"Till you stop faffing around and tell us the truth."

"I did not kill Michelle. I did not kill the other girl. I've never even heard of her."

He sounded genuine, but then he would. God, thought Bev, why wasn't it like cops-on-the-box, all cut and dried in an hour?

"I may have met Michelle," he conceded. "I meet a lot of people. But I sure as hell never came across the Kent girl."

He must have. Whoever killed Michelle had also killed Louella. It was all or nothing. He was leaning forward, his hands on the desk as though closer proximity would add credence. Bev returned to her seat, regretting that the guv's magic appeared to have vanished. They could do with another evidence bag of tricks.

Charlie glanced at his watch again.

"What's up?" Bev asked. "Expecting visitors?"

He flashed a smile. "What a sense of humour! Must be great compensation when you're such a dog."

His veneer of charm had slipped. She tilted her head. "How kind."

Byford cleared his throat. "I want to take you through your statement step by step. We've spoken to most of the people whose names you gave us. But there are one or two…"

Bev tuned out, struck by a sudden thought. She narrowed

her eyes. It was wing and prayerish. She hoped it wasn't a flight of fancy. As she saw it, Charlie Hawes was better groomed than a stable: manicured, pedicured; coiffeured. So how come his all-over tan wasn't? How come he had a tidemark to rival Annie Flinn's?

"When did you have your hair cut, Charlie?" she asked softly.

"What the —?"

"How long was it, Charlie?"

"Sod off — "

"Tied it back, did you, Charlie?"

"Fuck you."

"You first."

She got up, stood in front of him, invaded his space. "You see, Charlie, we found a scrunchy near Louella's body. It had lots of long dark hair in it. Long dark hair just like I bet yours used to be. And you know what? We're going to get a match."

For the first time, he looked unsure. "Can't be. I've never been near the girl."

"That's what you said about Michelle."

"I'm being framed here."

"Said that before too." She smiled sweetly. "Didn't you, Charles?"

Byford gave her a nod, scraped back his chair. "I'm suspending this interview for the time being." She barely noticed the wind-down spiel for the tape; her focus was on Charlie and his growing unease. It increased further when the guv spoke again. "You need to consider your position very seriously, Mr Hawes. I strongly recommend that when we resume you have your solicitor present."

32

"You look like a bleedin' solicitor. What you playin' at?"

Bev looked nothing like a brief. Not the Max Viner variety anyway. Charlie's legal representative, the smooth-talking Mr V, was currently at Highgate earning his doubtless massive remuneration. Jules's was on the patch looking to make a few quid. Her comment wasn't so much a reflection on Bev's sad-git gear, more a disappointment that she wasn't a punter.

Bev had driven to Thread Street straight from work. It was a bad move. Jules's face was still falling.

"Got me hopes up there," she whined as Bev joined her at the railings. "Haven't had a john since Tuesday."

"Another quiet night on the Thread Street front?"

Jules gave an eloquent eye-roll. "Apart from Cyanide Lil and Marathon Man."

"Marathon Man?"

"The runner. That bloke you saw the other night? Set your watch by him, you can. Oh! And a cheeky sod in a three-wheeler. He offered me a fiver. Said he'd settle up on pay day."

Bev grinned. "What did you say?"

"Told him I didn't do charity cases and how come he's always hangin' round the job centre."

Bev glanced at Jules. "How'd you know? You looking for work or something?"

She sniffed. "Could be."

The crossed arms and tapping foot warded off further questions and anyway, Jules's job prospects weren't the reason Bev was here. "You on your own?"

"Yeah. Val's got somefin' on..."

"Makes a change."

"...and the others are still twitchy."

She watched as Jules scanned the street. The fake-leather coat was no match for the February cold. Jules was shivering and her bare legs looked like slabs of brawn. Bev was bringing good news, but it could be better. It could be Hey Jules, you've won the lottery, you'll never have to freeze your ass on a street corner again. Yeah, yeah. Yada yada.

"Look, love, I can't say much at the mo but it looks as if it'll all be over soon. Perhaps you can let the others know?"

Jules looked stunned. "You got someone banged up?"

"You could say that." What with Charlie protesting his innocence and Ferguson still protesting his guilt, the cells had a glut of bad guys.

The momentary thrill had gone. Jules was staring at her wedgies. "If you're talkin' Charlie Hawes, you'll never pin anythin' on him."

Bev narrowed her eyes. "I want a word about that." It had been bugging her off and on since she'd left Val's. "How come you knew it was Charlie being pulled in? As far as you lot were concerned Charlie Hawes didn't exist, you'd never heard of him, you wouldn't know him from the invisible man."

"Got a fag?"

"Don't change the subject."

"Well, what do you expect? Who's dumb enough to admit knowin' Charlie?"

"What's so special about him? He's just a bloke, Jules. And with a bit of luck, he's going down. And staying down."

"It'll take more than a bit of luck. He's got this place in his back pocket. Anyone who crosses Charlie's gotta be tired of life."

Bev sighed. The girl seemed to have shrunk. The feistiness had vanished. How come men like Hawes held such sway over girls like Jules? She'd seen it time and again: cases falling down because a woman won't stand up in court; sleazeballs walking free, then forcing their girls to pay. Women either backed off or lied through their teeth; more often than not, teeth the bastard had broken. But not this time. This time was different.

"We're nearly there, Jules. We're nearly there."

"Yeah. Well, forgive me if I don't hold my breath."

33

It had not been a good night. She'd arrived home curiously depressed after the conversation with Jules. Morriss Towers didn't help. It was warm and cosy but – as always – empty. Times like that, you needed to talk. Perhaps she should get a lodger? She'd recced all the rooms but the new locks had deterred visitors, authorised or otherwise. She was reduced to talking to herself. Again.

"Okay, Bev, the evidence against Charlie isn't enough for a conviction, but it's early days. He's not asbestos man and this time, he's gonna burn."

It took three large Grouse and a microwaved chicken Kiev before she actually began to believe it, and she'd woken next morning with a head that had a mind of its own. It had issued warnings about imminent death without immediate oxygen. An early run seemed the only option.

It wasn't as much fun without Frankie, not having anyone to talk to, but it was great for getting rid of the cerebral cobwebs. Wouldn't like to do it on her own all the time, though. Loneliness of the long distance runner and all that. Not that three miles qualified.

"Two down, one to go, Bev." God. She must stop talking to herself. Not that there was anyone around. Not when the grass was skimmed with ice and her breath was like something out of the Flying Scotsman. Still, you noticed things more when you weren't rabbiting on about tasty blokes or wankers at work. Rustic touches like a trail of paw prints or baby snowdrops sprouting in a crop of cotton buds. Crop of cotton buds? Pass the sick bag! What about all the glue-sniffing gear and empty cans of Special Strong Brew. Mind, it was good to be about when the park was quiet. Couldn't see the point in getting out later, pounding pavements, dodging lippy schoolkids and smoking exhausts. Still, horses for courses and all that. Jules's Marathon Man didn't mind the fag end of the day. Set your clock by him, she said.

She stopped dead, heard her breathing in the still air as disjointed thoughts fell into a sort of focus. The Thread Street runner. It was his patch, as much as the girls. Had he been interviewed? Had he seen anything? Had he come forward? And if not, why not?

It took a couple of false starts but Bev was propping up Marathon Man's sink before he'd downed breakfast. Cyanide Lil had eventually pointed her in the right direction. There weren't many locals the old dear hadn't clocked in her time and Bev was banging the bloke's front door in line with the eight o'clock pips. He lived in a redbrick bed-sit. Like many in Balsall Heath: gross on the outside, inside what you made it. Jack Crane hadn't made much of it. He hadn't made much of himself; his cheap grey tracksuit was out at the knees and he'd obviously cut himself shaving. Either that or he had strange ways with bog roll. At thirty-something, he had a schoolboy fringe that fell into deep blue eyes. He wasn't one for clutter: bare walls, empty shelves, no knick-knacks or newspapers. She thought maybe he'd just moved in but the packing cases were Jack Crane's idea of a dining suite.

He hadn't stopped gabbing since he'd opened the door. He'd apologised for the mess, offered her a bacon sarnie, explained how the wife had kicked him out and how he was on benefit. All this in the time it took to cross the cracked lino into what passed for a kitchen. Yet she didn't get the impression he was jumpy, just saw a lonely guy glad to have someone to talk to, even if she was a copper.

"Sure I can't get you something? Piece of toast? Coffee?"

He was hovering like an anxious waiter.

She shook her head. "I'm fine. Finish yours."

He perched on the only stool, self-consciously forking scrambled eggs. "I eat as well as I can."

She nodded. Bloke sounded almost apologetic. "Have to. Running like you do."

"I love it. Keeps me going in more ways than one. I don't smoke, don't drink. Can't afford a telly. I'd go mad if I stopped in this place all day."

"That's what I want to talk about. Your evening runs."

She waited while he swallowed. "Thought you said it was to do with a murder inquiry?"

"It is. You may have seen something that could help us."

"Happy to. When did it happen?"

Bev studied his face. Was it possible he didn't know? "Not it. Them. Two girls. You haven't heard anything?"

"Should I have?"

"It's been in the news a lot. Loads of people talking about it down the pub, that sort of thing."

He shrugged. "Not my scene."

She gave him edited highlights, concentrating on dates, times. His face was rapt, set in concentration.

"Can't help you with Tuesday. There was a big protest in Thread Street. Threw me off my regular course."

She nodded, impatient. "What about the Friday before?"

He had a mobile face, she could see him playing the events of the evening in his mind. Come on, come on.

"No." He shook his head. "Couldn't have been…"

"What?" The outburst filled the tiny space. "Sorry, Mr Crane. What couldn't have been?"

He was so slow. This was so painful.

"I didn't see any girl. Nothing like that." There was an unspoken but. He frowned, met her gaze. "He seemed a nice bloke."

"Who did?"

"Said he'd had a fall."

"Who did?"

"This bloke. Looked all shook-up. Had quite a tumble. I took him for another runner. Lot of blood on his top."

"Can you remember what he looked like?"

"Good-looking sort of chap. Very dark. Very fit. Long hair. Had it tied back."

Gotcha! "This man, Mr Crane, would you recognise him again?"

"Yes. I rather think I would."

34

Charlie was lying back, hands behind his head, stirred and shortly to be shaken. Bev carried the image with her as she took the stairs, two at a time, to the governor's office, whistling *Who's Sorry Now?* between her teeth.

For the moment, she could barely contain her excitement. She'd missed the briefing yet again but hell, so what? She'd got filling in of her own to do. She'd bring the guv up to speed, get the go-ahead for an ID parade then send a car for Jack Crane. Should only take a couple of hours. By then, Mr Asbestos Hawes would be toast. She was so keen, she forgot to knock.

"Where the hell have you been?" He was half in, or out, of his coat.

"Sorry, guv, I didn't want to pull you out of the briefing."

"There wasn't one." Definitely in. "Something's come up."

She frowned. "Right." Where was he going?'

"I want you with me."

"Well, actually, guv, there's a few points…"

He glanced at his watch. "You've got two minutes."

What was his problem? "I've been to see this bloke, he was in Thread Street the night Michelle was killed and it looks like he can finger Charlie Hawes."

"Oh yes?"

"Yeah. He's a runner, see, and…"

She was babbling and Byford wasn't really listening, he was collecting papers, putting them into a file. Her initial excitement was giving way to irritation. "So you see, we need an ID parade. This bloke can get here any time. Thought I'd send a car just after lunch."

"Not sure how useful that would be, Sergeant."

"Christ, sir. The man's painted a bloody portrait of Charlie Hawes. What more do you want?"

"The killer."

"I'm sorry?" She wasn't; she was seething.

"I don't believe Charlie Hawes killed anyone."

"You're not still thinking Ferguson?"

"I know it's not Ferguson."

His certainty didn't even register. "Thank God for that. Let's concentrate on Charlie."

"You're not listening, are you?"

She was listening, just not believing.

He took car keys from his pocket. "Just for once, will you concentrate on something else? Forget Charlie Hawes."

"Forget! How am I supp –?"

Byford was already opening the door. "Because Charlie Hawes is in custody, Sergeant. So, answer me this; how come another girl's been knifed?"

A tip-off from the General: a teenage prostitute with throat wounds. That's all they had. The drive to Casualty passed in a blur. Pictures of the girls were kaleidoscoping in Bev's head; next the image would be a fruit machine with the kids' faces: Jules, Patty, Smithy, Vick. She glanced at the guv now and again but he didn't like talking and driving. By the time they arrived at the hospital, she could have done with a bed herself.

He held the door back. "You all right, Bev?"

She nodded. At least he'd dropped the Sergeant bit. The A & E Obergruppenführer was being arsey, but Bev spotted a familiar face heading their way. "Christ, doc, don't you ever go home? You do more hours than me."

Doctor Thorne sighed. "Tell me about it."

Bev introduced Byford, who'd already clocked the woman's

name badge and by the smile on his face a few other things as well.

"Superintendent?" The doctor arched an eyebrow. "You'll be on your best behaviour, then, Bev?"

She inclined her head. "As ever."

The doctor glanced at her watch. "You should be able to see her in a bit."

"Who is it, doc?" Bev asked. "They didn't say."

She led them to a bench, stood while they sat. "She won't give her name."

"She's conscious then?" Byford asked.

"Very much so. The attack happened last night. She got herself to a friend's house and the friend brought her in."

"This friend?" Bev asked. "A woman? Quite a bit older? Big hair?"

"That's right. You know her?"

"I reckon." So much for sisterly solidarity. Val could at least have given her a bell.

"Brought her here in a cab about an hour ago, said she had to get back. The girl's lost a lot of blood but she'll be okay. Her hands are in a state. She put up a hell of a fight. Been giving us a hard time as well."

That figures, thought Bev. "What's she said about the attack?"

Dr Thorne sighed. "As little as possible. Tried to make out it was an accident." She glanced from Bev to Byford and back. "She doesn't want the police involved. But given what's happened…"

"Thanks," Bev said. "Appreciate it. When can we see her?"

"Ain't there no tasty docs round here?" The voice had lost little of its cheek. Bev located its source behind the screens of a cubicle, mouthed a silent prayer of thanks. Gratitude, it appeared, was the last thing on the patient's mind. "How come I get landed with an old slapper like you?"

"Watch your mouth or I'll stitch that as well."

Bev's lips twitched. Couldn't have put it better herself. No point mollycoddling a kid like Jules. That's what she'd told herself last night, driving away from Thread Street; but she'd been haunted by the memory of a pair of skinny legs in the driving mirror. She got to her feet, had to put out a hand to steady herself.

Dr Thorne turned all professional. "What is it, Bev? Are you okay?"

"Blood rush. I'll be fine." Relief rush more like, God knew what her stress levels had been up to on the way in, added to which she'd done a run and skipped breakfast.

The doctor was clearly concerned. "You look tired. Take it easy. Yes?"

Bev gazed at the woman's face: the eyes had dark circles under them, and not so much bags as a set of luggage. "I will if you will."

She inclined her head. "Touché."

"Okay if I pop my head round?" Bev asked.

"If you don't mind bitemarks."

Bev considered for a second. "Her bark's worse."

Byford stood, fastening his coat. "If you know this girl, it's probably best I leave you to it, Bev."

"Scared you off, has she, Superintendent?" Dr Thorne winked. Bev's eyes widened. Byford just grinned.

"Shaking in my boots, Doctor Thorne."

"Nasty," she smiled. "I could probably give you something for that."

Gooseberry or what? The woman was actually flirting!

"I may take you up on that." The guv was at it now! "Something wrong, Sergeant?" Bev wiped whatever expression was on her face. "Good. I'll be off then. Let me know what's happening."

"Seems like a nice man." The doctor watched as Byford saluted before disappearing round a corner. "Married, is he?"

"Yeah. Six kids. Wife's an invalid."

"You're joking."

"Had you going, though, didn't I?"

She laughed. "Come on. I'll see if she's ready for a visit."

"Ready or not, she's getting one."

"Where's me grapes, then?"

Bev had to stop herself racing across the cubicle and giving the poor kid a cuddle. Frail and lonely on a massive trolley, both hands swathed in bandages, she looked like a boxer waiting for a pair of gloves. Sixty-odd stitches across fingers and hands and superficial wounds on her neck; the medicos wanted to keep her in. They had a battle on their plate but despite all the fighting talk, the sheet had more colour than the girl's face and her dark eyes were brimming with tears.

Perching on the edge of the trolley, Bev said: "I'd have bought you some grapes. But they might have been sour."

The girl turned her head as far as the dressing allowed. "Too clever for me, that."

"Jules," Bev asked softly, "why didn't you phone me? Or get Val to put in a call? I thought we were getting on okay, you and me. I'd have brought you in, got it sorted."

"Sorted!" She glared. "You couldn't sort post." Bev's own words were thrown back; Jules even did the voice. "'Can't say much at the mo, love, but I reckon it'll all be over soon.' Over? I'll say it was over. All effin' over me." She turned her head again. "Fat lot of good you were."

Bev didn't argue. "Tell me what happened, Jules."

She was still staring at the wall. "I only wanted a packet of fags. I'd have had a lift in your poncey motor but I hadn't got any dosh. Needed a punter. Just the one would have done."

Bev swallowed hard, closed her eyes. What a price for a pack of twenty. Health warning needed an update. "I'd have given you a few quid. You only had to ask."

She turned her head back. "Yeah."

This time Bev looked away, studied her nails. "I'm sorry, Jules." Sorry you're on the game, sorry your life's shit, sorry I let you down.

"No worries."

Bev counted them, ran out of fingers. And toes.

"The bloke who attacked you. Punter, was he?"

"Nah. Johnny Depp. Wants me in his next film."

Bev clenched her fist. "I know you're hurting. And I know you're scared. And I know you don't have a lot of time for me at the mo – "

"Correction: no time, any moment."

The barb stung worse than a slap in the face. Bev hit back. "Blame me if it makes you feel any better, kid. But it isn't going to find the bastard who did this to you."

She watched as Jules lifted a hand gingerly to her eyes and gently rubbed. The bandage came away with black streaks from her kohl. She kept her eyes down and her voice flat, picking and pulling loose ends from the frayed edge. "Got took short, see. Desperate for a pee, so I go into the park. There I am squattin', next thing there's a blade at my throat. Thank God I didn't have no knickers on. I put me hands up like this," Bev nodded, "then I shoot up and I catch his chin with me head. Reckon it saved me. He loses his footin' so I kick him in the balls and do a runner. Didn't even hurt till I got to Val's. Then it stung like shit."

"You did good, Jules."

"Yeah?"

"You bet," she smiled. "This bloke. What's he look like, then?"

She shrugged. "It was pitch black out there and he come from behind." She was still fiddling with bits of thread. "Anyway, I was scared shitless."

Disappointment vied with despair. "What about a voice? Did he say anything?"

"Not a word."

"Had you been aware of anyone around? Anyone watching?"

"Come on, Bev, you were on the patch. It was turkey town on Christmas night."

Bev nodded. But it wasn't. Jules's attacker had been there, hiding in the shadows.

Watching, waiting, biding his time. Had he seen Bev as well, seen her talking to Jules?

"You look knackered, kid. How about I let you get some shuteye?"

Jules looked up, the fear back. "You gonna be around?" She disguised it quickly with something more casual. "Case I remember somefin', like."

"I've got a few things to…" She baulked at the word *sort.* "…see to, but I'll do an Arnie."

"You what?"

"I'll be back."

Jules's face dropped.

"Don't worry." Bev made to pat her hand, thought better of it, ran a finger along her cheek. "No one's going to get to you in here. Safer than a stainless steel condom, this place."

It could have been a smile, more likely a grimace. Bev tousled the girl's hair. "I meant what I said. You did really well, kid." Bev frowned: it matched the new expression on the girl's face. "What is it, Jules?"

"Hair." She looked at Bev. "He must have had long hair."

"You said you didn't see him."

"I didn't. All I saw was the knife. But somethin' brushed against the side of my face. Tickled a bit. Not that I was laughin' at the time. Shittin' meself, more like." She looked at Bev seeking confirmation. "It must have been, he had long hair? There was a smell an' all. Could have been shampoo. Not too sure."

Bev was almost afraid to ask. "Jules? The clothes you were wearing last night?"

"They're at Val's." She lifted a hand to an O-shaped mouth. "I told her to get rid of them. The stink was makin' me heave.

Apart from the blood an' that," she looked down at the covers, "I was sick as a dog." Bev waited. "I was scared, Bev. Real scared."

"You're okay, now, kid." She leaned across and kissed the girl's forehead. "Get some zeds in. I'll get someone round to Val's place, see what's what." She'd already got a little list for Ozzie; one more job wouldn't hurt.

The girl lifted her hands. "Know what really pisses me off about this?"

Bev turned her mouth down. "You'll never play the piano again?"

Jules rolled her eyes. "Daft sod."

"Give us a clue."

"Think about it." Bev watched, bemused, as Jules made a cack-handed attempt at a bit of hand relief. "Tools of the trade, ain't they? It'll be ages before I'm up to speed."

There was no answer to that. Bev smiled, slowly shook her head. "I'll catch you later."

"Yeah." Jules grinned. "And don't forget the soddin' grapes."

The hospital caff had left Bev longing for a Greasy Spoon; greasy anything, in fact. She'd bolted down a bowl of All-Bran and prunes and come away more ravenous than virtuous. Fast food to keep her going. The notion was amusing but she'd have preferred black pudding and baked beans. She'd been tucked away in a corner with the mobile clamped to her ear for much of the meal, an increasingly tetchy Oz at the other end. She'd considered her few requests well reasonable until he'd asked if he should stick a broom up his backside and give the floor a good going over at the same time. It was her absentminded agreement that had really rattled his cage. Still, he'd acceded. Had no choice. Not when she'd used the C-word in every sentence. As in Constable.

Now she was sitting at Cassie's bedside; had been for an hour or so. She'd swapped places for a while with Alison who was doing a stint with Jules. Bev was beginning to feel like the lady with the lamp. She just wished it would shed a bit more light on the case. It was like Jules's bandage: all loose ends and unravelling threads. It got her thinking cobwebs and Charlie Hawes, a malevolent spider enticing unwary flies parlourwards. Except this spider was still banged up. It didn't make sense.

She jumped a mile at a tap on her shoulder. "Not nodding off, are we, Sarge?"

She turned to see Ozzie grinning down, an armful of files in his grasp.

"Thinking, Constable. The word's thinking."

"Yeah, right." He dumped the papers in her lap. "Bit of bed-time reading for you. Ma'am."

She pulled a face, then grinned back. "Thanks, Oz. You're an angel."

"There's a couple of reports you might not have seen. Came in this morning. I copied them as well." He had a glint in his eye which she doubted stemmed from paperwork. It didn't. "I'd have got away sooner but there's a bit of a stink on back at the ranch."

"Oh?"

"Yeah. Something to do with DI Powell. The guv's had him on the carpet. No one really knows what's going on, but you know what that place is like. You should hear some of the rumours."

All manner of Powell's shortcomings sprang to mind, but that was down to him being a pillock. Professionally, far as she knew, he toed the line. "So what's the smart money on?"

Ozzie shrugged, inspected his shoes. He didn't go in for bad-mouthing, so this must be a biggie.

"Go on, Oz." Bev did not share his misgivings. "You must have heard something."

He was hesitating and she was about to ask again when he spoke. "Ferguson's name keeps cropping up."

She blinked, mind whirring. Duncan Ferguson, fruitcake of

this parish; hobbies included confessing to murder and making death threats. Powell had certainly spent a fair bit of time with the bloke. He'd spoken to him on the night of Louella's murder, been to his home, led the interviews back at the nick. So what had Powell done?

"I give up," she said after a few moments. "Give us a clue."

He spread his hands. "Honest, Sarge. I'd tell you if I knew."

She snorted. "You'd be the only one round here who does, then."

Ozzie glanced round, clearly eager for another subject. He nodded at the girl in the bed, her fingers wrapped round Paddington's neck. "Poor kid. Must've been quite a looker before some bastard got his hands on her."

Bev put a finger to her lips, beckoned him closer. "She's probably listening to your every word. She's just being arsey. I'm hanging round cause I need her to give me a steer."

"Hope you have better luck than me," Oz said. "I called on your mate. Val? About the clothes? She's burnt the lot. Said they were covered in blood."

Mate? Bev wasn't too sure about that. It still rankled that she hadn't put a call in about Jules. It seemed even the oldest profession closed ranks. More importantly, it scuppered any chance of forensics finding a thing, let alone a stray hair or three to match the others that had surfaced elsewhere. "What you up to now, Oz?"

"I'm still digging."

She looked puzzled.

"Steve Bell," he explained. "Apparently he was at Thread Street Comprehensive a few years back. I'm having a word with the caretaker up there at lunchtime. Oh, and the guv wants me to organise this ID parade you were on about."

"Really?"

"Yeah. I think he just wants to put the wind up Hawes."

"I can think of other things I'd rather put up him."

Oz wasn't listening properly, glancing at his watch, his lips in a rather fetching pout. "I should just have time," he muttered to himself.

"Time for what?" she enquired.

"Desperate Dan."

Bev looked blankly at him.

"The bloke duffed up a couple of days back?" Oz prompted. "He's in here. Men's Surgical."

It was ringing a vague bell. "He the one Gazza's been baby-sitting?"

Oz nodded. "Thinks he might talk but Gaz is otherwise engaged today."

Bev looked at Cassie who was still doing a Sleeping Beauty, mouthed the query "Funeral?"

Oz nodded. "Anyway, the guv wants me to pop my head round while I'm here."

Seemed a strange request. It was nothing to do with the case.

"I know what you're thinking, Sarge. But this bloke's in a bad way; any worse and it'll be murder, not attempted."

She lifted a few files. "Catch you later, then. This'll keep me going."

She ferreted out the fresh stuff first, browsed through. And froze. No wonder the guv wanted to go ahead with the ID parade. The hairs on the scrunchy found near Louella's body matched Charlie Hawes. She grabbed at the next print-out, fingers fumbling in the rush then stopping dead. It didn't make sense. Scraps of hair caught under the girl's nails were definitely not Charlie's. Neither had they found a match for the tiny particles of fibre. Fibre contaminated with minute traces of oil. She held the papers in her hands, staring ahead as if the answers were about to show up. She was back to loose threads, unravelling ends, but at the same time, a gut feeling that it was all here if she knew where to look.

She flicked through the rest of the reports, reread interviews and witness statements. She was as still as the comatose patients, a patch of calm surrounded by constant sound. She cut out the beeps and hums, ignored the occasional swish of cotton against nylon, the trill of a phone. She was miles away, head full of thoughts that one second seemed to connect and the next were as far apart as ever.

"Ain't you got a home to go?" The voice startled Bev. She glanced at Cassie whose wide yawn showcased the benefits of fluoridisation. Shame about the gap in the front but even fluoride was no proof against a fist in the mouth.

"You're not still knackered, surely?" Bev smiled.

"Need me beauty sleep, don't I?"

Bev told her about last night's attack on Jules, said she'd be around for a while yet.

"I've been thinkin' 'bout what you said." Cassie was staring at her hands. Bev held her breath. "It was all crap. You're on completely the wrong track."

"Put me on the right one then, Cass."

"Charlie Hawes is a mad bastard but he ain't stupid. He ain't gonna kill his girls, specially not a bird like Shell. Makin' him a fortune, she was."

Bev put her head in her hands, felt like putting them over her ears. She didn't want to hear this. Heard it before; from the horse's mouth, only yesterday. She sighed, looked at Cassie again. "I thought you were going to help me."

The silence lasted a few seconds. "I don't have to tell you anythin'."

"No, 'course not — "

"Will you shut the fuck up!" Bev took a deep breath. She couldn't remember the last time she'd seen a kid so angry. "I don't have to tell you anythin'. You can see it for yourself. On tape. There's half a dozen of 'em. Buried, in the park. They were gonna be Shell's passport out of the game. I told her blackmail was wrong but she reckoned these tapes were gonna take her to a better place. They did that all right. Only trouble is she can't never come back now, can she?"

The girl was telling the truth, it was in her voice, Bev just didn't want to believe it. If it wasn't Charlie Hawes, she'd been wrong since the start.

"So Charlie…" She got no further; Cassie was still seething.

"What was it your mate just said? Must have been a looker before some bastard got his hands on her? Well, for bastard read Charlie Hawes." She was crying now. "Get him for what he done to me."

It was something, but it wasn't the biggie. "So the tapes. Who –?"

"An old fart from up at the school. Shagging the arse off some bugger."

An old fart from up at the school? Bev was in a state of shock, mesmerised by her racing thoughts and the silent tears streaming down Cassie's cheeks.

"Go and dig 'em up. Your lot get off on a bit of porn, don't they? Have a good laugh. Then go get the bastard who really did kill our Shell."

35

Bev recognised the location from Cassie's description: an old, rotting tree stump, a stone's throw from Bogart's Pool. The same pool she'd thrown up in, the same stump on which she'd sat waiting for the waves of nausea to recede after the sight of Louella's body. It had been night then, but even now in the middle of the day the park was dark and dank. Darker in places; last time there'd been emergency lighting.

Trembling, she looked round; detected a hint of menace. Whether it was in the damp air or her fevered imagination, she wouldn't like to guess.

She gazed down, knowing the answers were beneath her feet, a shroud of black plastic giving protection from wet earth and voracious mouths. There was no rush. Oz hadn't put in an appearance yet.

She lit a cigarette, one of several items she'd bought en route from the General. She inhaled deeply, savouring the forbidden weed, refusing to consider it yet another failure. On her current rap sheet it didn't register. The nicotine hit made her dizzy, nauseous. She took another deep drag, then another and another. She threw away the butt only after lighting another cigarette from the glowing end. The nausea passed; at least she'd mastered that. She was watching, waiting, making sure he wasn't around, half-hoping he was.

A boring old fart up at the school.

Only he wasn't. Bev had made the same sort of mistake as Cyanide Lil. Only worse. Much worse. Lil wasn't a cop; just a harmless old biddy who'd seen Henry Brand as a 'real gent'. Bev knew he was a pervert with a taste for S&M. She'd just never seen him as a killer. She'd only ever seen one man as the killer. She'd been backing the wrong horse from the start. The favourite had faded before the finishing post. A rank outsider had come up from behind. Digging out the tapes would confirm what she was sure she already knew.

It had started to make sense in the car on the way over. There was no sudden flash, no specific spark. The complex threads had simply started drawing together; a gentle tug here, a little pull there, and the loose ends had begun to fuse. She didn't know everything but —

A sudden noise. She twisted her head; recognised it as the thud of a decaying branch falling onto a lush carpet of rotting vegetation. She relaxed again. No, not relaxed: shifted focus, then zoomed in.

Cassie had talked her through the videos. Shell had nicked them from Charlie. They made the tape Ozzie took look tame. Henry Brand in shot throughout and in the shit forever. Shell had threatened Brand that the movies were going on general release unless he wanted exclusive rights. Bev covered her face with her hands. No wonder the poor kid thought her boat had come in; she'd probably seen a whole fleet. All Shell had to do was keep her mouth shut and she'd make a killing. Brand couldn't afford *not* to pay. That was the theory.

Bev lifted her head, suddenly alert. The sharp crack had come from the upper branches of an old fir. She listened again. Nothing.

Her cigarette was almost out. She snatched a last drag then flicked the butt into the water. It was so quiet in the park she heard the hiss. She toyed with the idea of lighting a third. No. She'd waited long enough.

She rose, reached for the spade. The price tag was still attached, not that she'd be writing it off on expenses. This wasn't just part of the job. Anyway, a few quid bore no relation to what she felt she owed the girls and the guv. Her obsession with Hawes had cost everyone dear.

She sighed, felt an unbearable weariness. 'Course, she could call out a plod for the donkey-work, and by rights the boss should be here. Somehow it felt better like this, though. She'd been out on a limb from the start; ending it on another seemed fitting. Okay, she'd called Oz, but that didn't count. They'd come a long way together. She glanced at her watch.

The earth was still soft after Tuesday's downpour. Nothing to work up a sweat. She wondered if Shell and Cassie had found it easy or if they'd had to take it in turns. Maybe one kept lookout while the other dug.

About a metre down, Cassie had said. Bev looked into the hole; halfway there then. A worm, gross in its fat whiteness, was struggling on top of the soil, protesting about the intrusion, the light, whatever pissed worms off. She felt like killing it, cutting it, really giving it something to whinge about. Wrong target: she tossed it aside in the next clod.

She was working more carefully now, alert for a glimpse of black plastic. Did plastic still shine after a month's interment? Better not risk it: she went down on her hands and knees. The earth's dampness seeped through her tights, on to her skin.

It was there. She could see it. Maybe she should hang fire till Oz got here? Nah. He'd cover her back with the guv. Christ, she'd back-covered big time for Oz. She scraped at the earth with her fingers, revealing more of the sack beneath. Nearly there now. The soil was blacker, more cloying, smelt stronger.

And then it was closer. Too close. Far too close.

She'd seen nothing, heard nothing but now she was face down, head down, a foot hard on her neck. She was winded, fought not to gasp for the breath that had been knocked from her lungs.

How had he known she was there?

With her head down, Brand's voice was muffled. Her body was making competing noises of its own: blood rushing in her ears, heart pounding against ribcage. She was terrified, fighting a rising panic. She was afraid of the earth; afraid it would fill her mouth, her nostrils, she wouldn't be able to speak, wouldn't be able to breathe.

The pain was excruciating. For a second she feared blacking out. Then she remembered what he'd done to Michelle and Louella; tried to do to Jules. There'd been enough victims.

There was very little time. That was all she knew. The park wasn't much used at this time of year but he wouldn't hang around. He'd gone to extraordinary lengths to keep them off his back; he wouldn't take more of a risk than he had to now. Think, girl, think. He could snap her neck like a twig whenever he liked, but she didn't think he'd go for that. Not his style. So which hand held the knife?

Every nerve was charged, every muscle taut. She sensed a lessening of the pressure on her windpipe. He'd have to crouch to use a knife; was he going for the kill?

Was the pressure easing, or was her neck going numb? Her eyes were accustomed to what little light there was. She'd only have one chance of a pop.

A second? Two? That's all she had. The fist-sized rock was just within reach. If she could grab it when he lifted his foot, she might just be able to…

His hot rank breath was in her ear. "Don't even think about it, bitch."

Oz was running. He had to get to Bev. Boy, had he got news for her. He'd just left Men's Surgical. It was all in his notes. Desperate Dan, a k a Danny Glover, hadn't so much grassed on Charlie Hawes as covered him in turf. As a former heavy of Hawes Danny's words carried weight. Talk about putting a smile on Bev's face. Oz couldn't wait. His own face fell when he saw the empty space at the girl's bedside.

"Hi, Cass. Where's Sergeant Morriss?"

"Bev?" Cassie lifted her glance from a dog-eared copy of *heat*. "Dunno."

Oz turned but something in the girl's expression gave him pause. "You sure, Cassie?"

She turned a page ostensibly intent on some Hollywood C-list celeb.

Oz tapped a foot. "Come on, love. I need — "

"Did you mean what you said earlier?" He hadn't a clue what she was on about. "You said I must have been a looker before..."

"Look, love, I'm in a bit of a hurry—"

"Bugger off, then."

He shook his head; didn't like women swearing. God knew why he liked Bev so much. "Tell me where she is and I will."

"She buggered off an' all. Soon's she got — " She'd shut her mouth but couldn't hide the look on her face.

"Got what?" Oz asked. What had Bev got? And where had she gone?

"It doesn't matter."

So why was Oz's instinct telling him it did. He looked more closely at the girl. She'd been crying. The whites of her eyes weren't, and tears had left salt trails on cheeks the colour of damsons. It would be weeks before the bruises faded.

"Okay. Have it your way." He saluted her and this time made it to the door before turning. "Tell you something, though, Cass."

She licked a finger turned another page.

"You're still a looker in my book."

He closed the door gently behind him. He was halfway down the corridor before she called him back.

The man's breath was on Bev's neck. He'd shifted his foot; the pressure she felt now was from a hand. Which one? She desperately tried to recall which he favoured. It would determine the direction of the knife. That he had a blade she had no doubt. She could even describe it: small, sharp, serrated. She saw again the damage it had already inflicted.

She felt his fingers tightening. What was going on in his sick mind? Why hadn't he stabbed her already? Knifed her in the back? It would be easy. No. Of course. She knew then. He was going to cut her. The way he'd cut Shell; the way he'd cut Louella. He'd go for her throat.

The pressure eased as he grabbed her hair to yank her head back. She jerked forward; the self-inflicted pain was preferable to a blade. Her hair was too short. He couldn't get a grip. Bev's reverse jerk was equally quick. Her head whacked into the side of his face. She heard a crack like a twig snapping.

She was on her knees now struggling to get to her feet. She was in agony. Her spine, her neck, her head all hurt like shit. There was dirt in her eyes. They stung like hell. She could hardly see. Had he dropped the knife? She hit out in the direction of his heavy breaths.

"Bitch."

The hiss helped. She lashed out again. Then kicked. Her boot made contact. The scream could have come from either of them. Bev's eyes were streaming. She dashed a hand across them, desperate to get some vision back, more desperate that the knife wasn't heading her way. It took seconds for her to identify the noise. It couldn't be. "Fuck."

He was getting away. She caught a soft-focus glimpse of Brand heading for a line of trees, dragging one of his legs. It wasn't the only thing she saw. The knife lay on the ground at her feet. So did the fist-sized rock she'd envisaged smashing into his skull. She'd never catch him. She could barely stand let alone give chase. She had no choice. She made a grab, aimed and threw. Then the pain, the dizziness overwhelmed her. The earth rushed towards her as she fell to the ground.

Oz was in the car spitting feathers. What the hell was she playing at? He'd been gagging to share Dan's dirt with her, but oh no. According to Cassie, Bev would be in the park by now digging up videos crucial to the Lucas inquiry. He glanced at the dashboard clock. An hour she'd been gone. On her own. Without so much as a whisper. Teamwork, or what? He had a damn good mind to call it in.

He started the motor, still undecided whether to go to the park or back to the nick. Why had she left him out of the loop? It was out of character: those parts of her character he thought he knew. He had time for Bev, recognised her strengths, tolerated the odd fault. Morriss-the-Mouth some of the blokes called her. But Oz reckoned the smart-lip stuff was mostly a front, a distraction. She felt things deeply did Bev. He'd picked up on that straight away. He'd also recognised a sliver of ice inside a core of steel. She was her own woman; refused to be one of the lads; ploughed her own furrow.

He snorted. How apt. He could see her now digging away with her little spade. Of course, she'd covered her back: left a message on his mobile. For God's sake, he was only down the corridor. She'd known precisely where he was.

He tapped an angry beat on the steering wheel, then the image shifted. Bev was still digging, head down, leant forward. Back not covered.

"Oh shit."

He put his foot to the floor, told himself not to be stupid. Repeated it half a dozen times on the way. The killer wouldn't be there. There was no reason for the killer to be there. He told himself that as well. By the time he arrived he almost believed it.

There were two bodies. Bev was on her side near the pond. A man was lying face down over by the trees. Oz was so out of depth, he felt he was drowning. He knew the procedures. There were systems in place. Call it in. Cordon it off. Don't contaminate the scene. The books didn't say anything about Bev being down. He ran through wet grass, sticky mud, stumbled, almost fell.

She was on her right side. Her face, hands, clothes were filthy. There were holes in her tights; one shoe had come off. She was very still. He lifted her hair to feel for a pulse, saw the livid bruising and blood on her neck.

"Bastard." His voice was a whisper.

"Get your fucking hand off. It hurts." So was hers.

"Bev." He swallowed; couldn't speak.

She tried to sit but waves of pain forced her back. She put a hand to her head. It hurt to open her eyes. "Bastard got away." Her voice was a rasp. It hurt to talk. It hurt to open her mouth.

Oz's was open in shock.

"Brand. He's the killer." She lifted a hand to her throat. "Call it in. Get an APB out."

"I don't think so."

"What?"

"There's a bod — "

"What?"

"By the — "

"Help me up. Now."

"I'm calling an ambulance first. I'm not sure you should be moving at all."

She was struggling to sit. She'd just spotted Brand, recalled what happened in the seconds before she'd lost consciousness.

"Sarge?" Oz laid a hand on her arm. She shook it off.

"Is he dead?"

"I've not — "

"For Christ's sake. Check it. Now."

The waiting lasted a lifetime. If Brand was dead, she wasn't sure how she'd live with that. He was a murderer, but if she'd killed him – what did that make her? Tentatively she tried standing. There were bumps and bruises. Nothing broken. She felt sick. It would pass. Oz was walking towards her. She examined his face, searching for clues.

She could wait no longer. "Is he dead?"

Oz shook his head. “No.”

She closed her eyes, mouthed her gratitude.

Oz was in front of her, regarding her closely. His face creased in concern. “He’s not dead. But, Bev. It’s not Brand.”

She felt the colour drain from her face. She didn’t believe it; forced herself to approach, to see for herself. Oz had applied cuffs and placed him in the recovery position. The face was partially obscured. The long dark hair had come adrift. The unwittingly comic effect of the wig was underlined by the swelling on the back of the head. It put Bev in mind of a shiny pink egg. She imagined the rock would be around somewhere.

She knelt. Maybe she needed a closer look; maybe she needed to confirm the snot rag was still alive.

He was. He shook hair out of his eyes and spat in her face. Charlie Hawes was a looker. Steve Bell bore little resemblance.

36

The soup was grey, greasy, gross. *Of the day* it said on the board. It didn't specify which day. Not this one, Bev thought. This had been the longest day she could recall. It was ending in the canteen at Highgate because she was too depressed to face an empty house, too scared to be alone with her thoughts, too wired to switch off. Oz was opposite, forking an omelette round his plate. Bev's throat wasn't up to anything more solid than the consommé; her appetite wasn't even up for that.

"Come on, Sarge. You've not tasted it." He handed her a spoon.

Her smile was shaky, matched by the fingers she was trying to close round it. She slammed it down, watched crumbs jiggle on the plastic cloth. She was pissed off. Not with the cutlery. She leaned her elbows on the table, rested her head in her hands.

She shouldn't be there by rights. She knew that. They'd wanted to keep her in the General overnight but she'd walked, desperate to be in on the preliminary interviews with Bell. Byford – a seething Byford – had refused. She couldn't get it out of her head.

He had thrown not so much the book as the library. He hadn't raised his voice; hadn't had to. The thunderous look on his face was enough. She'd shown scant – make that no – regard for procedure. She'd kept colleagues in the dark and could have got herself killed. She'd endangered DC Khan, and potentially damaged the force.

Part of her had silently rebelled; the tirade was unfair. Bell was in a cell for Christ's sake. Then she recalled not only her time-wasting obsession with Hawes but her utter conviction that Brand was the killer. That led to a flashback in the park: caught between a rock and – for hard place, read knife. She'd come *so* close to the knife. It was a place she didn't want to go.

Sure that Byford was going to kick her off the squad – perhaps all the way back to uniform – she'd kept quiet, glad when the storm eventually blew itself out and he'd told her to get out of his sight.

That was then. This was now. And Oz had recently emerged from one of the later interviews. They were by a radiator and she had a Blues scarf round her neck. She still had the shakes. She leaned forward, hands clamped in armpits.

"Talk me through it, then."

He took a bite; couldn't speak through rubbery egg. She knew his game: playing for time. She sighed. He actually felt sorry for her. She'd got it so wrong she could go on Mastermind. Name: Beverley Morriss. Specialist subject: cocking it up.

"Come on, Oz. I'm a big girl now."

He laid his fork on the plate, took a sip of water. "Look, Sarge, anyone could've — "

"Cut the crap, Oz. Anyone didn't. Just me. It was me who made the mistakes. Jumped – no, make that leapt – to conclusions."

She looked round, met the curious glances of a couple of plods three tables away. She gave a less than regal wave but at least used all her hand.

"You hadn't seen the tapes," Oz said. "You only had what Cassie gave you."

Cassie had confirmed the boring old fart's identity but knew nothing about Henry Brand's co-star. Bev blamed herself. She should have pushed the girl harder; got a description, age, anything. No. She'd hared off to retrieve the videos – ignoring the bigger picture.

Unlike Oz. He, she'd since learned, had gently drawn out Charlie's erstwhile minder Danny Glover. The man had coughed enough to put the pimp behind bars till he picked up his pension. Charlie was already in custody getting a taste for porridge. Living off immoral earnings was the least of his worries. Not when there was porn, blackmail, extortion, abduction, kidnap and attempted murder.

One of Danny's tip-offs had led to a police raid on a house in Balsall Heath. Vicki Flinn was there, in a bad way but alive. Seeing Lucie would be the best treatment. Arrangements were in hand. Annie Flinn had taken the baby to her sister's. But only after Charlie Hawes had *borrowed* Lucie for a night, a little chilling reminder to Annie what could happen if she blabbed.

It was all second-hand news to Bev. Vicki refused to see her, let alone talk to her. It was another stick Bev was beating herself with.

Oz handed another. "Why'd you leg it like that? You knew where I was."

She gazed at her blackened nails; scrubbing had only touched the surface. She didn't know the answer. Leaving a message on a mobile was pathetic. There were signs all over the hospital telling people to switch the damn things off. She'd known he wouldn't get it while he was in the building. She'd done it deliberately. But why? It was another place she didn't want to go.

She shrugged. It was a cop-out. He acknowledged it with a shrug of his own.

Bev delved in her bag and came up with a crumpled pack of ciggies. He pushed his chair back and for a second she thought he was leaving. He must have seen her face.

"You'll be wanting an ashtray."

God. It must be worse than she thought. Oz loathed smoking. He came back with a saucer and a smile of sorts. She lit a Silk Cut, took a deep drag. It had been small beer so far. Now it was time for the brewery.

"Come on, Oz. You were in there for hours. What's the scum-bag saying? What's he putting his hand up to?"

"It was weird. At first he wouldn't open his mouth, then – " Oz's hands traced floodgates opening.

Oz reckoned it boiled down to greed and revenge. Bell had been one of Hawes's hired hands. Charlie had brought him on board to service the gay brigade. Enter Henry Brand. Bell had been Brand's favourite whipping boy for years. Paid well over the odds. Bell certainly couldn't afford to let Michelle take a cut of the fairy cake.

"Bell said she was cutting her nose off to spite her face." Oz shook his head. "Can you believe that?"

Bev snorted. "He's an arse. I can believe anything. Why did he kill her? Why not just rough her up?"

"He was after Charlie as well."

Bev nearly choked. "What?"

"Bell hated Charlie almost as much as he hated Brand. He reckoned they were both buggering him about."

She groaned at the awful pun.

"Yeah, okay. Bad choice." Oz waved away a puff of smoke. "Fact is, Bell had been multi-skilling. He'd turned into Charlie's regular blue-eyed bully-boy. It gave him a fix on Charlie's dealings: massage parlours, illicit videos, blackmail. Bell reckoned he was in line for promotion. Junior partner at least. But Hawes wasn't coming to the wicket."

If Oz said anything about maidens over, she'd bop him.

"Bell killed Michelle to protect his source of hard-earned cash," Oz said. "But he'd make sure Charlie went down for it. He had it all planned. He was biding his time, waiting for the right moment. Shell's argument in the street with Brand brought it to a head. Lil wasn't the only witness. Bell saw it too. It was Shell's death sentence and – if Bell's plans had panned out – Charlie's life sentence."

Bev nodded, mentally ticking Bell's duff pointers. The

scrunchy with Charlie's hair. Michelle's blood in Charlie's motor. The wig to copy Charlie's look, and conceal a shaven scalp. Bell had been doing his worst to point the police in the wrong direction – and she had obligingly followed the signs.

She saw a few more then, not erected by Bell. A dodgy bike-chain soaking in Annie Flinn's sink. Tiny particles of fibre contaminated with oil. Dark stains on Bell's jeans. She shook her head. Jack Crane hadn't seen a jogger. He'd bumped into Steve Bell fleeing the scene of Michelle's murder. Bell with long dark hair. Like Charlie.

From Bell's point of view, she supposed it had a sick twisted logic. But why Louella? Where did a girl like Louella fit in? She asked Oz . There was a pause before he replied.

"It had nothing to do with her dad being a cop. She took a shortcut. Bell was hanging round the park. He needed another victim. He had evidence to plant. Heat to turn. Hawes to burn."

Bev closed her eyes; still saw Louella; saw all the girls.

Oz leaned back, folded his arms. "As for the rest of it, Bell's buck-passing so fast you can't see his hands move. He's laying everything at Charlie's door. The attack on Cass. The death threats. Your postcard."

"Regular Postman Pat." Bev sniffed.

"And Freddie Florist. Hawes was behind all that, according to Bell."

"You don't sound too sure."

He looked at Bev. "Yeah, well, Hawes hasn't opened his mouth yet."

"What about the attack on Jules?"

Oz hesitated. Either he didn't know or he didn't want to tell.

"Come on, Oz. Give."

"Bell's admitted to it. He'd been following you. Saw you talking to her."

She closed his eyes; saw another stick.

"It's not down to you, Bev." Oz reached out a hand but

stopped just short of touching her.

"But why risk it?" Bev's puzzlement made her voice tight. "Surely he'd have known it would destroy everything he'd done to frame Charlie. Hawes was in custody at the time. By attacking her, Bell was letting the scumbag off the hook."

Oz shook his head. "Ah, there's the irony. Bell isn't the sharpest knife in the box..."

She winced but didn't interrupt.

"...He didn't realise that we had enough to hold Charlie. He thought Hawes was back out on the streets. Said he needed one last push to convince us that Charlie was the killer. "

Bev groaned as the implication sank in. "Convince *me*, you mean!"

Oz tried to smile reassuringly, but she could see the pain.

"If you ask me, it's all bollocks," he insisted. "I think he'd lost it by then. Bell just didn't care. He was getting off on it. Couldn't control himself. Listening to him in there, Sarge, he was enjoying it all. Bragging, showing off, know what I mean?"

"No. Thank God." She shivered at the thought. "Did he say anything about the night outside my place?"

"Oh, that was a co-production. Charlie's idea, but Bell was only too willing to oblige. He was on a nice little earner for that. £500. You were lucky."

She widened her eyes. "I was?"

"Yeah. Charlie only wanted you scared. If Bell'd taken you out Charlie would have broken his neck."

"Shame he didn– " She saw Oz's face. "Yeah. Right. Okay."

"Anyway, when Bell's not buck-passing, he's snivelling. Blaming everyone but himself. To hear him talk, he's as much a victim as the girls."

"Go on."

"You name it, he's had it: abuse, violence, neglect, bullying."

"Suing everyone in sight, is he?"

"No." Oz said. "Just you. Joke," he added, a tad tardily to Bev's way of thinking.

"Frankly, my dear," she drawled through a yawn. "I don't give a damn."

Oz rolled his eyes. "Don't tell me. 'Tomorrow is another day.'"

Another day. She smiled. She liked the sound of that.

37

The Fighting Cocks was throbbing, for want of a better verb. Big Val swayed like a tipsy queen, her lilac Bet Lynch a tower of quivering candy-floss. Bev smiled ruefully. The big woman had more hair-pieces than Madame Tussaud's; shame they hadn't rung a bell earlier. Bell, it turned out, had quite a collection himself. They'd found the dreadlocks behind a false wall at Annie Flinn's place. Bev tried not to think about it; this was supposed to be a party.

Cassie was missing the fun, and Jules's hand-me-down grapes weren't much compensation. Still, Jules and the rest of the girls were out in force, come to that, so was the force. Even the guv had said he'd try to pop in for a swift half. To Bev's way of thinking, if he didn't show he still hadn't forgiven her for nearly getting herself killed.

Frankie hadn't. She'd gone apeshit. Looking at her now, it was hard to believe such profanities had passed such lips. She was on the floor, sheathed in slinky black, belting out *Search For The Hero.*

Bev's mouth twitched. Val was already exploring. Her fingers were tracing lines along Ozzie's thigh. Politely, he kept removing them but back they'd creep. Bit like Bev's thoughts. She shoved them aside and laughed perhaps a touch too loudly.

She glanced round the table. It wasn't exactly tarts and vicars, but who needed dog collars at a knees-up? She downed the rest of her Grouse.

"Get you another, Sarge?"

It was more plea than request. She looked at Ozzie, spotted Val's latest digital foray, winked and said ambiguously: "I'll give you a hand."

It was a parting-of-the-waves job to get to the bar. Once there, Ozzie propped it up and looked back appreciatively. "Your mate, Frankie. She's got a cracking voice."

Bev nodded. "Crystal. Twenty paces."

He cocked his head in the direction of their table. "What about the Spice Girls? Same again?"

She glanced over. Jules was regaling Patty and Smithy with a blow-by-blow account of her big scene in the park, heavily bandaged hands adding weight to the drama. Jo and Chloë were taking the piss, aping every move.

She nodded, smiling. "And Oz," she added mischievously, "don't forget Val's pork scratchings."

He swallowed hard, wiped his top lip with a paisley handkerchief. "Shame Vince isn't here. Get on like a house on fire, him and Val."

"Hot, isn't she?" Bev murmured.

He shoved a couple of drinks across the bar. It was the only answer she was getting.

"Cheers, Oz." Val relieved him of the tray, then patted the bench at her side. "Been keeping it warm for you, chuck."

Bev grinned. Last time she'd seen him so flushed was at Marlene's place. Mind, the lights had gone out at Marlene's. They'd been pulling plugs all over the city. All those massage parlours and covert film studios. All part of Charlie Hawes's 21st Century Fucks. They'd seized enough movies to keep Blockbusters going for years; not that Blockbusters would be in the market for them. Charlie had other clients, of course. Customers he had by the short and curlies. Big time. Talk about a money spinner. Come into my parlour.

"Penny for them, Bev?" She turned to see whose hand was on her shoulder. The woman looked even more stunning without the white coat.

"Believe me, doc, you don't want to know." She glanced round, motioned to a chair. "Grab a pew. Glad you could make it."

"How you doing?" It was more than small talk. The woman's gaze was on Bev's neck, and it wasn't admiring the scarf.

Bev flapped a dismissive hand, tried not to flinch. "Flesh wound, mate. Just a little prick."

Val had obviously caught the tail end. "Had a few of them in my time, kid."

Doctor Thorne drew up a seat and plonked a bottle of Bolly on the table. "That's for later."

The wild applause was a bit OTT, then Bev realised Frankie had finished the song. The whistles and catcalls were for the opening bars of *Money's Too Tight To Mention.*

Jules drawled, "Tell me about it."

"Glad to see you're feeling yourself," Bev said.

"All I will be feeling with this lot." The beer-stained bandages looked worse for wear. Bev reckoned the girl was secretly proud of them.

"Where's your boss, then?" The doc's question was casually posed but it didn't fool Bev. She'd love to see him walk through the door herself.

"The night is young." She smiled to hide a sadness that wasn't just down to Byford's absence. Shell and Louella would never be coming back, and there was another missing face. Vicki was still refusing all Bev's calls. She mouthed a toast to absent friends and drained her glass, made a mental note to switch to mineral water. When it boiled down to it, Vick's attitude was the same as Val's. "You're a great bird, Bev, but you're still a cop."

It partly explained why Val hadn't played straight. She'd been a damn sight more scared of Charlie than she had of the Bill. She'd lied through her bridgework for Hawes: the death threats; the Brighton line; Vicki's baby. Christ, she'd even minded the kid one night. Charlie might be banged up, but Bev still hadn't persuaded the big woman to give evidence against him. Mind, she was working on it.

"Cheer up, chuck. It might never happen."

Bev lifted her glance from the bottom of her glass. What if it already had?

"My round, I think." The doc was on her feet. "Bev?"

"Large Grouse. Cheers." The mental abstinence note was lost in a stack of others. Taking work home was one thing, bringing it here was something else. Again she tried switching off but it was still ticking over.

She glanced at her watch. 10.20. The guv was cutting it fine. He'd come down a notch during the day, from seething to steaming. He'd let her sit in on a couple of interviews, and take a look at the tapes. Talk about frightening the horses. She could see she'd been well out of order, going off on her own. On the other hand, the buried treasure equalled a closing case. Make that cases. It would be months before they got to court and God knew how many worms would crawl out of the woodwork before then. Ferguson the Confessor had crept back to his hole. His fifteen minutes of fame had been forced on him. Charlie had propelled him into the spotlight with a lethal combination of threats and promises. Hawes had been playing for time. Ferguson would get done for wasting it.

As for Powell, he had a little of it on his hands. The DI had been sent home, pending an internal inquiry. Word was, that while interviewing Ferguson he'd mentioned the tenners in Michelle Lucas's shoe. Short of divine inspiration, it was just about the only explanation for Ferguson knowing. Powell denied it, of course. Bev didn't know what to think. The man was a plonker, but she didn't have him down as a bent plonker. It was possible – however unprofessional – that he'd let it slip accidentally. She glanced at Oz, recalled the night in her place and Henry Brand's tape in her player. Anyone could make a mistake.

Brand certainly had. They were still working on the charges he'd face. Enid Brand's overdose was one they might have to drop. Brand still insisted it was self-inflicted. Bev had doubts. Fact was, the woman was worth more dead than alive. A tempting prospect for a man with a faulty cashflow.

It all looked puny compared with Bell's charge account. Bev wrapped the scarf gently round her neck and resisted the urge to look over her shoulder. Ridiculous. The sleaze ball was behind bars. Mind, he'd been on her back long enough. It was Bell who'd been in New Street that day. She hated to think how he long he'd been trailing her. Paid off for him though. Not only had she led him to the spoils, she'd even dug the bloody things up for him. Still. Bell would be going down: two counts of murder and the attempted murder of a police officer.

"'allo, 'allo, 'allo. Evenin' all!" Vince Hanlon's bulk was blocking the light. "Room for a little 'un?" he asked.

"Brought one wiv yer?" Jules countered.

"Sit here, Sarge," Ozzie offered with alacrity. "I'll give the doc a hand."

Bev grinned as she caught what sounded like "Hello, big boy" from Val. She glanced round. She'd never seen the place so full. Frankie was on good form.

"You givin' up the day job then, Bev?" The question was from Jules, but all the girls were smirking.

"Be a shame," said Patty. "Now we've shown you the string."

"Ropes, Patty, ropes," they chorused.

"Have to ask the boss 'bout that," Bev said.

"That'd be a first."

She glanced up; Byford was at her shoulder.

"Ask the boss about what?"

Bev jumped to her feet. "Guv. Sit down. What you having?"

"It's on its way." He nodded as Ozzie and the doc made their way back with a couple of trays.

"Not sure you'd make it," Bev said.

"Press got wind of the story. I've been doing interviews."

"You gonna be on the telly?" asked Jo.

"Maybe." He smiled, then looked at Bev. "Makes a change from the rack."

"Cheers." She lifted her glass. The Grouse was working its magic. She relaxed for the first time in ages; sat back, watched her mates, listened to the music. Frankie finished with *Holding Back The Years.* The song always had the same effect on Bev.

"You okay, chuck?" Val asked.

"Bit smoky in here." They were all looking. She changed the subject. "Another, anyone?"

"My shout," said Byford. "Same again, Bev?"

Better not. She was sure to regret it. "Large Grouse, guv. Ta."

The horrific events were beginning to recede. She was moving from 'Life's A Bitch And Then You Die' into 'All This And Heaven Too'. A touch of the hard stuff always softened her up. Good job Frankie was about done or she'd be joining her at the mike.

The girls clapped louder than anyone and Smithy's two-fingered whistle warranted earplugs. Jules shuffled along the bench to make space for Frankie, which had a knock-on effect on Val and Vince. Bev listened to the chat, lounged back further, lost herself in the amber glow.

"Still with us, our Bev?" Val tapped her knee. "It's last orders. Want another?"

Better not. "Yeah, why not?"

"Large one, Sarge?" Oz asked.

No way. "You bet."

She could feel an Indian coming on. She smiled; with Oz around, that wasn't the best way of putting it.

"What's tickled you, Bev?" Jules asked.

"Nothing." She was still grinning.

"This'll give you a giggle." Vince reached into a pocket, brought out a neatly folded piece of paper.

"What you got there then, Vince?" she asked.

"Hold on. Just have a listen." He cleared his throat, lifted a hand for silence.

"There was a young sergeant from Highgate
Who went off one night on a blind date.
She'd been warned by her mummy
Don't mess with a dummy
And ever since then she's been celibate."

When the catcalls eventually died down, Bev pursed her lips. "That is the biggest pile of dog-doo I've ever heard. It doesn't rhyme. It doesn't scan. It's not even funny."

"Me thinks the lady dith protest too much," Oz intoned.

"Doth," she corrected automatically. "Hold on a minute." She'd heard that somewhere before. She narrowed her eyes, kept them on Oz. "Who did you say wrote that crap, Vince?"

"Dunno. No name on it."

She was still glaring at Oz, but the man had no shame. He asked Vince what the prize was.

"What's it to you, Constable?" she snapped.

"Just wondered," Oz said.

"Now then, children." Vince was at his avuncular worst. "The winner gets a balti for two. Jewel in the Crown."

Bev's glare was now a glower. "Make that snake in the grass."

Into the silence, Patty piped up with a timorous, "What's celibate?"

No one answered. Or if they did, it got lost in the laughter.

Bev still had a smile on her face in the morning. Her memory of the night before was a little hazy. She vaguely recalled the guv leaving the pub with an arm round the doc's waist. Or it might have been a dream. Waking in the arms of a celebrated bard was definitely not a dream. He was still here, sleeping like a baby. Though when she considered the potential complications, it could turn into a nightmare. Bit late now. She snuggled closer. "Celibate," she whispered, "I don't think so."

EPILOGUE

It was no diss any more not to wear black. Kinda lucky, or the girls would be standing there in their undies. As it was, they were lined up like exotically plumed birds on a clothes line. Bev, who'd dug out a dark suit from the back of the wardrobe, was on the opposite side of the grave. They were soaked. It didn't always rain at funerals – Bev's dad had been buried in a heatwave – but right now it was tipping down.

There'd been just the eight of them in church plus some under-manager from the home. A fatherly vicar had said nice things about a fifteen-year-old prostitute he'd never met. They'd all sung *The Lord's My Shepherd* and *Abide With Me.* Now it was nearly over.

The first earth struck the coffin. Bev didn't see who'd thrown it. Could have been the vicar. Might have been Val. The dull thwack startled her. She stiffened, blinked furiously, glad then for the stinging downpour.

She tried to stop herself, but her eyes were stripping away the cheap wood. Shell was down there and the fury and sadness were like a knife in her stomach. She felt a gentle squeeze on her hand. Jules. Words weren't needed. Couldn't trust herself to speak anyway. The pressure was there again. She looked down.

The girl was handing her a Kwik Save carrier bag, she leaned close, whispered in Bev's ear.

"Cassie wants Shell to have it."

She peered inside. Paddington's fur was matted now and the peg had come off his duffle coat. Bev nodded. Shell deserved more. They all did.

"We're off now," Jules said. "Catch you later."

She nodded, watched them totter away on their wedgies, wondered who they were waving at. Hoped it wasn't the vicar. It wasn't. When she got back to the MG, Vicki Flinn was perched on the bonnet.

"Wotcha, Bev."

"Vick."

Bev made the first move. They stood for a while, arms round each other in the rain. "I tried to find you."

"I know." She didn't want to talk about it. Bev couldn't leave it alone.

"I heard what Hawes did."

She shrugged. "Over now, innit?"

"I thought he'd kill you, Vick."

"He probably would, if it hadn't been for Lucie."

"How do you mean?"

"Told him she was his kid, didn't I?"

Bev couldn't help looking aghast. "And is she?"

"Could be. Who knows?"

More action-packed crime novels from Crème de la Crime

A Kind of Puritan

Penny Deacon

ISBN: 0-9547634-1-6

Dead and dumped. Jon was nobody … no money … no influence. So who dropped him in the river?

Bodies are bad for business so when one is dredged up the Midway Port developers want it buried. Deep. But Humility found the body and she's not going to let it go. Not until she knows who killed the guy everyone said was harmless.

She's a low-tech woman in a hi-tech world and no one wants to give her any answers. But with her best friend's job on the line, a series of 'accidents' at the Port, and the battered barge she lives on threatened with seizure, she's not going to give up.

The mystery leads her to the cruellest parts of the city where people kill for the cost of a meal and it's dangerous to get involved. When she has to seek help from the local crime boss she knows his price is likely to be high.

It's a world where she's not sure anyone is who they claim to be, and where one death leads to another… and the next one could be hers!

No Peace for the Wicked

Adrian Magson

ISBN: 0-9547634-2-4

Old gangsters never die … they simply get rubbed out! But WHO is ordering the hits? And WHY?

Hard-nosed female investigative reporter Riley Gavin is tasked to find out. It's an assignment that follows a bloody trail from a windswept south coast seafront to the balmy intrigues of Spain's Costa Del Crime – and sparks off a chain of grisly murders.

As she digs, Riley uncovers a deadly web of vendettas, double crosses and hatred in an underworld that's at war with itself. The prize? Control of a faltering criminal empire.

But this is one story that soon gets too personal – as Riley discovers dark forces that will stop at nothing to silence her. Dodging bullets, attack dogs and psychotic thugs, she fights to unravel the threads of an evil conspiracy.

And suddenly facing a *deadline* takes on a whole new chilling meaning…